KT-153-069

Praise for Nick Brown and *Agent of Rome: The Black Stone*

'Brown has joined the elite legion of top-notch Roman history-mystery authors, dishing up feasts of blood-soaked soldiering, thrilling political intrigue and an addictive and compelling brand of military cynicism and comradeship... superb.'

Lancaster Evening Post

'[Nick Brown's] writing is always top-notch, his plots seamless and his narrative excellent... [*The Black Stone has*] well-written and plotted and thoroughly realistic character progression... Go get this series and read them through. You will not be disappointed.'

SJA Turney, author of the *Marius' Mules* series

'*The Black Stone* is as violent an adventure as its predecessors, although Cassius himself handles a weapon only once... There are plenty of swordfights and action of all sorts.'

The Historical Novel Society

'This series just gets better and better and *The Black Stone* is the best book so far... a cracking read, the plot is fast paced and the action scenes very exciting.'

Reading Gives Me Wings

NICK BROWN

Agent of Rome: The Black Stone

HODDER

First published in Great Britain in 2014
by Hodder & Stoughton
An Hachette UK company

First published in paperback in 2015

1

Copyright © Nick Brown 2014

Maps by Rosie Collins

The right of Nick Brown to be identified as the
Author of the Work has been asserted by him in accordance
with the Copyright, Designs and Patents Act 1988.

All rights reserved. No part of this publication may be reproduced,
stored in a retrieval system, or transmitted, in any form or
by any means without the prior written permission of the publisher,
nor be otherwise circulated in any form of binding or cover other
than that in which it is published and without a similar
condition being imposed on the subsequent purchaser.

All characters in this publication are fictitious and any
resemblance to real persons, living or dead, is purely coincidental.

A CIP catalogue record for this title is available from the British Library.

ISBN 978 1 444 77911 0

Typeset in Plantin by Palimpsest Book Production Ltd, Falkirk, Stirlingshire

Printed and bound by CPI Group (UK) Ltd, Croydon CR0 4YY

Hodder & Stoughton policy is to use papers that are natural,
renewable and recyclable products and made from wood grown
in sustainable forests. The logging and manufacturing processes
are expected to conform to the environmental regulations
of the country of origin.

Hodder & Stoughton Ltd
338 Euston Road
London NW1 3BH

www.hodder.co.uk

Dla mojej kochanej Mileny

THE ROMAN EMPIRE
in 272 AD

Mare Germanicum

Oceanus

BRITANNIA

GERMANIA INTERIOR

BELGICA

LUGDUNENSIS

GERMANIA SUPERIOR

RAETIA

NORICUM

PANNONIA SUPERIOR

AQUITANIA

DAL

GALLIA NARBONENSIS

ITALIA

HISPANIA TARRACONENSIS

LUSITANIA

BAETICA

MAURETANIA TINGITANA

MAURETANIA CAESARIENSIS

NUBIA

AFRICA PROC

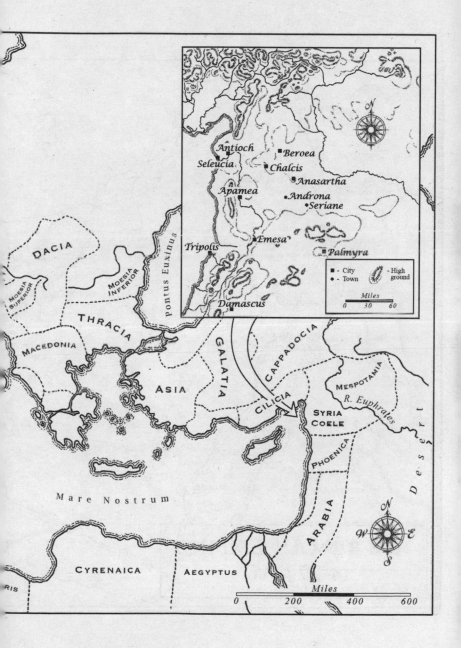

Antioch

Beroea

Seleucia

Chalcis

Anasartha

Apamea

Androna

Seriane

Tripolis

Emesa

Palmyra

Damascus

■ - City
● - Town
- High ground

Miles
0   30   60

DACIA

MOESIA
SUPERIOR

MOESIA
INFERIOR

Pontus Euxinus

THRACIA

MACEDONIA

ASIA

GALATIA

CAPPADOCIA

MESOPOTAMIA

R. Euphrates

CILICIA

SYRIA
COELE

PHOENICA

ARABIA

Desert

Mare Nostrum

CYRENAICA

AEGYPTUS

Miles
0   200   400   600

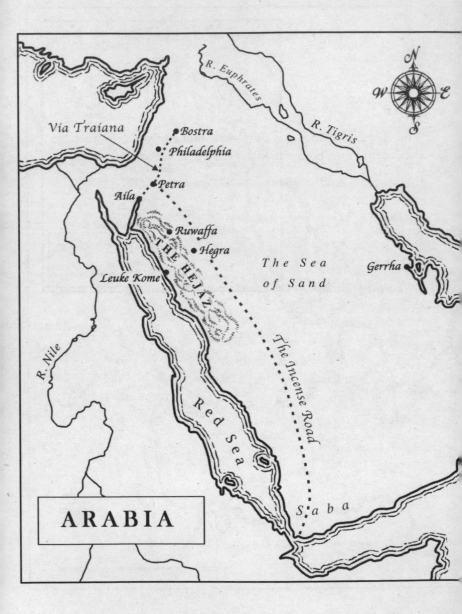

Via Traiana

Bostra
Philadelphia

Petra

Aila

Ruwaffa

THE HEJAZ

Hegra

The Sea
of Sand

Leuke Kome

Gerrha

R. Euphrates

R. Tigris

R. Nile

Red Sea

The Incense Road

Saba

ARABIA

TIME

The Romans divided day and night into twelve hours each, so the length of an hour varied according to the time of year.

The seventh hour of the day always began at midday.

MONEY

Four sesterces (a coin made of brass) were worth one denarius.

Twenty-five denarii (a coin made partially of silver) were worth one aureus (partially gold).

March AD 273

Ursus took his mug from the bedside table and turned back towards the girl. Like him she was naked, lying on her front, feet atop the bunched-up blankets. She was sleeping now, head resting on her crossed arms, sleek black hair splayed between her shoulder blades. Sipping the honey-sweetened wine, Ursus surveyed her body and allowed himself a triumphant grin: as shapely a back as he'd seen; narrow waist; pale, inviting buttocks; and legs slender and shapely enough to drive a sculptor to distraction.

He'd spotted her a few days ago, several weeks into the posting at the temple and long after the more forward of the men had taken up with the more forward of the local girls. Such arrangements were as old as the hills; in return for a few coins every month, they would offer their favours plus the odd bit of sewing and the occasional home-cooked meal.

Ursus was pretty sure none of the legionaries had been near this one, though. The younger men were too interested in powdered faces and low-cut tunics to bother with her. But he'd been around long enough to take his time, seek out a nice girl who hid her assets well and wouldn't cause him any trouble.

Even so, he'd taken the precaution of bringing her to his quarters only after dark (the men had been told to keep their dalliances completely away from the barracks). It was best all round if the priests didn't find out. Holy men could be funny about that sort of thing and he didn't want any trouble when the tribune next visited. In fact, he didn't want any trouble full stop. Army postings didn't come much better than this one.

3

The candle on the other side of the bed flickered, casting watery light over the girl's skin. Ursus commended himself once more; he really had outdone himself this time. Who else would have noted the statuesque curves beneath the dull, shapeless clothing? He moved down the bed and ran his tongue over her hip, then sucked at the soft, yielding flesh of her bottom.

She gave a little moan then opened her eyes and turned over. 'Is there more wine?'

He passed her the mug and continued kissing: her side, her belly, then up between her breasts to her throat. Giggling, she stretched over him and put the mug down.

Ursus lay back and let out a long breath. 'So was I right? Did you enjoy yourself?'

'Oh yes, sir. Yes I did.'

'Tertius, please.'

'Tertius.'

She hissed the second syllable and ran her fingers through the thick hair upon his chest. He hoped she wouldn't notice the few grey ones that had appeared in recent years.

'Tertius.' She caressed the bunched muscles of his left shoulder.

Staring up at the shadowy ceiling, Ursus reminded himself to give her some of that herb concoction he'd bought in Gerasa. The officers there had sworn by it, told him it never failed. The last thing he needed was a girl with child.

She lay back and nestled against him. Ursus checked the hour-glass by the candle but then remembered he hadn't turned it since she'd arrived. Judging by the impenetrable dark beyond the window and the lack of noise coming from the barracks, it was late. Agorix would have come to tell him if any of the men were causing trouble but it was a relief to know they were asleep. Most would be drunk, of course – that was to be expected on the last night of the Festival of Mars – but they would still have to be up early, ready to take over from the unfortunates currently on duty.

All Ursus could hear was the girl breathing. He thought about putting his hands on her again, getting her wet for a second bout, but he too had downed a jug or more and he couldn't leave everything to Agorix the next day. Better to sleep and be up in time to get her safely away unseen. He'd make sure she didn't leave without some of the concoction, of course. Couldn't forget that.

Settling into his pillow, he flicked the blanket up over his feet and closed his eyes. He knew he'd sleep well anyway but routines were routines and this one rarely failed him.

Ten squads to a century, six centuries to a cohort, ten cohorts to a legion, ten squads to a century, six centuries to a cohort, ten . . .

He awoke, shivering.

'A call to the temple?' the girl mumbled. 'Now?'

The ringing of the bell was frantic and at a higher pitch than the one used by the priests. Ursus hazily remembered it had been his idea – to be used only in an emergency. And now someone was ringing it in the dead of night.

'Blood of the gods.'

He half-clambered, half-fell out of the bed. Finding himself sitting naked on the chilly floor, he grabbed one of his boots and pulled it on. 'There's a lantern below the window. Light it.'

'What?'

'Light it! Use the candle.'

Ursus put the second boot on and made sure he tied the laces well. The girl was up but stumbling around.

'Use the candle,' he repeated. 'Lantern's on the floor below the window.'

He snatched his tunic from the hook closest to his bed and pulled it on over his head. The bell was still ringing. And was that shouting in the distance? On the second hook was his belt. Once he'd buckled it, he turned; the girl had the lantern's shutter open and was now lighting it. On the third hook was his sword belt. He grabbed it and threw it over his shoulder. He hurried around the bed and the girl handed him the lantern. 'What is it? What's going on?'

He ran back across the room and wrenched the door open. 'Stay here.'

He stepped outside and pulled the door shut. Despite the clanging of the bell, the parade ground was empty, the only light provided by the torches mounted at each corner. He turned to his left and gazed past the barracks. The army post was separated from the temple by two hundred yards of path surrounded by woodland. He saw dots of light – torches on the move. He heard more shouts, then a man scream.

Lantern held out in front of him, Ursus ran into the barracks and along the central corridor. 'Get up! Boots and swords!'

There was no time for anything else; he just had to get to the temple with as many legionaries as he could muster. 'Get up! Boots and swords! Every last man. Up!'

He darted into the closest room, which stank of bodies and wine. All eight beds were occupied but only one soldier had made it onto his feet. Naked but for a loincloth, he winced at the light.

'Get your weapon, man!'

'Yes, sir,' replied the legionary, staggering towards the equipment rack by the door.

Ursus reached for the closest man still in his bed and bodily dragged him out onto the floor. 'Get dressed. Get your weapon!'

The still-drunk legionary grunted something but Ursus was already back outside and pounding along the corridor again. 'Get up! Every man! Up!'

A few of the soldiers were out of their rooms and awaiting orders. A slight figure pushed between two of them and approached Ursus. 'Centurion.'

The soft Gaulish accent of Agorix, the younger and more able of the two guard officers.

'What's going on?'

'Sounds of battle from the temple, sir. We're under attack.'

'Get them up, get them outside.'

'Yes, sir.'

Ursus ran on, bellowing as he passed the remaining rooms, half a dozen men now behind him. In the last doorway on the right, one soldier was struggling with the straps of his segmented armour.

'Forget that.' Ursus pulled him into the corridor.

Just as he exited the barracks, a figure came bolting along the path. Ursus was about to draw his sword when the man tripped and fell in front of him. He was clad in long robes, his hair cut in a childish fringe. The young priest cried out as Ursus grabbed him.

'You – what's going on?'

The priest shook under the centurion's grip.

'Speak!'

The youth uttered a garbled stream of Aramaic. Ursus didn't understand a word. He let go and moved away from the barracks door to let the others out.

'Sir, what's happening?' someone asked. Ursus ignored him; he was counting the men as they filed out. Eight were armed and ready to move and a couple had even found time to strap on their helmets. A ninth came through the door and instantly dropped down to tie his boots. Ursus slapped him on the shoulder. 'Wait here. Tell Agorix to bring the rest and meet me at the temple end of the path.'

'Yes, sir.'

'You others, follow me.'

Ursus tightened his belt two notches and set off, the men behind him. At his insistence, torches had been put in at sixty-foot intervals: each stuffed with branches and covered in enough goatskin and oil to keep them burning for hours.

The bell had stopped and there were no more shouts. Cencius (his second guard officer) was on duty with twenty men. Could they really have been taken out so quickly? Were the raiders already inside? Had to be a large, well-organised force.

As Ursus passed the fifth torch, one of the legionaries cried out.

'Sir, look there!'

A man – a man running towards them – flashed past the next torch and was then swallowed up by the dark once more. Ursus slowed. He could hear quick steps, panting breaths.

'Draw!'

He gripped his sword hilt tight and eased it out of the scabbard. The legionaries came up on either side of him, blocking the path.

The man spoke. 'The Pillars—'

Ursus completed the password: '—of Hercules. Who's there?'

The soldier ran up to him, sword in hand, face wet with sweat beneath his helmet. Ursus knew him well: Bradua, a decorated veteran of the Palmyran campaign – not a man to run from a fight without good reason. 'Sir, they're in the temple. By the time I got there, they'd already surrounded the place. There are scores of them.'

'Cencius?'

Bradua rubbed his eyes. 'Didn't see him. Lot of men down, sir.'

Agorix had caught up; accompanied by another small group. 'Everyone follow me.'

Ursus ran on once more. Past the seventh torch, then the eighth. As the trees thinned out, he could see the vast, angular bulk of the temple over to the left. Torches flickered close to the great columns, sparking off armour and blades. More lights were scattered across the courtyard and by the main gate. Ursus could hear whinnying horses and hooves on stone.

He shuttered the lantern and slowed to a walk. 'Quiet.'

Approaching the tenth and last torch he moved to the left side of the path, well away from the light. All he heard from his legionaries was their boots scuffing the ground as they narrowed into a line behind him. Just as he reached the low wall that surrounded the temple complex, a shout rang out and the torches closest to the building began to move away. Ursus crouched behind the wall, Agorix beside him. They were close enough to hear voices now.

'What language is that?'asked the guard officer.

'Not sure.'

'Palmyrans?'

'No idea. But the bastards know what they're doing. Covert approach, quick . . . and attacking during the festival – they knew we'd be a mess.'

'I count thirty torches, sir. Even if only every other man has one, that's sixty.'

Bradua dropped down close to them. 'Sir, I saw a cart. Big, reinforced thing – like we'd carry artillery loads in.'

'Just one?'

'Yes.'

Having gathered in the middle of the courtyard, the raiders now began to move right, towards the gate.

'How?' said Agorix. 'How could they have got in and out already?'

'Because they knew what they wanted and they left the rest,' said Ursus. 'They've got the rock.'

Hearing a sudden rush of movement, he and the others shot to their feet as a figure burst out of the darkness. The man ran straight into the wall and fell over it, landing in the midst of the legionaries.

'Is that Bolanus?' someone asked.

The soldier was writhing around on the ground, clawing at his face. The side of his helmet had been split by a blade and the same blow had carved a line across his face. Blood welled between his fingers and his mouth puckered like a landed fish.

'Jupiter save him,' said one of the men as two others knelt down and tried to hold the stricken soldier still.

Agorix was gazing at the courtyard. 'They're on horseback, sir. 'We've only half a dozen mounts, none of them ready.'

'They'll stay with the cart,' reasoned Ursus. 'The cart will be slow.'

The other men closed in around him, listening in.

'The road curves around that old guard tower at the edge of the wood. We can cut through the trees and get ahead of them.'

From the temple came a long, piercing wail, then another and another. It was the priests, mourning the loss of the sacred object they had pledged their lives to.

Ursus watched the last of the torches pass beneath the arch of the gate.

'Sir, we're badly outnumbered,' said one of the soldiers. 'Is it really worth it for some lump of—'

Though he saw the punch coming, the legionary was unable to avoid it and Ursus's fist struck his jaw with a dull crack. Fortunately, the centurion had no intention of doing any real damage. 'You can lead the way, Maro.'

9

Maro pressed his hand against his jaw but took the lantern offered to him.

'Turn left after the closest light, then head south-east towards the road. Go!'

'Yes, sir.' Maro ran back down the track.

'Agorix, you go last. Put the torch out and take it with you.'

'Sir.'

Ursus did a quick head count as the men departed. Eighteen, including the two trying to help Bolanus.

'Leave him.'

Unlike Maro, the legionaries knew better than to argue.

Ursus knelt beside Bolanus, who was lying on his side, head at rest in an ever-expanding puddle of blood. He was still now, and with each breath came an agonised whimper. Ursus put a hand on his shoulder. Bolanus was a local lad; he'd put in a leave request a few days ago – asking for two weeks off to help his mother on the family farm. Ursus turned him onto his back and stood. He took a moment to aim, then slashed downward with his sword, cutting the young legionary's throat.

'Gods forgive me.'

It didn't take him long to catch up with the men but once in the trees, the going became difficult. Low, dense bushes carpeted the ground and – with the canopy blocking out most of the moonlight – they had only the lantern to guide them. Keeping his steps high, Ursus powered past Agorix and the others, urging them on. 'Stay close together. Pick up your feet.'

As he closed in on the middle of the group, a man ahead of him fell, grunting as he struck the ground. Ursus grabbed him under one arm and hauled him to his feet before charging away again. As they entered a clearing, he took the opportunity to get to the front.

Maro was still leading the way. Ursus snatched the lantern from him and altered their direction slightly: by heading further south, they would have more time to get ahead of the raiders. On he ran, holding the lantern as steady as he could to keep the light aflame. As twigs snapped under his boots and birds scattered, he looked left. He could just make out the angular silhouette of the tower: the torches of the raiders hadn't passed it yet. Fifty paces more took him close to the road and there was still no sign of a light. He crouched next to a tree, closely followed by Bradua and Agorix.

'Bradua, here – guide the men in.' Ursus swapped the lantern for the torch. 'Agorix, you'll take five of them across to the other side of the road. I'll halt the lead horses. As soon as they stop, try and get the mounts down, then hit the men.'

'Yes, sir.'

As the rest of the legionaries arrived, Ursus tapped five on the shoulder in turn. 'You're with the guard officer.'

The men gathered around Agorix. Ursus gave the Gaul one last order. 'Remember – mounts first. The other animals will panic and you might just block the way.'

Agorix led his squad down a grassy bank then across the road.

Ursus looked through the trees towards the tower. A dozen torches were visible now, bobbing along as the column advanced. The first riders were no more than a hundred yards away.

'That everyone?' he asked, turning back towards the remainder of the men.

'Numonis fell, sir. Done his ankle.'

'All right, listen. Agorix will strike the front. We head along the side of the column and go for the cart. If we stop it, they can't take the rock with them. If they can't take it, there's no point fighting on. Hit fast, hit hard . . . and remember who we toasted tonight. Mars is with us.'

Though a couple nodded, most of the legionaries just stood there, trying to slow their breathing, probably fighting the urge to run. All in all, Ursus considered them a decent bunch, but there was a smattering of new recruits and some others whose only experience of fighting was mopping up Palmyran irregulars. He had little idea how they would do.

Apelles came forward. He was a bearded, brawny Thracian who had somehow managed to equip himself with both spear and shield. He offered the shield to his centurion. Ursus knew

11

he'd have a few of his beloved throwing darts mounted close to the handle.

'Here, sir.'

'Thank you, Apelles. But you keep it.'

Ursus moved up to a position between two trees at the top of the bank. The noise of the horses rumbled along the paved road and he cursed as he saw that the rear of the column was still coming past the tower. Sixty? More like eighty.

Glad to see no trace of Agorix and his squad, he ordered Bradua and Maro forward. Maro was the only man wearing a cloak.

'Take that off. We need it to hide the flames. Bradua, light the torch.'

The veteran opened the lantern shutter and carefully removed the candle. Maro held up his cloak, which was easily wide enough to prevent the light being seen from the road. Bradua crouched beside it and put the candle to the torch. The goatskin and oil took light easily and in moments the whole thing was aflame.

'Draw swords.'

Ursus armed himself once more and peered around the closest tree. The lead trio were twenty yards away, sitting high in their saddles, the middle man carrying a lantern. The raiders were armed with swords and wore pale, long-sleeved tunics. A few were also equipped with mail and helmets, all of a rudimentary design. What he saw told Ursus absolutely nothing about who they were or where they came from. Presumably that was the idea.

He counted five more ranks of riders before he saw the cart. The vehicle seemed to fill the road and was drawn by four stout horses. All he could see in the rear was a dark shape.

'Get ready.'

As the lead riders drew level with their position, Ursus grabbed the flaming torch from Maro and threw it into the road.

The raiders pulled up, one man already wrestling with his reins as his mount backed away from the flames.

'Now!'

By the time Ursus reached the bottom of the bank, Agorix and his men were already on the road. The Gaul went straight for the middle horse and hacked his blade deep into the animal's neck. As Ursus bolted along the side of the column, he glimpsed the mount rearing and the rider being thrown.

There was a strange moment of hesitation while the raiders struggled to react to what they were seeing. The second and third ranks did nothing more than watch Ursus run past them. The closest man in the fourth rank urged his horse out to block the Roman's path but Ursus nipped up the bank and around him. He was then confronted by another horse and a spear-point coming at him.

The spear suddenly fell to the ground and the attacker slumped back in his saddle, a small metal object sticking out of his throat.

'With you, sir!'

Apelles still hadn't drawn his sword but already had another of the throwing darts ready. The driver of the cart was trying to control the horses and spied the Romans just before the second dart lodged itself in his chest. He dropped the reins and tried to pull it out.

Sitting to his left was a tall, broad man wearing a fine metal chest plate. The wounded driver turned to him for help but the man did no more than glance at the soldiers then drop down onto the other side of the road.

As Bradua and another legionary arrived, Ursus went for the lead horse on his side. With the column stationary, the beast had nowhere to go. Like the others, it was bucking against the reins, eyes rolling, mouth frothing. Ursus chopped four times into its throat. Chunks of flesh and hair and gouts of blood spilled noisily onto the stone. Mortally wounded, the horse fell to its knees.

As the animal stench filled his nose, Ursus looked back along the road. The rest of his men were just behind him. One was trying to pull a rider out of his saddle. Another was felled by some unseen strike.

As Ursus moved up to the cart, a spear clattered along the road, narrowly missing his feet. To his left, Apelles was flanked by Bradua and the other legionary, all three trading blows with the raiders. Ursus raised his blade, ready to cut the reins and disable the riding gear.

But he faced an unexpected danger. The driver had managed to pull the dart out of his chest and was now clutching a dagger.

As he flung himself off the bench, Ursus simply ducked. One of the driver's boots caught his head but the rest of him crashed heavily onto the road. Ursus spun around, booted him in the side then drove his sword down into his unprotected heart. Pulling the blade free, he turned back towards the cart and peered at the closest wheel. It was as solid as any he'd seen, the wooden spokes two inches thick. His sword would barely scratch it.

He looked up at the stone; it had been covered by a sheet. While he was trying to think of another way to disable the vehicle, another spear struck its side. He checked to the right again. More of the raiders were off their horses and engaging the Romans. Only two of his men were left on their feet. They – and he – had only moments.

'Centurion!'

Ursus turned back in time to see Bradua knocked to the ground, his head cracking against the road. His neck had almost been severed by a deep, dark wound. The other legionary was already down, lying next to the rear wheel of the cart.

Apelles fought on alone. As Ursus went to help him, the Thracian's shield suddenly flew high into the air, landing several yards up the bank. Towering over him was the tall man from the cart; head now encased in an angular helmet – bronze like his armour. Apelles swept at his foe but the blade bounced off the chest plate. The riposte was so quick that Ursus didn't even see the tall warrior's weapon. Apelles staggered, then fell, hand clutching his chest.

Ursus snatched a last look down the road. The raiders were advancing, stepping over the bodies of his fallen men. As he turned back, he wondered about Agorix, though he knew he must be dead too. The odds never had been good but they'd fought well to a man.

As the warrior came forward, the raiders behind him stayed

where they were. He was a foot taller than most of them, and in his hands was an immense double-bladed axe, the wooden handle reinforced with bands of metal. Ursus now saw that while the others were from the eastern provinces, the tall warrior had the face of a man from the northern part of the world. His eyes were pale, and the few tufts of hair poking out below the rim of the helmet were fair.

'Nice try, Roman. A commendable effort.' His voice was a low rumble, the Latin impeccable.

'My men,' said Ursus. 'You'll leave them as they lie?'

He wanted them to be found with their swords and – as importantly – the lead identity tablet each wore around his neck.

'We will.'

'The army will find you. And they'll kill you.'

'No more talk. You've delayed me long enough as it is.'

Ursus took a deep breath. By the great and honoured gods he was going to hurt this big bastard if he could. A bit of armour would have been handy, though, shield and helmet too.

The warrior stomped forward, axe held high. Ursus looked for a weak spot but the man clearly took his personal protection seriously; he was also wearing arm-guards and greaves.

Ursus stepped back. He'd just realised he didn't particularly want to die at the end of some barbarian's dirty, bloody axe blade.

'The army will find you.'

He turned his sword upward and placed the tip against his throat. The last thing he saw was the warrior lower his axe.

Ursus drove the blade in. Cold iron gave way to warm blood and he slumped to the ground, his head coming to rest on Apelles's leg. The sound of the raiders' voices and their boots on the road grew faint as the black fog took him.

His last thought was of the girl. She was probably still waiting in his quarters: alone, confused and scared. It was not a good thought. Not good at all.

Gutha looked down at the Roman and shrugged. A centurion, perhaps. Hardly a glorious death but he *had* led a glorious charge; and he seemed like a man who'd done his fair share of fighting for the Empire. At least he'd chosen the manner of his death. Gutha could understand that.

'Any of them left?' he shouted in Nabatean. The only replies were the moans and prayers of the injured. He walked over to the bank and wiped his axe blades clean on the turf, then placed the weapon in the cart. He unbuckled his helmet, removed it and put it beside the axe.

He pointed at Reyazz, his second in command. The young man had already sheathed his sword and was flicking blood off his hands.

'Place ten riders in a cordon around us until we're ready to move. I don't want any more surprises.'

Reyazz relayed the orders.

Gutha walked up to the front of the cart. The men were struggling with the other horses, all of which were desperate to get away from the dead animal. Gutha could see that some of the riding gear had been damaged. Another warrior came up from the front of the column.

'They did the same to us, sir. We're clearing the horse out of the way now.'

Gutha turned to Reyazz. 'How long before you can get us moving again?'

'Half an hour?'

'Make it a quarter. Who did you send to check the barracks?'

'Syrus. Commander, please, don't—'

Unsure where the man was, Gutha shouted: 'Syrus, come here!'

He heard a cry and saw a man running up from the rear.

As he waited for him, Gutha watched the others checking the fallen. From the looks of it, not one Roman was left alive.

'You.'

The closest man turned round, a hulking fellow with a patch over one eye. 'Commander?'

'Put the Romans on the other side of the road. Nobody is to

take anything from them. Our dead and those too hurt to move – lay them here on the bank.'

'Yes, sir.'

Syrus came to a stop, breathing hard, already chewing his lip.

Gutha rested his hands on his belt and looked down at him. 'You were sent to check the barracks?'

'Yes, Commander. My men and I got very close. There wasn't a single soldier. You were right: the festival, the drink—'

'You were told to wait. To watch. To send a runner if anyone appeared.'

'We did wait, sir. But we saw no one. We returned—'

'Too early. Far too early.'

Syrus dropped to one knee. 'My apologies, Commander. The fault is entirely mine.'

'I'd say so, yes.'

Gutha watched as a fifth injured warrior was laid out on the bank. 'That the last of ours?'

'Yes, sir,' said the man with the eye-patch. 'Plus six dead.'

'Strip all but their tunics.'

'Yes, Commander.'

Only two of the wounded were moving. One man's tunic had been slashed open, exposing a glistening cut across his chest.

'Water,' he gasped. 'Water.'

'Thing is,' Gutha told Syrus, 'we can't take him and the other four. We're in enemy territory. We need to move quickly, without drawing attention. And we can't leave them alive because they know too much.'

Syrus was still down on one knee.

'Get up.'

The younger man did so.

'Best get to it,' added Gutha.

'You mean—'

'Yes. All five.'

Syrus gazed up at the heavens and muttered a prayer. He drew his sword.

'Water,' pleaded the injured man. 'Please.'

Syrus walked towards him then stopped. 'Sir, could I at least give him some water?'

'No. Best to be quick. Merciful.'

The men attending to the horses had stopped to watch Syrus. 'Keep at it!' Gutha ordered.

Syrus stood over the injured man. As he lowered the blade towards his throat, the warrior tried to swat it away.

'Why?' he asked. 'Why?'

Syrus stuck the blade in. The slick of blood that soon striped the warrior's tunic was made black by the moonlight. His eyes remained open, even when his body became still.

The next man stirred. Despite the numerous messy injuries to his belly and groin, he managed to roll away. Syrus tried to pull his blade out of the first man but it was stuck. Something crunched as he twisted it this way and that before finally wrenching it free. Gutha heard a whimpering cry and initially thought the warrior was still alive. But the noise had come from Syrus. He composed himself then moved on to the next man. Gutha ran a hand across his head and cursed.

All this for a rock.

They rode on through the night, putting ten miles between them and the temple. At dawn, the bulk of the column continued south while Gutha, Reyazz and two others sheltered at a previously requisitioned barn, then moved on the following day. Numbers were now more of a hindrance then a help and, with the cart's precious load hidden beneath a stack of reed-bales, they hoped to reach friendly territory.

It took nine days to reach friendly territory. Nine tense, long days spent avoiding army patrols, customs officials and curious locals. Once beyond the reach of the legions, they reunited with the main force and Gutha found the last few days of the journey far less taxing. He was looking forward to delivering the rock to his employer; partly because the long, complicated operation would be over, but also to see the mad bastard's reaction.

The final obstacle was the lengthy mountain road, particularly the steep stretch that led down to the town. But the cart and its load survived intact. As they halted at the outer wall, the escort was dismissed, every last man having sworn an oath of secrecy. Once through the noisy, busy streets, they reached the inner wall. Only Reyazz was permitted to remain alongside Gutha. As the guards closed the doors behind them, other men came forward to take control of the horses. Gutha jumped down to the ground and looked around him, glad to be in familiar surroundings.

To the left of the gate was a sloping path cut into the rock which led up to a cavern. Within was the vast network of ancient chambers that Ilaha had now claimed for his headquarters. Gutha heard a cry, and saw the man himself rush out into the light, his purple cloak a vivid splash of colour against the pale rock. He looked almost giddy as he ran down the path, eyes fixed on the cart.

Gutha had worked for him for three years; and when they'd first met he'd gone by a different name. He'd been no more than an up-and-coming tribal chief then, with perhaps only a couple of hundred swordsmen at his command. Ilaha had always been a tad eccentric but there could be no denying his drive and energy, nor his ability to lead. Yet Gutha had observed a dramatic change in him – a change that seemed to gather pace with every passing day – and he now knew what to expect when he was in his priestly garb.

One constant remained, however: for Gutha the only factor that really mattered. The man paid well. Unusually well.

Holding up his cloak as he ran, Ilaha reached the bottom of the slope. The men had by now finished removing the reed-bales from the cart. As Ilaha approached, they and Reyazz withdrew, leaving Gutha alone with him. Ilaha lifted the sheet and peeked under it, then backed away, as if barely able to believe what he had seen.

His cloak was embroidered with gold thread, the back covered by a lustrous sun. Though he was wearing a tunic and trousers underneath, Gutha could tell that he'd lost yet more weight. A wonderful rider and formidable swordsman, Ilaha hardly ever seemed to carry a blade these days and spent little time outside. And the weight lost from his fair, almost androgynous face made him seem gaunt, though his dark eyes had not lost their compelling power. It took him a long time to drag them off the rock.

'You did it,' he said in Greek. 'You brought it to me.'

He dashed forward and grabbed Gutha's tunic, then pulled him down and kissed him on the cheek.

'I heard it, Gutha,' he whispered. 'I heard it. I knew you had it. It's been speaking to me for days.'

Ilaha abruptly let go and yelled at the men. 'Where are those logs and ropes? Get it inside at once!'

Gutha was sleeping when the guards came for him. He swiftly dressed and followed the pair back through the town to the inner gate. They escorted him as far as the cavern, then silently joined the other sentries there. Gutha peered inside, at the rows of mounted torches that narrowed into the passageway beyond. The scent of blood – rust and rot – breathed out into the night. He took a last gulp of fresh air and entered.

After fifty paces, the passageway reached the high-roofed chamber that Ilaha now referred to as the temple. Braziers had been lit, casting a fuzzy orange glow. Gutha smothered an oath as he realised that what he had taken for statues were in fact Ilaha's priests. All ten of them were there, heads bowed, each man wearing an identical scarlet cloak and cowl. They stood in a circle around the rock. Gutha knew he should have kept walking to the passageway opposite but he still hadn't taken a good look at the thing. The priests – who were allowed to speak only to Ilaha – did not react as he walked over, stopped between two of them and gazed at the black stone.

It seemed small: the conical top no more than five feet high, the rounded base no more than six across. The composition was unlike anything he'd seen: a honeycomb pattern topped by a grey, almost metallic sheen. Etched upon the surface was marking upon marking but every time he thought he saw a familiar word or letter or image, the lines seemed to shift. He moved around it, past another priest, and the very colour and shape of the rock seemed to change. He blinked; and put it down to tiredness or a trick of the light.

Gutha looked down. The rock was mounted on a plinth surrounded by a circular basin filled with water. Connected to the basin were four channels that ran out to the chamber's walls, each ending below a large iron hook. Gutha saw the blood in the water and went to see which animals had been sacrificed to the sun god.

He found a calf, a goat and a lamb; and smelt the shit they had voided when their throats had been cut. Having traversed the whole chamber, he approached the last hook.

The yellow-beaked eagle was still breathing. It had been tied on by its wings, its neck merely nicked to ensure a slow death. The bird's chest was twitching weakly, but as Gutha came nearer, its talons scraped the air, vengeful claws desperate for something to tear into.

Gutha watched it a while longer, then continued on towards Ilaha's quarters. He passed two closed doors. The third was open.

'Gutha?'

'Yes.'

'Come in.'

A small, sparsely decorated cavern. Ilaha – now barefoot and without the cloak – was sitting at a hexagonal table. In front of him was a jug and some fine glasses.

'Please, sit.'

Gutha did so and cast a wary glance towards the rear of the room. The old woman was sitting in a chair by the hearth, facing away from them.

Ilaha called her 'Mother' but Gutha couldn't believe she was a day under eighty and as Ilaha couldn't be much more than thirty, he reckoned she was actually his grandmother. Gutha was glad she was well away from him. Apart from the fact that she stank, he hated even looking at her. Her face was more lines than skin, her eyes opaque and yellowed, yet her white hair was as thick as his and hung down as far as her waist. Despite her age, she was never ill and always available to advise and guide her 'son'. To Gutha, her very existence seemed unnatural.

'Wine?' said Ilaha.

'No, thank you.' As Gutha settled into the chair, the frame groaned under his weight.

Ilaha looked tired and pale but those dark eyes somehow still shone. 'Did you feel it? Did you feel its power? I believe I can hear it beating like a heart.'

'I am relieved it is finally here.'

'Reyazz did well?'

'Exceptionally. He thinks the real stone is lighter than the one we practised with – that's why they were so quick. Twelve minutes in and out. There was a little trouble getting the frame on but the rollers and the ramp worked to perfection.'

'So everything went to plan?'

'Pretty much.'

'I've warned you before about lying.' The crone sounded like a little girl with hands around her throat. 'What about the man who spilled the blood of horses and then his own?'

Gutha was never quite sure how she did that; was she really a sorceress or just exceptionally well informed?

'Centurion, I think. Ambushed us on the way out. Lost a few men but they didn't slow us down for long.'

'There's no possibility that someone could have followed you here?' asked Ilaha.

'Not a chance.'

'I want them to know I have the stone, but at a time of my choosing.'

'The Emperor will have heard of it by now. He is coming east to put down the Palmyrans himself.'

'He knows,' said the old woman. 'He knows what he has lost.'

'It was well guarded,' said Gutha. 'I imagine he'll do whatever's necessary to get it back.'

Ilaha looked irritated. 'I believe we have been through this before.'

'We have. But there can be no turning back. You have started along a dangerous road now.'

'I?'

'We.'

Ilaha leaned forward onto the table. 'There will be no turning back, Gutha. It is good that the Emperor comes east now. The invincible god of the sun aids us by bringing him here. It will only hasten his demise.'

Gutha didn't like the sound of that. The man wasn't just becoming more unstable and more arrogant; he was becoming more ambitious.

'I have been busy while you've been away,' Ilaha continued. 'Our allies have been summoned.'

'*Potential* allies.'

Ilaha ignored him. 'They will gather here on the last day of the month; and when I show them what I have, every last one will pledge himself and his men. But even before then we must show them that the tide is turning, that Rome has already lost control. We must stay in the shadows no longer. All of Arabia must see that our time has come.'

'You wish to send another message?'

'I do.'

Gutha didn't much like the sound of that either but they both knew he would do as he was bid. Ilaha did pay well. Unusually well.

'I'm sure we can come up with something.'

Ilaha glanced at the door. 'You came through the temple. How's the eagle?'

'Still alive.'

Ilaha grinned. 'Not for long.'

23

I

'Damn you, Simo. Damn you, damn you, damn you.'

Cassius Quintius Corbulo sighed and shook his head. The helmet's bronze was greasy and dull, the crest needed combing and there was a dead spider stuck to the cross-piece.

'Sir?' Muranda appeared in the doorway.

'Didn't I ask you to clean this?'

The chubby maid hurried forward and took it. 'I thought I had, sir.'

'By the gods, look at it, woman. You must polish it – I want to see my face in there.'

'Yes, Master Cassius.'

The housekeeper waddled out of the bedroom, sandals slapping on the floor. Cassius was convinced that if she worked a bit harder she might lose some weight off her bottom half.

'Just come back soon, Simo,' he whispered. 'Please.'

His Gaulish attendant had finally taken the leave long promised to him and journeyed to Antioch to visit his father. The Syrian capital was a week away so Cassius had allowed him three weeks in total. But twenty-four days had now passed. He knew Simo had arrived safely yet he had heard nothing since. Cassius felt as if his entire life were in utter disarray.

Seeing the state of the hourglass did nothing to improve his mood.

'And why didn't you wake me sooner?' he shouted. 'The meeting is in a quarter-hour!'

After only a couple of days without Simo, Cassius had grown tired of putting all his clothes and belongings away, so in order to find things he'd decided to leave them all out where he could see them. Muranda occasionally popped in to take some washing but she seemed to have a gift for missing the dirtiest items.

So far that morning, the only clean item Cassius had managed to locate was a long-sleeved scarlet tunic. He looked around for a cape but the only one in view had a stain down the front.

'Tunic'll do,' he said to himself. 'Now, er . . . sword belt, sword belt.'

This at least was easy to find: it was lying on a chair by the doorway. Cassius grabbed it and lowered the strap onto his right shoulder, more at ease with the weight of the weapon now. The regular lessons with Indavara were really starting to pay off and he was almost beginning to enjoy handling the blade, though the bodyguard continued to insist it was too big for him. Cassius inspected the ornate eagle head at the base of the hilt and tutted: it too was unclean. He grabbed a loincloth and gave it a quick rub.

'Er . . . satchel, satchel.'

The deer-hide bag was hanging from a candelabra. Cassius undid the buckle and checked he had some paper and a stick of charcoal. He seldom made notes at these meetings with the governor but it always paid to appear conscientious. He slung the bag over his left shoulder and hurried out into the atrium.

The curtain to Indavara's room was open; an empty plate left on the bed. Wondering where he'd got to, Cassius hurried into the kitchen, expecting to find Muranda there. But, apart from the mangy cat that had taken to wandering in, the room was empty.

'Muranda!'

She came shuffling in from the courtyard. 'Here, sir. Sorry. I needed the light.'

Cassius took the helmet from her. 'Well, at least the spider's gone.'

As Muranda stroked the cat – which had jumped onto the bench beside the kitchen table – Cassius did his best to straighten out the rough bristles of the crest. He couldn't fault the maid's manners but she really was a useless creature.

'Shall I prepare a dinner for later, sir?'

The very mention of the word made Cassius long for the

innumerable dishes Simo could conjure at speed, every one adapted to suit his palate. By contrast, Muranda seemed unable to invest any foodstuff with a pleasant taste.

'No. I'll eat out.' He aimed a finger at the cat. 'And keep that wretched thing out of here. Yesterday I found a hair in my dates.'

'Yes, Master Cassius.'

He strode back across the atrium to the front door. Mounted on the wall close by was an oval, silver-framed mirror. After a few hurried adjustments to his hair, he looked at his nose. Simo kept telling him the break had reset perfectly and Cassius had almost believed him until Indavara cracked a joke about it one night. Now he could barely look at his face without fixating on the knob of bone. Apart from cosmetic considerations, he hated the fact that he'd been left with an inescapable reminder of his last assignment: a brutal confrontation with a rogue centurion.

Muttering curses, he stepped outside, only just resisting the temptation to slam the door.

The villa faced onto the Via Cappadocia, the wide street which – a stone's throw to the left – led straight into Bostra's legionary fortress. Beyond the marble arch of the gatehouse and the high wall lay the sprawling complex: headquarters of the Third Cyrenaican, Arabia's only standing legion. Two sentries holding spears and in full armour flanked the gate. Above them a large red and gold standard hung limply from its pole.

'Afternoon, sir,' said one of the men as Cassius reached the pavement.

'Afternoon.'

Given the villa's location, Cassius had come to know the faces of the sentries and this fellow was unusually cheery. The second soldier just about managed a nod. Cassius imagined he – and most of the others – weren't overly concerned about impressing an officer of the Imperial Security Service, long-standing rival of the regular army.

Setting off along the street in the opposite direction, Cassius realised he no longer worried as much about such things. The attitude of his compatriots, ranks and officers alike, was something he could do little about; and the benefits of a life free from the punishing grind of conventional soldiering still outweighed the disadvantages, for the time being anyway.

The morning was bright and windless, his light linen tunic ideal. This was Cassius's third spring in the eastern provinces and it was a pleasant time: little rain and plenty of sun, but without the stifling heat of the summer.

He, Indavara and Simo had arrived in Bostra three months earlier. Though the city lacked the grandeur and history of Antioch, there was a fine theatre, several excellent baths and some decent inns. The occasional appearances of the desert folk – the Saracens – added something to the place, as did the myriad colours of the native clothing and the exotic smells of the spice market.

All in all a reasonable posting, except that much of the province's army had been despatched to assist with fresh rebellions brewing in Syria and Egypt. The Third Cyrenaican was now down to just six cohorts; fewer than three thousand men. Worse still, the Tanukh – a confederation of Arabian tribesmen traditionally allied to Rome – could no longer be relied upon; rumours abounded of dissent in the south.

'Officer Corbulo. Officer!'

Over the wall of the villa he was passing, Cassius spied a familiar figure bustling along the path. He stopped outside the gate just as Mistress Lepida opened it, already smiling.

Most of the residents on the Via Cappadocia had some connection to the army and Lepida was the wife of a tribune who'd been transferred to Egypt. According to Muranda, her husband had lost interest in her long ago and she freely sought her pleasures elsewhere. Even so, Cassius had resisted her advances. It was rarely advisable to indulge with the wives of fellow officers, and though she was in good shape for her age – which he reckoned was about thirty – the large mole on one side of her nose was singularly off-putting.

'Good day to you, sir.'

'Good day, Mistress Lepida.'

Cassius was all set to walk on when he saw a younger lady exiting the villa.

Lepida didn't seem overly concerned by the speed at which he shifted his gaze. 'May I introduce my cousin, Miss Helena Umbrenius.'

'Miss Helena.'

Cassius stepped into the garden and took her hand; and a well-manicured hand it was too. She was rather short but slim with it; and far darker than Lepida. She looked like the local girls, in fact, with jet-black hair and remarkably white teeth.

'Helena arrived from Qottein yesterday. She is staying with me for now because of the troubles. Any news, Officer? There's talk that the rest of the legion might be recalled.'

'I'm really not sure.'

'I thought you were supposed to know about these things.'

'As you know, I deal mainly with logistics.' Cassius smiled. It was a running joke between them.

'Come now, Officer.'

'Cassius, please.'

'Very well – Cassius. Enough of this pretence. I have been an army wife for more than ten years and I am fully aware that it is the job of the Service to know things before everyone else.'

'I wish that were true,' he replied honestly.

'Officer Corbulo was born in Ravenna,' Lepida told her cousin. 'He hails from one of the old families and is related to Gnaes Domitius Corbulo, the great general.'

'You are kind, Mistress Lepida, but I'm sure Miss Helena doesn't want to hear about me.'

The look on the young lady's face suggested otherwise. Cassius guessed she was around his age. Almost certainly unmarried or Lepida would have mentioned it by now.

He continued: 'Tell me, have you had a chance to look around the city? The theatre is really quite impressive.'

'Not yet,' the girl replied shyly.

'Are you attending the performance tonight?' asked Lepida.

'*Brutus*?' replied Cassius. 'I thought that had been cancelled.'

'It's back on. Apparently the governor gave specific instructions that all should continue as normal.'

'Ah. Well, Accius has always been a bit broad for my tastes, but—'

'Perhaps you would escort us?' asked Lepida.

'Why not?'

A bell rang out from the fortress, marking the start of the third hour.

'Gods, sorry, I'd better be going.'

'Is that an arrangement, then?' asked Lepida.

'Certainly. Shall I call in at the twelfth?'

'Perfect.'

'Good day, ladies.'

They answered together: 'Good day.'

Feeling his spirits rising by the moment, Cassius placed a steadying hand on his sword and jogged away along the street. He didn't like being seen to hurry in public but he liked being admonished for tardiness even less.

Up ahead, a double line of cavalry had just turned onto the road, bound for the fortress. They were trotting along at quite a speed and several locals had to take evasive action. One unfortunate tipped his little cart onto the pavement. Bounding over a cascade of watermelons, Cassius nodded politely at the cavalry commander. The officer returned the gesture and bawled at the poor vendor, who bowed repeatedly as he recovered his wares.

Once past the last pair of riders, Cassius crossed to the other side of the street. At the corner, he turned left onto the Via Petra and passed the city's largest sanctuary. Equipped with an immense central fountain, it functioned as spring, retreat and meeting place. Water-carriers bearing jugs or skins gathered by the numerous pipes while richer folk walked the gardens or sat sunning themselves.

Another hundred paces took him under the imposing arch commonly known as the East Gate. Squatting in the shadows were a pair of legionaries and four city sergeants. Noting his approach, they whispered warnings, but when Cassius ignored them they returned swiftly to their dice. Turning right up a narrower street, he heard a desperate cry of 'Dogs? Again?' Cassius grinned; the gambler had rolled four ones – the lowest possible score.

A smaller arch marked the entrance to the governor's residence. The two guards outside had been slouching but straightened their spears and their backs as Cassius strode past. 'Good day, sir.'

'Good day.'

The residence was known locally as Rabbel's House – palace of the last king before the annexation of Arabia by the emperor Trajan. Cassius thought it appropriate that few people actually used the word palace. Despite two colonnaded storeys, it was a blocky, rather anonymous building, and several of the city's richer inhabitants could boast far grander homes. The governor had, however, done his best to improve the place: it was surrounded by a colourful strip of flowerbeds and watched over by Trajan and several other of Rome's most revered emperors. Hurrying between life-size bronze renderings of Hadrian and Marcus Aurelius, Cassius approached the passageway that led to the palace's central courtyard.

Standing there with another sentry was one of the staff; an aged attendant holding a waxed tablet and stylus. 'Officer Corbulo, good day to you. The governor is holding his meeting in the Table Room. Do you—'

Cassius didn't break stride. 'I know the way.'

The courtyard was large – forty yards from corner to corner – and today contained two groups of people. One was a huddle of toga-clad men: senior administrators deep in discussion. The others were centurions, helmets cradled under their arms as they listened to another officer reading from a sheet of paper. None of the men looked up.

Cassius passed through a portico then turned right into a corridor. Two maids were on their knees, rolling up a heavy rug. They were about to scramble out of Cassius's way but he held up a hand and nimbly turned sideways to get past them. Slowing down as he approached the Table Room, he checked his helmet, straightened his tunic, and walked in.

The room was well lit by three grilled windows and dominated by the eponymous table – a rectangular monstrosity far too big for the space that housed it. On the interior wall was a fading fresco; the inevitable seven hills of Rome. At the near end of the table stood two young clerks, silently sorting through some papers. Sitting at the far end were Governor Calvinus, Tribune Pontius and Chief Nerva.

'Ah, Corbulo.' Calvinus beckoned Cassius forward then addressed the clerks. 'You two leave us. Shut the door behind you.'

As the clerks complied, Cassius placed his helmet on a table next to Nerva's (which looked in rather better condition) then slipped the satchel from his shoulder. The governor occupied the chair at the end of the table, the others to his right. Cassius took a seat to his left.

Directly opposite him was Pontius: a tall, striking man. At twenty-six he was five years older than Cassius and the legion's senior tribune. His light woollen tunic was of unmistakable quality, the wide purple stripe running from shoulder to belt. Pontius was a senator's son, putting in his time in the provinces before returning to Rome to take up a political career. With the prefect away leading the legion's crack cohorts in Syria, he was now effectively commander of the province's forces. Brash and direct, Pontius was also a renowned rider, having won several prestigious contests. Cassius had tried to ingratiate himself with all those he dealt with at his new posting but Pontius remained as unreceptive as Chief Nerva – possibly the only thing the two had in common.

Though technically a centurion, as the man in charge of the fortress, Nerva enjoyed a status only just below Pontius. Unlike the tribune – who might be back in Rome within a year – he had served with the Third Cyrenaican for two decades. Jowly and squat, his red tunic was far more faded than Cassius's and looked at least a size too small. Pinned to his chest was a miniature silver spear: symbol of his post; and around both his wrists were broad gold bands: decorations for distinguished service.

Calvinus was a little older: well into his fifties. According to local lore he had shunned the possibility of a future career in Rome because of his love of the province and its inhabitants. His broad face was topped by a thick head of silvery curls, his cheeks lined with red veins. He was said to like his drink but there was never any at these meetings. Cassius was a tad hungover, and wouldn't have minded pouring himself some water from the jug on the table. But it was too far away and he was last to arrive, so he sat up straight and waited for the governor to begin.

Calvinus ran a knuckle across his brow. 'Chief Nerva passed

this news to me early this morning. Pontius, Corbulo – you are the first to know. Five days ago the legionary fort at Ruwaffa was attacked. Burned to the ground. It was efficiently done – the fire was started in several places and the gates blocked from the outside. Almost the entire century perished. The three men that escaped had to climb over the walls. They eventually made it to Humeima from where Centurion Ignatius immediately despatched a message.'

'By the gods,' said Pontius. 'This is an outrage.'

'And unprecedented,' said Calvinus. 'In all my years here.'

Cassius had several questions running through his head but remained silent. Upon finding out he would be taking the job, he'd been relieved – pleased to accept an administrative position at last. But he was still getting to grips with both the role and the situation. He planned to listen, learn and keep his head down.

Chief Nerva broke the silence. 'Without wishing to go over old ground, sir, it's no coincidence that the frequency and severity of these attacks have risen since the legion was dismembered. Our enemies know we are weak.'

'Dismembered? Must you use such dramatic language, Marcus? What we must focus on is finding out exactly who these enemies are.'

'Could be brigands,' replied the centurion. 'Some splinter group within the Tanukh? Palmyrans, even?'

'Perhaps our resident spy has something to add?' said Pontius, staring across the table at Cassius.

Nerva weighed in before he could reply. 'Unlikely, Tribune. To find out anything useful one might actually have to leave Bostra.'

Pontius sneered, then continued the attack. 'Well, Corbulo? Isn't it your job to anticipate such events?'

The governor intervened. 'I shall remind you both that Officer Corbulo has been here only a matter of weeks. He is no more a soothsayer than you or I.'

Cassius decided he had to say something, if only to be seen to contribute. 'Sir, was there any further information regarding the attack in the letter? Any evidence or—'

'No,' said the governor. 'Just the bare facts.'

Nerva picked up a sheet in front of him and slid it across the table. 'Here.'

Cassius examined the letter – a few sentences scrawled hastily on a well-worn page.

Calvinus continued. 'Ruwaffa is – was – our most southerly presence. Now we shall know even less about what is going on down there.'

'What *about* the Tanukh, sir?' asked Nerva. 'Any progress?'

'Whatever their other concerns, the thirteen chiefs do not currently seem particularly interested in meeting me.'

'What is wrong with these bloody Saracens?' uttered Pontius. 'We have safeguarded this province for almost two centuries. They should be coming to us, not the other way around.'

'With respect,' said Nerva, 'you weren't here when the Palmyrans hit us. The Tanukh's reward for fighting alongside us was to see their villages and towns razed, their caravans robbed. When the Emperor defeated Zenobia we told them that was the end of it; that we could guarantee a period of peace. And now? Palmyra up in arms again. Egypt? No wonder they've turned their backs on us.'

'Is there no more we can do, sir?' asked Pontius.

'My emissaries are working hard but we have heard almost nothing,' said Calvinus. 'You know how it is with these nomads – always on the move. Let's go over the numbers again. If this attack presages a wider problem, I want to know just how bad it could get if the Tanukh do turn against us.'

'Sir, I think that's extremely unlikely,' said Pontius.

'Based on what?' replied Calvinus irritably.

'The fact that they have fought beside us before, been our allies for many years.'

'That's right. They have. I consider some of these men my friends. I have eaten with them, ridden with them, seen their children grow up. And they are ignoring me. That silence frightens me more than anything. '

Nerva swiftly outlined the deployment of the Third Cyrenaican. 'The first and tenth cohorts of course remain here in Bostra, the sixth outside Petra, the seventh at Aila. The eighth is divided between Gerasa and Philadelphia. The ninth currently man the fortresses in the south of the province. Based on current strength returns, we can muster a total of around two thousand six hundred men.'

Nerva saw the look of surprise on the governor's face.

'This outbreak at Gerasa, sir. A third of Modius's men are laid up. Half his officers too.'

'Auxiliaries?'

'Viridio's camel-riders are in as good a shape as ever. Strength returns for the other cohorts are adequate.'

'That's something, I suppose,' said Calvinus. 'Now what about the Via Traiana? It's an obvious target for whoever's behind the attack. The road *must* stay open. Trade must continue, taxes must be collected and the general staff must be assured of free movement across our territory.'

Calvinus and Nerva turned to Pontius.

'No incidents reported to me. Clearly, protecting the entire road is a virtual impossibility but we are ready to mount extra patrols and put squads into the way-stations if required.'

'And your report on potential placements for these patrols and squads? Wasn't it due last week?'

'My apologies, Governor. We are doing our best but where previously the chiefs would have provided us with intelligence, we are now rather in the dark. I must confess I am bemused as to what Officer Corbulo has been doing for the last few weeks.'

Cassius had been reading the letter for a second time while keeping one ear on the conversation. He lowered the sheet as the three senior men looked at him.

'As you know, my predecessor Verecundus wasn't the most conscientious of individuals but I have been in contact with a few of the men he employed as informers.'

'And?' asked Pontius.

'I have obtained nothing that could be described as actionable intelligence,' admitted Cassius. 'Some refused to meet me, others claim that the tribesmen are spending less time in the north of the province. None were prepared to cooperate.'

Pontius snorted.

'How I love the Service,' scoffed Nerva. 'About as useful as a candle in a snowstorm.'

'Actually, sir, what I have learned is quite useful, in a way.'

'Knowing nothing is useful?' countered Pontius. 'Then you must consider yourself an expert, Corbulo.'

'The fact that Verecundus – by all accounts a lazy, disorganised fellow – was able to gather information, yet I have not, is in itself instructive. It reinforces what Governor Calvinus has already told us. The situation has changed. I would surmise that some or all of the informers are withholding information out of fear. Perhaps because the attitude of the less loyal Saracens towards Rome is now at best unfriendly, at worst hostile.'

Pontius seemed determined to assert himself. 'We must get a grip of the situation, sir. Allow me to march the tenth cohort down to Humeima. We shall investigate the Ruwaffa attack and bring those responsible to justice. Once there are a few dozen bodies hanging by the road these bastards might think twice about attacking again.'

Nerva was nodding. 'If we can restore order, the chiefs may come back to us.'

Cassius made a noise, and realised the governor had heard him only when Calvinus looked at him.

'Corbulo? Something to say?'

'Er, well, sir . . . I'm not sure the situation is as chaotic as it first appears. I've been working through the documentation regarding the various incidents as you instructed. The majority may well be due to the reduction in troop numbers and a consequent breakdown in order. But a few – and I wouldn't be surprised if this attack on Ruwaffa is the latest – share certain common characteristics.'

'Go on.'

Cassius knew he should have been spending six hours a day on the paperwork Verecundus had left behind. In fact he'd been doing about two hours, but he was most of the way through it and sure of his conclusions.

'Sir, I shall refer only to incidents where our people have been killed. You will recall that a tax collector was murdered outside Aila last March.'

'Hardly a rarity,' said the governor.

'Usually two or three a year,' added Nerva.

'Four last year,' said Cassius. 'The other three were investigated by local legionaries and brought to a conclusion – all disgruntled taxpayers as I recall. The Aila murder wasn't solved. Then, last October, a legionary patrol was ambushed outside Humeima.'

'Palmyran irregulars, wasn't it?' said Nerva.

'That's what Verecundus wrote it up as,' replied Cassius. 'But I checked the original report from the optio down there. There was no evidence of Palmryan involvement. There was no evidence at all. Verecundus just wanted a neat conclusion to his investigation. Then there was the robbery of the wage cart at Udruh in January. Six men killed this time, several thousand sesterces taken. Verecundus made no progress identifying those responsible. All three incidents were roughly the same time apart, all struck directly at symbolic Roman targets and all were carried out with a high degree of professionalism.'

'And you chose not to mention this before?' asked Pontius.

'I did mention it,' Cassius replied quickly. 'It was in the preliminary report I prepared for the governor. Your office should have received a copy.'

Pontius turned to Nerva, who nodded.

'Bloody useless clerks,' said the tribune, reddening.

'Now this attack,' said Cassius, tapping the letter. 'Again, a few months after the last incident and, judging from what we know so far, again carried out efficiently.'

'Do you have a theory about who might be responsible?' asked Calvinus.

'No, sir. Frankly, I don't know enough about the province. All I can say is that there seems to be a guiding hand at work. Someone who is becoming more brazen, more confident.'

'Governor,' said Nerva. 'You know the chiefs better than any of us. Are they really capable of this?'

'Knowing so little of their present state of mind, it's difficult to say. But a few were certainly more reluctant allies than others, and some still cling to the hope of a return to the old days.' Calvinus flicked his head upward. 'When old King Rabbel lived under this roof and the desert folk came and went as they pleased.'

'This person is an opportunist,' said Cassius. 'They might have waited for years, even fought alongside the legions.'

'We have always been so vulnerable here,' said Calvinus. 'Thousands of miles of ungovernable territory to our south and east; and always dependent on the Saracens to provide information and security.'

'Well, sir?' said Pontius, still anxious to regain some ground. 'I could have that column on the move within days, down to Humeima in a couple of weeks.'

'Show our faces,' added Nerva. 'Discourage a further escalation.'

Calvinus didn't seem convinced. 'I will not risk such a move yet. Not until I know more. If the Tanukh *are* involved, retaliation may make things worse and the chiefs can each count on at least a thousand swords; if they turn against us we are outnumbered five to one. I shall look into this Ruwaffa incident myself. Pontius, I want that deployment report – use what information you have. Nerva, keep a close eye on those centuries with a large intake of new recruits – we may need them sooner rather than later. Corbulo, your priority must be these informers. One way or another, we must find out what the chiefs are up to.'

'Yes, sir.'

Calvinus continued: 'Also, I have instructed the magistrate to pay special attention to any disruptive elements within the city; anyone even mentioning the word revolt will find themselves up on a charge. Talk of the attack will get out eventually – it always does – but for now keep it to yourselves. Oh, and as of today, all leave is cancelled.'

Cassius stood. Pontius and Nerva were already on their way out. Calvinus moved his chair away from the table and ran his fingers through his silvery curls. 'Corbulo, wait.'

Cassius turned towards him, hands clasped behind his back.

Calvinus crossed his legs and rearranged the folds of his toga. He spoke only when he was sure the others were gone. 'You defended your corner well, young man, and I cannot fault your analysis. But if the present informers aren't doing the job, recruit new ones. Get out there. Find out what I need to know. If you require more personnel, more funds, tell me.'

'Yes, Governor.'

With that, Cassius picked up his satchel and left, collecting his helmet on the way out. The courtyard had emptied and – as he exited the residence and passed the sentries – he saw Chief Nerva striding away towards another exit, accompanied by two other officers.

As he neared the East Gate, Cassius heard the clatter of hooves behind him. He moved to the left side of the road but as the noise grew louder, something told him to turn. A tall, broad horse was bearing down on him.

Cassius threw himself out of the way, striking a low wall and half-burying his head in a bush.

By the time he'd recovered himself, the rider was well past. Tribune Pontius turned and gave a sly grin, then rode on.

'Bloody idiot!'

Cassius kept the volume of his shout down so that the tribune wouldn't hear, then felt ashamed for doing so.

'Bloody army!' He kicked away a nearby lump of wood, then checked himself for damage – just a few scratches on his arm.

Cassius continued on his way, still cursing. He resented always having to swim against the endless tide of army antagonism towards the Service but he was determined to prove himself. According to the demands of his father, he still had two more years to serve, and he planned to fulfil his duties as well as he could (preferably without taking any more risks than was necessary).

Thinking of the stack of paperwork awaiting him back at the villa, he quickened his pace. He would have to work hard for the rest of the day if he was to keep his evening appointment with the ladies.

II

It was the noise that did it. The previous rounds of the archery competition had been held in the morning, with only a few dozen inside the hippodrome. But the final was to commence at the eighth hour and over five hundred tickets had been sold. Before being introduced, the finalists waited inside one of the stalls usually used by chariot teams.

Indavara stood at the back, staring vacantly at clumps of horsehair stuck in the planks of the wall. There hadn't even been a cheer yet but he could hear that low buzz of excited anticipation. His hands were clammy, his throat tight; and for a moment he considered walking straight through the swinging doors and out of the stadium. But with little else to occupy him in the last few weeks, he'd put in hours and hours of practice and he was determined to see it through. Sixty-four entrants were now four and the winner stood to collect ten aurei plus a silver trophy.

One of the other competitors – a cocky Egyptian named Eclectis – was removing the remains of his lunch with a toothpick. Two others – both local men – stood close to the front, peering over the doors. Outside, the organiser of the event, Taenaris, was warming up the crowd. The two locals exchanged a few barbed comments about him then shared a drink from a jug of wine.

Indavara walked forward and checked the first few rows of benches for Sanari, the maid from next door. She had promised she would come. Corbulo had said the same but Indavara doubted he would be there, especially without Simo around to remind him. Though they shared a roof, Corbulo rarely needed his services these days and was usually busy with work or his social life.

Belatedly realising that examining the sea of faces was only making him feel worse, Indavara turned away and tried to control his breathing.

'Nervous, big man?' asked Eclectis. The Egyptian had been calling him that since the quarter-finals. Every one of the competitors was by necessity broad chested and strong, but most were leaner than Indavara. They were mainly ex-auxiliaries. Eclectis, however, was still serving and always brought along dozens of his fellow soldiers.

'Just want to get out there,' said Indavara.

'My advice – enjoy yourself now. This is as good as your afternoon's going to get.'

Eclectis had won the competition for the last three years and it seemed a good proportion of his winnings went on clothes. He was wearing a pale blue tunic decorated with two vertical bands of silver thread. The bands were not solid but composed of a series of miniature arrows arranged nose to tail. His belt buckle was, of course, in the shape of a bow.

Taenaris had almost finished the preamble. His two assistants came over, their sandaled feet visible under the swinging doors. Eclectis and the local men lined up beside Indavara.

'People of Bostra, please welcome . . . the competitors!'

The assistants pulled the doors apart. Eclectis was out first and soon bowing theatrically to the crowd gathered to their left. The surge of clapping and shouting was almost too much for Indavara, who hung back behind the others. He looked forward at the range.

The four targets had been set up on the crowd's side of the 'spine' – the high, stone structure that formed the centre of the chariot course. Precisely one hundred yards away was the rope from where the competitors would fire their arrows. Taenaris stood there, beaming.

Indavara glanced at the crowd and noticed a few city sergeants on the front row of benches, clubs laid out on the sand in front of them – ready for any trouble. Lads carrying trays were trotting around, selling palm leaves stuffed with sweet and savoury snacks. There were bookmakers on the move too; each trailed by a clerk clutching a handful of papers or a writing tablet.

Indavara was glad to be farthest from the crowd. Each competitor had been given a circular table for his equipment. The two others were between Indavara and Eclectis, who was still enjoying the attention too much to worry about actually getting ready. His cronies were already on their feet and shouting his name.

Indavara checked his gear. His leather case was propped up against the table, on top of which lay his arrows and the bow he had purchased the previous year in Syria. The string was a few weeks old – fresh enough to maintain elasticity but worn in enough to be consistent. The other archers had laughed when they saw he would be taking his arrows from the table. As seasoned auxiliaries they plucked theirs from a quiver on their back or hanging from their belt. Indavara owned one but wasn't used to it yet; he preferred his own method for now.

He ran through a few stretches and started to feel better. As he swung his arms to loosen up, Taenaris came over. The Greek was short – barely five feet – and remarkably hirsute, with black hair sprouting above his tunic collar. 'When they've quietened down I'll introduce you by name. Where are you from again?'

'Er . . . Antioch.'

'And a bodyguard, yes?'

'Yes.'

'No family name.'

'No.'

Indavara continued his exercises.

Taenaris turned to face the crowd. 'Welcome once more! Welcome all, to the twenty-second annual Bostran archery contest. And a fine one it's been this year, with competitors from six different provinces, all vying to win the much-coveted Silver Archer, not to mention ten – yes, ten – golden aurei.'

One of Taenaris's men held the figurine up to the crowd, then the bag of coins.

'Eclectis has spent half of it already!' yelled someone. The Egyptian chuckled along with the crowd and Taenaris waited once again for the noise to fade before continuing. 'First, making his debut this year: the man who set a record-equalling score in the semi-finals – twenty-six points from ten arrows. Hailing from Antioch and currently employed as a bodyguard – I wish I could afford him! – Indavara!'

Muted applause; mostly from a small group of girls sitting close to the front. Indavara had a quick look but couldn't see Sanari. The girls were soon shouted down by the auxiliaries with cries of 'Get back to work!', 'Stick to cleaning!' and a few more vulgar insults.

'Now, now, gentlemen,' cried Taenaris. 'Everyone is welcome here.'

He went on to introduce the two locals, one of whom was a previous winner. Eclectis listened proudly to every word of his introduction, which was so lengthy and flattering that Indavara reckoned he'd probably helped write it. By the time Taenaris eventually called out his name, the auxiliaries were joined on their feet by much of the rest of the crowd.

One of the Greek's men ran off to station himself by the targets, while the other inspected the competitors' equipment. Sitting at another table close by was a clerk of the Bostran court; a respectable-looking man in charge of scoring. Assisting him was a lad standing next to a large wooden frame facing the crowd. He had written the names of the competitors on paper sheets and now slotted them into openings on the left side of the frame. Next to each name was a row of holes. Once the contest started, coloured pegs would be placed in the holes to allow the onlookers to keep track of the score.

'Is Bostra ready?' asked Taenaris.

Indavara tapped his fingers against his belt; this tiresome routine had preceded the start of every round.

'I ask once!'

'Yes!' bawled the crowd.

'Twice!'

'Yes! Yes!'

'Thrice!'

'Yes! Yes! Yes!'

'Let's loose those arrows!'

A final roar, amplified by stamping boots.

'Gentlemen, ready yourselves,' said Taenaris, taking a small hourglass from the clerk's table.

Indavara selected an arrow and stepped up to the rope. He took a long breath and a long moment to gaze at the target, then turned side-on and nocked the arrow.

'Usual rules for the first round,' announced Taenaris. 'Our competitors have five minutes to fire ten arrows. At the end we will count up the scores. The competitor with the lowest score drops out and we move in to round two. As ever, an arrow stuck in the white scores one, an arrow in Hades' Eye scores three. Are the competitors ready?'

Indavara nodded, facing away from the crowd and the other men.

'Five minutes, then,' said Taenaris. 'I am turning the hourglass . . . now.'

Eclectis always got a shot in quickly to intimidate the others and – judging by the shouts – he'd struck red.

Indavara knew he had plenty of time and little to fear from the other two but he could feel his fingers shaking as he drew back the string. He stopped at three-quarters of a full extension: all he needed for a shot of three hundred feet.

He closed his left eye and slowly breathed out.

He took aim, then let go. The string snapped tight and he knew instantly the shot was low. The arrow clattered into the frame below the target, drawing a groan from the crowd.

Indavara grimaced. He'd missed only once through all the hundreds of shots in the previous rounds, and then only because some drunk had thrown a bottle onto the range. He lowered the bow. The others were already onto their second or third shots.

All those people watching. The pressure, the tension. It felt like the arena.

This is different. It doesn't matter. You can walk away whenever you want. You are a freedman. Free.

The tightness in his throat eased. He took his flask of water from the table and drank, continuing only when he felt ready. By the time he loosed his second arrow the others had all fired their fourth. It was a decent hit, not far from the three-inch circle of red.

From then on he did well: white, white, red, white, white, red, white, red. His pace improved too; and he finished just after the locals. Eclectis had been done for some time and wandered over to take a seat on the front row. The Egyptian had scored five reds and five whites, giving him an impressive total of twenty.

Thanks to Simo, Indavara's mathematical skill was now sufficient for him to count up his score, and even before Taenaris announced the result he knew he was through to the next round. His total of fifteen was matched by one of the locals but nerves had obviously got the better of the other competitor; he hadn't hit a single red. With a quick salute to the crowd, he collected his gear and sloped off.

Taenaris then brought out a comedian; entertainment for the short break before the next round. Eclectis stood there, listening and laughing along, having sent a lackey to fetch his arrows. The other competitor asked one of Taenaris's men to get his. Indavara chose to recover his arrows himself.

The walk gave him a chance to calm down but halfway along the range, he heard a woman call his name. He turned to his left and saw Sanari. She and a couple of friends had followed him; away from the benches and along the protective wall that ringed the chariot course. The young maid had that ever-present smile on her face. Indavara couldn't help grinning back.

'Well done!' she cried. 'You're through.'

'Just about,' he replied, feeling his cheeks glow. He was so relieved she hadn't shouted out to him in front of the other archers.

'You can do it. I know you can!'

The other two girls shouted encouragements too, then all three set off back towards the crowd. Indavara waved a thank-you and walked on.

He had never met anyone who smiled so much. Sanari was nineteen – a bit younger than him – and worked for the army administrator two doors down. She had first spoken to Indavara while he was doing his exercises in the back garden and she'd been hanging out washing. Corbulo reckoned she was too chubby and that it wasn't a girl's place to talk over a wall to a stranger but Indavara didn't mind any of that. They had taken a few walks since then, and he'd told her he would buy her the biggest bunch of flowers in Bostra if he won.

Shaking his head to dispel such distractions, he reached the target and plucked out the arrows. One had hit the shaft of another and was no longer usable but the rest were fine. Careful not to touch the flights, he walked back along the range. Unable to spot Sanari, he found himself looking at the images carved into the pale stone of the spine. Most of the carvings showed racing chariots and athletic contests. One, however, showed two gladiators standing toe to toe, swords raised. Indavara looked away and hurried on.

It's different. You have nothing to fear now. You are free.

He told himself these things a lot. Often at night; when he awoke and thought he was back in his cell beneath the arena at Pietas Julia. If he wanted to get back to sleep he would have to go to a window or door so that he could see something – reassure himself he really wasn't there.

He felt sweat form under his arms; and as he approached the tables he thought again about walking straight out through the gate.

No. He couldn't let himself down like that in front of Sanari. He wanted to beat Eclectis. And he wanted to beat the fear.

He didn't even listen to the comedian's last few japes; he was busy examining the arrows, selecting for the next round. Once Eclectis and the other man were ready too, Taenaris turned the hourglass over and the second round commenced.

Indavara got off to another poor start – three whites – but he forced himself not to look at either the spine or the crowd. He imagined the range as a tunnel down which the arrows would fly, straight into the eye. Of the next seven shots, five hit red. He finished shortly after Eclectis, who had registered precisely the same score. The third man was slower and needed two reds from his last two arrows to equal the others. He managed only whites and uttered a stream of imaginative curses as he took a seat in the front row.

For the next break, Taenaris had recruited a juggler and a pair of acrobats. Feeling rather calmer, Indavara even left the table and watched their alternating routines, which drew cheers and whoops from the crowd. Spying some frantically waving hands, he spotted Sanari and her friends and summoned a smile. He was grateful, but he really wished Simo or Corbulo were there.

Eclectis sidled up to him, running his hands through his shiny mane of hair. 'Now we can get down to the real fight, eh, big man?'

Indavara did not reply.

'Nothing new to you, I'm guessing.'

Indavara watched the juggler, pretending not to listen.

'All those scars. Never seen so many on such a young man. Too young to have got them all in the army, so I'm guessing maybe you're used to contests of a different kind.'

Indavara tried desperately not to react.

'Thought so,' continued Eclectis. 'So you should be used to all this. The sand, the heat, the noise. Except you look a bit nervy to me, big man – have done since you got here. So I'm thinking maybe you haven't been back in a contest like this for a while. And now it's starting to get to you a bit.'

'You think you're the only one who notices things?' Indavara replied, trying to keep his voice steady. 'Four times I've seen you compete and not once before did I see you try to put someone else off. You must be worried.'

He returned to the table. There was one easy way to shut Eclectis up and he wanted it now more than ever.

'We come to the final round,' announced Taenaris. 'Sixty-four are now two and only one man can walk away from here victorious.'

Indavara realised he had forgotten his prayers. He reached down and touched the little figurine of Fortuna nestling behind his belt.

Dear Fortuna, goddess most high, make my hand steady, make my aim true.

'Eclectis and Indavara will take turns with their ten arrows,' continued Taenaris. 'When both are finished, we will have our champion. In the event of a tie we move into "sudden death". Are the competitors ready?'

Indavara nodded. When Taenaris didn't continue, he glanced left.

Eclectis was facing the crowd, bow held casually in one hand. 'I am sometimes known as the Hawk, because of my unerring eye. It seems only fair that our new friend has his own title. I suggest the Maid – because he likes to take things from the table!'

Eclectis's acolytes weren't the only ones to laugh. Face glowing once more, Indavara kept his back to the crowd, eyes locked on the target. As the noise faded, a high-pitched voice yelled a response: 'And now he will *take* your prize!'

The auxiliaries' attempts to shout Sanari down were drowned out by the noise from the rest of the crowd. It took several efforts by Taenaris to restore order.

'As the competitor with the highest total score, Eclectis wins the right to choose who shall loose first.'

Smirking, Eclectis jabbed his bow towards his rival.

Indavara started well, the first arrow landing only an inch or two above the red. The smile finally off his face, Eclectis matched it.

Though there was noise after each arrow hit the target, the crowd remained respectful as every man took his turn. By staying focused on the imaginary tunnel, Indavara found he became calmer and calmer. Both he and Eclectis had struck red with their second shot and hit white only twice more with their next six arrows.

At this point, Taenaris broke in: 'A tie, with only two shots left!'

Most of the crowd was now standing. Taenaris held up a hand to Eclectis and Indavara; the bookmakers wanted time to register a last few wagers.

Eclectis took a couple of steps towards Indavara. He smiled for the benefit of anyone watching and kept his voice low. 'Seeing as you got out alive, I'm thinking you must have been quite a killer. That right, big man?'

Indavara just wanted to get on with it.

'Always wondered what it must be like,' continued the Egyptian. 'Standing over some poor bastard with a blade in your hand, waiting for the decision. Feel good, did it?'

Images flashed into Indavara's mind. So many men. All hurt, all bloodied, all lying in the sand.

The betting was over. Taenaris addressed the competitors. 'Indavara will loose first.'

Eclectis was already back at his table, the picture of innocence.

Indavara nocked the arrow. He raised the bow and pulled the string back. A thick bead of sweat dropped onto his right eyelid. He shook it off and adjusted his aim.

Feel good, did it?

That rush of relief, the glow of victory? Oh yes. Once the decision had been made you just got on with it. Didn't even think about it. Just did what you had to. The guilt came later.

Indavara gulped, lowered the bow, took a breath.

A few murmurs from the crowd.

He adjusted his feet slightly, raised the bow once more. He closed his left eye.

A single image returned: that poor bastard who had just lain there; his slimy, smelly guts hanging out of him, crying like a child. *Mama, Mama, Mama.*

Complaints rang out from the crowd, demanding he hurry up. Taenaris tried to silence them but the shouts continued.

Indavara tried to shut it all out. He drew back, exhaled, let go.

A white. A bad white, close to the target's edge. At least he hadn't missed.

Mild applause.

Eclectis, calm as ever, went through his smooth routine and let fly. A red.

The crowd erupted.

Indavara took a drink. Eclectis was two points ahead. Only red would do. He picked up the arrow and readied himself.

Sanari waited for a gap in the shouts. 'You can do it, Indavara! You can do it!'

I can. I can. It's all in the past. I am free.

He closed the eye, exhaled.

Mama, Mama, Mama.

He noticed something moving in front of him. The iron point of the arrow was trembling. Worse, his arm was starting to shake from the effort of holding the string.

He blinked and looked at the target once more; repeated his routine, let go.

High. So high in fact that the arrow struck the top edge, spun several times in the air, then landed in the sand.

The auxiliaries were already celebrating. Indavara put a hand to his head, suddenly dizzy. The moment passed. He looked up at the bright blue sky and suddenly the thoughts and images were gone. He couldn't believe he'd let the bastard get to him like that.

Eclectis put his bow down then turned to the crowd, arms high, lapping up the acclaim.

Indavara threw his bow onto the table and walked towards him, fists clenched.

Eclectis yelled back at his supporters, 'Just another year! Just another year!'

Sensing that their attention had shifted, he turned and grinned at Indavara. 'No hard feelings.'

'This'll feel pretty hard.'

The head-butt struck Eclectis just above his nose and knocked him clean off his feet. Indavara barely noticed the spike of pain and when his eyes cleared the Egyptian was lying in the sand, mouth hanging open.

Then came the shouts. The auxiliaries charged off the benches, knocking several people over. One man was ahead of the pack. As he drew his knife, his trailing leg caught the clerk's table and he hit the ground three yards away.

Indavara ran.

III

Cassius stood over the desk, gazing down at the piles of paper. He was determined not to let the unpleasant incident with Pontius affect him. Calvinus's vote of confidence had given him a boost and he intended to repay the gesture. Provincial governors were generally an ambitious, manipulative bunch – mostly senators in the making – but, owing perhaps to his advancing years, Calvinus seemed like a decent, thoughtful man. Cassius admired his commitment to Arabia and its people. Here was a leader in the tradition of the Republic – a man more committed to Rome than himself. It was hard not to contrast him with Cassius's commander in the Service – the ruthless, underhand Abascantius – though he was just as dedicated in his own way. Cassius hadn't heard anything from his superior since being assigned to Bostra, which was fine with him.

After a bit of rummaging he found the list of informers Verecundus had left. Rolled up with the page were the notes Cassius had made while trying to re-establish contact. He'd secured meetings with only two of the men; one had never turned up, the other had blankly refused to discuss anything relating to the Tanukh.

Cassius dropped the pages and sat down. How could he help the governor find out more about the Ruwaffa attack and the chiefs? Calvinus had his emissaries, but they moved through official channels and seemed to have made little progress.

If in doubt, make a list. His mother's maxim for taking on a big task had always served him well so he reached for a blank sheet. He had no idea where his pen case was so he fished the charcoal out of the satchel and started writing.

Informers – check again. New ones?
Spice market – ask around, or get someone else to.
Moneylenders?
Army scouts?
Merchants?
Will need bribe money. A lot.

Cassius felt something brush his ankle. He looked down and watched the cat slink past. Imagining fleas jumping from its fur onto his exposed leg, he waved a hand at it.

'Clear off, you.'

When it came to the animal kingdom, Cassius really only liked horses – as long as he didn't have to look after them, of course. Dogs and cats he detested equally, and he had no idea why anyone would want to keep the accursed things as pets. The cat sat down and stared at him.

This time he used Greek. 'Piss off!'

Cassius was about to throw the charcoal at it when he heard shouting from the street. Then the front door crashed open.

'What in Hades?'

Grabbing his sword belt from a nearby couch, he hurried out of the study and into the atrium. Indavara had just slammed the door shut. He rammed the bolt in and turned round. He was breathing hard, his face flushed and wet.

'What—'

The bodyguard held up a hand. 'Just listen. You have to do something. I think they mean to kill me.'

'Who? Why?'

'Auxiliaries. I head-butted their friend.'

Cassius could hear more shouts and rushing footsteps outside. 'Again – why?'

'Long story.'

Someone hammered on the door, which fortunately was a robust slab of hardwood framed with iron.

'We know you're in there.'

'Come out and face us.'

'Show yourself.'

A red face appeared at one of the grilled windows. 'I think I can see him!'

Cassius joined Indavara behind the door, which was now shaking, the bolt rattling in its mount. Despite the situation, Cassius couldn't help being slightly amused by the look on the bodyguard's face; it was unusual to see him so scared.

'You'd better utter a prayer to Cardea,' he advised.

'Cardea?'

'Goddess of door hinges.'

'There's a goddess of . . . forget that, do something!'

Cassius looked down at the sword belt in his hand. He drew the blade and held it up so that the eagle-shaped hilt was visible. He then motioned towards the door. 'Open it.'

'What?'

'Open it.'

'Are you sure?'

'I'm sure.'

Indavara retracted the bolt. The mob quietened.

'He's coming out,' said one man in Greek. Others were talking in what sounded to Cassius like Nabatean.

Indavara lifted the latch and eased the door open, careful to stay behind it.

Cassius stepped forward, ensuring he kept the sword high. Every inch of space between the doorway and street was occupied. There were twenty men at least: some holding clubs, a few daggers. Cassius guessed most of them noted the red tunic first, then the pricey blade with the eagle head.

The fight went out of them quickly. Shoulders sagged, a few groaned, and some began to retreat. Not the man at the front, however. He was a flabby individual with a snub nose and beady eyes, his fat fingers clutching a fighting stave.

'Where is he?' Snub asked in Greek.

Cassius offered his best flinty glare. 'Perhaps you are unused to addressing officers of the Imperial Army. I suggest you try again.'

Snub looked confused.

One of the others tapped him on the shoulder. 'Sir. Say sir.'

'Where is he, sir?'

'He's here.'

Indavara was leaning back against the wall, still hidden by the door. Cassius took a step to the right and gestured for him to come forward. Indavara did so, warily eyeing those outside. 'I'm sorry. I—'

'No, no, don't speak,' interjected Cassius.

By now, the two sentries outside the fortress had wandered over and were questioning some of the men.

Cassius called out to them. 'Leave this to me, thank you.'

The legionaries desisted but stayed to listen in as Cassius addressed the mob. 'I am Officer Corbulo of the Fourth Scythican Legion and currently a member of Governor Calvinus's staff. This man is part of my household and therefore under my protection. Any dispute is between him, the party concerned, and me. Not you lot. You should therefore leave immediately.'

'But he—'

'Finish that sentence and you'll find yourself up before the municipal court before the day is out. If your idea of a pleasant evening is to be tied to a post and have the skin flayed from your back then by all means continue!'

Cassius had spoken with such ferocity that a dollop of spittle landed on Snub's tunic. This was not the first time he'd admonished a large group of men – soldiers and citizens – and he always followed the advice of a centurion he'd observed to be particularly good at it. *Get in quick and sell your anger. Think of them as children or animals. They must believe it.*

Checking first that no one was aiming a weapon at him, Cassius stretched out his arm and pointed the tip of his sword at Snub. 'Now, I think it's about time you vacated my doorway.'

He took a step, and if Snub hadn't retreated, the blade would have struck his face. The others withdrew too. Cassius walked them all the way onto the road, stopping only when he reached the gate.

'Disperse! Quickly if you know what's good for you – I have a remarkable memory for faces.'

Only then did Cassius remember he was barefoot. As the muttering men trudged away along the street, he spotted Lepida and Helena watching from a window. He gave what he hoped was a genial shrug and returned to the house.

Indavara was leaning against the wall, recovering.

Cassius shut the door then sheathed his sword. 'I must admit I rather enjoyed that.'

'Thanks.'

'Pleasure. Nice to be able to return the favour once in a while. So what happened?'

'Don't worry, just . . . thank you.'

He walked into his room and pulled the curtain shut behind him.

⬤8➤

Cassius spent the rest of the day in the study (forgoing his usual trip to the baths) and finally finished sorting out the papers. He didn't find much else of use other than an older list of informers with some different names to follow up. He was trying to decipher some of Verecundus's scrawled notes concerning a previous agreement between Calvinus and the Tanukh when Muranda came in carrying a lamp.

'Here, sir, you'll hurt your eyes reading in this gloom.'

Cassius put the sheet down. 'I should start getting ready now anyway.'

'Out again tonight, sir?'

'The theatre. Apparently *Brutus* is on after all.'

'Who's that one by, sir?'

'Accius.'

'Mmm. I'm not one for the theatre really. I do love a good mime, though.'

'Can't stand them myself.'

As Cassius placed some paperweights on the various piles, Muranda closed the shutters.

'Sure you won't be wanting any dinner, sir?'

55

'Quite sure.'

'Not really worth cooking then, I suppose. Not if it's just going to be me.'

'Well, I doubt Indavara will be going out, and when have you ever known him to miss a meal?'

'He said he's not hungry, sir. Just sitting in the kitchen he is, miserable as I've seen him. Must have been what happened earlier.'

'He didn't tell you what had caused it all?'

'No, sir. I daren't ask how he got on at the contest.'

'The archery? The final? That was today?'

'Yes, sir.'

'Shit.'

Indavara was perched on a stool by the kitchen table, close to the hearth. He was staring at the flames, idly stroking the cat. As Cassius walked in, the bodyguard gave him a wary glance, then went back to looking at the fire.

Cassius decided to let the cat stay where it was. 'Drink?'

Indavara shook his head.

'I insist.'

Cassius found two clay mugs and made up a mix of two-thirds wine, one-third water. The wine was the local stuff – a tad bitter for his taste but good and strong. He handed a mug to Indavara then pulled the bench out from under the table so he could sit opposite him.

'The contest – apologies. I forgot.'

Cassius now recalled that Simo had left him a note reminding him to try and make the semi-finals. Now he'd missed the whole thing, including whatever had led to the trouble.

'You don't hit people without good reason. What happened?'

Indavara sipped his drink and continued stroking the cat.

From the fortress came the sound of bellowed orders, a noise they had become used to.

'Come on. Tell me.'

'I might be leaving soon.'

'Leaving? Why?'

'There's nothing for me here.'

'Of course there is.'

Indavara looked at him. 'You have things to occupy you – your job with the governor, chasing women. Simo has his work, his friends at the church-house. What do I have?'

'You have a place with us. With me, with the Service.'

'What do I care? Just another job.'

Cassius hadn't heard him talk like this before. He'd always assumed Indavara had little affection for Rome – no surprise in an ex-gladiator – but he thought their experiences together had created quite a bond. Cassius also knew Indavara had no one else; no family, no other friends.

'What about that girl, Nasari?'

'*Sanari*,' replied Indavara sternly. 'I might as well forget her. What must she think of me now?'

'Gods, man – just tell me what happened. It's not sensible to keep all your problems bottled up. Perhaps I can help.'

Even as he spoke, Cassius admitted to himself that his concern was not solely for Indavara's well-being. For someone in his line of work, a good bodyguard was essential; and Indavara had repeatedly shown himself to be nothing short of irreplaceable. But he was a troubled man, and Cassius now realised he had erred in neglecting him.

Indavara took a long breath before speaking. 'I was doing well, but this bastard Eclectis—'

'I remember the name – the current champion.'

'He worked out I'd been a fighter, started riling me – made me remember things. Things I've tried to forget.'

'So he played dirty. You must have had him worried.'

'Still worked, though. I couldn't control myself. I lost.'

'And then you hit him.'

'Yes.'

'Listen, memories such as you must have would stay with anyone. I've a share that haunt me too – as you well know – but your situation is unique. You remember nothing else before the arena. Perhaps that's why those thoughts remain so strong.'

Indavara downed the rest of his wine and slammed the mug onto the table. The cat sped silently out of the kitchen.

Cassius drank. Given what he knew, he really had been stupid not to notice the poor sod struggling. But perhaps there was a way to make up ground. 'I've been thinking about something. The first thing you remember is the arena, correct? At Pietas Julia?'

Indavara nodded.

Cassius had first considered this idea months ago but had never got round to mentioning it. 'There's bound to be a Service officer there. I can write to him, ask him to do some investigating on your behalf. You mentioned a man once, the organiser of games. He might know more about where you came from.'

'As if he would help.'

'You know how persuasive the Service can be. It may take time and it may not lead anywhere, but we could at least try.'

'You would do that?'

'Absolutely.'

Indavara gave a little smile. 'Absolutely – it means to be certain. Like a pledge or promise.'

'It does.'

'That's what you said about the contest. You said you'd be there. Absolutely.'

He stood up and walked out of the kitchen.

'Indavara . . .'

As Cassius flicked the rest of his wine into the fire, he heard the front door slam.

The theatre was only a quarter full, which still amounted to over a thousand people. The steeply angled tiers of seating were arranged in a semicircle facing the stage. Most of the bowl-like structure was composed of the local black basalt but the colonnaded front was pale limestone, which helped the stage stand out in the gloomy dusk. There had been a brief, light rain-shower earlier in the day but that was unusual for the season and unlikely to be repeated. Dozens of torches and lanterns were alight, shrouding the place in a greasy glow.

'How about here?' said Lepida as they walked down the central aisle. She was pointing at some empty seats to the right, about ten rows back. They would be close enough to hear the performance but also able to talk if they wished.

'Fine with me,' said Cassius. 'Miss?'

Helena gave a polite nod. She had said little on the walk over and Cassius guessed he would have to play the gentleman to make any progress. But – after what had been a fairly taxing day – he wasn't actually sure he could be bothered. It was all very well messing around with tavern girls but relationships of any kind with young ladies were fraught with difficulty. It was hard to get your hands on them without at least hinting at the prospect of marriage and that was the last thing on Cassius's mind. A bit of kissing and groping was usually as far as it would go, unless you got very lucky.

He waited for his companions to sit down, then did so himself, careful to ruffle his cloak up under him. The ladies, of course, both had cushions with them, once again reminding Cassius how much he needed Simo. No one would bat an eyelid at a servant carrying a cushion for his master but an army officer simply couldn't be seen with one, so he would have to contend with a cold backside for the evening. He had, however, remembered to wear an under-tunic, and the thick, woollen cloak would help too. The ladies were both in hooded capes and long stola that reached down to their ankles.

'Lucky me,' he said, 'a thorn between two flowers.'

Lepida moved in immediately, her left breast against his arm, the haze of perfume engulfing him. Cassius was glad she was sitting to the right – he wouldn't have to look at that ghastly mole. During their last trip to the theatre, her hand had wandered up his tunic and he'd had to be quite forceful to fight her off.

59

But tonight, with the fading light to cover them, he fancied he might not resist. The theatre had one notable advantage over other forms of entertainment; it was one of the few places where men and women were permitted to sit together.

'Ah, I do love that scent,' he said.

Down on the stage, a lad was sprinkling saffron water: a long-standing theatrical tradition that could have unfortunate consequences – few actors managed to get through their career without an embarrassing fall or two.

Lepida leaned forward to address her cousin. 'Officer Corbulo did some acting as a youth.'

'Really?'

'An ignoble profession, of course,' said Cassius. 'But I must admit I did enjoy it at times.'

He stifled a grin – the main source of enjoyment had been the dressing up and spying on girls getting changed.

Lepida continued: 'He also has a remarkable memory for poetry.'

'Please, Mistress,' said Cassius, 'you're embarrassing me.'

Fortunately, the play was about to begin and a corpulent actor in a green tunic had just appeared on the stage. Behind him was the first set; several screens decorated to resemble a forest. The actor held both hands high.

'Pray, silence!'

The hum of muted conversation died away.

'Thank you and welcome. Hail to the gods who watch over us!'

'Hail!' replied the locals, Lepida included. Cassius refrained; he could never quite bring himself to shout along with a crowd.

'Hail to the governor, who has ensured that tonight's performance goes ahead!'

'Hail!'

'Hail to the Emperor, Lucius Domitius Aurelianus!'

'Hail! Hail! Hail!'

Cassius felt obliged to at least mutter this.

'And now,' added the actor in his most portentous tone, 'best

of order, please. The Bostra Players proudly present *Brutus*, a
tragedy, by Accius of Pisaurum.'

He withdrew and was swiftly replaced by three of his compatriots, all dressed in luxurious robes and carrying wooden
swords. Before even the first word was spoken, Cassius felt warm
fingers upon his right knee.

Indavara hunched forward on the stone bench, chin propped up
with his hand, gazing at the statue. Simo had told him about the
sanctuary a few weeks ago and he'd already visited it twice.
Because of the darkness he couldn't see much more than the
silhouette of the crowned head but that didn't matter; he just
hoped Fortuna might help him make up his mind.

To begin with, it had seemed as if life in Bostra might be good.
He liked the idea of living in the house with the other two; having
his own room, settling down in one place for a while. And parts
of it were good; he would often help Simo with his work and in
return the attendant would help him with his numbers and letters.
But Simo had been away a while now and he'd been stuck in
the house with Muranda most of the time. She was a nice woman
but she talked too much and asked far too many questions, so
whenever he could, Indavara escaped to practise his archery.

As for Corbulo, they shared the odd laugh when they were
training but he was always busy, asleep or at the baths. And now
that he knew him better, Indavara realised he was too tied up
with himself to ever worry about anyone else. It was true he
treated Indavara better than when they'd first met and − underneath the arrogance and vanity − he was a good man. But he
was also a rich Roman; and Indavara reckoned Corbulo would
always think of him as an employee, as his inferior.

The best thing about the last few weeks had been meeting
Sanari. She didn't seem to mind about his disfigured ear and all
his scars, or that he knew so little of the world; they just seemed
to get along. They'd been together when he saw the advertisement

for the archery contest. Sanari couldn't read but Indavara knew enough Greek to work out the basics and he'd later asked Simo to confirm the details. How he wished he'd never bothered now.

He stamped down on the ground, sending some birds fluttering away. That sly bastard Eclectis; he'd knock him down again if he could.

Indavara tried hard not to think of the arena but he suspected Corbulo was right – he usually was about that sort of thing. He could remember almost nothing before waking up there so it was no surprise that such thoughts were never far away. Little things reminded him: the clang of an iron door or that first breath of fresh air. Or the noise of a crowd.

Even so, he knew he'd have got through the contest if not for Eclectis. Indavara toyed with the idea of hunting him down. Facing his cronies wasn't a concern; he would knock plenty of them over too before they stopped him.

He thought of the mob at the door. He had to admit Corbulo had done his best for him there. And perhaps things would be better when Simo came back. But he didn't know how he could face Sanari now. What he had done must have seemed so cowardly, so weak. And how could he ever explain? Not without telling her it all.

Indavara heard shouting from somewhere. Nabatean? Aramaic? He could never tell the difference. He didn't like this city much, or the province. It was too dry and too hot. He'd always preferred green lands with hills and rivers and forests. If he knew one thing about his origins it was that he came from one of the northern provinces, somewhere far, far from here.

He was also sure that Corbulo had offered to investigate his past only to make up for forgetting the contest. Indavara doubted there was anything to be discovered and he certainly didn't want to return to Pietas Julia; not after what had happened in that inn.

Perhaps it was just better to keep moving, find a new life somewhere else. He had taken the job with Abascantius because the money was good, but he'd never intended to stay with Corbulo and Simo for so long. He had plenty of coin now; enough to take him as far as he wanted to go.

Brisk footsteps on the path to his right. Two men strode out of the shadows: city sergeants, clubs resting on their shoulders as they walked. Indavara looked down at the ground, raising his head only when they were well past.

He stood up and walked across the path, closer to the statue. The goddess's face had always seemed to him how a mother would look: kind and forgiving. He knelt down.

'Dear Fortuna, goddess most high. Tell me what to do.'

Although he had missed his afternoon trip to the baths, Cassius found he was now feeling quite relaxed. The play was even worse than he remembered but the actors were rather good, their eloquent delivery making the most of the crude, melodramatic dialogue.

Even more expert was Lepida's technique. Though Cassius had taken Helena's hand, Lepida had managed to get under his cloak and up his tunic without her cousin noticing. As he caressed Helena's fingers, Lepida tightened her grip and increased her stroke. Cassius felt his breathing accelerate and shifted his right arm to cover his groin. He hoped Lepida would slow down but if anything she was going faster.

He coughed (largely to avoid making a noise of another kind) and gave the older woman a nudge. She let go, then withdrew her hand. Cassius coughed again.

'Are you all right, Officer?' asked Helena. 'Perhaps we could get you a drink?'

'No, thank you, I'm fine.'

Cassius turned to his right in time to see Lepida put her left hand to her mouth and lick her fingers.

'Officer,' said Helena in her soft voice, 'please tell me what's going on.'

'Sorry?'

'The play. I was following it up to a few moments ago but now I seem to be lost. The masks on those two actors are rather similar. Which is the daughter, which is the mother?'

'Ah. Er . . .'

Cassius heard boots clattering down the aisle steps. Looking over his shoulder, he saw a legionary hurry past. Torches weren't normally permitted in the audience and scores of people had already turned around. The legionary continued past them, then held the light up as he peered at the multitude. In such circumstances it was customary to pass on the name of the individual being sought and the people below soon did so.

'Corbulo, Corbulo.'

'Is there a Corbulo here?'

'Anyone know Corbulo?'

'It seems you are a wanted man,' said Lepida.

'Indeed,' said Cassius. 'Excuse me, ladies.'

He stood – grateful a little time had passed since Lepida had released him – and walked down the steps to the legionary. 'You there, looking for me?'

'Officer Corbulo, sir?'

'Yes.'

'Message from headquarters. There's another officer wants to see you immediately.'

'Typical.'

He hurried back up the steps to Lepida and Helena. 'I'm afraid I have to go. Army business. My apologies.'

'We will see you again soon, I trust?' said Lepida.

'Absolutely.'

He hurried away up the steps with the legionary. 'Who is this officer?'

'Sorry, sir, I can't remember the name. I did see him ride in, though. Big man, with marks on his face.'

'Marks?'

'Yes, sir. You know, scars . . . from spots.'

'Overweight, thinning hair?'

'That's him.'

Cassius sighed. 'Caesar's balls.'

64

IV

They were just yards from the fortress when Cassius heard someone shout his name. Peering back towards the villa, he spied a heavyset figure holding a lamp just outside the door. There was enough light to make out the sneering visage of Shostra, Abascantius's ever-present attendant. Cassius dismissed the legionary then trudged back along the street.

Shostra gestured at the doorway and grunted, 'In here.'

'As cordial as ever, I see,' said Cassius. 'Try addressing me correctly next time. And by the way, I don't really need an invitation to enter my own house.'

The Syrian – an ex-wrestler with the manners of a monkey and a face to match – grunted again and crossed the atrium to the kitchen.

The aching hollow that had been forming in Cassius's stomach as he marched back through the city streets now seemed to burn hot along with the rest of his body. He wiped his face and took off his cloak, then shut the front door behind him.

'By the favour of the great gods,' he whispered. 'Nothing too perilous, please.'

Cassius had made a concerted effort to worship of late and had even surmised that this might have contributed to his peaceful few months in Bostra. But a visit from Aulus Celatus Abascantius inevitably meant trouble. He draped the cloak over an unused candelabra and walked through to the kitchen.

'And here he is – the Service's best and brightest.'

Abascantius was sitting by the hearth in the dwelling's only comfortable high-backed chair. Resting on his lap was a plate stacked with bread, cheese and dates; and he was already well into a large mug of wine.

'I would get up, Corbulo, but my arse is absolutely killing me.'

Muranda – who was standing behind him – giggled.

Shostra, loitering in the shadows with his arms crossed, looked on impassively as Cassius walked over and shook his superior's forearm.

'Good evening, sir.'

Abascantius gave a sour smile. 'Hardly the warmest of welcomes, Corbulo, but I've become used to a chilly reception over the years.' He nodded down at the plate of food. 'Your girl's sorted me out, though, as you can see.'

'Sorry, sir. How was the journey?'

'Long and hard. We've been through four horses and I've barely slept a wink. Fortunately we were already in Epiphania but it still took five days. I hear that Christian slave of yours is up in Antioch. What about our quiet friend?'

'I'm not exactly sure, sir. There was an . . . incident today.'

'Oh? Well, you can fill me in later. There is a rather more pressing matter to discuss.'

'I thought there might be.'

'Mar . . .'

'Muranda, sir,' volunteered the housekeeper.

'Muranda, pour your master some wine. We may be here for a while. And shut that door – I've a nasty draught on my back.'

'Yes, sir.'

Cassius was too concerned about what was coming to summon much outrage at the way Abascantius had made himself at home. He pulled out the bench again and sat opposite the agent, who had turned his attention to Shostra.

'Get back to the fortress and make sure they've sorted out my room. And send a message to Calvinus requesting a meeting first thing tomorrow. I'll be over later.'

The Syrian departed silently.

'Indavara hasn't been back?' Cassius asked Muranda.

'No, sir,' replied the maid as she shut the back door.

'Leave us alone, would you? Tidy my room up or something.'

'Yes, sir.'

Chewing a lump of cheese, Abascantius watched the departing housekeeper. 'You need to work her harder, Corbulo. Last thing I saw with a rear end that size had a trunk and tusks.'

Cassius forced a grin. Abascantius wolfed down some more food then dumped the plate on the table and picked up a leather folder. After wiping his hands on his tunic, he opened the folder and rifled through the sheets inside.

As usual, Cassius was struck by the singular ugliness of the man. His plump legs and arms were covered with moles; his broad face by pockmarks. He seemed to have lost even more of his straggly grey-brown hair but Cassius also observed another change in him.

'I do believe you've lost weight, sir.'

'It's the worry.'

Abascantius took out a sheet and gave it to Cassius. It was composed of the finest Egyptian paper and addressed to him. His eyes ran down to the signature and wax seal at the bottom.

'From Chief Pulcher,' said the agent.

Despite his fears, Cassius couldn't ignore the slight tingle of excitement. The commander of the Imperial Security Service was not known for readily doling out praise but even a brief glance at the letter revealed its tone of genuine gratitude.

'An official commendation,' continued Abascantius. 'For your efforts in tracking down those responsible for the death of Deputy Chief Memor.'

'Thank you, sir.'

'Your report was very detailed. That murdering piece of shit Carnifex sounds like quite a foe. You did remarkably well.'

'I had a lot of help, sir.'

Abascantius replaced the folder on the table and retrieved his wine.

'I must admit I didn't expect a lot when I put you and our ex-gladiator friend together all those months ago, but you have proven yourself a potent combination. The affair with the flag must of course remain secret but this last investigation – Pulcher tells me there's even been talk of it in the Senate.'

As Cassius placed the letter on the table, the tingle of excitement became a pulse. He took a long drink and wondered whether any of the talk had reached his father. At last, something for the old man to be truly proud of.

Abascantius raised his mug and gave a toothy grin. Excitement turned to trepidation once more as Cassius realised the flattery was purely to soften him up. Now the agent would work his way round to what he was really doing in Bostra. The Emperor himself was currently leading his legions east and would soon be arriving in Syria to deal with the second Palmyran revolt. What could be important enough to drag Abascantius away from his duties in Antioch?

The older man belched, then reached into a money bag on his belt. He took out a handful of coins then leaned towards the fire, looking for one in particular. When he found it, he threw it to Cassius. 'Tell me what you see.'

Cassius put down his wine and shuffled along the bench so that he too could see it better. 'An old denarius.'

The obverse was quite worn; he couldn't read the legend around the portrait. 'Not sure which emperor that is.' He turned the coin over and examined the reverse. The image on this side was clearer – four horses leading a cart with a round object inside. Beneath was a single word. *ELAGABAL.*

'Ah. Elagabalus. The Syrian boy priest who somehow ended up emperor. If memory serves he liked to wear women's clothes and set up a brothel in the palace. Ended up dead in a sewer after four years in charge. My grandfather, and many other people, consider him to be one of the worst emperors of all time.'

'And in the cart?'

'The fabled black stone. He'd worshipped it as a child then took it with him from Emesa to Rome. A sacred rock that spoke with a voice from above.' Cassius handed the coin back. 'Or some such rubbish.'

'Given the views of our current ruler, it might be wise to keep statements like that to yourself.'

'It's true, then, sir? Aurelian really does favour the solar religions of the east now?'

'I don't know about "favour". He's certainly interested in them, though unlike Elagabalus he's too wise to elevate them above Jupiter and the other great gods. But he has recently set about acquiring the most notable icons associated with Sol or whatever name you wish to give him and placing them in the Palatine temple. The black stone is perhaps the most well known of them all. Aurelian intends – was intending – to add it to his collection.'

Cassius took a longer swig of wine to steady his nerves. 'Something tells me that what comes next might bode ill for me. This is starting to remind me of our first conversation regarding a certain missing flag.'

Abascantius glared at him. 'May I continue?'

'Sorry.'

'After the demise of Elagabalus the stone was returned to the great temple at Emesa. It has remained there for the last five decades, watched over by a brotherhood of priests. When the Emperor recently elected to lead the second campaign against Palmyra himself, he also decided to take the stone back with him to Rome. A detachment was assigned to guard the temple and await his arrival. When I left Antioch, the grand army had just crossed into Cilicia. The Emperor will reach Syria in a few weeks; and the attack on Palmyra will commence soon after. Once that is concluded, he will move on to Emesa. The unfortunate Governor Gordio will have to inform him that the stone is no longer there.'

Cassius's headache had begun as soon as he entered the kitchen and was worsening by the moment. He closed his eyes and massaged his brow.

'You needn't despair just yet, Corbulo. I know where it is.'

Cassius put down his hand.

'Here,' added Abascantius. 'In Arabia. Where exactly I'm not sure, but I know a man who does.'

'Sir, please. I beg you not to continue. There *must* be someone else who can take this on.'

'I haven't told you what I want you to do yet.'

'Find the stone?'

'Well, yes, but—'

Cassius could control himself no longer. He shot to his feet and lashed his boot back onto the bench. It hovered for a moment, then crashed noisily to the floor.

Abascantius looked up at him, stunned. 'What in Hades do you think you're doing, you little turd? Sit down!'

Cassius heard himself say, 'No.'

'What?' The agent put down his wine.

'Sir, this is simply not fair. You have asked me to shoulder a great deal already. I do not see why I should be responsible for sorting out every single problem that—'

Despite his size, Abascantius moved with surprising speed. He leaped out of the chair, grabbed Cassius's tunic and pushed him back against the wall beside the hearth.

'It seems I shall have to remind you of a few things, Corbulo. First – you do not question me. Understood? Don't say anything, just nod.'

Cassius nodded; and tried not to inhale any of Abascantius's putrid breath. The agent's fingers scraped across his chest, pulling his tunic tight around his neck.

'Second – recall that you are still a man making up for lost time – the two years you spent avoiding your Service duties by hiding in Cyzicus.'

It had actually been twenty months, but Cassius wasn't about to quibble.

'You may have covered yourself in glory of late but things change. Things can always change.'

Abascantius let go and took a step backwards. He flattened Cassius's tunic down and placed a hand on his shoulder. 'Look at me.'

Cassius did so. 'Profound apologies, sir. I didn't—'

'Just listen, lad. I have two words for you. One is deserter. The other is hero. Which do you prefer?'

'Certainly not the former, sir. But I am no hero.'

'False modesty doesn't suit you. Sit down.'

Abascantius took Cassius's drink and pushed it into his hand, then coaxed him down onto the bench.

Muranda looked in through the doorway.

'It's all right,' said Cassius shakily. 'On with your work.'

Abascantius sat down. 'And for the record, I've only actually given you one assignment that turned out to be dangerous. You took on the Memor investigation yourself.'

'Yes, sir.'

'Why?'

Cassius shrugged. 'The local magistrate was an idiot. Memor's family were bereft. Somebody had to do something.'

'There, what did I tell you? A hero. By Mars, Corbulo, you even have the looks for it – especially now you're starting to roughen up around the edges.'

Cassius took another drink as Abascantius continued.

'Believe me, I would take charge of this myself if I could but I must ride directly from here to a meeting with Prefect Venator. The Fourth Legion is to lead the counter-attack against the Palmyrans and Marshal Marcellinus has tasked me with the scouting operation.'

'Sir, it's just that I had begun to settle in here. The province has its own problems and the governor has given me the task of acquiring information on the tribal chieftains. Essential work.'

'I'm sure. And under normal circumstances I wouldn't take you away from it. But you have shown yourself to be a natural at investigative work.' Abascantius leaned forward. 'This is for the Emperor himself, Corbulo. He believes, he must win and secure the favour of Sol. And what *he* believes, *we* must believe. You called Elagabalus one of the worst emperors of all time. Quite right, but in this Dacian we might have one of the best. A few have come and gone in my time but finally we have a man worthy of the purple. Pulcher tells me he may even be planning a move into Gaul, to crush the usurper Tetricus. You and I have taken an oath to serve him. Do not forget that.'

Though he resented Abascantius's rather obvious attempts at manipulation, Cassius found himself nodding. Aurelian was an aggressive, astute commander yet also a man dedicated to peace and prosperity for the Empire. If that could be achieved, all would benefit, Cassius included.

'Sir, please forgive my outburst.'

'Already forgotten. Now, time's getting on. I need a bath and a good night's sleep. I'll see Calvinus in the morning, then call in here and give you the details.'

'Very well, sir.'

'I will, however, say this. All must do their duty and their share but – yes – it could be argued you have already done more than yours. How much longer must you serve under the agreement with your father?'

'Almost exactly two years, sir.'

'Then I offer you another agreement. If you recover the stone, I'll guarantee you six months behind a desk. How does that sound?'

There was a sudden thump against the front door.

Muranda ran through into the kitchen. 'Someone's outside, sir. Could it be those men from earlier?'

'What men?' asked Abascantius as they stood up.

'I'm sure it's nothing, sir.'

Even so, Cassius kept his hand on his dagger as he hurried across the atrium. 'Who's there?'

From outside came a strange groan.

'Indavara?' Cassius opened the door. Abascantius had grabbed a lamp and he held it over the figure lying across the path.

Indavara's top half had crushed a shrub. He gazed up at the light, eyes glassy.

'Gods.' Cassius knelt down and checked him for injuries.

'Is he hurt?' asked Abascantius.

Cassius inhaled a heavy waft of wine. 'Drunk.'

'Ah. Does he do this often?'

'Never. Can't take more than three or four mugs.'

Abascantius gave the lamp to Muranda. 'I'll take his legs. Let's get him inside.'

'By Jupiter, he's even heavier than he looks,' spluttered the agent as they finally lowered Indavara's limp form onto the bed.

'This end's even worse.'

Though his eyes were closed, Indavara waved at something, then turned onto his side and promptly began to snore.

Abascantius eyed the livid pink scarring upon his right shin. 'That new?'

'From Cyrenaica. The fight with Carnifex. It got badly infected a while back but Simo dealt with it.'

The agent turned his attention to the arrangement of the bed. It had been pushed up against one wall and was corralled by the rest of Indavara's belongings.

'He always does that,' explained Cassius. 'Simo thinks it's because he was in a cell for so long. It's strange – I'd have thought he'd want as much space as possible.'

'Fought for three or four years, didn't he? Not many survive the arena that long.'

'Six. Six years.'

'Remarkable. So you think he got drunk because of what happened today?'

'Probably,' replied Cassius as they left the bedroom.

'Come. I need to stretch my legs – you can tell me about it.'

As Cassius pulled the curtain across Indavara's doorway, Muranda appeared outside the kitchen.

'I'll be back shortly,' Cassius told her. 'Keep all the doors locked.'

'Yes, sir.'

Upon reaching the fortress gate they met the two sentries. Though in theory the men should have asked for some identification or at least the day's password, the officers' red tunics – or perhaps Abascantius's reputation – saw them through without a word. Once inside, the agent sauntered along one side of the parade ground, Cassius beside him.

'So?'

Cassius related what Indavara had told him about the incident at the hippodrome and the pursuit of the mob.

'Could have been nasty. You need to keep a closer eye on him, Corbulo. Surely I don't need to remind you about the importance of keeping him in our employ. Indavara is a valuable asset. I advise you to treat him as such.'

'There is something else, sir. Something he told me in Cyrenaica. It too perhaps explains his troubles.'

'Go on.'

'I – I felt when he told me that it's not something he would want passed around. Simo knows, but—'

'Who would I tell?' snapped Abascantius. 'Continue.'

'Indavara has no memory of his life before the arena. He was hit on the head somehow and the first thing he remembers is coming to there. The only man that knew him from before was killed not long after. All he knows is his name.'

Abascantius stopped and gazed at the torches lining the barracks on the other side of the parade ground. 'By the gods, that does explain a lot.'

'That naivety he has about him, sir, that innocence. Whatever earlier experiences he had, he cannot draw upon them. All he has known is those six years then the time after.'

'He remembers *nothing*?'

'Not a thing. I've offered to help by contacting his former owner in Pietas Julia – where he came from. Perhaps we might find some answers for him.'

Abascantius set off again. They turned at the corner of the parade ground and continued along beside a high wall. 'Perhaps. But such a distraction would be in neither of our best interests.'

Cassius felt a little guilty; discussing Indavara's fate while the poor bastard slept. But the situation had to be resolved somehow.

'Honestly, sir, I think he's better off with us. Simo gets on well with him; he's teaching him to read and write and count. But this incident, clearly it has affected him. He spoke of leaving for good.'

'We cannot have that. I will double his payment for this operation.'

'Sir, I'm not sure that's the issue. Apart from weapons he has no real interest in possessions; no one to spend it on. In fact, money just makes him more independent of us – more able to leave if that is his wish. He spoke of having no place in the world.'

'Yet he has already risked his life for the Service. For Rome.'

'He has risked his life for myself and Simo, yes. And for others. But not for Rome. Earlier today he told me it was just another job.'

As they approached the barracks, Abascantius stopped again. 'That needs to change. We must make him feel wanted, Corbulo. We must give him his place.'

V

'About bloody time. I was just coming to kick your bed again.'

A bleary-eyed Indavara tottered out of the kitchen towards Cassius, who was taking his breakfast in the courtyard. Slumping down on a stool, he eyed his plate.

'Go ahead,' said Cassius, pushing it across the table. 'I don't want any more anyway.'

As the bodyguard pulled a roll apart, Muranda appeared in the doorway. 'Morning, Master Indavara.'

Indavara managed to raise a hand as he stuffed the bread into his mouth.

Cassius held up his mug. 'Another, Muranda. And plenty of water for him.'

As the sun reappeared from behind a cloud, light filled the courtyard. Indavara bowed his head and kept eating, fringe hanging over his eyes.

'How did I get home?' he murmured.

'No idea,' said Cassius, leaning back and crossing his legs. 'We found you passed out in front of the door. Where'd you go?'

'Some tavern.'

'You're lucky those men didn't find you.'

'I wish they had.'

'Don't be idiotic, man. Oh, by the way, you owe me six sesterces.'

'Why?'

Muranda returned, carrying a steaming mug of hot wine for Cassius and Indavara's water.

'We had an early morning visit from the city sergeants regarding your misdemeanour at the hippodrome. One was a senior man – wouldn't take any less than six to drop it.'

'I'll get you the coins later.'

Indavara thanked Muranda then took a long drink. The house-keeper put her hands on her hips and looked down at him. 'Look at the state of you. Shall I put a bowl of water and a towel in your room?'

'Do so at once,' said Cassius, waving her towards the villa. 'You need to freshen up and get your tunic on. A messenger called in just before you roused yourself. We are expecting an important visitor.'

'Who?'

'A rather overweight gentleman who arrived in Bostra last night. Odious features, appalling manners and known affection-ately across the length and breadth of the eastern provinces as "Pitface".'

'He's here?'

'He's here.'

⸺ 8 ⸺

Abascantius suggested they meet in the study. As Indavara brought in two extra chairs, Cassius dug out the map of the province the agent had requested (Verecundus had left behind a decent copy – thick paper mounted on a wooden frame). Indavara placed the chairs in front of the desk and sat down. Cassius watched him watch Abascantius, who was still in the atrium, doling out a stream of instructions to Shostra. Indavara wiped some residual water off his hair and rubbed his eyes. As Shostra left via the front door, Abascantius strode in.

For once he was attired like an officer, though his scarlet cloak was rather threadbare. The helmet was in rather better condition and – uniquely in Cassius's experience – boasted a black crest. Abascantius had earlier confided to him that this had been his idea; apparently the Praetorian Guard wore the colour many centuries before and he liked the way it unnerved other officers and ranks. He deposited the helmet on the table then thumped his hands onto Indavara's shoulders.

'Look at this lad. Built like a brick shithouse, eh, Corbulo?'

He lowered his bulk into the chair and grinned at the bodyguard. 'Tell me – how in Hades do you stay in such good condition?'

'Just keep up with my exercises, sir.'

'Two hours a day,' added Cassius. 'Often more.'

'Remarkable commitment,' said Abascantius. 'Wish I had the time. So, have you seen the commendation?'

Indavara looked at him blankly.

'From Chief Pulcher,' continued the agent. 'Expressing his thanks for what you and Corbulo did in Cyrenaica.'

'I have it here,' said Cassius, pointing to the letter. 'I'll read it to you later.'

'Well, Indavara can probably read it himself now. I hear you're doing well with your numbers and letters.'

'It's difficult.'

'You are progressing, though,' said Cassius as he sat down. 'Simo says so.'

Abascantius leaned forward and shook Indavara's forearm. 'Young man, I want to thank you personally for what you did. I knew Memor well. You and Corbulo not only found his killers but avenged his death.'

'Miss Annia gave me a medal,' said Indavara.

'The daughter? You did that family a great service.'

Indavara looked thoughtfully out of the window behind Cassius.

'To business,' said Abascantius. 'You two have been lounging around here in Bostra too long; time to set you to work once more. Corbulo, you told Indavara about the stone?'

'I did. Sir, you said there was a regular army garrison at Emesa. Surely they have been searching for it since it was stolen?'

'Indeed, but without success. The commander there was a centurion named Ursus – from the Sixteenth under Prefect Sanctus. Apparently, this Ursus made a valiant attempt to stop the raiders but virtually his entire force was wiped out. Sanctus refuses to have any Service officers attached to his legion so his recovery efforts have been . . . well, let us say unimaginative. He also has limited numbers of troops available because of the Palmyrans.'

'But you have made some progress, sir?'

Abascantius had the leather folder with him again. He took out a small sheet of paper. 'I've lost count of the people I've paid for information over the years. I get letters every week offering some essential piece of intelligence, always demanding money in return, of course. Most of it is useless. I hadn't heard from this fellow for ages – to be honest I thought he was dead – but this arrived nine days ago.'

He handed the letter to Cassius. 'Ulixes was a legionary for a few years and a spy for many more. A rogue and an inveterate gambler but he appears to have stumbled on something.'

Cassius read the letter through. When he finished, he found Indavara staring at him expectantly.

'One of Ulixes's old informers was heading north from the western coast of the province several weeks ago and tried to enter a town, but was refused entry because it had been taken over by a chieftain and some kind of cult.'

'Which town?' asked Indavara.

'Doesn't say,' replied Cassius. 'It'll become clear why in a minute. This man continued north and stopped at a cistern to water his horse. A large party of heavily armed horsemen riding south towards the town stopped there too, led by a big, fair-haired northerner. The informer stayed out of their way but noticed they appeared to be guarding a large cart, even though it seemed to contain nothing but reeds. Eventually he arrived back in Damascus and related the tale to Ulixes. Ulixes thought no more of it, but a few days later he met some scouts from the Sixteenth outside the city and one officer recognised him from his army days. Knowing he had worked as a spy, the officer told him what they were searching for and asked if he knew anything. Ulixes told him nothing, then contacted Master Abascantius.'

Cassius returned the letter.

'Why not tell them?' asked Indavara.

Cassius gave him a knowing look.

'Because the sly bastard wants money,' said Abascantius, 'and he knows I pay well. I received a second message from him while in Epiphania. In return for a certain amount of coin, he will disclose the name of this town.'

Abascantius got to his feet. 'Let's have a look at the map.'

Cassius turned it so that all three of them could see.

The agent pointed at the southern region of the province below Petra. 'Depending on the informer's route north, it might have been any of these towns in or close to the Hejaz mountains. I would assume quite far to the south.'

'Because it has been taken over by this chieftain?' said Cassius.

'Yes – well beyond our reach. I met with Calvinus this morning. He briefed me about the attack on Ruwaffa and the wider situation but knew nothing about any particular chief or cult.'

'Might we be able to narrow the possible location based on the temples and sects in each town?'

'Unlikely. Most, if not all, have connections to one of the sun gods. I imagine all would covet the black stone.'

'Why take it, though?' asked Cassius. 'Why risk a conflict with Rome?'

'Perhaps they think they *are* beyond our reach down there; that we've little chance of finding the stone. And they would probably have been right if not for Ulixes. The gods have favoured us with this stroke of luck. We must use it.'

'*If* he's telling the truth,' countered Cassius. 'What if he heard the troops were looking for the stone, then invented this tale about the informer. I'm sure he stands to earn a considerable sum.'

'He is expecting one hundred aurei. We shall give him half.'

'But it could so easily be a ruse.'

'The thought had occurred to me, Corbulo,' said Abascantius sharply. 'And I might agree with you were it not for one particular detail. I managed to get a look at Prefect Sanctus's report regarding the theft of the stone. One of the few surviving witnesses was a young priest. He was unable to speak for several days afterward but when he did, he offered what has turned out to be a vital piece of information. He watched the raiders as they set about removing the stone from the temple. He saw their leader without his helmet – a tall man with fair hair. This northerner. Ulixes is telling the truth.'

Cassius leaned back and considered what he'd heard.

Abascantius let his belt out a notch, lowering the flabby rolls of his gut. 'I told Ulixes to be in Petra in seven days' time. He will be at the Temple of Atargatis at midday. You are to meet him, get the location and pay him. You will then proceed south and attempt to recover the stone.'

'Might I ask how, sir?' asked Cassius, trying not to sound incredulous. 'Will Calvinus let us use men from one of the southern garrisons?'

'He might. But I wouldn't dream of using conventional forces. Word would travel several days ahead of you: whoever has the stone would have ample time to make their escape.'

'What's the alternative?'

'A covert squad of around twenty soldiers – small enough to avoid detection, big enough to grab the stone. You will masquerade as a merchant and they as your local help.'

Cassius couldn't even reply; the assignment was sounding more perilous by the minute.

Indavara spoke up. 'You said soldiers. Not legionaries?'

'To move freely through that area the men will have to pass as natives. They will need to speak Nabatean and know the ways of the desert and its people. We will use auxiliaries from one of the cohorts based here in Bostra.'

'*Auxiliaries?*' repeated Cassius.

'Yes. And if that pompous arsehole Pontius has done his job, some volunteers will be waiting for us in the fortress right now.'

Abascantius stood. 'Come, we must choose our twenty. There will be an officer to lead them. Don't worry, Corbulo, only an optio – local, apparently. I think we both know field operations aren't your strength, so I thought it seemed wise.'

Cassius couldn't deny that; in fact he was relieved. 'Fair enough, sir.'

'Swiftly then, I have only today to help you prepare. I need to be back on the road tomorrow.'

As Abascantius and Indavara left, Cassius remained behind for a moment and examined the map. South of Petra was a region dominated by desert, where only the hardiest creatures and men could survive. Three centuries earlier, the emperor Augustus had launched an expedition under a general named Aelius Gallus to cross the barren wastes and reach the kingdom of the Sabeans, a people who had grown rich through producing incense and spices. The expedition had ended in disaster and Gallus had been forced to retreat, defeated by the conditions and the treacherous locals.

Cassius stared at the bottom of the map, beyond the last known settlements and roads. It was blank.

— 8 —

The fortress was virtually empty. So far they'd seen only a handful of men, mainly clerks and other specialists exempt from regular duties.

'Manoeuvres going on apparently,' remarked Abascantius as he led the way along the main avenue. To their left was a long, timber-built warehouse, to their right the hospital, a stone building with a wide entrance that opened out into a courtyard. Cassius looked inside as they passed, noting a herb garden and several men lying on beds in the shade.

'This place is huge,' said Indavara, who had never accompanied Cassius on his few trips inside.

'Has to accommodate the best part of an entire legion,' replied Abascantius.

At the centre of the complex they came to the legion head-quarters: a two-storey structure from which a pair of large standards flew. One bore the SPQR legend topped by an eagle; gold thread on thick scarlet cloth. The other was for the Third Cyrenaican: above the legend was a prowling lion; gold thread on black. Two more sentries guarded the main door, both in helmets and armour.

At each corner of the headquarters was a neatly trimmed acacia with sap lines running down its silvery bark. Arising from squares of earth between the paving slabs, the trees looked rather

82

incongruous amongst all the brick and stone. Under one was a young gardener tilling the soil. Beneath another stood a soldier. He stepped out of the shadows and marched towards them.

'Officer Absacantius?'

'You Mercator?'

'Yes, sir.'

Mercator was a serious-looking fellow of around thirty, with a few grey flecks in his light beard and thick hair. His flattened nose had been broken more than once and he had the thin, pursed lips of a man who rarely smiled. He was a similar size and shape to Indavara, if a couple of inches taller and a few pounds lighter. Though the metal rings of his belt gleamed, his dagger and sword were mounted in plain, undecorated sheaths. Upon the sleeves of his tunic was a double red band, signifying his rank. If first impressions were anything go by, Cassius adjudged the optio a solid choice.

Abascantius didn't offer his forearm, but instead gestured to Cassius. 'Officer Corbulo. You'll be working for him.'

Cassius winced at that phrase. He readied himself for a forceful grip but Mercator was no more than politely assertive. Cassius observed the older man glancing at his helmet, noting its poor condition perhaps.

'Optio Secundus Sidonius Mercator – third century, first auxiliary cohort.'

To Cassius's surprise, Abascantius also introduced Indavara, describing him as 'another of my operatives'.

'The volunteers are waiting as you ordered, sir,' said Mercator. 'The senior officers and I have already weeded out a few but there are still sixty for you to choose from.'

'Excellent. Lead on.'

Just as they set off, there was a loud bang from behind them. Turning round, they saw a second window shutter rebound off the headquarters wall with equally loud results. Behind a grille up on the first floor was the face of Chief Nerva. 'Aulus! A word.'

Abascantius made no attempt to hide his annoyance but waved to Nerva before addressing Cassius. 'Go and make a start. Don't mention any details. I'll be along presently.'

As he hurried back towards the headquarters, the others continued along the avenue, Mercator setting a swift pace. 'I see you wear the crest, sir. I'm never quite sure of the rank of you Service men.'

'It is rather confusing,' admitted Cassius. '"Officer" and all that. I do, however, hold the rank of centurion, and I am attached to the Fourth Scythican. I previously commanded a fort during the first Palmyran revolt.'

Cassius didn't often trot that one out – it brought back too many unpleasant memories – but Mercator was probably already taken aback by his age; it seemed sensible to try to win him over.

'And yourself?' asked Cassius. 'Aiming for centurion eventually, I presume?'

'I am.'

'I do appreciate that a crest is rather harder to achieve via the conventional route.'

Mercator seemed to accept this in the spirit it had been intended.

'How do you find the auxiliaries?' Cassius asked him.

'Fine. I have local blood on my mother's side, which helps. There were no optio posts available in my cohort so when I wanted to move up from guard officer it was the best alternative.'

'You and your men are housed here?'

'No, the auxiliary cohorts are based at the old fort, about a mile or so away. We're not needed for the manoeuvres until tomorrow.'

'You don't mind the prospect of leaving your century at such short notice?'

'They can do without me for a few weeks.'

'You volunteered yourself?'

'Yes.'

Cassius said nothing but he found this odd. An ambitious officer prepared to abandon his cohort for a risky operation with the unpopular Service? It didn't make much sense and he made a mental note to question Abascantius about it later.

The auxiliaries were waiting between two of the barrack blocks. Some had been sitting but upon seeing the officers they got to their feet and joined the others in three neat lines, hands behind their backs. Aside from their more obviously local features, they were barely distinguishable from legionaries. As he got closer, however, Cassius did note a lack of tattoos, a preponderance of sandals over boots, and a number of curved daggers housed in ornate sheaths.

Mercator addressed the auxiliaries. 'At ease, men.'

He turned to Cassius. 'You have some specific criteria, I believe?'

Cassius answered quietly. 'It is most important that they're able to pass as hired swordsmen from the province: fluent Nabatean, of course, and a good understanding of local customs and habits. Other than that, we need competent riders, able fighters.' He lowered his voice to a whisper. 'And no idiots. They may have to keep up the pretence for several weeks – the smallest detail might give us away.'

'Understood, though I wish I'd been told all that before.'

'I heard of this plan less than an hour ago myself.'

'May I use your name?'

'Go ahead.'

Having worn his helmet quite regularly in recent weeks, Cassius was finally beginning to get used to the weight of it, though the itchy leather strap still annoyed him. Reminding himself not to fiddle with it, he stood up straight and met the eyes of the men before him.

Mercator began. 'Morning. For those of you who don't know me – I am Optio Mercator of the Third. This is Officer Corbulo, Imperial Security. As you've been told, we are looking for volunteers for a special assignment lasting around a month. A substantial additional payment is being offered but first we must go through some requirements. You will need to know Nabatean. Please raise your hand if you consider yourself fluent.'

Every single man did so.

Cassius turned to Mercator. 'I don't believe it. Sure they all know what fluent means?'

'The majority are Arabian but there are a few Egyptians and Syrians. Plus some come from Greek-speaking areas. I'm sure they all know the basics, but—'

'Can't blame them,' said Cassius, lowering his voice again, 'they want the money. You *are* fluent, I take it?'

'Of course.'

'Then I suggest you go through them one by one – dismiss anyone who isn't up to scratch. I can continue from the front here.'

'Very well.'

Mercator walked around to the rear line and began quietly questioning the first man.

'You will also need to be able to ride,' Cassius told the auxiliaries. 'For an extended period, probably across some difficult terrain; and I know men drawn from an auxiliary infantry cohort will not all be expert riders. I will be leading a drill later and anyone not up to standard will be dismissed. Do not waste my time or yours; drop out now if you're not up to it.'

Five men stepped out of line and sloped away.

'Straight back to your centuries!' barked Mercator, who was already conversing with the next man.

'Don't worry,' Cassius said quietly to Indavara with a grin, 'I'll excuse you from the riding drill.'

'And yourself from the sword drill?' replied the bodyguard. 'If this lot see how you handle a blade they'll probably all drop out.'

'Most amusing. On that topic we must fit in another lesson before we leave.'

'You're assuming I'm coming with you.'

Before Cassius could respond, he saw Abascantius approaching. The men all cast curious looks at the overweight figure with the unusual black crest. Cassius heard a few whispered comments, several of them mentioning 'Pitface'.

'How are we doing, Corbulo?' asked Abascantius, rings of sweat already staining his tunic around the armpits.

'Mercator's assessing their Nabatean, sir. We've also just got rid of a few poor riders.'

Abascantius took his helmet off and wiped his brow, then walked up to one of the men. 'Ever seen action, lad?'

'Yes, sir. Palmyran revolt. Fought alongside the legion right here in the city.'

'Good, good.' He moved on to the next man. 'What about you?'

'No, sir. I joined up a year ago.'

'But eager to do your bit, I'm sure.' Abascantius took a few steps backward. 'If you've struck an enemy of Rome with your blade, raise your hand.'

About half the men did so.

'Could be worse, I suppose,' Abascantius said to Cassius, before addressing the auxiliaries once more.

'Listen here, I'm not going to tell you my name – just know that I'm in charge. This job will be tough. You'll be a long way from home and a long way from help. You'll be drawing those blades, more than likely blooding them. However, you will have good men leading you; and we'll be making it worth your while. But if you'd rather stick to what you know, stay with your century. There's no shame in it. If it's not for you, you can leave now with your head held high.'

Another nine men left. Despite Abascantius's words, all looked rather ashamed.

'You and I can work through the rest from the front,' the agent said to Cassius, unconcerned about keeping his voice down. 'Get rid of any you don't like the look of. The last thing you're going to need is troublemakers.'

Half an hour later they were down to thirty-two. Mercator had dismissed six more whose language skills were deficient, while Abascantius had got rid of another five, one of whom he bodily threw out of the line for asking his name. Cassius had rejected two, one because his equipment was inexcusably shoddy, another because both his Greek and Latin were atrocious. He'd also had to refuse another man after Indavara noticed that he appeared to have an infected leg wound.

'Well, that'll do for now,' Abascantius told Cassius and Mercator, scratching his chin as he surveyed the depleted lines. 'You can use the drills to whittle them down to twenty. We might as well tell them what they'll be getting.'

He turned to the men once more. 'As I understand it, you auxiliaries receive four hundred denarii a year. Now, the twenty that progress from today's drill to become the final squad will receive the same amount for this assignment alone. But it will be paid as sixteen golden aurei. Four will be given to you before you leave the day after tomorrow, the balance when you return.'

Several of the men smiled.

'However,' added Abascantius, 'if the officers here have a single problem with you during that period the final amount will be reduced. Substantially. You will be given more details about the operation in due course but I can assure you that it is of the greatest importance to this province and the Empire.'

Cassius smothered a grimace. The operation was evidently important to the Emperor but it was hard to avoid the conclusion that the auxiliaries might be better employed protecting the province and their own people. Only Indavara saw his reaction; he was standing several yards away, silently looking on.

Abascantius continued: 'In recognition of your commitment to Rome, I am also offering the final twenty something else.'

He reached into a bag hanging from his belt and took out a small, two-leaved bronze plaque. 'I'm sure you all know what this is. Most of you can expect to receive your discharge certificate after serving twenty-five years, entitling you to a full military pension and other benefits. It is what you are all striving towards. I can bring it closer. Ten years closer. Governor Calvinus has agreed to make the arrangements.'

This caused even more excitement than the money. Many of the auxiliaries exchanged smiles and comments.

Cassius was still looking at the discharge certificate in Abascantius's hand. It had given him an idea.

VI

Organising the riding drill took an annoyingly long time. Most of the horses were being used for the manoeuvres and Nerva had refused to provide any more than three. Abascantius confided to Cassius that the chief centurion's long-standing enmity towards the Service meant that they could expect little assistance from him. Pontius, however, had been helpful, even going as far as to personally recommend Mercator. As a man with serious political ambitions, the tribune had to take rather more care how he treated Abascantius than the veteran Nerva.

'That stubborn prick,' said the agent as he and Cassius watched some lads lead the horses onto the fortress corral. 'He *demanded* to know what we needed the men for. As if I would disclose Service matters to the likes of him.'

'The governor knows, though, sir?'

'Of course. I had no choice there. Just hope the old boy keeps it to himself.'

'He seems a decent man.'

'Better than most. Can you take it from here? I have some other matters to attend to.'

'Yes, sir.'

Abascantius plucked his helmet off a nearby fence post and pulled it on. 'When you're done here, start thinking about logistics: mounts for the journey, supplies, weaponry . . .'

'Yes, sir.'

As the auxiliaries parted to let Abascantius through, Cassius quietly cursed. Organising all that needed doing in little more than a day would be a struggle, especially with no Simo to assist him. The thought of leaving Bostra without the capable attendant was deeply depressing. Cassius was trying not to think about what they might face in the southern desert. He now knew from experience that the only way to get through the next few weeks would be to negotiate a day at a time.

'Right, first three men – in you go and get ready.'

With the lads holding the horses, the auxiliaries walked through the open gate and onto the mix of sand and bark that covered the ground. Cassius noticed a few jumps and other obstacles piled up in the middle of the oval-shaped corral but he didn't plan to make things complicated. All he needed to know was whether the men could handle a horse properly.

As the trio hesitantly mounted up, he looked over at Indavara's group, who'd occupied the empty space between the corral and the road. Mercator had earlier collared an armourer, who'd furnished them with some wooden practice swords. The bodyguard and the optio were now assessing the fighting skills of the other half of the auxiliaries.

Despite his apparent lack of enthusiasm, Indavara had perked up at the prospect of the sword drill. Cassius wondered how he'd fare with the auxiliaries – he was hardly the most vocal of men, after all. But, as he looked on, Indavara raised a sword and gestured for one of the soldiers to come at him. The man seemed keen to impress and darted this way and that, striking from different angles and positions. Indavara held his ground, seeing off every thrust with smooth parries and sidesteps. After a while the deflated auxiliary gave up, but Indavara encouraged him to continue against another man and moved on.

'Sir?'

The auxiliaries were ready; the lads out of the corral.

'Right. Circuits. Nice space between you. Keep to a walk for now.'

As they began, one of the other auxiliaries came up to the fence. 'Sir, it's been a while since I've ridden. I should tell you, I might—'

Cassius cut him off with a palm held up to his face; he wanted to watch the others. Two were passable but one man had taken up a terrible posture, his weight too far forward.

After two circuits he ordered a trot. The third man was still struggling to control his mount and seemed to have no clue how to speed up. As he approached the gate, Cassius ordered him to stop. Even this was a challenge and one of the lads had to intervene and grab the reins.

But the auxiliary was determined to persist. 'Another go and I'll get it right, sir. Honestly.'

'Dismount. You won't be coming with us.'

The Arabian muttered an oath, no doubt imagining those precious gold aurei slipping through his fingers.

'I told you to dismount.'

The man did so.

Cassius called out to the remaining riders. 'Gallop!'

The auxiliary struck his leg with frustration, then walked over to the others.

'Thank you for volunteering,' said Cassius, conscious that the men would also be sizing *him* up, seeing what kind of officer he was. 'Back to your century.'

As the auxiliary complied, Cassius ordered the riders to make a turn and trot in the other direction. Both managed this with little difficulty and he decided he'd seen enough.

It took him half an hour to watch the rest of the recruits. By the end he'd lost three more, which left him with twelve competent riders. As the last of the rejected men departed, Cassius led the auxiliaries over to the second group.

Indavara and Mercator had only four pairs still fighting, the sound of their scuffing boots mixing with the sharp crack of wood on wood. The others were sitting down, watching.

'Easy there,' said Indavara to one wide-eyed soldier who looked as if he thought he was in a real battle. 'Your shoulders are all tensed up. Watch the blade, not the man.'

Mercator looked on with arms crossed.

'Well?' Cassius asked him as the men sat with their compatriots.

'I've decided to leave it to your friend there. Where did you find him anyway?'

'Long story. By the way, I see we've got a couple of guard officers with us.' Cassius had noted the single red band on their tunics.

'That's Yorvah with you – good soldier. He'll have no trouble with the sword. How was his riding?'

'Excellent. It will be useful to have one or two squad leaders. And this man here?'

'Andal. He'll not struggle with the riding either.'

Cassius moved on to Indavara. 'What do you think?'

Indavara nodded at the men already sitting down. 'They're all decent.'

'Decent?'

'A lot better than you, not as good as me.'

Cassius was at least grateful Indavara had kept his voice down. 'I suppose that's clear enough. What about these others?'

'Some of them were originally recruited as archers. It shows. How many can we lose?'

'Anyone who's not up to it.'

'There are four.'

'Tell them.'

'You tell them. I'm not even in the army.'

'Which ones?'

'The young lad, that pair at the end, and the fat one.'

'That'll do, men,' said Cassius. Once the auxiliaries had lowered their swords, he pointed in turn at the four Indavara had selected. 'Thank you for volunteering. I'm afraid you won't be joining us. You can head back to your century.'

Two of the men placed their swords on the ground and left immediately. Another looked for affirmation from Mercator before joining them.

The young soldier, however, didn't move an inch. 'That's not fair.' He aimed the sword at Indavara. 'Why's he deciding? He doesn't fight like we've been taught anyway.'

'Perhaps you'd like to take him on and we can see whose way is best?' suggested Cassius.

'The decision's been made,' said Mercator. 'The others were stronger. On your way.'

Realising he wasn't going to get anywhere, the auxiliary added his sword to the pile and left.

'Right,' said Cassius to the sweating swordsmen. 'Over to the corral, you lot.'

He turned to Indavara and Mercator. 'Remember we need twenty. No more, no less.'

Half an hour later they had them. While the men filled up their canteens from a barrel of water supplied by Mercator, Cassius took the optio and the two guard officers aside. 'We aim to leave the day after tomorrow. If you and the men have any affairs to tidy up, now is the time to do it. But do not discuss the operation with anyone.'

'With respect, sir,' said Andal, the older of the two, 'we don't know enough to discuss anything.'

'It will have to stay that way for now.'

'Might be a few drop-outs before we leave,' said Mercator.

'Why?'

'Some of them have women, family. Given a bit of time to think about it they might decide they'd rather stay here in Bostra.'

'Well, we have a few reserves we can call up,' said Cassius. 'Now, we've covered horses and supplies. What about weapons? What would a bunch of desert warriors be carrying?'

The three Arabians looked at each other. Yorvah touched the curved dagger at his belt. 'One of these, certainly.'

'All the men have one?' asked Cassius.

'Just about,' said Mercator.

'Make sure they *all* do. What about swords?'

'Actually a lot of the Tanukh carry legionary-issue blades; thousands were handed out during the Palmyran war.'

'You can keep your own, then. What about bows?'

Cassius glanced at Indavara but he again seemed content to observe in silence.

'We have some archers,' said Andal.

'Useful to have a few,' said Mercator.

'Indeed,' said Cassius. 'Tell those that have them and are happy to carry the gear to bring them. What about armour?'

'Occasionally a helmet or a bit of mail,' said Andal. 'Generally the nomads travel light.'

'Then I'm afraid we must do the same. No armour.'

'We' would not include Cassius. In disguise or not, he would be taking his pricey copper alloy mail-shirt.

'Other than that,' he continued, 'each man may bring what he thinks he'll need, but remind them – nothing else issued by the army. No canteen tins, no entrenching tools, no military belts. Which brings us onto clothes.'

'Not a problem,' said Mercator. 'Forgive me, Officer, but something tells me we'll have a lot less trouble blending in down there than you will. You have some kind of cover story, I presume?'

'You presume correctly. Anything else?'

The three locals shook their heads.

'Mercator, we will need to meet again tomorrow. My villa is the third on the right outside the main gate. Will you come along at the second hour?'

'Of course.'

'Very good. Thank you for your help, gentlemen.'

With that the trio turned away.

'Oh, one more thing,' said Cassius. 'I've noticed these desert folk are a hairy bunch. Anyone without a beard must grow one.'

As Mercator and the auxiliaries collected up the swords and left, Cassius walked over to Indavara, who was cleaning his dagger blade with a cloth.

'You seemed to rather lose interest once the fighting stopped.'

Indavara shrugged. 'Back to the villa?'

'Yes.'

Once on the avenue, they turned left. A squad of cavalrymen trotted by, roaring at some jape.

'What do you think of our auxiliaries, then?' asked Cassius.

'Not bad.'

'I'd prefer the pick of the legion. Some good sword-hands?'

'Like I said, not bad.'

Indavara kicked a stone that skittered away into the end of a barracks. They walked on in silence: past the headquarters building, past the hospital and the warehouse, then onto the empty parade ground.

'Long ride down to Petra,' said Cassius. 'And who knows how far to wherever this bloody stone is.'

Indavara stopped briefly to scratch his shin; the skin there was yet to fully heal.

'Twenty men,' added Cassius ruefully as they walked on. 'The raiders had many more than that when they grabbed the stone. I wonder how many protect it now? Probably a lot more.'

'Probably.'

'Mercator and the guard officers seem capable at least, eh? Good to have them with us.'

This time Indavara didn't even reply.

Cassius stopped in the middle of the parade ground.

Indavara took a few more steps then halted too. 'What?'

'You *have* to come. You *have* to. Not having Simo will be bad enough. I cannot go on my own. I just *cannot*. Tell me you're coming.'

'I haven't decided yet.'

'Abascantius thinks you're coming.'

'He may be in for a surprise.'

'Must I beg?'

'You wouldn't beg.'

'Actually that's true, but I *am* asking. One friend to another.'

Indavara gave a slight grin and walked towards the gate.

'What does that mean?' asked Cassius. 'Is that a yes?'

'It means I'm hungry,' replied Indavara as he quickened his pace. 'It's lunchtime.'

Cassius stood there, watching him. 'Gods, give me strength.'

—◆8◆—

Indavara was less critical of Muranda's cooking than Cassius, but he decided to buy his lunch on the street. One stall sold some excellent spiced sausages and after two of these, followed by a handful of mixed nuts, he felt considerably better. Watching a long column of carts leaving the fortress, he walked slowly back towards the villa along the Via Cappadocia.

Fortuna hadn't helped him much this time. Sometimes just asking her for guidance steered him to his own decisions and once or twice he thought he'd actually heard her voice, but he still couldn't make up his mind. He wouldn't admit it to Corbulo or Abascantius, but the prospect of hunting down this mysterious stone sounded a lot more interesting than sitting around in Bostra, especially now he'd ruined things with Sanari.

Nearing the villa where she worked, he looked over the front wall, hoping she might be there. The small, neat garden was empty. Before he realised it, he'd stopped and put his hands on the wall. He looked at the six windows in turn, hoping to glimpse her face. He saw only darkness beyond the shutters. He thought about walking up to the door, asking to see her. But it was a busy household: her employer had a wife, three children and several other servants. Indavara wouldn't know what to say, and he'd probably get Sanari in trouble – then she'd definitely never talk to him again.

Suddenly the door opened. Indavara hurried along the street but after a few steps glanced back. The old steward had appeared. He always looked very serious, though Sanari said he was a good-hearted man. In his hand were some rolled-up papers. Indavara continued on his way.

'Hey. Hey, you.'

The steward came up the path and spoke without looking at him. 'She's in the alley there. Hurry up, I don't want Mistress to see you.'

The old man continued along the street towards the fortress. Indavara doubled back, then jogged down the alley that separated the villa from Lepida's place. A door opened and Sanari slipped outside. As he hurried up to her, she carefully shut the door. There was no smile this time.

'Are you all right?' he asked.

'Why didn't you come and see me?' she replied, arms wrapped around herself though it wasn't cold.

'I – I didn't know what—'

'Why did you do it? Why did you hurt him like that?'

'He was saying things to me. Trying to put me off.'

'I heard he didn't wake up for almost an hour. He hasn't been out of his bed since.'

'I didn't know that.'

Indavara just looked at her. He'd never seen her face like this.

'What did he say to you?' she asked.

'It doesn't matter. I shouldn't have done what I did. I know that.'

Someone walked past the end of the alley. They both looked, but whoever it was had already disappeared.

'You shouldn't hurt people like that. It isn't right.'

'Can I see you later?'

Sanari looked down at the ground. 'People are talking about you. It will be difficult for us now.'

Indavara was about to reach for her hand when someone called her name.

'I have to go.'

'Will I see you again?'

'Sanari!' It was a woman's voice; a well-spoken woman.

Without another word, Sanari opened the door and hurried inside.

Indavara stared at the scarred planking of the door for a while. He heard her talking to someone then the voices faded. He looked back along the alley and wished more than ever that Simo would return. He would know what to do.

The last thing Indavara needed now was another earful from Corbulo.

The sanctuary? Yes, there.

— 8 —

Shostra emitted a loud grunt as he dumped the little barrel in the atrium. Abascantius shut the front door behind him as Cassius came through from the kitchen.

'A gift, Corbulo.'

At a signal from his master, Shostra wrapped his remarkably long arms around the barrel and tipped it on its side. Cassius peered down at the bottom and saw a small stopper. Shostra unscrewed it and pulled it out. Abascantius gestured to the barrel. Cassius squatted down and looked inside. Seeing something glinting, he plucked out a gold aureus. The coin was in pristine condition.

'Where's Fat-arse?' asked Abascantius.

'Outside dusting the carpets. Don't worry, she's harmless.'

Abascantius shut the kitchen door. 'She likes to talk.'

Cassius was still examining the coin. On one side was an image of Aurelian, on the other two crossed swords.

'Only a few weeks old – fresh from the mint at Cyzicus,' added the agent. 'There are two hundred in there. And some wine in the top half in case anyone gets thirsty. Or curious.'

'Two hundred?' Cassius struggled to keep his voice down.

'Fifty for Ulixes. The rest is to use as you see fit. An amount like that will buy you a lot of information. Or cooperation. Obviously the men needn't know, Mercator included.'

Cassius replaced the coin. 'Ingenious.'

While Shostra put the stopper back in, Abascantius handed over a small sheet of paper with a few lines written on it. 'You'll have to sign for it, of course.'

Cassius took the paper into the study.

'Find somewhere to hide that,' Abascantius told Shostra before following Cassius. 'Where's Indavara?'

'Not sure, sir.'

Cassius signed the sheet and handed it back to him. 'Actually, on that subject . . .'

'Yes?'

'He's talking about not coming. I suspect it's a bit of a ruse for attention but I can't be sure.'

Abascantius grabbed a handful of sunflower seeds from a bowl Muranda had left on Cassius's desk. 'He was doing his bit with the auxiliaries today. Seemed quite keen.'

'I need to be sure, sir. Otherwise I might find myself travelling alone with two hundred aurei and twenty men I hardly know.'

'That wouldn't be ideal.'

Chewing noisily on the seeds, Abascantius leaned back against the desk. 'So still no word from that Gaul of yours?'

'I shall wring his fat neck when I see him. To be late is bad enough but to send no word. It's an outrage.'

'How late is he now?'

'Four or five days.'

'You do realise he may have left you.'

'Simo? Never.'

'Be realistic, Corbulo. It happens all the time. You think he adores attending to your every need so much that he's never thought of having a life of his own?'

'He comes from a line of slaves. He has known nothing else.'

'These Christians put ideas in their heads. They don't worship our gods, they don't worship the Emperor, but you expect him to worship you?'

'Simo's not like that. He wants to follow their teachings, I know; and he wants to do good, but—'

'There – he wants to do good. Will he be able to do what he would consider good working for you; in our line of business? No, it'll be a wrench to start with, good slaves are hard to come by, but you need someone who can do more than wash your loincloths and cook up a good meal. That's women's work. You need someone who can really help you. You should get yourself down to an auction tomorrow and buy a man. Take some of the gold if you need a bit of help. Any self-respecting merchant would have a slave so it won't affect your cover.'

Cassius found the idea horrifying, and not just because of the financial implications of losing a slave and having to buy another. The prospect of Simo not returning and replacing him with some brute like Shostra was truly awful.

'There must have been some delay. He'll be here.'

'You don't have time to wait around. Anyway, that's your problem – we were discussing your other troublesome employee.'

'Sir, what you said last night – about giving Indavara his place. I think there's something more we can do. Something concrete.'

'Go on.'

'Ask him to join the army.'

'But he's a bodyguard – hired help.'

'It's unconventional, I know, but I think it might work. Do you know what happened to him in Pietas Julia, at this inn?'

'No.'

'Because he was well known from the arena, people wouldn't leave him alone. One night he was cornered by a group of men. He ended up killing one of them. The magistrates came after him and he had to leave; I believe that's why he headed east. As a soldier he'd be free from prosecution. We can offer him a proper wage, get him an identity tablet, enter him onto the books of the Fourth Legion with me.'

'I suppose I could sort out the paperwork. He'd have to take the oath.'

'I know. It's a gamble. He might say no. The whole thing might scare him off. But if he agrees, he'll have his place . . .'

'. . . and we'll have him.'

'Sir, it might be best if the offer comes from you.'

Abascantius grinned. 'Best for you?'

'For all of us.'

'Very well, Corbulo. You know him better than me. We'll try it.'

VII

Gutha laid the charred, tattered flag on the floor. There was a single patch of red left, upon it an eagle's wing embroidered in golden thread.

'I thought you might like this.'

Ilaha smiled. 'I shall use it as a doormat.'

Gutha straightened up and looked around the cavern.

'Don't worry,' said Ilaha. 'She's not here.'

Feigning indifference, Gutha examined his hands. He had been holding reins for so long that bits of leather had stuck to the lines in his palms.

'Shall I have something fetched for you?' asked Ilaha. 'Food? Drink?'

'No thank you, I'd just like to get back to the inn.'

'I really don't know why you insist on living in the town. There are hundreds of these caves. I could have one furnished to your tastes.'

Staying here – close to the temple and the old crone – was not a prospect Gutha considered appealing. 'I just wanted to give you the flag.'

Ilaha was standing in front of a table covered with gems, figurines, jewellery and other assorted valuables. Below it were stacks of wooden boxes overflowing with coins. In amongst the trinkets was a circular golden mask bearing the narrow features of a young girl.

Gutha moved closer. 'That death mask, it's not Gerrhan, is it?'

'The expert who checked it for me thinks so. From the lost city – perhaps more than a thousand years old.'

'Do you know what one of those would fetch in Rome or Alexandria?'

'I do. Fortunately my men don't. Please ensure it stays that way.'

'Of course. But where did you—'

'Let's not get distracted, Gutha. The operation – did you lose any men?'

'Not one. I allowed some of the legionaries to escape as you ordered.'

'Bostra will know by now that they face a serious threat.'

'They will.'

'You still think this was premature?'

'We cannot be sure how they will respond. And I am concerned that you continue to draw so much attention to yourself.' Gutha jutted his jaw at the treasure. 'More "donations"?'

Ilaha gave a sly grin.

'Raiding these temples – it does you more harm than good. Your men do not take the precautions I do. Word will get out. You will make enemies of those you wish to become allies.'

'I need money. My army needs money.'

Army. That was new.

'Besides,' continued Ilaha, 'there is no place any more for temples to false idols, or Persian gods or Roman gods. There is only . . .'

He paused; and Gutha realised his face must have betrayed his feelings.

'What?' said Ilaha.

'Nothing.'

Ilaha's hand drifted to an amulet around his neck, a yellow gem mounted on a silver chain. 'You do not believe as I do. As the others do. I know that.'

'You do not pay me to believe. You pay me to offer counsel and do your bidding.'

Ilaha walked away, through one of the shafts of light angling down into the floor from the small, high windows.

'The new arrivals in the town concern me too,' added Gutha. 'We chose this place because it is remote. Safe.'

Ilaha turned as he spoke, a note of irritation in his voice. 'Is

it not a cause for celebration? These men are not even affiliated
to the loyal chiefs but they have heard what is happening here.
They are curious, eager to join us.'

'To join what exactly? I am concerned that you intend to go
beyond what is practical, what is possible.'

'Mother told me you would try this.'

'Try what?'

'To dissuade me. Limit me.'

'My view has stayed consistent throughout. There *have* to be
limits. I did not agree—'

Ilaha held up a hand. 'Your agreement is not required, Gutha.
You have given your counsel. And I have heard it. Now, will you
do my bidding?'

Gutha bit his tongue, even though Ilaha had never previously
treated his advice with such disdain. To protest more would risk
a permanent rift between them. Ilaha might not be governed by
pragmatism, but he was.

'Of course.'

Ilaha walked back through the light. 'Mushannaf has agreed
to come and see me in a few days' time but I have it on good
authority that he means not to attend the meeting of the chiefs.
I want him dealt with before the others arrive.'

'That situation is in hand. If you cannot persuade him, I will.'

'Mushannaf is influential. He has no interest in the divine and
his people are little more than money grabbers – but he commands
many swords.'

'He won't be a problem.'

'Excellent. Now, you must rest.' Ilaha walked up to Gutha and
put a hand on his chest. 'You deserve it.'

Gutha had never particularly minded the fact that Ilaha sometimes touched him. But he now found himself struck by an urge
to reach down and crush those slim fingers under his.

'Thank you.' He stepped back, Ilaha's hand slipping off him
as he made for the passageway.

'Oh, Gutha.'

He stopped and turned.

Ilaha took the amulet from his neck and offered it to him. 'Please.'

Gutha didn't want the thing, didn't want it anywhere near him in fact. But he had gone too far earlier; it seemed wise to accept the gift. He put out his hand.

'No, let me.'

Glad they were alone, Gutha bowed his head. Even so, Ilaha had to stretch to his full height to get the chain over his neck.

'Perhaps it will help you.'

'Help me?'

'To believe.'

—◦8►—

When he awoke later, the amulet was the first thing Gutha saw. The chain was hanging from the chair next to his bed, the gem catching a little light from outside the inn. He imagined the crone's eye somewhere within – spying on him, trying to enter his mind.

'Get hold of yourself, man,' he muttered, grabbing a blanket and throwing it over the gem.

He looked out of the window and guessed it was early evening. He was still stiff from the ride but not tired enough to sleep through until morning. He was, however, hungry, and hopeful that Qattif would be back that evening to meet him as planned.

He pushed himself up off the bed, the timbers protesting noisily. He always half-expected the thing to collapse but the innkeeper insisted he could find nothing stronger. Gutha would have settled for longer; only by sleeping diagonally could he fit his entire frame on what was supposed to be a double bed.

He splashed water onto his face from a bowl then pulled on his trousers, a sleeveless tunic and a pair of sandals. Bowing his head – as he had to do everywhere other than the inn's parlour – he stepped into the corridor. There was no need to lock or even close the door. He rented the entire second floor and each of the four rooms contained some of his gear: clothes, riding equipment, weapons; one was devoted entirely to his armour. Most of his time with Ilaha had been spent on the move and he found it quite pleasant to have a base at last. Even so, he kept only a fraction of his money there. Every few weeks he would send Qattif or another lackey to various moneylenders outside the province. That way he could always leave at a moment's notice, confident the bulk of his earnings were secure.

Downstairs, the parlour was surprisingly busy. As Gutha entered, a group of youths sitting by the hearth became suddenly quiet. They looked like desert folk: dusty robes, home-made knives at their belts and not a sword or a decent pair of boots between them. They stood and bowed to him.

Gutha acknowledged them with a nod, then went to sit on his usual stool at the bar. The other customers were all warriors – about fifteen of them, some familiar faces – and they also bowed. Gutha was still unsure how it had all started – the bowing. The gesture had never been sought by him or suggested by anyone else. The first time he'd really noticed it was after that scrap with the Palmyran cavalry. Gutha admitted to himself that perhaps it wasn't that surprising – he had pulled five of the bastards off their horses and slain a dozen in all.

Alome, the innkeeper's wife, leaned on the bar opposite him and tutted. 'You kill a jolly atmosphere quicker than a leper, Master Gutha. You'll be costing my husband money.'

'Take it off my bill,' replied Gutha with a grin. He liked the old girl – she was the only one who treated him like a normal person.

Alome scratched a blotchy insect bite on her cheek and gazed at him. 'Those locks of yours – so pretty.'

As a child growing up in Gerasa, he'd got used to having the only head of blond hair in the entire city. He'd had a pretty face then too.

'Shame about the rest, eh?'

'Not so bad,' she replied. 'Rugged.'

'That's one word for it.'

Alome took a jug from a shelf and poured him some wine.

'What's for dinner?' he asked.

'Yesterday's lamb stew or today's chicken and vegetables.'

Gutha tried to make up his mind as he took his first drink.

'Stew always tastes better the second day,' said Alome as she retied her apron.

'Stew it is.'

'Oh – Qattif came in earlier. I told him you were sleeping so he said he'd be back this evening.'

As she went off to fetch the food, Gutha became aware of someone standing over his left shoulder. 'It is inadvisable to creep up on me. Stand where I can see you.'

The young warrior came forward. Despite his brazen approach, he was wringing his hands. 'My apologies, sir. Might I speak with you for a minute?'

'As long as you keep it to a minute.'

'We arrived this morning, sir, and wish to join the forces of Lord Ilaha.'

Forces? Lord? Gutha had heard those words a few times recently too. Who came up with this stuff?

The youth's beard was patchy; his face soft and unmarked. 'Why?'

'Lord Ilaha is the most powerful of all the chiefs, sir. They say he will protect us from Palmyra, from Persia – even take our lands back from Rome. The sun god wants him to rule us. We know that you are a great warrior, that—'

'You should go to the tower. See Commander Theomestor or Commander Oblachus.'

'I will, sir. Would we be able to—'

Gutha turned away. 'Minute's up.'

The youth returned to his friends.

Gutha looked at the other warriors, thought of the other full inns and the men billeted across the town. No wonder Ilaha was feeling so full of himself. Perhaps he was right to seize the moment.

But things were moving fast. Too fast. If they didn't control events, events would control them.

He had just finished his second plateful of stew when Qattif came in. The Saracen hung his sand-encrusted cloak on a hook, greeted Alome and her husband, then made his way over to Gutha. Qattif was of nomad stock like the youngsters: a tall, stringy specimen with a beak of a nose and a heavy beard greying below his chin. He brushed sand out of it, then sat down. 'Nasty wind getting up.'

As Gutha downed the last of his bread, Alome took his plate and whistled. 'By Our Lady of Light, in my old village that could have fed a family for a week. Anything else?'

Gutha licked a gravy-stained finger. 'Bowl of dates for my room.'

Alome cast a speculative look at Qattif.

'The usual,' he said, looking around the parlour as Alome withdrew to the kitchen. 'Lot of new men coming in. I heard even Chief Uruwat is with us now.'

'Apparently.'

'Exciting times.'

Gutha snorted as he washed the stew down with a mouthful of wine. 'Well? You have what I asked for?'

'I do.'

'Took you long enough.'

'Wasn't easy. Almost got caught twice.'

Qattif reached into his tunic and retrieved a small leather bag tied with twine. Gutha took it and tucked it behind his belt.

'And that other matter?'

Qattif flicked sand out of his cavernous nostrils. 'That was even harder. I had to tread carefully. People don't like to talk about him, even the warriors that have fought with him for years.'

'And?'

Qattif waited for Alome to put down his wine and walk away. No one else was within earshot.

'There's a fellow called Gallani who was born in the same village – little place about a day's ride from Emesa. Said he remembers the old woman. Said Ilaha lived with her in a house there – small place out on its own. Apparently, she looked just like she does now. She can't be his mother, just doesn't add up.'

'Did this Gallani mention any other family?'

'Just the old woman. She was quite well known in the area. The locals were all petrified of her. They called her "the queen".'

'Who says peasants don't understand irony?'

'It seems she told the villagers she really had been a queen. One woman mocked her for it and the old bitch attacked her – clawed out one of her eyes. Her husband and her sons went to the house to have their revenge. Never came back.'

'That has the ring of an old wives' tale.'

'Sorry. All I could get.'

'Could you find this village?'

'You know me. I can find anything.'

'I want you to go there, dig up whatever you can and come straight back. I need to know the truth about her. And him.'

Qattif exhaled loudly.

'Your usual rate – and a half,' said Gutha.

'Very generous. I will leave—'

'At dawn.'

'I will leave at dawn.' Qattif swigged some wine, then wiped his mouth. 'If there's nothing else, may I go? This place is rather quiet for my liking.'

'You may.' Gutha reached out and clamped his hand over Qattif's arm. 'But do not breathe a word of this to anyone.'

'You know you can trust me.'

'I hope so. Because if I ever find out otherwise I will tear your spine out of you and use it as a backscratcher.'

Qattif seemed rather impressed by the threat. Even so, he made sure he met Gutha's gaze. 'Understood.'

Qattif had nerve. Gutha had always liked that about him. He let him go.

VIII

When it came to worship, Cassius preferred to keep things simple. He couldn't see much point in dividing his efforts amongst the lesser gods so had recently decided to devote himself to Jupiter and never ask for too much. As countless others would be seeking the favour of the god of gods, he considered it wise to limit one's expectations.

He had long been aware that requests for a quiet, easy life were unlikely to elicit results. Upon being told by his father that he was to join the army he had embarked on a frenzied – if brief – period of worship; all to no avail. And considering how things had gone since that point, it seemed the denizens of the heavens were intent on putting him through trial after trial until he succumbed. Since arriving in Syria three years ago, he'd often felt like a bottle tossed around on a sea; and eventually he'd been tempted to forgo worship entirely.

But he had survived. And he knew that in many ways the gods had been kind. They had given him a rich, powerful family; a healthy, handsome body; and a mind that invariably outperformed those around him. He wasn't perfect – swordplay and other martial skills didn't come naturally, and he had a damaging tendency to lose all sense where women were concerned – but the latter was a common affliction and he was trying to address his other weaknesses.

This new-found sense of clarity had led Cassius to ruminate on the words of Marcus Aurelius: *Nothing happens to anybody that he is not fitted by nature to bear.*

Had the gods placed him in these situations to serve Rome? Set him these challenges precisely because he was well equipped to deal with them?

An appealing concept, but one that rather fell down in the face of logical appraisal. His own poor judgement had twice set in motion events leading him to face danger and death; that and the demands of Abascantius and Chief Pulcher. On the other hand, his arrival on Rhodes at precisely the right time to take up the Memor investigation had suggested a divine hand.

As he queued in front of the Temple of Jupiter, waiting to buy a libation, Cassius tried to put such questions aside and concentrate on the here and now. Whatever the gods' intentions, they seemed determined to place him in harm's way again. So be it; but Cassius reckoned he was owed something in return for his previous accomplishments and was prepared to spare an hour of his evening to make one important request.

He handed over a coin and took the clay cup of wine, then hurried up the steps and between the two gargantuan columns on either side of the entrance. The wooden doors were each a foot thick and studded with massive iron bolts. Two young priests whispered prayers as every worshipper entered.

Cassius liked the cool air of temples; the quiet, too. He'd remembered to change into his soft walking boots and he strode swiftly across the immaculate marble floor, past the interior colonnades to the podium at the rear.

Another pair of priests flanked the platform, silently watching over a dozen of the kneeling faithful. Cassius didn't enjoy having to mix with commoners but there was nowhere else to go if one wished to commune with Jupiter. The altars here were not intended for sacrifice, merely to accommodate the hundreds of libations offered daily. Cassius found a space for his cup, then a space below the podium for himself.

Lifting his scabbard to make sure it didn't scrape on the floor, he knelt on one knee. He didn't want to look up at the statue until he was ready to speak but it was hard to ignore the whispered entreaties filling the air:

'God of gods, let Aurelia be freed. We have waited so long.'

'A son, a son, a son.'

'Not bronze, silver. Mighty Jupiter, let it be silver.'

'Father of the gods, I beg you to cure him.'

To Cassius's dismay, more worshippers arrived and surrounded him. One man was clad in little more than rags, his sandals held together with rotting lengths of twine. He immediately embarked on a swift and remarkably articulate request for nothing more than enlightenment. More distracting still was a legionary. This man offered a cordial nod to Cassius, then bowed his head and whispered his prayers. His right arm was a stump that ended six inches below his shoulder. It was heavily bandaged and spotted with yellow and red.

Admonishing himself for wasting time, Cassius gazed up at the statue. It was a fine rendering, perhaps twice life size, composed of pale grey marble. The heavily bearded god was sitting, eyes no more than hollows in the stone, bronze sceptre held in his left hand. Cassius extended his arms upwards and whispered the words.

Father Jupiter, revered god of gods, I come with an offering, one of many I have given in recent times. I pledge to come again to your dwelling-place whenever I can and give for the rest of my days. In return I ask only for one thing. Do not let me face this journey alone.

———◦———

'Where have you been?' asked Indavara as Cassius walked into the atrium.

'I could ask you the same thing.'

'Just walking.'

Cassius had no intention of telling him what he'd been doing. 'There's hardly time for that. We must get ready for the journey.'

Indavara avoided his gaze.

'I swear you're enjoying this,' said Cassius.

'Corbulo, I am not your slave. I am a free man. I'll tell you when I've made up my mind.'

'No sign of Simo still, I suppose?'

'I just got back.'

'Muranda!'

'Yes, sir?' came the reply from the kitchen.

'Nothing from Simo?'

'No, sir.'

Cassius sighed. It seemed he could expect little help from above. Muranda walked into the atrium. 'There was this note, though.'

Cassius unrolled the sheet. The message was from Abascantius. He had made the preparations and was waiting for them at the headquarters building.

Indavara was already on his way to his room.

'Wait.' Cassius held up the note. 'From Master Abascantius. He has a proposal for you.'

'Proposal? About what?'

'Let's go and find out.'

—◆8◆—

Abascantius concluded the tour of the headquarters with the armoury, a miniature version of the main building where a special cache of weapons was kept and maintained. Inside, one man was sitting on a stool polishing a bronze hilt without a blade. Another had a spear held in a vice and was fitting a new head. Indavara couldn't help stepping up to the doorway and running a professional eye over racks full of pristine spears, swords and shields.

Abascantius had also shown him and Corbulo the small shrine where the senior officers worshipped and a large, colourful map of the eastern provinces. Indavara hadn't been able to make much out of it and was still unsure what they were doing there.

'Come, you two,' said the agent. 'I've had a room put aside for us.'

They passed three servants carrying trays of steaming food and entered a small chamber equipped with a square table surrounded by chairs. In one corner was a shelf overloaded with scrolls tied with multicoloured string. Abascantius shut the door behind them and gestured to the table. Three mugs of wine had already been filled from a jug and there were bowls of dates, raisins and walnuts. Next to a lamp was a small cloth bag.

The trio sat down and sipped at their wine. Indavara thought

112

Corbulo seemed unusually quiet and didn't particularly like the way he and Abascantius were looking at him. The agent plucked a bag of coins from his tunic and pushed it across the table to Indavara.

'Let's get this out of the way now. I don't want it to influence your decision. Corbulo's had his. It's the balance for the Cilicia job and the rest's for the Memor investigation.'

'Thank you, sir.'

'You're probably wondering what all this is about,' said Abascantius. 'Well, I've been very impressed by your work since taking you on last year. I've seen a lot of bodyguards and other operatives come and go over the years and it's quite clear to me that you are an individual of great skill and courage.'

Indavara shifted his gaze to the wall. It was difficult to look at people when they gave you compliments, but he didn't mind hearing them.

'Helping Corbulo find that Persian flag, for example. You two helped us keep the peace – possibly even averted a war. And ridding Cyrenaica of Carnifex and his like. Noble acts, greatly appreciated. And yet Corbulo here tells me you're thinking of leaving.'

'Maybe.'

'Might I ask why?' Abascantius was speaking much more quietly than usual.

Corbulo was leaning back in his chair, trying to look uninterested.

'I never really planned to stay on. I thought I'd keep moving, take another job somewhere.'

'That's up to you, of course, but Corbulo and I need a decision now. We need to know if this operation is going ahead with or without you. And I have an offer that I hope will help you make up your mind.'

Indavara nodded.

'A place in the army,' said Abascantius.

'As what, a soldier?'

'As bodyguard to Corbulo and an agent of the Service.'

Indavara had seen enough to know that being a free man didn't count for much if you had to follow orders. 'So I'd have to do whatever the army told me to.'

'You'd have to do whatever the Service told you to.' Abascantius aimed a thumb at himself. 'Meaning me.'

'Soldiers have to give an oath,' said Indavara. 'I can't give an oath to Rome.'

'Why?'

'I'm not a Roman.'

'What are you, then?'

Corbulo coughed. Abascantius looked at him.

Indavara took another drink before replying. This was exactly why he didn't like being stuck in rooms and being made to talk. Too many difficult questions.

'You know what I was.'

'The arena is not Rome.'

Indavara wasn't sure what to say to that. There had always been soldiers at the arena in Pietas Julia, and wasn't the governor also the chief of a province's legions?

'The army didn't put you there,' added Abascantius. 'The contests grow less popular every year. Not everyone agrees with them, you know.'

'Corbulo doesn't. He's never even seen one. But you . . .'

Indavara stopped himself. Abascantius was a hard man to like but he'd been good to him. He didn't want to insult him.

'Go on,' said the agent. 'You can speak freely.'

'What about the man who had the Persian flag – Scaurus? You had him torn apart by dogs in the arena at Antioch.'

'That man was a criminal and a traitor.'

'Perhaps I was too.'

Indavara wished he hadn't said that. In his first weeks at the arena he'd been haunted by the thought of it; many gladiators were criminals after all. But over time – though he still didn't know what he had been – he had become sure it wasn't that.

'Well, were you?' asked Abascantius. 'You never speak of your past.'

Corbulo leaned on the table. 'That's all water under the bridge now, sir. Shouldn't we focus on the present?'

Indavara was grateful to him for intervening; and that it seemed he hadn't passed on what he knew about Indavara's memory loss.

'Indeed we should,' agreed Abascantius. 'Indavara, taking the oath brings great advantages. You will receive a wage and be exempt from most taxes. If you serve for several years we can give you a discharge certificate like the one I showed the auxiliaries. You will be awarded a large lump sum or an area of land. Ex-soldiers go on to head councils, own concerns. They have great status, much more than—'

'A bodyguard. Or an ex-slave gladiator.'

'Yes.'

Abascantius glanced at Corbulo then continued. 'And the army gives you protection. You cannot be brought before a court.'

Indavara could certainly understand the benefit of that. He had seen first-hand how Roman soldiers – Corbulo included – did as they pleased, often at the expense of others. But like the legionaries he'd encountered at the arena, they were a mix of good and bad. There were the evil bastards like Carnifex and his cronies but then there were men like that poor centurion Eborius in Cyrenaica. And then there was Corbulo. He wasn't a bad man, not really. As for Abascantius – Indavara hadn't quite made up his mind about him.

He still didn't like the idea of taking the oath but the army and the Service at least offered order and direction; better than working for some bloody crook or merchant as he had before being taken on by Abascantius. But then he remembered something.

'You said if I served for "several" years. Don't legionaries have to do twenty-five?'

'Exceptions can be made. Corbulo here, for example, has only two years left.'

Indavara couldn't make up his mind; there were too many things to consider.

For the first time, Abascantius looked annoyed. 'Do you imagine that we freely offer such things to hired men? I have never done this before. I am showing you how highly you are valued. I am offering much but I need something in return. Your loyalty.'

'Might I suggest a compromise?' said Corbulo. 'The oath to the army is taken every year. Why not write into Indavara's contract that his service is on a year-by-year basis. In that time he would enjoy the benefits and – if he completed an extended period – the other rewards of service.'

'How does that sound?' asked Abascantius.

'So I could leave after a year?'

'If you wanted to.'

Abascantius reached into the cloth bag next to the lamp and pulled out two small items. The first was a miniature spearhead about three inches long with a pin on the back. 'We use these when the full-size version is impractical. You walk into a room wearing this, you'll get people's attention. Solid silver.'

Indavara picked up the spearhead and turned it around, catching the light from the lamp. The intricate carving was remarkably detailed; he thought it rather beautiful. Then Abascantius showed him a small rectangular tablet. It was about the size of a thumb and composed of a duller metal.

'Lead. I've already had it inscribed.'

Indavara was amazed to see his name etched into the metal in neat, precise lettering.

'May I?' said Corbulo, examining it. 'Gods, they did a better job with this than mine.'

Indavara liked the tablet too, but he couldn't help thinking of the brands slave-owners sometimes burned onto the skin of their slaves.

'We need to know now,' said Abascantius.

'I'll have to sign this contract, then?'

'Yes.'

'I'll read it to you,' said Corbulo. 'Make sure it's what you want.'

Indavara looked up at the ceiling. He had money. He could leave the next morning if he wanted to – just keep walking north. But what then? It would be just like the first day he left Pietas Julia.

And there was something else too. He didn't much enjoy sitting around doing nothing. And as a bodyguard protecting someone else there'd been a lot of that. Well, standing around mostly.

The last time he'd really felt alive was when those auxiliaries had been after him. Scared, yes, but alive. Standing around wasn't for him.

'We want you with us,' said Corbulo.

Abascantius nodded. 'We do.'

—8—

The ceremony was carried out in the shrine. Night had come and the chilly room was lit by shifting splashes of candlelight. While he and Corbulo waited for Abascantius to return, Indavara looked down at the three bound sheets of paper lying on a writing block. He had understood only a little of the contract, but Corbulo had assured him it was in line with what they'd discussed.

Abascantius came back with two tribunes. They exchanged greetings with Corbulo then stood at the rear of the room.

Indavara listened carefully as the agent began. 'He who joins the legions pledges himself to Rome. He who joins the legions honours Jupiter and Mars and all the great gods. He who joins the legions bows before the Emperor Lucius Domitius Aurelianus and offers his sword, his service and his life. Do you give your oath?'

'I give my oath.'

Abascantius grinned.

'Is that it?'

'Not quite.' The agent pointed at the bronze pen beside the writing block. 'You must sign all three pages.'

For Indavara, this was the worst part; having to write his name with the four of them watching. When he was finished, he showed it to Corbulo. 'Is that all right?'

'It's fine.'

Abascantius clapped him on the shoulder. 'Congratulations, lad, you are now on the books of the Fourth Scythican Legion under Prefect Oppius Junius Venator.'

The two tribunes came forward and shook Indavara's forearm. One examined his signature. 'Just the one name, eh? Very mysterious.'

'Congratulations,' said the other man, 'you must down plenty of wine tonight in celebration.'

Indavara noticed him wink at Abascantius.

The agent said, 'Thank you, both.'

As the tribunes left, Abascantius handed over the identity tablet and the miniature spearhead. 'Yours to keep, though I'm afraid you won't be able to take them with you on this operation.'

'Well then,' said Cassius. 'What about that drink?'

'You two go ahead,' said Abascantius. 'I'll call in tomorrow before I leave. If there's anything else to discuss we'll do so then.'

'Come on,' said Corbulo, leading the way out of the shrine. Indavara followed him, the spearhead in one hand, the tablet in the other.

'I think the occasion merits a bit of that Surrentine.'

Cassius reached to the back of the cupboard and took out the flask, which had been left in the villa by Verecundus. He removed the stopper and looked inside. 'Muranda, have you been drinking this?'

The housekeeper was sitting on one of the benches, polishing a candelabra between her legs. 'No, sir.'

'I'm sure there was more.'

'You drank some when you came back from that dinner party last week.'

'Oh. Right.'

Cassius took the wine over to the table and poured some for him and Indavara. The bodyguard was standing, staring thoughtfully down at the fire. At certain points in the evening, Cassius had felt the odd twinge of guilt about his and Abascantius's scheming but such thoughts had now been subsumed by a warm flood of relief.

Indavara took the mug offered to him. 'Corbulo, this doesn't change anything between us. If I have something to say, I'll say it.'

'I would expect nothing else. Let's drink. A busy day awaits tomorrow but that tribune was quite right – we must celebrate.'

Just as they sat down, the courtyard door rattled open. 'That'll be my sister's girl,' said Muranda. 'Come to help me with the bronze.'

Something heavy thumped down on the floor then a large figure filled the doorway.

'Simo!' cried Indavara, spilling his wine as he jumped to his feet.

The big Gaul stepped over his saddlebags and walked wearily into the kitchen. His hair was in a tangle, his tunic coated with dust. He gave a brief nod to Indavara and staggered forward, eyes wide with nerves. 'Master Cassius, a thousand apologies for this disgrace. I will make amends in whatever way you see fit.'

Simo seemed on the verge of tears but watched along with the others as his master calmly got up, walked around the table and stopped in front of him. Cassius looked him up and down and shook his head. But when he could contain himself no longer he smiled and gripped Simo's heavy shoulders. 'By the gods, you had me worried there, you big bastard. Welcome back.'

Simo's head dropped.

'Look at the state of you,' added Cassius. 'Some Surrentine will see you right.'

'Sir, please, no. I deserve nothing.'

'Nonsense.'

Indavara shook Simo's hand and coaxed him onto a bench, even though he insisted he was too dirty. Muranda looked rather perplexed by this turn of events but welcomed Simo back and brought in his saddlebags.

Cassius turned away to pour the wine. He raised his eyes to the heavens. *Thank you, Jupiter. Thank you.*

IX

'Time to wake up, sir.'

Cassius actually smiled as he heard those words spoken in Simo's sunny, reassuring tones. He opened his eyes and saw him already at work, sorting through the clothes strewn across a chest of drawers.

'Water's there, sir. Nice and fresh.'

As he drank, Cassius was relieved to note he had no headache. 'I'm glad we stopped after three mugs.'

'Me too, sir. I imagine we have a busy day ahead.'

'Extremely. Having concluded one unpleasant journey, Simo, you must now embark upon another. Damned bad luck with those two lame horses. I still think you could have sent a letter on but I appreciate it can be difficult to find someone reliable.'

Simo said nothing as he put the window shutters back on their hooks. The dawn light revealed the full extent of the mess.

'You should probably start with some washing,' suggested Cassius. 'At least with this sun it'll be dry by tomorrow. Then we need to think about our horses and, believe it or not, I'm going to have to outfit myself like a merchant. There's a hundred and one things.'

Simo dropped a cape on the dirty pile then looked at his master and rubbed the back of his neck.

Cassius knew what that meant. 'What is it?'

'A difficult matter, sir.'

'Your father? Didn't you say all's well with him?'

'It's not that, sir. What I told you about why I was late.'

'Spit it out, Simo.'

'I lied, sir.'

Cassius put the water down. 'By Jupiter, first you disappear and now this. What's happening to you?'

'I barely slept, sir, thinking of how I deceived you. I thought it better to tell the truth now.'

'I suppose that's something. Well?'

'As you know, I have now reached the stage where I can receive direct instruction about the teachings of the Lord. I should have done so far earlier but we have been rather busy of late. I needed a letter of recommendation from Antioch so that I might be taught here in Bostra. Elder Nura was away so I had to wait for him to return and sign the letter. It delayed me by four days. I am sorry, sir. Deeply sorry.'

Cassius threw his blanket aside and got up, naked but for his loincloth. 'I wonder sometimes if you know how lucky you are. Upon hearing something like that, many a master would take a whip to your back. Lies, deceit – just the beginning, I expect. Soon you'll be running off to join your Christian "brothers" permanently.'

'No, sir. I would not do that.'

'Perhaps I have been too weak. Allowing you the leave seems only to have encouraged disobedience. Well, you can forget getting any more coin for the time being. I expect you wasted everything I gave you on charity as usual.'

'Not entirely, sir. I bought two medical texts.'

Cassius crossed his arms. 'We have always been open with each other, Simo.'

'Yes, sir.'

'If we lose that, we lose trust. I have enough uncertainty around me. Can I be certain of you?'

'Yes, sir.'

'Do you know, yesterday I thought I might have to go and find myself another attendant. Buy a new man at an auction.'

The very mention of the word drew a marked reaction from the Gaul. Satisfied he'd made his point, Cassius pointed at the pile of dirty clothes. 'They're not going to wash themselves.'

'Shall I fetch your hot water first, sir?'

'Do so.'

—◼8▶—

'Well, well. Reunited at last.'

Abascantius walked into the atrium and inspected the trio, then pointed at Simo. 'So what happened to you? You had your master very worried.'

'Sir, I—'

'Simo was unlucky with transportation,' interjected Cassius. 'But now he's back with us I'm sure he hasn't a minute to spare.'

With a bow to the agent, Simo hurried out through the front door clutching a list of supplies.

Abascantius wore his riding trousers and a light cloak over his tunic. He had dispensed with his helmet and was now virtually unidentifiable as a military man. He turned his attention to Indavara. 'And how's the Fourth Legion's newest recruit?'

Indavara offered a cordial nod.

'Not saying much today, eh? All that talking last night perhaps. Corbulo, the auxiliaries have been paid and the rest of the money is with Pontius's clerk. Mercator assures me they'll all be ready tomorrow morning and he'll be along presently. He has a few questions for you.'

'And I for him.'

'Any for me? Last chance.'

'This Ulixes character, sir. He didn't sound particularly reliable. What if he's not in Petra or his information turns out to be false?'

Abascantius took a step forward. 'Let's be clear, Corbulo. You must do your utmost to locate and recover that stone, whatever happens in Petra. I expect your next letter to me to be one that brings a smile to my face.'

'On that subject, sir, where should letters to you be directed? I assume you'll be on the move.'

'Address them to the chief clerk of the Fourth at Raphanea. I will ensure he knows where I am at all times.'

'Sir, if we do recover the stone – where should it be taken?'

'Ultimately, here. But considering where you're going, the fortress at Humeima should perhaps be your first stop. It's just south of Petra. The walls are three feet thick and there are never less than two centuries stationed there.'

'One other thing, sir – Mercator. Seems rather odd for an ambitious optio to leave his cohort for an assignment with us. Any explanation?'

'It's very simple. Inside the headquarters office is a list – a list of those optios ready to take over when one of the legion's centurions is killed, gets ill, or retires. Despite the resistance of Chief Nerva, I have successfully moved Mercator from somewhere near the bottom to somewhere near the top.'

'I see.'

'It's interesting,' said Abascantius, struggling to straighten the lines of his cloak around his paunch, 'I found our little ceremony in the shrine rather inspiring. Last night I gave offerings to the great gods, asking them to assist this operation. It's been a while since I did that.'

He grasped Cassius's forearm. 'Remember what you stand to gain, Corbulo; the appreciation of the Emperor and some time to yourself. That enough for you?'

'Yes, sir.'

Abascantius held onto his arm. 'For Rome.'

Despite himself – and the usual whiff of rancid breath – Cassius felt a brief surge of enthusiasm. 'For Rome.'

'Here!' The shout came from outside.

Abascantius shook his head. 'At least that Gaul of yours has some manners.' He bellowed a reply towards the street. 'Out in a moment!'

The agent then put a hand on Indavara's shoulder and nodded at Cassius. 'You watch his back. Anything happens to him and I'll make sure something happens to you.' He grinned. 'And try not to argue. He's usually right.'

'Usually,' said Indavara.

Abascantius turned to Cassius. 'And the "wine" is safe?'

'Yes, sir.'

Indavara frowned.

'I'll show you later.'

Abascantius let out a long sigh as they walked outside. 'Ah, shit, another week in the saddle.'

Shostra was standing at the end of the path, trying to control the two horses, who'd been disturbed by a squad of cavalry trotting out of the fortress. Abascantius took charge of his mount, the same sturdy black stallion he'd been riding when Cassius had first met him the previous summer.

'He looks like he could do a fair few miles a day.'

'Antheon? Yes, he's served me well.'

Abascantius took hold of the saddle and hauled his heavy frame up. Once settled, he patted the horse's sleek shoulder. 'Farts every ten paces but that's not my concern. Old Shostra gets the worst of it.'

The attendant muttered something as he mounted up.

'Farewell, then, you two,' said the agent. 'May the gods favour you.'

'Farewell, sir,' said Cassius and Indavara.

As usual, Shostra ignored them.

Cassius tutted. 'The miles must fly by, sir, what with such stimulating company.'

Abascantius turned around and glanced at Shostra. 'Oh, he's not so bad. If you ask him nicely, he'll tell you one of his wrestling stories.'

'Really?' said Cassius. 'Interesting, are they?'

'Boring as shit. He lost most of his fights – why do you think he works for me?'

With Shostra still muttering – and Cassius and Indavara laughing – Abascantius guided Antheon away along the Via Cappadocia.

'So, what's this about wine?' asked Indavara.

'Ah yes, come, I'll show you.' Cassius was already on his way back inside. 'You may have to keep an eye on me, but we both have to keep an eye on this.'

———◄8►———

Mercator called in later as agreed. With Indavara busy cleaning his weaponry and Muranda out fetching firewood, Cassius spoke to him in the courtyard. The trusty charcoal and paper were already on the table. With time so short, almost everything had to be organised by the end of the day. He checked his notes.

'So what about your horses?'

Mercator rolled his eyes. 'Officer Abascantius insisted we not use army animals so Andal and Yorvah are with the men at the horse market right now. Lot of buying to do.'

'Legion mounts are branded. They might give us away.'

'Ah, of course,' said Mercator. 'Sorry, all this cloak-and-dagger stuff is new to me.'

Cassius didn't think it politic to confess just how new it still was to him.

Mercator crossed his bulky, vein-ridged arms. 'The prices will be high what with the army manoeuvres but I was thinking twenty-five horses and eight mules. We can travel fairly light but if we find ourselves down in the Hejaz there aren't many settlements or much grassland. We'll need to carry plenty of water and fodder.'

'Sounds about right,' replied Cassius. 'I'll be sorting out our mounts this afternoon. Do you think we'll manage it in five days?'

'As long as we keep up the pace.'

Cassius consulted his list again. 'What about accommodation?'

'Way-stations are out of the question, I suppose.'

'Correct. We must keep contact with soldiers to an absolute minimum. Someone will recognise someone and it'll get awkward. No, taverns would be better.'

'But twenty-four of us, with all that gear? What about tents?'

'Certainly more authentic,' said Cassius.

'Quite a bit more weight to carry.'

'Worth it, I think.'

'We will use the traditional type,' said Mercator. 'The men and I can have them up in half an hour. By the way, some of them were asking about identification. Leaving our tablets and papers behind is all very well but what if we have a problem with the army or some other official?'

'I will have my spearhead with me, my papers too – well hidden, of course. If there's no other alternative, that should be enough to get us out of trouble.' Cassius leaned forward. 'Leave your auxiliaries in no doubt. They are to bring *nothing* that can identify them as soldiers. I notice a few have tattoos – tell them to cover them up. No letters from wives, no mementos from home. Nothing.'

'What about sacred items: figurines and suchlike?'

'Which gods do your men worship?'

'The great gods, of course.'

Cassius knew he shouldn't have been surprised; it was often auxiliaries and provincials who showed most dedication to the Roman pantheon.

'All of you?'

'Most.'

'What about the desert people, the tribesmen?'

'A mix. Some worship local deities. Or Greek, or Egyptian, or one of the sun gods.'

'Then such items will also have to be left behind.'

Mercator scratched his chin. 'To ask them to forgo worship when they may be facing battle—'

'They can still pray.'

'It could be a problem.'

Cassius had seen this before too. Though generally tolerant of differing beliefs, the army encouraged joint worship – especially of Mars and Jupiter and especially amongst auxiliaries. The unifying benefits were manifest but the relentless routine of devotion sometimes made soldiers prone to superstition and – worse – more concerned with the gods than their immediate superiors.

'I trust you to ensure that it won't be, Mercator.'

The optio hesitated before replying. 'Yes, sir.'

Cassius checked the list once more. 'Now, where shall we depart from tomorrow morning?'

'Just east of the hippodrome is a piece of waste ground between two old temples. We can gather there out of sight and set off without drawing attention.'

'Sounds perfect. Let us say the third hour.' Cassius stood up. 'I must sort out these horses then get myself along to an outfitter who can dress me like a merchant. Anything else?'

'Just one thing.' Mercator stood too and adjusted his sword belt. 'Officer Abascantius didn't tell me much more than he told the men. I don't suppose you can give me any more details?'

'Not right now. When you need to know, you will. Let's just concentrate on getting to Petra.'

━━8━━

Organising the horses turned out to be a lot quicker than organising the clothing. As soon as Simo returned with two lads helping him carry the supplies, Cassius took him back along the Via Cappadocia. The attendant knew of a reliable Spaniard with a large stables from whom they secured three healthy-looking horses and a mule for a month; they would be brought to the villa first thing.

From the stables they hurried into the centre of Bostra and got the name of a Greek outfitter's just off the cloth market.

'Caesar's length,' moaned Cassius as they squeezed past a loud crowd of locals bidding for some colourful offcuts. 'I don't mind playing a role now and again but keeping this merchant act up for days and weeks will be a nightmare.'

'Sir, forgive me for saying so, but you also don't really have the colouring for a travelling man.'

'That had occurred to me. Well, I shall get plenty of sun on the way down to Petra.'

'You must be careful, though, sir, you know how you burn. Remember when we took that river trip in Cyzicus? Your knees were bright pink.'

'Yes, yes.' Cassius looked up at a sign above one of the wider storefronts. 'Here it is – Apri's.'

As they walked under an awning and into the store, a young lad scrubbing the floor got to his feet and retreated to the back. Standing there was a middle-aged couple examining a square of cloth laid out on a counter. The man hurried forward.

'Good day, sir, how may I be of assistance?'

Cassius blew out his cheeks. 'First of all, this needs to remain between us.'

'Of course, sir. Discretion is always guaranteed at Apri's.'

'Basically, I need to look like a merchant. A bit of colour, some patterning. You know how they are.'

'I see, I see. What exactly would you need?'

Cassius turned to Simo.

'Three tunics,' suggested the Gaul, 'a cloak, and some riding trousers.'

'That should do it.'

Apri's smile had broadened. 'Shall I measure you up first, sir, or would you like to look at some material?'

'Er, measure me.'

Cassius handed his sword belt to Simo. While Apri's wife brought in some rolls of material, the clothier took a knotted piece of twine from behind the counter and began. 'I'm wondering how much you would like to spend, sir. We have some excellent linens and cottons, then of course there's silk.'

'No silk,' said Cassius. 'I shall be on the move.'

Apri finished up, then gestured towards the cloth. 'Let's start with colour. We have some lovely spring shades here.'

Cassius looked over his shoulder and noticed a few locals peering into the store. Worse was to follow; two well-dressed young women strolled in and one looked vaguely familiar. As they examined hoods draped over wooden models, Apri's wife went to assist them.

'Well, sir,' said Apri. 'Which colour catches your eye?'

'I am an army officer,' stated Cassius loudly, 'fashion is not my strong point.'

'These yellows really are lovely.'

'No yellow. Yellow is for ladies.'

'Might be passable with some embroidery, sir,' suggested Simo.

'Green and blue suit me best.'

Apri replied: 'For the tunics perhaps a dark blue, a light blue and a light green.'

'That sounds fine.'

Apri lowered his voice. 'You will definitely need some patterning to convince as a merchant, sir.'

Cassius kept his voice low too. 'Very well. But no vertical stripes – they make me look skinny.'

It wasn't until the evening that Cassius found time to fit in some sword practice. He had no idea when there would be another opportunity and certainly didn't intend practising in front of the auxiliaries. He stepped out into the shadowy courtyard and looked up at a sky streaked with orange and pink. Indavara was knocking their two wooden swords together while he gazed at the wall.

'Still not spoken to her, eh?'

'Not so loud,' replied Indavara irritably.

Cassius started the stretches the bodyguard had showed him. 'Why not buy her some flowers or—'

'You want to practise, let's practise.'

Cassius eyed the swords. 'Back to *them*?'

'We haven't done anything for a week or two. Let's keep it simple.'

'I need to prepare for the real thing; we could be coming up against anyone.'

'If you think you know better, why not practise yourself?'

'All right, don't get touchy.'

'Finish your warm-up.'

Indavara did the same, then they moved onto a section of paving he'd cleared of all weeds and obstructions, giving them a square area four yards wide to practise in.

'Sweeps first,' he said, brushing his hair away from his eyes. 'What are the three things?'

'Speed, disguise, recovery.'

'Focus on speed to start with. Head and flank.'

Cassius began; and was soon enjoying taking out the frustrations of the day on the lengths of wood. Convinced he'd made progress, he assumed that eventually – in amongst all the thousands of traded blows – he might catch Indavara out or the bodyguard might make a mistake. But he was still waiting; and he wondered whether this was because Indavara didn't want to show even the slightest sign of vulnerability or because the gap between them was still so wide. He suspected a bit of both.

After a couple of minutes, Cassius was panting and wiping his forehead. Indavara insisted that he practise with a long, heavy sword to replicate his real blade and – even now – a few dozen sweeps and contacts sapped a lot of energy.

'You must get more into your swing,' instructed Indavara when they took a break. 'Use your height and those monkey arms.'

'What about disguise? A big swing means they see it coming.'

'I told you to focus on blade-speed. And you don't have to swing a long way to get power.'

'What was that thing you said about catching the shoulder?'

'With a sweep, most of the time you'll be going for the head, so the defender will keep his blade up high. With a bit of disguise, you can drop it low and into the shoulder. With a heavy blade like yours, you might even go through armour.'

'Really?'

'How many times have I told you? Until you get a bit of technique, if it comes to a scrap – just give it all you've got. You've put a bit of bulk on, and you have a long reach. If you're lucky you'll hit them before they can hit you.'

'So now what?'

'Recovery. Swing, then get your blade straight and central.'

Before Cassius could raise the sword, Simo stepped out of the kitchen. 'Sir, a note from Governor Calvinus. He wants to see you.'

'Now?'

'It says immediately.'

———◆———

Cassius stood alone in the Table Room, helmet under his arm, waiting. Given the speed at which events had developed, he'd hoped to get away without seeing Calvinus, though he'd planned to leave an appropriately regretful note. He wished he was back at the villa. The governor would be angry, he was sure of it.

He heard footsteps and voices. The men came closer, then stopped in the corridor, just out of sight.

'Yes, sir.' A tribune strode away past the door.

Calvinus walked in. He was wearing an immaculate white toga edged with purple. 'Corbulo.'

'Good evening, Governor.'

Calvinus turned and pushed the door to. 'I wanted to see you before you leave.'

'Yes, sir. I really am sorry that I won't be able to fulfil my duties here in Bostra.'

'Not your fault. And I think you still have an opportunity to assist me.'

'Sir?'

'It seems you will be journeying through the very lands we discussed here yesterday, perhaps beyond Ruwaffa. I will be most interested to hear what you find there.'

'Yes, sir. I will report to you as soon as I return.'

'Sooner, if you don't mind. The minute you're within reach of the imperial post.'

'Very well.'

Calvinus sat against the edge of the table. 'So, Pitface gives you barely two days to prepare, sends you off into the unknown, then promptly disappears again.'

'It seems time is of the essence, sir.'

'For Abascantius? Oh, I'm sure of it.'

Cassius thought it prudent to press Calvinus on this cryptic reply. 'I'm given to understand that the Emperor will shortly be arriving in Syria, sir. He wishes to see the stone recovered as soon as possible.'

'Perhaps. Unlike Abascantius, I wouldn't claim to know the mind of a man I'd never met.'

Cassius wasn't sure how to proceed, only that he needed to know what the governor was driving at. 'Sir?'

'The Emesan stone was being guarded by a unit of the Sixteenth Legion, yes?'

'Yes, sir.'

'So surely its recovery is the responsibility of Prefect Sanctus, not Imperial Security.'

'I suppose so, sir.'

Cassius wondered whether the governor knew about Ulixes. He certainly wasn't going to tell him. 'Sir, I think Abascantius believes a small, covert team has more chance of locating and recovering the stone.'

Calvinus examined the well-manicured fingernails of his right hand. 'I know Sanctus well. As young tribunes we fought together against the Persians. He is intelligent and resourceful. You think such an operation beyond him, with five thousand men under his command?'

'No, sir. But I was under the impression that the bulk of his forces are occupied to the north.'

'They are. Regardless, isn't it also possible that the army might not think it wise to cobble together a team of unproven auxiliaries for an operation in an area where an entire century was recently wiped out?'

'Indeed, sir. I see your point.' Cassius felt rather sick; he'd been foolish to get caught up even for a moment with Abascantius's enthusiasm. The chances of success were minuscule: more likely they'd all end up like those poor bastards at Ruwaffa.

'He told me what you did in Cyrenaica,' said Calvinus. 'And at that Syrian fort. Perhaps you do have a chance.' The governor stood up straight. 'But I repeat: why the Service?'

'Glory for Abascantius and Chief Pulcher? Getting one over the army? Currency with the Emperor?'

'Ah, almost there.' Calvinus smiled genially. He seemed to be enjoying this game.

Cassius continued thinking aloud. 'Or to atone for something. Some error or failing.'

'Remember Pontius berating you for failing to anticipate the attack on Ruwaffa? The army, and the Emperor, expects the Service to provide intelligence – prior warning.'

So that was it. 'Palmyra. The second revolt surprised everyone. It was Abascantius's job to see it coming.'

'His position and reputation are at stake. He wants you to help him restore it.'

Cassius wondered why he'd not considered it before; perhaps simply too much else occupying his mind?

Calvinus continued: 'That's not to say the Emperor won't be extremely grateful if the stone is recovered; we can't be seen to be outwitted by a bunch of thieves, after all. I mention this because I want you to realise it may not be simply the noble mission Abascantius made it seem.'

'I understand, sir. Thank you.'

'I'm sure you would have got there yourself in the end. And my motives are not entirely altruistic.'

The governor waited for Cassius to respond.

'You would prefer that I not focus solely on the stone.'

'You're a bright lad. Find out what's going on down there. I've spent the best part of my life protecting this province and its people; and for the first time in years we seem to have an emperor who knows what he's doing. I'm not about to let it all fall apart now. Get word to me as soon as you can.'

'Yes, Governor.'

Calvinus walked towards the door. 'Come, you need a good night's sleep and I've some dictation to attend to.'

'Sir, I wonder if I could ask for something – I don't have a portable map of the province.'

'I shall have one of my clerks send one over first thing in the morning.'

'Much appreciated, sir.'

Calvinus led him along the corridor and out to the courtyard. 'I spoke to my officers about this Optio Mercator. Sounds like a good man.'

'He does seems to be, sir.'

'I shall mention you both in my prayers. Your men too.'

'Thank you very much, sir.'

Cassius was surprised to see the governor offer his forearm.

'Come back alive. All of you.'

X

Though the entire household was up at dawn, a delay with the delivery of the horses meant that Mercator and the auxiliaries beat them to the meeting point. It was only a stone's throw from the hippodrome and, as they approached, Indavara glanced morosely at the enormous structure. It was the largest building in Bostra by a distance: walls formed of dozens of arches, the cavernous entrance flanked by two high towers. Today it was empty and silent, the only combatants some boys outside, wrestling in the dust.

Annoyed at being late, Cassius urged his horse between two basalt blocks and onto the grassy ground between the ruined temples. Mercator had the mounts neatly tied up and Cassius found himself rather taken aback by how large the group seemed with all the heavily laden horses and mules. Much of their load was water skins; the dry summer months weren't far away and previously full wells and cisterns would soon begin to run dry.

Although some of the beards would need a few days, the Arabians looked perfectly at home in their baggy tunics and hooded robes. Cassius, however, felt rather self-conscious in his merchant's outfit. He was wearing the pale blue tunic which had been hastily embroidered with several horizontal lines of lozenges. He had also purchased two large finger rings – one amber, one an imitation sapphire – and retrieved two gold bracelets from the hardwood box where he kept his valuables (his aunt had bought them for him years ago but he couldn't stand the weight and brazen opulence of the things).

Cassius dismounted and threw his reins to Simo, then hurried over to the auxiliaries, most of whom were sitting on a column lying on the ground. He nodded to Mercator, then gestured for the men to stay where they were. Cassius saw a good deal of tension and worry in their faces. Soldiers liked (and needed) routine and the twenty men had just been unceremoniously pulled out of theirs, with little idea of how the journey and mysterious operation would unfold.

'So,' he said, gesturing towards his garish tunic. 'Anybody want to swap?'

He gave an exaggerated shake of his head and was pleased to see a few smiles.

'That's the last time we're going to use Latin. Greek is fine but I suggest you men keep up with the Nabatean amongst yourselves – for practice if nothing else. As you will have surmised from our location we are heading south, bound for Petra. I would like to reach the Red City in five days and Thugrat by nightfall. We'll try to keep our heads down as much as possible but we haven't time to bypass towns and leave the roads. We will see locals, caravans and legionary patrols. If you think you've been recognised by someone, let myself or the optio know. Except he's not Mercator now, he is . . .'

'Mertan.'

'Mertan. And if any of the rest of you have Roman-sounding names, follow Merc – Mertan's example.'

Andal put his hand up. He already had a thick beard and, with his lined, nut-brown face, could easily have just walked out of the desert. 'And how shall we address you, sir?'

'Like that. You're supposed to be hired swords, so "sir" is fine. I am travelling under the name of Cassius Oranius Crispian – a Raetian merchant interested in the spice trade. Indavara and Simo – my attendant there – will go by their normal names. You men work for Mertan, who I hired here in Bostra to guide me south and provide protection. Any other questions?'

There were none.

'Then let's get going.'

➡8➡

135

South of Bostra, the Via Traiana cut through a fertile plain, with wheat fields and vineyards as far as the eye could see. The milestones were well maintained and the road smooth and even: compacted earth over paving slabs. The party rode two abreast, with Cassius and Mercator leading the way, followed by Indavara and Simo, then the rest of the men. Andal and Yorvah took it in turns to watch the rear.

Cassius was relieved to find his horse a placid beast. The Spaniard had passed on its name but he had already forgotten it. The mount – a tall, long-limbed grey – was carrying two weighty saddlebags and some rolled-up blankets that provided a convenient support for Cassius's back. There was nothing amongst his, Simo or Indavara's personal gear that could give them away. The mule trotting along behind Simo's horse, however, was carrying a precious cargo. As well as the 'wine' barrel, it was also bearing a sack of barley, at the bottom of which was Cassius's satchel. Inside were his spearhead (symbol of the Imperial Security Service) and his precious letters of recommendation from Chief Pulcher and Prefect Venator of the Fourth Legion.

The party was occasionally overtaken by the odd rider, including an army courier who sped past at a gallop. There was a remarkable variety amongst those they passed heading north: a gang of slaves chivvied along by some voluble guards; a toga-clad gentleman accompanied by his family and dozens of attendants; and itinerant farm workers trudging along with shouldered scythes and rakes. They saw a group of pilgrims too, easily identified by the wooden crosses hanging around their necks. Simo made no reaction but Cassius did note some disapproving looks from the auxiliaries, Mercator included.

Early in the afternoon, they spotted a small legionary fort a mile east of the road. According to Mercator, it was usually manned by a half-century but – owing to the current lack of manpower – now housed just a skeleton crew. They saw a flag flying but no trace of the legionaries.

Determined to use every hour of light, Cassius was extremely relieved when they finally saw the buildings of Thugrat up ahead.

Mercator had warned him that they should leave a bit of time for their first effort with the tents, and with thirty-one miles covered for the day, Cassius pronounced himself satisfied with their progress. The surrounding terrain had become rather bleaker – rocky ground covered by low grass – and at the first sight of a suitably flat area, he called a halt.

Mercator and the guard officers then took charge. The tents were rudimentary affairs: leather coverings hung over simple frames, with ropes and pegs to keep them stable. There were three: one for Cassius, Indavara and Simo and two larger ones for the men.

Once the shelters were up, Simo and Indavara moved the wine barrel and their bags inside. Cassius rid himself of the annoying jewellery and handed it to Simo, whose next job was to pour his master a drink.

'You saw those pilgrims, I suppose,' Cassius said quietly as he took the mug.

'I did, sir. We will pass close to Jerusalem on our way south, I believe.'

'Not that close. Do you still have that cross of yours?'

'Yes, sir,' said Simo, patting his tunic.

'Keep it out of sight. I've a feeling the auxiliaries may not be impressed. Do not mention matters of belief to them at all. If anyone asks, you worship only Jupiter and the great gods.'

Simo did not reply.

'Is that clear?'

'Yes, sir.'

Generally it took only the briefest mention of things religious for Simo to start rambling on about 'the kingdom' and 'the righteous' and how life should be lived in the service of 'the Lord'. Still bemused by the Christians' determination to indoctrinate others, Cassius had told Simo he was free to do so in his own time, but never in his presence. Sipping at the wine, he walked outside and met Mercator.

'We have a problem. One of the men, Sajjin, has told Yorvah he wants to go back to Bostra.'

'On the *first night*?'

'We can handle it if you want.'

'Physically?'

'You don't approve?' asked Mercator.

'In normal circumstances, I might. But I don't wish to sour things so early. We've a long way to go.'

'Apparently he got married last year.'

'You know him?'

'Not well. Yorvah says he's a decent soldier but . . .'

'Bring him to me.'

As Mercator left, Simo poked his head out of the tent. 'Sir, what would you like for dinner?'

'Something cold. We're not going to bother with a fire. And put as many layers as you can down for my bed – my backside is sore.'

When Mercator returned with Sajjin, the tall, handsome auxiliary was staring solemnly at the ground.

'Speak, then.'

'Sir?'

'Did you give no thought to your situation earlier? Why now?'

Sajjin looked up. 'I don't know, sir.'

'Your wife?'

'She was the one who wanted me to come – for the money.'

'And you?'

'I'd just as soon stay in Bostra.'

'By the gods, man, you have taken an oath to fight for the Emperor. Do you think you're the only one who'd rather stay at home?'

Cassius was briefly tempted to go farther, to tell him he hadn't seen a single member of his family in three long years, but he rarely spoke of that, even to Simo.

'Can you go on?'

'I don't think so.' Sajjin wiped at his eyes.

'You bloody coward.' Mercator grabbed his tunic and clenched a fist. 'You're a disgrace.'

Cassius held a hand up. Mercator pushed Sajjin away, breathing hard with frustration.

'All right, calm down,' Cassius said, conscious of the other soldiers looking on. 'Any more like him?'

'Not that I know of.'

Cassius considered his options, then pointed at Sajjin. 'Go and get your gear. Leave your horse.'

The auxiliary sloped away.

Mercator frowned. 'That's it?'

'Better he go now than disappear during the night.'

'We have to punish him,' insisted the optio, 'set an example.'

'Mercator, we are not at the fortress. This little group is going to be together for weeks. I'm not having a beating on the first night. Just see to it that he's quick.'

'As you wish.'

'By the way, you seemed to have slipped back into Latin again. The men will do as you do. Am I going to have to remind you every day?'

Mercator marched away.

Indavara ducked out of the tent, already munching something. 'Problem?'

'Not for you.'

The bodyguard winced as he straightened up. 'I'd forgotten how much I hate riding.'

'I expect your horse does too after today. You're still too tight on your reins and that poor beast's got to last you hundreds of miles.'

'You were going to help me, remember?'

'Remind me tomorrow. And didn't I tell you to speak Greek?'

'My Latin's better.'

'Not much.'

'You're a moody bastard, you know that?'

Cassius was about to fire an insult back at him but he reckoned Indavara had a point. 'Sorry. Do remind me about the riding.'

Cassius walked past the tents to where the soldiers were gathered. Most of them were watching Sajjin as he hauled a pack onto his back, head still down. Mercator was standing by a pile of food sacks with Andal and Yorvah. Cassius couldn't decide whether their unblinking glares were for him or Sajjin.

He spoke to the auxiliary, loud enough for all to hear. 'The moment you set foot in Bostra, report to headquarters. When I return I'll see you at the next session of the military court. Go.'

Sajjin walked away towards the road. One man offered him a gourd as he passed. Sajjin went to take it.

'Don't you dare,' ordered Cassius.

'He has no water,' said the helpful auxiliary.

'He can find his own bloody water.'

Sajjin continued onto the road and was soon lost to the fading light.

Cassius turned to Mercator. 'Two sentries. One facing the road, one watching the horses.'

'Yes, sir,' replied the optio, in Greek.

Despite his mattress of blankets, the endless howling of a fox and the combined snoring of Indavara and Simo, Cassius slept well. In the morning, Mercator and the men excelled once more and after the briefest of breakfasts they were away in time to miss the market traffic converging on Thugrat. There were no officials and no inspections at the gates and they continued on without delay for two hours.

The next town, however, Samra, was home to a legionary fort within sight of the road. Mercator had predicted a delay and they soon found themselves stuck behind a line of carts approaching an arched gate. Cassius – in his merchant's outfit once again – raised himself high in his saddle and looked along the road. Progress was slow because cart-loads were being checked by legionaries and money handed to a tax collector.

'This isn't going to be quick,' observed Mercator.

Cassius looked up at the cloudless, bright blue sky. The sun was already hot and he pulled up the hood of his riding cape. Ignoring a young lad offering date leaves full of something, he turned and looked back. The auxiliaries were lined up in orderly fashion – almost too orderly for a bunch of hired swords – and several were anxiously eyeing the gate. Thankfully the departure of Sajjin seemed to have been forgotten, and Cassius hadn't heard the man's name mentioned once. As he turned back, the cart in front trundled forward, but a few yards was the limit of their advance.

He sat there, nose assailed by flatulent horses and sweating men, growing increasingly hot and impatient, until finally – a good half-hour later – the senior legionary waved him and Mercator up to the arch.

'Business on the road?' asked the soldier in a bored monotone.

'I am a merchant,' Cassius announced, 'journeying south to investigate the markets of Petra.'

'Carrying trade goods?'

'No. Just our belongings.'

The legionary looked at the tax collector, who was now sitting behind a little table.

He was an unappealing individual with an unruly beard and beady eyes. 'Where are you from?'

'Originally? Raetia.'

'Your men aren't Raetian.'

'No. I hired them in Bostra.'

'Check the bags on every third horse,' ordered the tax collector. The legionary and his compatriots began with Mercator, who scowled as they unbuckled his saddlebags.

'Is this really necessary?' asked Cassius.

'It is for you,' replied the tax collector. 'I've manned this post for six years and I've never seen you before.'

'This is my first trip to Arabia.'

'A merchant with nothing to sell?'

'I told you. I'm here to buy. Samples of spice and perfume.'

'You're young for a merchant.'

'You're old for a clerk.'

'Watch yourself,' warned the legionary.

With a sour look at Cassius, the tax collector stood up and gazed along the line. 'Twenty-eight horses?'

'Yes,' confirmed Cassius.

A sudden shout from behind them. He turned along with the others and watched the senior legionary shake hands with one of the auxiliaries. The pair continued to talk as the other soldiers checked the baggage. Cassius took care not to look too concerned. The tax collector observed studiously until the check was concluded.

'Nothing,' said the soldier.

'You know that man?'

'I was stationed with him at Azraq a couple of years ago.'

'Doesn't look like he's done twenty-five years.'

'Discharged – lost a toe so he can't march.'

Cassius thought that rather inventive; it seemed at least one of the men was capable of maintaining their cover.

The tax collector walked back to his table and took a small counter from a pot. 'Without this you'll be charged again at every toll-stop along the road. Should be fifty-six but I'll call it sixty because of the rude remark.'

Cassius was tempted to root out the spearhead, show it to this greedy worm, then smack him about the face with it, but he instead told Simo to pay him.

Once he had the coins, the tax collector handed over the counter, which Simo passed on to Cassius. It was made of bark and marked with some kind of code.

The legionary caught Mercator's eye. 'Careful on the quieter stretches of the road. We've not many troops to spare. Few incidents of late.'

'Thanks for the advice.'

'On you go,' said the tax collector.

Cassius gave his horse a tap and set off through the gate.

◄■8■►

They passed through the town of Hadid, then the ancient city of Philadelphia. Like Damascus and nearby Gerasa, it was one of the Decapolis – the ten eastern frontier cities colonised by

Rome three centuries earlier. Though the provincial capitals were now more important, Philadelphia was still far larger and more populous than Bostra. Cassius found the impressive architecture reassuringly familiar, and as they rode on past busy side streets and squares, he saw several pretty sanctuaries. He got a particularly good look at one because of a collapsed cart that held up traffic for half an hour. While they waited, he gazed enviously at young men and women with nothing else to do other than lounge around on benches and talk and laugh. When they finally got under way again, he felt as if a black cloud of despondency had settled over him.

Since leaving Bostra, they had been skirting the highlands that bordered the Jordan and the Dead Sea. But as dusk fell, the Via Traiana neared the dark, rolling hills. Cassius was once again satisfied with the day's journey and they found a suitable place to camp with the next town, Madaba, already in view. A quarter-mile from the road was an area of dusty ground bordered on three sides by scrub. With the sun already lower in the sky than the previous night, Mercator immediately set the men to work.

Indavara and Simo gave a hand and – thinking it wise to be seen to be doing his bit – Cassius took it upon himself to unsaddle his horse, then pour some water for their three mounts. Yawning and wincing at his aching backside and thighs, he looked on as the men raised the tents. Yorvah began a Nabatean song and – after struggling on alone for a while – was joined by most of the others. During the delay in Philadelphia, Cassius had struck up a conversation with the younger of the two guard officers. Despite a nasty scar on his cheek that had rather ruined an otherwise pleasant face, he seemed a cheery fellow. The veteran Andal – who Cassius reckoned to be forty at least – was a more reserved figure, but clearly well respected by the men.

The song seemed to help the auxiliaries work even faster and the last tent was soon up. With Cassius and Mercator's approval, Andal got a fire going and some chickens were brought out for roasting. This prospect was enough to ensure Indavara didn't stray far and Cassius – circling the camp to stretch his legs – was glad to see the bodyguard sitting with the men. He didn't seem to be saying much but even the fact that he was mixing with them was a sign of progress. Cassius recalled their last assignment; how he'd been brought out of his shell by the camaraderie of Captain Asdribar and the crew of the *Fortuna Redux*.

He thought of the ship often. With the return of the sailing season the Carthaginian and his men would probably be heading for some exotic port, as ever occupied by their dual obsessions: superstition and turning a profit.

Cassius looked to the west. The Dead Sea was close now, just a few miles beyond the hills. He noticed a thick coil of smoke, drifting high.

Abruptly remembering how thirsty he was, he set off back to the small tent. Once there, he was surprised to see no light inside, but a faint glow coming from one side. He walked around the tent and spied a clay lamp on the ground. Facing away from him and kneeling beside it was Simo. He was whispering to himself.

'You'd better not be praying.'

Simo stood but didn't turn. When Cassius spun him around by his shoulder, he was still trying to push the cross down inside his tunic. 'A-apologies, sir. I thought if I kept out of sight—'

'You idiot, any one of the men could have seen you.'

'Sorry, sir, shall I fetch you some dinner? What about a—'

'Don't you dare try and distract me,' Cassius hissed. 'I told you specifically not to do this.'

'I am truly sorry, sir, there is—'

'You know what soldiers are like. If Mercator and the others take against you, then they might just take against *me*. You are supposed to help, Simo, not be a hindrance. I'm beginning to wonder if you might be more trouble than you're worth.'

'Sir, if I can—'

'Not another word. Get inside that tent and keep that bloody cross hidden.'

Simo bowed his head, then pointed west.

'What?' demanded Cassius.

'The smoke, sir.'

'What about it?'

'The martyr Pionius of Smyrna,' stammered Simo. 'He wrote of walking these lands and seeing scorched earth and bodies that wouldn't sink and smoke coming out of the ground. He believed them to be signs of hell. Sir, the Day of Judgement might come at any time. In Antioch all anyone talks of is sin and violence and the coming war. And in Egypt too. So much suffering.'

'"Day of Judgement" – that nonsense again.' Cassius held Simo by the shoulders. 'Pull yourself together. That smoke could be anything, there are hot springs in this area. War? What your people call sin? It's nothing new. And do you think your Christ was the first man crucified? I have ancestors, family, who died on the cross in the civil wars. Our gods, our traditions, go back a *thousand* years. This prophet of yours has barely been dead two centuries, yet you believe he and your one god have all the answers.'

Simo reached for the cross, then thought better of it.

Cassius let go of him.

'I am sorry, sir. But we are close to many holy places here.'

'Yes, and I expect you spent all your time in Antioch doing nothing but praying and listening to those fools who think the world will soon come to an end. There is more to life than worship, Simo. The gods do not always hear us. Sometimes they forsake us entirely. You have seen more than enough to know that.'

Simo bent down and picked up the lamp.

'I cannot control what goes on in your head,' added Cassius. 'And unlike your people, I am not arrogant enough to assume I can control what you believe. But you belong to me; and you must do as I tell you. Any more of this and I will have to consider letting you go. Now is not a good time to be trying my patience, Simo. I don't have much left.'

XI

'What is that smell?'

'Bitumen,' replied Mercator.

Cassius looked around. Apart from a single hamlet between them and the hills, the surrounding area was empty.

'Coming from where?'

'It occurs naturally – pools of it float to the surface of the Dead Sea. The locals go out in boats and scoop up all they can. It's worth a lot but doesn't appear very often so it's very competitive. They go armed to the teeth. People get killed over it.'

'Really? I must confess I had no idea.'

'What's bitumen?' asked Indavara, listening in as he rode along behind them.

'Black stuff, like pitch,' said Cassius. 'Used for proofing and glue.'

'It comes up from the bottom of the sea?'

'The Dead Sea's not actually a sea, technically speaking,' said Cassius.

'It's pretty big,' said Mercator.

'It's a lake,' affirmed Cassius. He turned and gestured to Indavara and Simo (who'd said almost nothing for the entire morning). 'We have been on several voyages across the Great Green Sea.'

Mercator looked impressed. 'I've still never seen it.'

'You'd never forget it if you did.'

'Squint and Captain Asdribar went farther than that,' added Indavara.

'Men we sailed with,' explained Cassius. 'They have been out past the Pillars of Hercules, seen the Great Ocean.'

'Does it ever end, do you think?' asked Mercator.

'They said it goes on forever,' replied Cassius. 'Hard to imagine.'

'I don't know,' said the optio. 'My first centurion once marched us to Damascus and back in five days. That felt like forever.'

—8—

Later that day they got a chance to see some of the bitumen up close. Running east from the Dead Sea and bisecting the Via Traiana were numerous tracks; and when they halted by one to rest the horses, a cart came along. The man driving it was with two lads and seemed wary at first but he reined in when Yorvah gave a friendly greeting. Cassius rather wished the guard officer had kept quiet but he was as bored and curious as the others and wandered over to investigate. When the auxiliaries offered to share some raisin cakes, the local climbed down and proudly displayed his cargo.

Tied to one side of the cart was a coracle made of reed and wood plus numerous pails and ladles. The bitumen itself had been stored in large amphoras. The driver introduced himself as Usrana and lifted out one of the containers. Inside was a thick, lumpy substance. One of Usrana's sons picked up a twig and dipped it into the black liquid.

'Like tree-sap,' said one of the men.

'Or honey,' said Indavara.

'Worth more,' volunteered Usrana with a sly grin.

'How much?' asked Cassius.

'For each amphora – about ten denarii.'

Some of the soldiers whistled.

'Not bad,' said Cassius.

'As long as I can get it safely to market in Dhiban.'

'Only five or six miles, isn't it?' said Yorvah.

'Yes, but the smell draws everyone. We got to the lake early and took what we could. But the big crews were already arriving when we left and some of them don't bother with boats. They just wait for poor folk like me to do the hard work then grab it.'

'No army round here?' asked Andal.

'There's a small fort at Haj but that's a way from here. You see the odd century marching along but that's about it.'

'By Jupiter,' said Yorvah, looking at one of the boys. 'I thought I ate quickly.'

The lad smiled. All that remained of the raisin cake were some flakes of pastry around his mouth. 'Got any more?'

The auxiliaries laughed; especially when Usrana clipped the lad round the ear. 'Greedy little beggar.'

The Arabian bowed low to Cassius. 'My apologies. Thank you for the cakes, sir.'

With a prod from their father the boys gave their thanks too. 'Well, we'd best be off.'

'Sure your horse is going to make it?' enquired Andal. The animal wasn't much bigger than a mule; and tasked with hauling quite a load.

'Don't you worry about her, she's done worse in her time.'

'Ride with us if you wish,' offered Mercator. He hadn't even glanced at Cassius, who swiftly quashed the idea.

'Usrana here is in a hurry,' he said. 'Our horses need a rest – we've been on the move since dawn.'

Mercator looked at him, brow furrowed.

'We shall stay a while longer, *Mertan*,' added Cassius.

'Well, thanks again,' said Usrana as Yorvah replaced the amphora on the cart for him. The men also helped him retie the rope so the load was secure. He and the boys climbed up and set off towards Dhiban.

While the men were still gathered, Cassius walked up to Yorvah. '"By Jupiter" – is that a common phrase amongst local tribesmen, do you think?'

Only then did the guard officer realise his error. 'Sorry.'

'He didn't notice,' said Andal.

'Maybe, maybe not,' said Cassius.

'They couldn't ride with us?' asked Mercator.

Cassius ignored him and addressed the others. 'The rest of you see to your horses. You have a quarter-hour.'

Mercator stayed where he was, arms crossed, staring at Cassius.

He at least waited for the men to disperse before speaking. 'Didn't you hear what he said? What if they run into some of these brigands?'

'What do we care?' countered Cassius. 'I am a merchant and you lead my hired swordsmen, so it's hardly our concern. Our concern is getting to the south of this province with our cover intact; a task which seems to be a sufficient challenge for you and your men.'

'No harm done,' said the optio.

'Rumour and gossip fly up and down roads like this quicker than the imperial post. I suggest you go and remind your auxiliaries of their obligations.'

'Perhaps they consider this playacting dishonourable.'

'Perhaps you do.'

Mercator looked away.

Cassius held up a hand. 'Listen, I admire the sentiment, really – wanting to help. But we have no room for sentiment. Understood?'

'Understood.'

———8———

As they rode on, the sun grew hotter. Cassius was grateful for the riding breeches protecting his legs and the hood protecting his head. He couldn't stop his fingers sweating on the reins, though, and eventually had to ask Simo for a towel.

With the horses visibly slowing, he became increasingly keen to get to Dhiban and give the mounts and the men (not to mention himself) some respite from the heat. As they neared the top of a crest, Andal and Mercator assured him they were close. Beside the road was a milestone: like the others a thick, six-foot post of rounded limestone. Cassius peered down at the carvings, checking that the distance to Petra tallied with his map. Some idiot had daubed paint on one side and he couldn't quite make out the figure. Waving the others past, he nudged his horse closer.

'Shall I get down, sir?' said Simo, who had come off the road behind him.

'No, I think I can see it. That's an eight, isn't it?'

'Look!'

The cry came from Mercator.

'What is it?' asked Cassius.

'Usrana – looks like he's in trouble!'

'Of course he is.' Cassius handed the map to Simo and trotted his horse up to the crest. About two miles to the south were the densely packed buildings of Dhiban. Closer, on the right side of the road, was a large farmhouse.

'See there,' said Mercator, pointing.

Usrana had just guided the cart behind the farmhouse. He jumped down and ran to the corner, then looked west. Riding hard across the flat, dusty ground towards him was a phalanx of around twenty horsemen.

'Sir?'

Cassius knew instantly he could not say no. If something happened to Usrana and the boys while they simply looked on, the men would never forgive him. Come to think of it, neither would he.

Indavara rode up beside him. 'I'll go. We'll see those thieving bastards off easily enough.'

Cassius looked at the horses. Most of the tired, heavily loaded mounts wouldn't make a mile gallop; and if the brigands weren't put off by the sight of them, they would reach Usrana first.

'Sir?' pressed Mercator.

'You and Indavara take Yorvah's squad. Drop all your bags.'

Mercator leaped down off his saddle.

'You heard the man!' yelled Yorvah as he and the others set about lightening their loads.

Cassius got down and helped Indavara, who was frantically untying blankets and bags.

'Take it easy. This isn't why we're here.'

'I know.'

Mercator was the first away, whipping his mount as he charged down the slope.

'Stay on the road!' shouted Cassius. 'That ground is rough.'

Indavara was next away, followed by Yorvah and the nine men of his squad.

Cassius winced as he saw the bodyguard hunched way too far forward, and hoped he'd make it to the farmhouse without coming off.

He turned to Andal. 'Load that gear up – quickly!'

—8—

Indavara cursed at his mount, imploring it to go faster as the auxiliaries sped past him. He was bouncing around all over the place and was pretty sure his horse was galloping only because the others were. Then he remembered what Corbulo had told him about gripping tight with his thighs, which seemed to help a bit. He snatched a look to his right as they neared the farmhouse – the brigands were close.

His mount seemed to sense he was distracted and slowed down. Indavara didn't like to kick it too hard and his half-hearted attempts made no difference. Thankfully, the horse followed the others as Mercator came off the road, heading straight at the brigands. Indavara glimpsed Usrana, still at the corner. He and the boys watched them fly past.

Mercator came up in his saddle and slowed to a trot. As Indavara copied him, he heard a shout then two loud thumps.

—8—

'Oh no.'

Cassius had just set off from the crest when he saw the horses go down. The men were thrown to the ground and the animals tumbled into the dust, legs flailing. A couple of the others looked back but they had other things to worry about: the brigands had fanned out to meet them at the edge of the property.

'Yah!'

Cassius's horse was the least heavily loaded. He lashed it with the reins and thundered away.

As the dust cleared, Indavara turned back and saw that one of the fallen riders was already up on his feet. The auxiliary went straight to his horse, which was lying motionless. The other animal hauled itself up by its front legs. Indavara couldn't see the second man.

'Stop,' ordered Mercator.

Indavara halted next to the optio. Some of the animals were wheezing and foaming at the mouth, barely able to keep their heads up.

The brigands passed through gaps in the patchy hedge that ran around the rear of the property. Dark, bearded faces framed by the folds of their hoods, they advanced across the dry ground. Indavara was relieved to see no bows or spears or other distance weapons.

'Twenty-one,' said Yorvah, 'and we've only ten.'

'Eleven.' The auxiliary who had recovered himself walked up behind them.

'Who's down?' asked Mercator without turning round.

'Druz. Looks bad.'

The brigands stopped at what Indavara reckoned to be about forty feet. He looked back at the road. Corbulo was ahead of the others but still a good half-mile away.

Two of the brigands exchanged a few words then one pulled down his hood. He was surprisingly young, pale eyes regarding those before him with cool contempt. He spoke in Greek.

'We want the black stuff. Give us the cart and there'll be no trouble.'

'I don't think so,' replied Mercator, who was breathing a lot harder than the brigand.

The leader spat into the ground. 'This is our territory. Who are you?'

'Friends of Usrana,' said Mercator. 'He's keeping the black stuff for himself – why don't you go and get some of your own?'

The leader gestured to his compatriots. 'We have the numbers. Just give us the cart and we'll let all of you go on your way.'

Indavara was listening but he was more interested in the fact that almost all the brigands now had a hand on their swords. He thought he'd done pretty well to stay on his horse but he wasn't about to try fighting on it. He patted its shoulder, then let go of the reins and dismounted. To avoid standing in amongst the other mounts, he took a few steps forward and stared at the brigand.

There was another reason he wanted to settle the matter quickly – judging by the noises Druz was making, he was badly hurt. Indavara had no intention of waiting around for this plundering bastard to make his move.

The brigand aimed a long finger at him. 'I would advise against provocation. Anything that comes out of the water around here belongs to us.' He nodded towards Usrana, who was still looking on from the corner of the farmhouse. 'And anyone who gets in our way ends up under the ground.'

'Enough talk, thief,' said Indavara. 'You want it, come and get it. If not, run along before I lose my patience and put *you* under the ground.'

One of the other men unleashed a stream of curses at him. Indavara didn't understand a word of it. He placed one hand on his sword and beckoned the vocal brigand forward with the other. Now that it came to it, he realised he might enjoy chopping his way through these parasites; in fact he was almost beginning to hope it would happen.

The leader scratched his chin and seemed to think for a while before replying. 'Luckily for you there'll be plenty more of the black stuff coming out today. You're not worth the trouble.'

'Keep telling yourself that,' said Indavara. 'It'll make you feel better.'

'Easy,' warned Mercator quietly.

The brigand pointed at Indavara again. 'I shall remember your face.'

'I've already forgotten yours.'

The loud brigand shouted more insults at him. The leader put out a hand and the man reluctantly quietened down. With a few more words, the leader turned his horse around and led the brigands back through the hedge. Some were slow to follow. Indavara and the auxiliaries watched them until the very last man had turned away.

— 8 —

As Cassius dismounted, Usrana hurried towards him.

'Thank you for sending your men, sir, thank you.'

Cassius handed him his reins. 'Watch my mount, would you?'

He jogged along the side of the farmhouse to where the horse and the injured man lay. The horse was on its side, breathing unevenly, bloody spittle bubbling from its mouth and nostrils. Bone had sheared through skin just above its front left knee. It would have to be killed.

Cassius reached the auxiliary at the same time as Indavara and Mercator. He was on his back, face wrinkled by pain, fists clenched. 'My back. Gods, I think it's broken.'

'You'll be all right, Druz,' said Mercator as he knelt beside him and took a gourd from his belt.

'Gods, gods.' Druz, who was one of the younger auxiliaries, reached into his tunic and pulled out a small, roughly cast iron phallus – a good-luck charm.

'Where's the pain?' asked Mercator, a hand on the younger man's chest.

'Everywhere.'

Indavara had checked the rest of his body. 'No other injuries I can see.'

'Give him some room,' Cassius told the others. 'Simo will be here in a moment.'

'Gods, gods,' wailed Druz. 'Some strong wine, please – something for the pain.'

'Here.' Usrana arrived with a flask. 'I was saving this for tonight. It's unwatered.'

Mercator pulled out the stopper and held it to Druz's lips.

As the auxiliary drank, Usrana looked up at Cassius and the others. 'Thank you again. Thank you all.'

XII

'Well?'

'Backs are very difficult to diagnose, sir,' said Simo. 'But I'd say he's damaged the lower part of it.'

'Can he ride?'

'Not a chance. We'll need to make a stretcher for him.'

Cassius looked at Mercator.

'What else could we have done?' said the optio. 'Let those thieving bastards kill Usrana and the boys?'

'I warned you about that ground,' replied Cassius, 'and you came off the road like it was a bloody cavalry charge.'

Mercator didn't seem keen to argue the point. 'I'll go and sort out the stretcher. We can bind some tent poles together, use panels for the sling.'

'Good idea.'

As he left, Druz continued to curse and groan. His cries had distressed the boys so much that Yorvah had taken them round to the other side of the farmhouse to play a game. There was no sign of any inhabitants; the place seemed abandoned.

'Any reason not to give him more wine?' Cassius asked Simo.

'No, sir. Unless we can get him to a surgeon, there's nothing I can do.'

'Then keep him drinking until he passes out. I can't take much more of that din.'

Cassius walked over to Usrana. 'You're *from* Dhiban?'

'Yes.'

'Do you know if there's a surgeon there?'

'I don't think so.'

'Any army? Administrators?'

'No, sir, just the odd tax collector now and again. There is the centurion – he's the richest man in the town and head of the council.'

'Centurion?'

'Retired. Name's Censorinus. He owns a big farm, employs dozens of workers.'

'Where is this farm?'

'About a mile south of the town. It's signposted from the road.'

After a failed attempt to mount the stretcher across two of the steadier mules, they decided to carry Druz the remaining two miles to Dhiban. Cassius placed the bearers in the middle of the party and kept one eye to the west all the way, fearing the brigands might return with reinforcements.

But in fact they saw no one, and with the men all taking their turn with the stretcher – Indavara included – they made reasonable time. Druz had succumbed to the wine and remained unconscious as they pressed on through the town, accompanied by Usrana and the boys until they reached the central square.

Dhiban was indeed a quiet place with no sign of any soldiers or officials, but Usrana assured Cassius that the brigands never ventured too close. He insisted on handing over all his remaining wine for Druz and promised that he and his family would offer prayers for him for the next hundred days. Farewells were exchanged and they went on their way.

Despite what Usrana had told him, Cassius asked several passers-by about a surgeon, but the only medical help available was from the usual opportunistic amateurs offering questionable advice and unreliable treatments. Cassius knew that only a well-trained, experienced physician would be able to do more for Druz than Simo. He didn't intend travelling any farther with the stricken auxiliary so all hopes now lay with this retired centurion.

Fortunately, the property was as easy to locate as Usrana had suggested. On either side of the track leading off the road were fields enclosed by fences and hedges, most containing goats or sheep. In the middle of one field were three boys who had stopped to peruse the new arrivals. They suddenly ran off towards the buildings.

Cassius led the auxiliaries to the scanty shade offered by a row of date palms, then told Mercator to wait there and rode on with Indavara and Simo. They passed numerous outhouses and pens before reaching what looked like the residence. The two-storey villa was large compared to most within the town, and was fronted by a wooden verandah. A maid cleaning the window shutters also ceased her work to watch the interlopers.

Hearing hooves on stone, Cassius turned to his right and saw four riders trotting up between two barns. Looking on from behind them were the boys. The leading rider was the oldest of the four and was wearing a wide-brimmed hat. To Cassius's relief, the expression under it was more curious than suspicious.

'Good day. I don't recall making any appointments for this afternoon.'

'Good day. Are you Censorinus, the ex-centurion?'

'Around here it is usual for the visitor to give his name first.'

'Of course. I am Cassius Oranius Crispian.' Cassius gestured back along the track. 'I have an injured man in my party and thought you might be able to help.'

'I am Censorinus. But what makes you think I'd be so willing to help a stranger?'

'Simo.'

The Gaul – who had already retrieved the spearhead – held it up. Censorinus nodded at the villa. 'You'd better come in.'

Cassius stood alone on the verandah and watched the men gather. Not his men – they were topping up their water supplies from a cistern – but the group Censorinus had swiftly assembled from his family and staff. In charge was one of his sons, a well-built fellow armed with spear and sword. There were two other sons, three nephews plus a dozen labourers. They had been tasked by

157

Censorinus with recruiting more sword-hands from Dhiban, then heading north in search of the brigands that had attacked Usrana.

The son gave a shout and led them away towards the road at a gallop, leaving a cloud of dust in their wake. The boys and women who had been looking on dispersed rapidly when they saw Censorinus exit the front door.

He too watched the group depart. 'I hope they find plenty of help. These thieves are growing in numbers and confidence – they even tried to take us on a couple of times recently.'

'The people are lucky to have you watching over them.'

'This is the first year I've had to do so alone.'

'No help from the army?'

Censorinus gave an ironic grin. 'You're the first officer I've spoken to in months. No, brigandage is generally kept under control by the local Saracen chief – we're on the western edge of what's long been considered his territory. No thief would dare rob one of the locals if they thought he would hear of it. But no one's seen him or his men in weeks.'

'Any idea where they are?'

Censorinus ran his hand across the few white hairs left on his head. 'Some say he's gone north to fight the Palmyrans, others that he's fighting *with* them. He never stays in one place for long anyway – he's heavily involved in the incense trade – but he'd always leave a few men behind to keep the peace. Seems like they've all gone with him this time.'

'This chief, he's part of the Tanukh?'

'I believe so.'

'I see,' said Cassius. It all tallied with what Calvinus had revealed about the apparent absence of many of the chiefs and their men. Where were they all?

Censorinus tapped his hat against his leg. 'I hope and pray the Saracens return soon. We haven't enough men in Dhiban to keep the brigands at bay for long and I need my employees working, not riding around the desert.'

'Apologies for the imposition. I didn't feel I had a great deal of choice.'

'No apology necessary. You did the right thing. That lad is in a lot of pain. I hope Eugammon can do something for him. He should be here by nightfall.'

'He is a good surgeon?'

'Yes. Greek. Old and hates to travel, but he knows I pay well.'

'Talking of money,' said Cassius, 'I will of course give you whatever you think is fair.'

'Keep it,' said the ex-centurion. 'I have more money than I know what to do with anyway.' He lowered his voice. 'Don't tell my wife I said that.'

'Trade is good?' enquired Cassius. Like all men of the upper class, his father had tried to engender an appreciation of agriculture in his son, but Cassius had never been able to get all that excited about crops or weather or animal husbandry. 'The land around here doesn't look particularly promising.'

'It's not. But with a bit of creative irrigation we've enough water and fodder for our four-legged friends.'

Censorinus waved a gnarled hand at the patchwork of fields between the house and the road. Most of the sheep and goats were sheltering from the sun by buildings or beneath trees.

'Twelve hundred head at the last count. We send hides and wool as far as Aila and Damascus. The meat and milk bring in a fair bit too. I started up with three goats, would you believe?'

'Impressive.'

'Few envious locals to contend with, of course.'

'Well, they have to pay all the taxes,' said Cassius with a grin.

'Indeed, but I try to balance the scales by helping out where I can.'

Cassius backtracked swiftly, anxious not to offend his host. 'I too have cause to be thankful for your generosity. It is much appreciated.'

'Least I can do for a fellow officer.'

'You don't mind helping a grain man?'

'My brother worked for the Service for a while; bit of secret stuff in Persia. We don't speak – he's an arsehole – but some of the others weren't too bad.' Censorinus nodded at Cassius's tunic.

'Talking of covert work, what's all this with the pretty colours and the gold?'

'It's complicated.'

'And confidential, I expect.'

'Well, yes. On that subject, I'm sure I don't have to—'

'Don't worry. Only my sons saw the spearhead. The others think you're a merchant.' Censorinus winked. 'And as you've probably already gathered, I don't tell my wife anything she doesn't need to know.'

He hurried down the steps. 'Come, let's see how those men of yours are getting on.'

With the horses refreshed and the water replenished, Mercator and the auxiliaries were soon ready to leave. The men were clearly concerned about Druz and Censorinus took it upon himself to put their minds at rest.

'Listen, he is badly hurt – there's no two ways about it. But there is an excellent surgeon on the way and he is currently in the hands of my wife, my daughters and the maids. He'll not want for attention.'

'I almost feel jealous,' ventured Yorvah.

'Watch it,' said Censorinus, playfully raising a fist, 'or you might also find yourself in a lot of pain.'

The men laughed.

Censorinus put his hat back on. 'If he's fit for travel we'll get him to Bostra.'

'If not we can pick him up on the way back,' suggested Mercator.

'Ah, wait there.' Censorinus strode over to the closest barn and went inside.

'Mount up,' ordered Cassius. As the others complied, he kept his horse out of the way.

Censorinus returned holding a well-filled sack. 'A few legs of lamb for you.' He handed the sack up to Simo. 'Here, you look like a man who knows how to cook a bit of meat. Add some salt and a few herbs and that'll do you nicely.'

Mercator raised a hand. 'Thank you, sir. Farewell.'

Indavara, Simo and many of the others added their thanks as the optio led them away towards the road.

Cassius and Censorinus shook forearms. 'Again, much appreciated.'

'Pleasure. We'll do our best for the lad.'

Cassius mounted up. 'Do you think we'll make Karak in daylight?'

'I should think so.'

Censorinus patted Cassius's horse and led it along by the reins. 'How far south are you headed?'

'Beyond Petra. A long way beyond.'

'Just remember – that's true Saracen territory down there. Whatever your mission, be careful, young man.'

'I will.'

'May the gods smile upon you.'

'And upon you.'

Censorinus handed Cassius his reins then stopped in front of the villa.

As he neared the road, Cassius looked back. He couldn't help wishing the kind, capable veteran was coming with them.

───◆8◆───

Not far south of Dhiban, the road dropped down into the valley of the Mujib Wadi, a broad watercourse that ran east from the Dead Sea. At the top the ground was barren and dry, but as they descended hardy greenery began to appear, along with several species of bird. Simo pointed out a copse of balsam trees with their distinctive multiple trunks and writhing branches; their oil was highly valued but they appeared untouched.

The stream was shallow enough for them to bypass the causeway and ride across. Though he was keen to keep moving, the water was so cool and inviting that Cassius called a halt and allowed the men half an hour to bathe.

The decision to take a break was soon vindicated by the steep climb out of the wadi; they had to stop several times to rest the mounts. Only a few hundred feet from the top, one of the men cried out and pointed at an animal upon a high ledge. Cassius couldn't identify the beast, which seemed frozen in a proud stance.

'What's that thing?' asked Indavara. 'Looks like a giant goat.'

'Pretty much,' replied Mercator. 'Ibex. Big male.'

The animal's coat was light brown, the crest of hair along its back darker. The formidable set of twisted, protruding horns were almost as long as the rest of it. Some of the auxiliaries offered a little bow and whispered a few words.

'It's sacred?' Cassius asked.

'Certainly to the nomads,' said Mercator. 'They call it the king of the desert – one of the handful of creatures that can survive in the southern lands. There is no trace of water there for hundreds of miles, just baking heat and the endless Sea of Sand. Amongst men, only the Saracens know the way across.'

'We're not going that far south, are we?' asked Indavara.

Cassius didn't reply. He took a last look at the ibex and moved off.

━ 8 ━

They almost reached Karak by nightfall, and made camp within sight of the wadi of the same name. With the darkness came a harsh wind. Exposed on the plain above the valley, they had to weigh down the tents with rocks and keep close watch on the animals. While the wind whipped at the tents, Cassius settled down to sleep at the end of what seemed a remarkably long day. He was at least again satisfied with the progress they'd made, having spotted a milestone just before they'd stopped. Fifty-nine miles to Petra. If they could avoid any more difficulties, they would reach the former capital in five days as planned.

XIII

Two days later, they left the Via Traiana for the first time. The road didn't actually enter Petra but bypassed it to the east, continuing south past the town of Udruh. Cassius thought it preferable to avoid Udruh anyway: the legionary fortress there housed the entire sixth cohort of the Third Cyrenaican – five hundred men, any one of whom might recognise one of the auxiliaries and cause an unnecessary complication.

They had been travelling through a mountainous wasteland since morning, the road passing bulbous, layered rock formations. The palette of colours reminded Cassius of shells on a beach and the aquatic analogy didn't end there. These were not hills or crags; to him they looked more like giant sea sponges squashed together then deposited on the ground, each a honeycomb of hollows and crevasses.

As the road became busier and hamlets appeared, Cassius knew they were nearing the city, but it remained hidden from view behind the towering natural defences of the landscape. Petra had originally been a retreat for the nomadic Nabateans, who'd made a home and fortress of the site over many centuries. The eastern approach was known as the Siq, a narrow gorge that led directly to the heart of the city.

A mile short of it, they came to a wide, flat area between sheer faces of rock. Built on either side of the road were two walled enclosures accessed by arched entrances. Within were dozens of bays containing horses, mules and camels. According to Mercator, this was a caravan station, where the travelling traders could safely feed, water and house their animals. The party would leave the mounts there and seek lodgings in the city, with Cassius hopefully meeting Ulixes the following day.

'Going through or putting in?' asked a loud voice in Greek.

A portly man with a tight belt around his robes had appeared in the middle of the road. Before either Cassius or Indavara could answer, another man stepped in front of him. This fellow had a multicoloured sash instead of a belt.

'One silver per mount per night! Best rate you'll find. Biyara's yard – on the right.'

'Don't listen to him,' advised the other man. 'Moab's is one silver per mount too, plus as much water as you need. Moab's – over to the left. Has to be Moab's!'

'They'll kill you with extras,' insisted Sash.

'Has to be Moab's – thirty years a family business!'

Cassius – exhausted after another day in the saddle – was leaning forward, resting on his mount's neck. He and Mercator looked at the enclosures. With dusk close, both were busy. Moab's appeared marginally less so.

'To the left?'

'Left it is,' replied the optio.

Sash was already looking for the next customer. Cassius hauled on his reins. As his horse lurched off the road he heard an angry shout. He turned and saw a camel just behind him. The animal brayed, showing a pink tongue and hideous yellow teeth coated with slobber. The rider was a plump man wearing immaculate white robes, a headband above his enraged face.

'Curses upon you!' he yelled in Greek. 'Watch where you're going!'

Cassius glared. The camel-rider looked at him, then at Mercator, then Indavara, then the auxiliaries, most of whom were staring back at him.

'My apologies. Please – you first.'

Cassius guided his horse towards the middle arch of Moab's, where half a dozen more camels were in a queue, waiting to enter. The riders had dismounted, reins in one hand, canes in the other. Each of the animals was heavily laden with clay jars secured by rope. Cassius had seen enough of them in Bostra to know most would contain frankincense – the precious gum harvested from the trees of Arabia Felix.

Unable to endure another minute in the saddle, he slid to the ground and almost fell when his right foot landed on a rogue walnut. Tightening his belt and bootlaces, he watched the others dismount.

Someone tapped him on the shoulder. 'Excuse me, sir. Did your party just arrive?'

The man was rather more presentable than the first tax collector they'd encountered, but the interrogative expression was the same. He was accompanied by a clerk holding a pile of waxed tablets and two bored-looking legionaries.

'Yes,' said Cassius.

'Are you a merchant?'

'I am.'

'With goods to declare?'

'Actually, no. I'm just down here looking for trade opportunities.'

Cassius retrieved the token and showed it to the tax collector, as he had at several settlements in the last few days.

'Mmm. You have a lot of men with you, lot of baggage too. Would you mind if the soldiers checked a few?'

'Go ahead.'

As the administrator and the legionaries went to do their work, Mercator walked stiffly over to Cassius. 'Not a lot of light left.'

'Two hours at most. I shall head into the city and find us some accommodation if you can organise things here.'

'Fair enough. I'll leave a man on guard. We can meet at the King's Tomb in an hour.'

'Where's that?'

'First building you come to – two-thirds of the way along the Siq. Trust me, you'll know it when you see it.'

Mercator walked away to brief the men, who had arranged themselves and their horses in an orderly line parallel to the road. The tax collector was examining a tablet with his clerk while the legionaries searched the bags.

Cassius's horse was unsettled by all the camels so he collared one of the young lads from Moab's and told him to look after it. Taking only his satchel, he walked over to Simo and Indavara.

'You two grab anything essential and stick the rest on the mule with the "wine"– that barrel's not leaving our sight. And hurry; I think there's still quite a way to go before we reach the civilised bit.'

━━●8●━━

Once they were ready, Cassius led the way along the road towards the Siq. Indavara and Simo were carrying almost as much as the mule.

'We're fine, thanks,' said the bodyguard.

'Good. Consider yourself lucky you don't have to bear the burden of leadership.'

Indavara glowered.

'That's called a metaphor,' added Cassius. 'Simo will tell you all about them some time.' As he walked, he pushed the annoying bracelets up his forearm. 'Sorry, but rich merchants don't carry saddlebags.'

'You can't take *anything*?' demanded Indavara. 'Patch looks like he's about to collapse.'

'Patch?'

Indavara nodded at the mule, which was plodding along, ears twitching. Upon its left haunch was a patch of white fur.

'Ten out of ten for originality. Why give a mule a name?'

Indavara tried to shrug but there was too much weight on his shoulders.

'Horses can have names,' said Cassius. 'But not mules.'

'Why not?'

'I don't know. They just don't.'

━━●8●━━

The Siq was no more than ten yards wide. Once inside, only a narrow strip of sky was visible hundreds of feet above. A steady stream of people were walking in both directions, many now carrying torches, ready for the coming dark. The sandy ground was almost white, the pink-grey walls seamed with black and dotted with the odd plant.

'Look how smooth the rock is,' observed Indavara, reaching out to run his hand along it.

'Must have been water flowing through here at some point,' said Cassius. 'Probably still does in the rainy months.'

Carved into the sides of the gorge were dozens of angular niches. Some contained wooden or metal figurines, some candles and lamps, others offerings of food and wine. Vendors who'd claimed valuable pitches beside this river of passers-by collected up their wares and joined the throng entering the city. Voices echoed off the walls, coalescing into a strange hum. They passed a flute player who seemed determined to use every last moment of daylight. He was producing a pleasing tune and his mug was half full of coins.

After about a mile, the Siq momentarily narrowed to five yards then opened out and bore around to the right.

'By the great gods, look at that,' said Cassius. 'Must be the King's Tomb.'

As the locals streamed past them, the three of them stopped to behold the monumental sight ahead. Hewn from the pale red rock was a vast, ornate façade at least two hundred feet high. The façade was made up of two sections, one above the other, and each boasting six colossal columns. Amongst the dozens of reliefs dwarfing the people below, Cassius picked out familiar gods and goddesses, griffins, eagles, even the writhing snakes of a Medusa head. In the middle of the bottom section was an immense, rectangular doorway; the largest he'd ever seen.

'I'd heard it was impressive.'

He glanced at Simo and Indavara, both of whom seemed oblivious to the curses and shoves of those hurrying past.

'First the Helios of Rhodes and now this,' Cassius continued. 'You two can't say I haven't taken you to some incredible sights. There's another tale for you to tell.'

Indavara shook his head. 'How could they carve that out of the rock?'

'Workmanship, time, and a lot of money. See the female figure up on the second layer, Simo? Like the Tyche of Antioch.'

They followed the road around to the right. Below the tomb's doorway, ten local guards stood on an equally massive set of steps, each armed with a sword hanging from a sash. Several of them scowled at the curious trio, as if even daring to look was an affront to their history and tradition.

'Well,' said Cassius as they walked on, 'only the ancient kings of Nabatea are allowed to sleep in there. I fear we shall have to do with something rather more modest.'

◆8◆

Remarkable though the city was, Cassius soon began to find Petra rather annoying. There seemed to be little structure to the place: buildings had sprung up wherever there was room and there was no clear network of streets – just the canyons, staircases cut from the rock and perilous, zigzagging tracks heading upwards to the gods knew where. Even so, he had to admire not only the former capital's enviable defensive position but also the provision of water. There seemed to be channels and pipes running everywhere; and even a few lush gardens fronting some of the larger properties. They did pass two symbols of familiarity: a colonnaded main street and a theatre – like Bostra's – housed in a huge basin carved from the reddish stone.

Cassius made a few enquiries and they were eventually directed to a street that ran below dozens of inhabited caverns. It was hard to tell whether they occurred naturally or had been fashioned from the rocky slope. From inside many of them came the glow of firelight and the odd cry or bark of laughter.

Beyond the last of the caverns, the street opened up into a circular space. At the far end was a high, ancient-looking wall. In front of it was a broad, two-storey building that didn't look much newer.

'Do you think that's it?' said Cassius.

'I can't see anything else large enough to be an inn, sir,' replied Simo.

Just then a small herd of black-haired goats trotted out of a ravine close by. Urging them along with a stick was a barefoot lad. Cassius got his attention and pointed at the building.

'Inn?' he asked in Greek.

The youth nodded and continued on his way, shouting at his charges in Nabatean.

'Gods,' said Cassius as they approached. 'Doesn't look very promising.'

'Who cares?' said Indavara. 'As long as there are beds.'

'I wouldn't count on it.'

To the right of the building were several unoccupied stalls for horses. In front of the door was a counter lined with bowls for serving food but they contained only dust and leaves. On the first floor was a timber-built balcony, from which several damaged planks hung. Cassius couldn't see a single light emanating from the place or hear a single sound.

'Simo, do the honours.'

The attendant passed the mule's rope to Indavara and put his saddlebags on the disused counter, then walked up to the door and knocked. They heard voices, then eventually saw a dim light through the numerous holes in the door. A latch was lifted and the door opened inwards.

The lamplight cast a murky glow across the wizened face of the elderly proprietor. He moved the lamp closer to Simo. 'Cretheus, is that you? By Allat – you've put on a few pounds.'

'Er, sorry, but we've never met. My master—'

'We need rooms for the night,' interjected Cassius. 'Are you open?'

'How many of you?' asked the man, tugging at his wispy white beard.

'Twenty-three.'

As the old man muttered something to himself, a woman bustled forward out of the shadows. Her face was just as wrinkled, her hair just as white, but she seemed considerably more energetic. She peered at Cassius and seemed particularly interested in his jewellery. Her Greek was obviously limited: 'Yes, yes. Come, come, yes.'

She silenced the old man's brief protest with a finger, then took the lamp from him and used it to light a lantern on a hook outside the door. She then wedged the door open and hurried back inside.

'You do have the space?' Cassius asked the old man.

'Yes, of course. My name is Jabbal. Welcome to our humble hostelry.'

'I hope the inside isn't as humble as the outside.'

Jabbal turned an ear towards him. 'Sorry?'

'Nothing. How long before our rooms are ready?'

'Yes, very cold.'

Cassius raised his voice. 'No – I said how long before our rooms are ready?'

'Oh, soon. Very soon.'

'Some hot food as well?'

'Of course, of course.'

'And a stall for the mule?'

'Of course.' Jabbal walked up to Patch and stroked the animal's neck.

'Simo, get yourself back to the King's Tomb and collect Mercator and the others.'

'I'll go,' offered Indavara.

'You'll get lost.'

'What? I have a good sense of direction.'

'In countryside you're all right. In towns, you're a disaster.' Cassius gestured at the mule. 'Why don't you help get your friend settled?'

Simo set off into the gloom past the caverns. Indavara sighed and began unloading the bags. The old proprietor seemed keen to help him.

'Jabbal, is it?' said Cassius.

'Yes, sir.'

'Tell me, are we far from the Temple of Atargatis?'

'Not far at all, sir,' said the old man, struggling with a saddlebag.

'Good. Perhaps your time might be better spent attending to those rooms. I need to lie down.'

━●8●━

The fourth hour of night was well under way when Cassius's head finally touched his pillow. Simo had swiftly returned with

Mercator and the auxiliaries but Jabbal's wife insisted on cleaning out the four rooms (three upstairs, one downstairs) before even allowing the men through the front door. A further round of mattress- and furniture-moving was required in order to fit them all in but eventually every man had a place to sleep. There was only one other guest at the inn; an aged goat trader who smelled remarkably like the animals that provided his living.

Because the parlour was so cramped, the wife put the food out then the men took what they wanted and ate outside. They seemed happy enough with what looked like some kind of vegetable soup but Cassius had no appetite and had retired immediately.

He, Simo, Indavara and two of the auxiliaries were sharing the downstairs room next to the parlour. Already in his sleeping tunic, Cassius was waiting for Simo to return with some warm wine. The straw mattress seemed barely thicker than the blankets he'd been lying on for the last few nights but with a pleasant flow of air from a nearby window, he was comfortable enough.

Yet he didn't expect to be getting to sleep any time soon because most of the men were still gathered outside, talking. They didn't seem keen on using Nabatean but as there had been no more lapses into Latin, Cassius wasn't inclined to complain. As he lay there, listening in, he also realised they were using Greek to include Indavara, who had made the odd, brief contribution.

The talk turned to the incident with the brigands.

'I sort of lost my enthusiasm when I realised how many there were,' admitted Yorvah.

'We used to have trouble with men like that round my old village,' said another man. 'Vicious bastards they are – care only for themselves and their kin. Not worried how they make their money.'

Another man laughed. 'They lost *their* enthusiasm soon enough when our friend here got off his horse.'

This provoked a few chuckles.

'What was it?' said Yorvah. 'Oh yes, "I shall remember your face – I've already forgotten yours." Ha – good one.'

More laughter.

'You don't say much, Indavara,' continued the guard officer, 'but when you do it's worth hearing.'

Andal spoke up next. 'That leader must have noticed you look like a man who's seen a few scraps.'

Indavara didn't reply. Cassius could picture the faintly embarrassed half-smile. He wouldn't be enjoying the attention.

'Where'd you learn your fighting?' asked a young voice. The others silently awaited the answer.

'Here and there,' said Indavara in his usual monotone.

'The arena, yes?' Andal again.

No reply.

Mercator spoke up: 'That's his business, not yours.'

'Fair enough, sir. Didn't mean to pry.'

'Just be glad he's on our side,' said Yorvah, puncturing the brief moment of tension.

'Drink?' asked someone.

'Thanks,' replied Indavara quietly.

The conversation continued but Cassius turned away and tried not to listen. He found himself rather jealous of the way Indavara had endeared himself to the auxiliaries. He'd noted such reactions to the bodyguard before; and it wasn't just about what he did. People were drawn to him. Cassius would have expected his damaged body and gruff manner to put them off but children invariably liked him, most women too; and not just the common sort either – their last outing had proved that.

And men? Most men feared him. But if they had no cause to, if they could feel close to him, they liked it. Cassius didn't pretend to himself that he was any exception; and he had no doubt that if Indavara joined a century he'd rise up the ranks far quicker than Mercator could ever dream of, especially if there were plenty of battles to be fought. It was as if the strength and resilience forged in the fire of the arena still cloaked the man in some supernatural glow. Cassius thought of what he'd seen him do in the brief time they'd known each other. He'd never met anyone like him. In fact, he doubted there *was* anyone quite like him.

XIV

'Caesar's balls, is the entire bloody population here?'

Having moved about a third of the way through Petra's spice market, Cassius, Indavara and Simo now found the street virtually impassable. Both sides of the market were lined by stores and warehouses but most of the space was taken up by temporary stalls and pitches. Also plying their wares were day traders selling produce straight from the amphora or sack.

The colours were remarkable: reds, oranges and yellows dominated but every possible shade could be found amongst the plants, seeds and herbs. The smell was incredible: an assault upon the nostrils within which Cassius had already detected garlic, cinnamon and mint. The noise was overwhelming: multiple languages, scores of urgent negotiations, dozens of bellowed invitations.

'By the gods.' He stopped and turned to Indavara. 'You first.'

'Knew I should have brought my stave.' The bodyguard shouldered his way between two men lugging amphoras, then pressed forward.

'I told you – we don't want to stand out.'

Eventually, the mass of buyers and sellers began to thin out and they reached a three-way junction beneath an outcrop of rock.

'Er, I think it's to the right,' Cassius told the others. Jabbal's directions had made sense for the first half-minute then descended into confusion and a heated argument with his wife.

Standing in shade beneath the outcrop and gazing back at the spice market were two soldiers. They were dressed and armed conventionally but had squares of red cloth sewn onto the front of their tunics. The badges bore the emblem of Nabatea's ancient royal house. Cassius had seen some of these men in Bostra; they didn't belong to any legionary or auxiliary cohort but to a small cadre of local troops who watched over important and sacred sites such as the King's Tomb. This select band had been permitted to bear the emblem ever since the annexation of the province; a long-standing gesture of respect.

'Excuse me,' said Cassius. 'Temple of Atargatis?'

One of the soldiers aimed a thumb to the right, at a path considerably less busy than the one leading left.

'Thank you.'

The path soon joined a narrow wadi that ran westwards, hemmed in by steep rock walls from which hardy vegetation sprung at unlikely angles. There was no water visible at the bottom, just a mass of lush shrubbery resplendent with pink and purple flowers.

As he walked, Cassius wondered how Mercator and the others were getting on. It had seemed advisable to give them some free time and – as most had never visited the city – he'd agreed they could take a look around, with the strict proviso that they kept to themselves and stayed out of trouble.

The Temple of Atargatis was about half a mile from the spice market. It too had been carved out of the rock though the entrance was singularly unimpressive compared with the King's Tomb. In fact the only sign that it was a temple at all was the image of the fertility goddess above the doorway. She wore a large crown and seemed to have leaves growing out of her body.

Waiting nearby was a young woman. A young man who had been walking behind Cassius and the others hurried over and kissed her, then the two of them continued along the path, hand in hand. There seemed to be no one else around.

Cassius checked the position of the sun. 'About exactly midday, I would say. Hope he's on time.'

        ◆8◆

There was something rather lupine about Ulixes. His shoulders were tight with tension and he seemed almost to be sniffing the air as he approached the temple. Somewhere between forty and fifty, he had high cheekbones and a long, angular chin. His hair was thinning in an unusual fashion, with several strands swept across his head and a lot of scalp visible underneath. He wore a ringed belt like the legionary he'd once been and a well-cut but well-used tunic.

He looked back along the path just before he stopped, then inspected the three of them. It had often occurred to Cassius that they must appear a rather strange trio at first sight. Interestingly, it was Indavara he spoke to.

'All praise Atargatis.'

Cassius had been given the correct response by Abascantius. 'Mother of all under the sun.'

Ulixes shifted his gaze.

'Good day,' said Cassius. 'Name's Crispian. Ulixes, I presume.'

Ulixes moved aside to let some worshippers out of the temple. 'At your service. Old Pitface's operatives are getting younger. And who are these two?'

'They work for me. I believe you have some information.'

'I do. I'll need to see the coin first, though.'

'I thought you might say that. Why are you so late? We've been waiting almost an hour.'

'Small spot of local trouble.'

'Such as?'

'Nothing a nice heavy bag of aurei won't solve.'

'I don't want any uninvited attention.'

'Then I suggest we get going.'

'Follow me.'

➤8➤

By the time they returned to the spice market, it was considerably less busy. Cassius walked alongside Ulixes, who was continually glancing around.

'This local trouble – care to be more specific?'

'Let's just say I owe certain people a certain amount.'

Cassius recalled what Abascantius had told him. 'Gambling debts?'

'Occupational hazard.'

'What's your occupation?'

'Gambler.' Ulixes's smile faded as quickly as it had arrived. He stopped and stared along the street. 'Crispian, do you have any of those golds with you?'

'No.'

Ulixes gulped. 'I owe a vicious bitch by the name of Zaara-Kitar. See the fellow looking around over there? Long hair.'

The man was wearing a sleeveless white tunic. His plaited hair reached almost to the black sash around his waist.

'I see him.'

'That's one of her sons. They do her dirty work for her.'

Ulixes looked back between Indavara and Simo, who had stopped just behind them. 'Shit. There's another.' Ulixes bowed his head. 'Did he see me?'

The second man looked remarkably similar to the first.

'Er, yes. I think so.'

'What's going on?' asked Indavara.

'Trouble,' said Cassius.

The second enforcer gave a shout and ran towards them. The first man heard it and spotted them too. Just as Ulixes looked across the street for an escape route, a pair of horses trotted by and a covered cart trundled to a halt. A third enforcer leaped nimbly out of the back. He had the same attire, same long hair, and – hanging from his sash – a very long knife.

'Exactly how many sons does this Zaara-Kitar have?' asked Cassius.

'Three, I think.'

Another man jumped down.

'Ah,' added Ulixes, 'maybe four.'

'You're a brave man,' said the new arrival in Greek, 'walking around in daylight. Thought you were safe after all these months, did you? You should know our mother never forgets a debt.'

'Now listen. I can get the money, I just need a little more time.'

'You're out of time.'

Cassius looked at Indavara, who was standing closest to the third and fourth enforcers. The second man had been delayed by a misbehaving donkey but would be there in moments. Indavara nodded.

Cassius pushed Ulixes away along the street. 'Run!'

The gambler did so.

'Simo, come on!'

Without waiting to see what would develop behind him, Cassius sprang away after Ulixes. Ahead of them, the first enforcer shoved a lad out of his way and drew his knife: half a yard of honed, glittering steel.

Indavara waited for the third man to move and had time to execute the trip perfectly. He caught his trailing leg in midair and had already grabbed the fourth enforcer before his brother hit the ground.

As he tried to wrench himself free, Indavara got both hands on his tunic and slammed him into the side of the cart. To his credit, the enforcer stayed on his feet and even tried to reach for his blade. But Indavara still had hold of him, and this time he threw him to his right. Hair whipping through the air, the enforcer sailed clean over a barrel and crashed head first into a rickety stall, showering the vendor with onions and ginger.

Cassius watched Ulixes snatch a big wicker basket and heave it at the first enforcer. It struck him on the chest and sent him sprawling onto a pile of empty sacks. But as Ulixes charged past, he stuck out a leg.

The gambler fell flat on his face. Cassius would have helped him up but he was more worried about the enforcer, who was trying to wrench his knife-arm free from the basket. Swiftly deciding he wasn't going to get the blade out, he let go and pushed the basket aside. As Ulixes got to his knees, the Arabian scrambled over and grabbed him around the neck.

Cassius and Simo stood there, watching. Cassius knew he should probably help, he just hadn't decided quite how.

Indavara's attention was now on the second brother, but when he heard the man on the ground behind him getting up, he drove a kick back at him without looking. His boot hit something and he heard the enforcer groan then strike the ground once more.

His brother was already cursing as he approached, knife up and angled at his foe.

'Sure you want that kind of fight?' said Indavara, knowing he couldn't match the weapon with his little dagger.

'Absolutely.'

Indavara backed along the side of the cart past the downed man, who was still struggling. The one he had thrown into the stall, however, was already back on his feet. Knife in hand, he took up a position beside his brother.

Cassius grabbed the first enforcer and tried to pull him off, but succeeded only in ripping his tunic. Still grappling with Ulixes, the man lashed out, his elbow catching Cassius on the jaw. Cassius staggered several yards backwards, then tripped and fell onto another pile of sacks. Rubbing his jaw, he found himself enveloped by a cloud of something. Suddenly his eyes and throat were burning. He looked down and saw a fine grey powder covering the ground. Pepper.

He raised his hands to defend himself but then realised the large, blurry figure coming towards him was Simo.

'Leave me. Help Ulixes – we need him!'

Indavara had backed past the cart and past the horses. Fortunately, the driver was too preoccupied with calming the animals to join the fight. The two enforcers stopped to help their brother up. He pulled out his knife with a shaky hand and lurched after them.

All the buyers and sellers had scattered, though some were shouting at the combatants. Still facing his enemies, Indavara withdrew into the mass of barrels and amphoras, looking around for a better weapon. One of the brothers said something and the men spread out, trying to surround him.

Ten yards away, Cassius blundered forward, snot dripping from his nose, eyes streaming. Simo had succeeded in pulling the enforcer off Ulixes and was stubbornly refusing to let go as the man reined blows down on his shoulders and head. Ulixes was still down.

'That's it, Simo,' cried Cassius. 'Hold him!'

Surprised by how enraged he was to see the peaceful attendant being struck, Cassius picked up an empty amphora. Wiping his eyes with his tunic sleeve to make sure he hit the right man, he brought the amphora down on the enforcer's head. It smashed into hundreds of pieces, several of which stuck in the man's long hair. Expecting him to drop to the ground, Cassius was surprised to see him shake his head, let go of Simo then turn around.

Cassius suddenly remembered how Indavara had handled an uncooperative individual in Antioch. Before his enemy could strike, he formed a fist with his right hand and punched the man on the ear.

'Ow!'

The enforcer crumpled. Cassius felt a grin form on his face as he helped Ulixes up.

Still retreating, Indavara had just stopped by an old woman's stall. Next to her set of iron scales was a box containing weights. He took out the largest one he could see but it was little more than a marble.

As the enforcers closed in, one of them laughed.

'Try these,' said the old woman, lifting a heavy box up from behind the stall.

'Stay out of it, hag,' spat one of the brothers.

'Up yours!' yelled the old woman. 'You bullies think you run Petra – it's good to see you get your arses kicked for a change.'

'Thanks,' said Indavara, grabbing a weight that almost filled his hand. He took aim at the closest man and let fly. The iron ball hit the enforcer on the chest with a loud crack. He initially seemed unaffected, but then sank to his knees, teeth grinding.

'Who's next?'

One took up the invitation by leaping over a row of amphoras and charging. Indavara couldn't miss. This weight was even heavier and struck his foe on the thigh. The shock of the impact caused the enforcer to drop his knife and lose his footing. He careened past Indavara and into the stall. The old woman chuckled as a tray of something green and leafy landed on his head.

Indavara drew his dagger and moved into a small circle of open space. The last man came on, crouching low, knife out in front of him. Indavara stood his ground and looked over the Arabian's shoulder.

The enforcer smiled smugly. 'You don't expect me to fall for that, do you?'

'Up to you.'

Cassius had plenty of time to line his second victim up and punch his ear. This time, however, the result was somewhat different.

The man cried out but recovered quickly and launched a wild swing at his assailant.

Cassius saw the blade flashing towards him but it never arrived.

As Indavara's elbow connected with his head, the enforcer dropped like a stone, the knife clattering to the ground between Cassius's feet.

He was still standing there, wide eyed and shaking, when Indavara grabbed his arm and guided him towards the street. 'What was *that*?'

'Just trying to help.'

'Didn't ask for it, didn't need it. Come on.'

'Well done, young man!' cried the old woman.

'Ah, shit,' said Indavara as they neared the street.

Simo was standing just in front of the cart, looking on helplessly.

There was a man standing behind Ulixes: white sleeveless tunic, long hair, black sash. He was holding a knife to his captive's throat.

'Sorry,' said the gambler as Cassius and Indavara approached. 'I forgot. There are five.'

◄8►

The atmosphere inside the cart was rather tense. Cassius, Indavara, Simo and Ulixes sat on one side, three of the brothers on the other – all still holding their knives. The man Indavara had elbowed in the head was struggling to keep his eyes aiming in the same direction, the second kept checking his ear, and the third looked as if he were about to be sick.

'Could have sworn there were four,' murmured Ulixes.

One of their captors yelled something in Nabatean and jabbed his blade at him. Cassius didn't particularly enjoy getting a close look at the sharpened steel but he couldn't help admiring the handle; embedded in the ivory grip were a sapphire, a ruby and an emerald.

When the enforcer eventually leaned back, Cassius glanced at the others. Simo was mouthing prayers to himself. Indavara was looking out of the back of the cart. The brothers had pulled down the covers but there was a narrow gap in the middle.

After a while, they halted briefly and Cassius noticed a section of pink rock outside. They'd been on the move for at least a quarter of an hour and he could no longer hear the noise of Petra's busy centre. The cart then headed up a steep, twisting incline, the driver berating the horses while the vehicle rattled and the iron-rimmed wheels squeaked.

When the ground eventually levelled out, they stopped. Two of the brothers guarded their charges while the third tied the coverings back and climbed down.

'Move it!' he ordered. 'One at a time.'

Cassius was last out behind Indavara, who was already receiving special attention: a blade pressed against his neck.

They were on one side of a wide courtyard. In the middle of the space was an impressive fountain topped by a fine bronze Venus. The goddess seemed to be looking into the adjacent garden, where more statues poked up out of a sea of pale green fig trees and snowy almond blossom.

'Over here,' said one of the brothers, nodding towards the fountain. Cassius noted that he was not only the oldest but also the first man he'd attacked. The ear still looked red, even with his brown skin.

As he followed him, Cassius caught his first sight of the villa. Built in the shadow of another immense rock face, the building wasn't particularly large but every wall was coated in dazzling white paint, the marble columns veined with silver and gold. Three male attendants filed out of the main door. Two went to help the driver with the horses while a third listened to some instructions from the older brother then trotted back inside.

The five enforcers lined the captives up in front of the fountain, facing the house. Cassius now saw that the family resemblance went far beyond the long black hair. Little more than an inch or two in height separated them and they all possessed the same muscular build, heavy brow and deep-set eyes. The eldest brother approached Cassius, knife at the ready.

'Kushara, don't do anything hasty,' said Ulixes. 'Remember it was *you* that jumped *us*.'

One of the other brothers darted forward and tickled Ulixes's chin with his knife. 'Shut up or I'll skewer your tongue to the top of your mouth.'

Ulixes obeyed.

When Kushara got within a yard of Cassius, Indavara stepped in front of him.

The enforcer stopped, knife close to the bodyguard's belly. 'Move.'

Indavara did not.

'Kush!' The female voice came from the villa. Cassius looked but could see no one. She shouted a few more words in Nabatean and Kushara reluctantly withdrew.

He spat at Indavara's feet then waved his blade at the front door. 'Inside.'

———■8■———

If anything, the villa's interior was even more luxurious than the exterior, the atrium stuffed with well-polished furniture, exotic glassware and a spectacular set of wall paintings. The artist – or perhaps the owner – seemed to have a preference for birds and cherubs. Even the floor was ostentatious; hexagonal stones coloured blue and green.

Cassius, Simo, Indavara and Ulixes sat together on a long couch. The other four brothers had disappeared but on the couch opposite were Kushara and a bulky, middle-aged man who was missing virtually all his teeth. Attached to the other end of the studded leash in his hand was quite possibly the largest dog Cassius had ever seen.

'Molossus,' he whispered to Simo.

'Sir?'

'Used for hunting wolves.'

It was essentially an oversize mastiff; hugely powerful in the shoulders and neck with pale fur and a fleshy black muzzle. Cassius wasn't fooled by its dopey expression.

'My uncle had one,' he continued, 'though not quite so big. One day it decided to attack my aunt's cat. They had to stick eight spears in it to stop the bloody thing and even then they couldn't get the teeth open.'

'Oh gods,' said Ulixes. 'Here she comes.'

Though certainly over forty, Zaara-Kitar moved with a purposeful, sensual grace. Her sleeveless, dark green tunic reached almost to her ankles and was embroidered with swirling gold as bright as the dozens of bangles upon her wrists. Her hair was cut short at her collar and almost as black as her sons'. Only when she came close did Cassius see the powder upon her face and the wrinkles on her upper arms. Wrapped around one of them was a silver serpent. Trailing along in her wake, head down, was a young maid clothed in the dullest, most shapeless tunic imaginable.

Kushara and the other man stood up.

Zaara-Kitar headed straight for Ulixes. She bent over, put her hand softly on his cheek, then raked her nails down it.

'Uh! Gods, you—'

Rage flashed in the lady's eyes. 'You *what*? Say it – I dare you!'

'M-my apologies,' stuttered Ulixes.

The dog was growling. Zaara-Kitar glared at the gambler, her narrow chest heaving. Cassius spied streaks of blood upon one of her nails. He also noticed that one of the fingers on her other hand was missing. She pushed a strand of hair away from her eyes.

'I don't believe I have *ever* been made to wait so long for a debt to be repaid.' Her voice was a soft purr, her accent that of an easterner for whom Greek was a foreign language. 'I hope for your sake you have something for me.'

She turned to Cassius. 'Who is this handsome fellow?'

'Master Crispian,' said Ulixes. 'A business associate.'

Zaara-Kitar seemed rather amused by this concept. She turned her attention to Indavara, examining him from head to toe. 'And you're the bodyguard. It has been known for certain individuals to put one or two of my sons down but I don't recall anyone ever managing four. Are you available for hire?'

Indavara shook his head. So did Kushara.

Zaara-Kitar pointed at an ornate high-backed chair which the maid brought over. She sat down and crossed her arms. 'I have an appointment at the ninth hour.' She turned towards Ulixes. 'Give me a number.'

'Fifteen aurei.'

'My bookkeeper tells me twenty-five, when the correct amounts of interest are taken into account. Considering the trouble you have caused me and the incident today we shall call it thirty.'

'My original debt was five!'

She turned to her son, who – like the dog handler – had sat down again. 'I do believe he's arguing.'

Ulixes held up both hands. 'No, good lady. I am not. May I discuss the matter with Master Crispian?'

'You may.'

Cassius and Ulixes were sitting at opposite ends of the couch. With a wary glance at the mastiff, Ulixes got up and swapped places with Simo.

'Well?' he whispered, brow now beaded with sweat. 'Do you have that much?'

'Yes. But you do understand it will come out of your fee?'

'Of course.'

Ulixes looked across the atrium at a small central courtyard. He wiped his brow and turned to Zaara-Kitar. 'We have it.'

'I don't see it.'

'We can have it here in—'

'One hour,' said Cassius.

'You two will stay here,' said the lady.

Cassius gestured for Indavara and Simo to get up. 'Be as quick as you can.'

Zaara-Kitar clicked her fingers and aimed a finger at an hourglass on a table. The maid turned it over.

The moneylender smiled at Cassius. 'Quite right, Master Crispian, because if there aren't thirty gold coins here before that sand runs out, your "business associate" will be taking a trip to the garden.'

'What?' asked Indavara.

'Just go!' ordered Cassius.

As the pair hurried away, Ulixes clasped his hands and appealed to his host. 'Please, no. Don't even say that.'

'People talk,' said Zaara-Kitar as she stood. 'They know you owed me. They know you didn't pay. You have made me appear weak.'

She walked over to Cassius. 'Do you see my missing finger, Master Crispian? I shall tell you how I came to lose it. My father loved sayings, expressions. He used them to teach us. Well, that and some other methods. As a child I loved honey; I couldn't get enough of it. I won't touch the stuff now – for reasons that will become obvious – but it was my favourite thing in the world. So sticky, so sweet. When I was three my father caught me dipping my finger into a pot. He sat me down and told me that if I ever did it again he would chop that finger off. I didn't believe him. So I did it again. And he did exactly as he'd said he would. Can you guess what my father's favourite expression was?'

Cassius shook his head.

'Actions speak louder than words.'

With that she strode out of the room, the maid not far behind.

Cassius looked at Ulixes. 'What's in the garden?'

The gambler was too busy praying to reply.

Kushara threw his head back and unleashed a throaty, savage laugh.

XV

Indavara thought he and Simo had done pretty well. Once at the bottom of the villa's drive and back in the city streets their only real obstacle had been a busy slave auction. Once through this, a combination of asking directions and educated guesswork got them back to the inn.

'How long did that take?' he asked as they jogged past the auxiliary Mercator had left on guard.

Simo had to take a deep breath before replying. 'Fifteen, maybe twenty minutes.'

Ignoring old Jabbal – who was sweeping up – Indavara hurried along to their room. He dropped down, reached under his bed and pulled the barrel out. Once the stopper was unscrewed, he began clawing out the coins. Simo grabbed a skin of water and poured its contents down his throat.

'Come on, Simo, I need you to count.'

The Gaul knelt beside him. 'What shall we put them in? Master Cassius's bag?'

'That'll do.' Indavara took the satchel from the table and emptied out the contents.

Simo had already finished counting. 'Thirty.'

Indavara scooped the coins into the satchel. 'Let's go.'

──◆──

Cassius reckoned at least half an hour had already passed. On the couch opposite, Kushara was cleaning his fingernails with the tip of his knife. The dog handler was alternating between picking his nose and stroking the dog. The Molossus was sitting upright, drooling onto the floor.

Head in his hands, Ulixes continued his prayers. Having so far invoked all twelve of the great Roman gods, he'd also appealed to a few local deities and was now working his way through the Greek and Egyptian pantheons.

Arriving back at the slave auction, Indavara was dismayed to see that the crowd had trebled in size. He soon saw why: upon a high platform were three young women being paraded before the crowd. Clearly from some distant northern province, they were tall, fair haired and clothed in short, low-cut tunics. The auctioneer's voice could barely be heard above the whistles and shouts.

'Balls,' said Indavara. 'It'll take ages to get through there.'

'Perhaps we can go around?' said Simo between breaths.

Keeping a tight grip on the satchel, Indavara retraced their steps then ran along a parallel street. At the far end was an open gate, but as they got closer he realised it was the side entrance to a private townhouse. The three-storey building was still under construction and encased by wooden scaffolding. Next to the gate was a pile of sand and stacks of limestone blocks. Labourers were carrying the blocks in for other artisans working with chisels and hammers.

Indavara could see right through the property to the gate on the opposite side. Beyond was an alley. If they could get there and cut right, they'd be only a stone's throw from the villa's drive.

'Straight through?' he suggested.

'There are a lot of workers in there,' replied Simo anxiously.

'So hopefully no one will notice two more.' Indavara waited for the next labourer to pick up his block and return through the gate, then took one for himself. It was quite heavy but he got it up on his shoulder easily enough. 'Quick.'

'Oh, Lord.' Simo took a little longer to raise his stone.

'Come on, we're running out of time.'

The labourers had walked off to the right to deposit their loads but one was already on his way back. 'Who are you?'

'We're . . . er . . . with the other crew,' Indavara said as he came through the gate.

'Oh.'

Indavara winced but hurried on towards the side of the villa, Simo close behind. They walked up some steps and through a doorway into an unfinished atrium where more men were working on a floor mosaic. Just as the pair exited the other side of the villa, they heard a shout.

'Hey! Hey, you!'

'Oh no,' said Simo.

Spying a trio of labourers coming after them, Indavara dumped his block and ran past a mound of rubble to the side gate. It was identical to the other one – except it was shut and secured by a padlocked iron chain.

'Shit.'

As he and Simo turned round, the labourers piled out of the villa. One was the man Indavara had spoken to.

Another, older fellow spoke up. 'Take us for cretins, do you? There *is* no other crew. Least now we know who's been stealing our supplies.'

'Not us,' said Indavara.

'What in Hades were you doing with the stones, then?'

'Listen.' Indavara patted the satchel. 'I have some gold coins in here. If I give you one will you let us go on our way?'

The leader looked at the others, then all three laughed.

The jollity didn't last. The leader stalked towards Indavara and pointed at Simo. 'Balbus, you watch Fatso. We'll take care of this one.'

Balbus – a bearded giant even taller and heavier than Simo – approached the Gaul. Simo tried an appeasing smile, to no obvious effect.

Indavara looked over his shoulder. The wall was high and he could see no way over. He glanced at the villa. The wooden scaffold was between the side of the building and the wall. The alley beyond was narrow, the houses opposite close.

'Hundreds of sesterces you thieving cocksuckers have cost us,' said the labourer, pulling a hammer from his belt. 'It's time for some payback.'

'Sorry, Simo. We don't have time to mess around.'

Indavara ran: through the lowest level of scaffolding, along the side of the villa, then inside through a low window. The mosaic-makers watched as he bounded up the staircase.

On the first level there were little more than walls and floor-boards. From below came several shouts as the labourers gave chase. He raced up the next staircase; on the top level there were only floorboards.

Once at the edge of the structure he looked down through the scaffolding. The sloping roofs of the townhouses opposite were about ten feet below. He reckoned the distance across the alley to be no more than fifteen feet. Close enough.

He heard the labourers on the first floor. He ran back to the staircase and looked down. The leader was charging up at him, face red, still gripping the hammer. Indavara looked back at the scaffold. Enough of a run-up? It would have to be.

'Put that down.'

Simo took the block from his shoulder and held it across his chest. He could hear the men yelling as they chased Indavara but all he could think about was that horrible villa and those horrible people. Surely the hour was almost up. What would they do to that man Ulixes and Master Cassius? He had to get away too.

The bearded labourer seemed to see the change in his expression. 'Don't even think about it.'

'Lord, forgive me.'

Simo heaved the stone at the man, who had no choice but to try and catch it. He got both hands on it but overbalanced and fell backwards, the stone landing on both stomach and groin.

'Sorry!' Simo looked down the long drive that led to the villa. At the bottom was the main gate, which was open. He set off at a jog, sandals splashing through muddy puddles.

—8—

Indavara checked the satchel was secure then sprinted away from the staircase. He touched the planks of the scaffolding only once – a driving step that launched him high into the air and over the alley.

A rust-coloured roof flashed towards him.

He spread his arms and legs but the impact shattered dozens of tiles and drove the breath from his lungs. His boots landed just above the edge of the roof and he instantly began to slide. His left foot slipped off. He pressed down with his hands but both were stinging. His right foot dropped over the edge, then both knees.

He heard tiles smashing on the ground. Spying an exposed wooden beam, he gripped it with his left hand and held himself against the roof-edge with his right arm. Legs hanging, he sucked in some air then looked down – surely there wasn't far to drop.

But whoever owned the house was clearly keen on security. The wall directly below was topped with triangles of glass.

Two young children – a boy and a girl – had stopped in front of the house and were standing there, watching him.

'What are you doing?' asked the boy.

'Indavara!'

He twisted his head the other way and saw Simo trotting along the street. The Gaul raised both hands in desperation. 'How did you . . .'

Simo then looked back the way he'd come. The three labourers weren't far behind.

'Here,' said Indavara, slipping the satchel from his shoulder and flinging it into the street. 'Take it. Get to the villa.'

Simo picked it up. 'What about you?'

'I'll work something out. Just go!'

As Simo fled, Indavara looked down again at the wall. He might just be able to swing forward and land inside it, but that would risk catching his back or head on the vicious edges of the glass.

'Well, well.'

The labourers had arrived.

'Got yourself in a bit of a mess there, haven't you, mate?'

The leader was carrying a length of wood which he threw at Indavara, catching him on the side. Indavara stifled a cry as it clattered to the ground.

'What fun this is going to be!'

The next thing that struck Indavara was smaller and harder; the labourers were now using the broken tiles. Another one caught him between the shoulders. His left arm was going numb.

'Ha. Simpler than catching fish from a barrel!'

The men came up to the wall to make their task even easier. The moment they did so, Indavara realised he had a chance. His landing had damaged several columns of tiles but the adjacent columns were intact. He reached over to his right and pulled away the lowest tile on the nearest one. The tiles above all slid after it and rained down on the labourers, one smashing on the leader's head.

'Ow! You sneaky arsehole!'

———◆8◆———

Zaara-Kitar returned with her other four sons. She twisted a strand of hair around a finger. 'It's funny what a sense of anticipation will do. I do want my money but now I find I'm almost hoping they don't make it. Your friends are certainly cutting it fine.'

'Where are they?' wailed Ulixes.

Cassius shrugged helplessly.

The moneylender picked up the hourglass. 'Oh. I'm afraid time's up.'

'What?' cried Ulixes. 'No.'

She held it up to show him. Kushara and another brother took one arm each and lifted him off the couch.

'Just give them a little more time,' he pleaded.

'Sorry. An hour is an hour.'

'Crispian, do something!'

'Oh, he'll do something,' said Zaara-Kitar. 'He'll watch.'

With one eye on the dog, Cassius stood. 'If you hurt him, I won't pay.'

Again, she seemed amused. 'What makes you think you're in a strong bargaining position? Hurry, boys, I have that appointment.'

One of the other brothers went to stand by the door that led to the garden. Next to it was a long cane and a pail with a slab of stone across the top. Zaara-Kitar gestured to the dog handler, who passed the leash to one of the sons. The beast growled as Ulixes was dragged past.

'Please, no. Please!'

Cassius looked out at the courtyard but there was no sign of Indavara or Simo. Surely the villa wasn't that far from the inn. What were they doing?

'Not this,' begged Ulixes. 'Please, not this.'

'So you've heard of the garden, then?' enquired Zaara-Kitar, still twirling her hair.

'Everyone has.'

'It pleases me to know such measures have an effect. Afterwards I'll have the boys dump you near the dice dens. Word will spread quickly, I should imagine.'

Cassius's thoughts had turned from his subordinates to his superior; how exactly would he explain allowing Ulixes to be killed an hour after meeting him?

'All right, how much more?' he asked. 'How much more to keep him out of there?'

Zaara-Kitar came closer and looked up at him. 'I suggest you stay quiet from now on, Master Crispian. This worm has escaped the consequences of his actions for long enough.' She gave a nod.

In the middle of the door was a small window. The dog handler looked through it, then unbolted and opened the door. The brothers dragged Ulixes forward then shoved him into the garden. As the door was locked behind him, Ulixes turned and examined his surroundings.

'Come,' Zaara-Kitar told Cassius, walking over to a long, grilled window. 'This should be rather entertaining.'

The handler reclaimed his dog and positioned himself close by as Cassius stood behind the moneylender and her sons.

The garden didn't contain any trees or flowers. The square space was about twenty feet across, enclosed on all sides, with the door the only way in or out. In the middle was a smaller square – a shallow pit of sand, half of which was covered with low bushes. Cassius also noticed two water bowls.

'We've used a few different animals over the years,' said Zaara-Kitar, as if she were describing her choice of paint or rug. 'Hyakinthos isn't just a dog handler, he knows how to keep all manner of creatures. We've had scorpions, spiders, all sorts. But you know, Master Crispian – people really do hate snakes. Oh, there's one now.'

The reptile's rear half was hidden in a bush. It was thick in the body, its scales varying shades of brown and white. The rounded head came up off the ground and bobbed from side to side, thin black tongue licking the air.

'Southern Arabian adder,' continued Zaara-Kitar. 'There are, what, six now? These were all born in captivity but Hyakinthos says they can't really be tamed. He feeds them rats – just enough to keep them alive. They have no real reason to attack humans, yet they do. Hyakinthos says it's because they're territorial. Personally, I think they just enjoy it.'

Ulixes moved away from the snake, sliding along the wall up to the window. He turned to the onlookers, face pale and clammy. 'Please let me out. I'll get you double. By the end of the day. I swear on my mother. On the gods.'

'Watch yourself,' advised Kushara.

The snake slithered off the sand and onto the stone.

'Their teeth can go through leather,' added Zaara-Kitar as Ulixes moved away. 'In fact, the bite is often enough to kill smaller prey. A mercy really. But of course it's the venom we humans have to worry about. It's strange, we never seem to see the same results twice. Sometimes the skin swells, sometimes it bleeds; some are paralysed, some can still move; some vomit and collapse immediately; others seem fine at first but after a few hours their skin turns black and green. One man lost all the fingers on both hands. There's only one consistent factor – the pain. You do have a good chance of surviving one bite, but once you're down on the ground, the others usually join in.'

The snake was no more than three feet long. Its head came up, and it let out a long, malevolent hiss.

'Oh my gods,' breathed Ulixes. 'Please let me out. I beg you, I beg you!'

Kushara and his brothers laughed.

Cassius felt an icy tingle across his shoulders and spine.

'Master Crispian.' Zaara-Kitar turned from the window and showed him the silver snake on her arm. 'Do you see? I had it changed to look like the adders. Do you see?'

Simo thought he was about to expire. As if running to the inn and back hadn't been enough, he was now on the steepest part of the slope, the satchel banging against his side as he ran. The journey up the drive had never seemed this long in the cart. He wiped his face and ploughed on, sandals slapping on the road. He was so exhausted he'd even forgotten to pray.

Indavara's left arm was no longer numb. In fact, numb was starting to sound pretty bloody attractive. The pulsing ache stretched from his elbow to his fingers and his grip was weakening by the moment.

The labourers were continuing their onslaught so he stretched out his right arm and pulled off the bottom tile of the next column, forcing the trio into evasive action. With more of the roof frame now exposed, he could reach up and grab another of the vertical beams with his right hand. As a tile struck his backside, he hauled himself up and wedged a knee on the roof-edge. With one last effort, he was able to climb up, turn and lie back against the beam.

His assailants didn't look too happy about it and continued to throw their missiles. Indavara could have done with a minute to recover but the temptation was too great. He dodged a couple of tiles, then plucked more off the roof beside him and launched his own attack. His volleys were both harder and more accurate. The labourers were soon retreating.

Then he heard a door open below and a woman's voice. 'What's all this noise? What's going on?'

Indavara clambered up the frame towards the peak of the roof.

— 8 —

Zaara Kitar had decided they would be able to observe better by moving to another window. Cassius looked on – Hyakinthos and his slobbering friend still behind him – as she and her sons exchanged comments on the unfolding events in the garden. Cassius had little doubt they were enthusiastic attendees at gladiatorial contests; he wanted to be far, far away from this vulgar house and its repellent residents.

'Oh look, there's another one, see him?'

'Ah yes, that's the big fellow who killed one of the others. He can be especially nasty – keeps biting until there's no venom left.'

'I don't think that branch is going to do our friend much good.'

Ulixes had given up on pleading and was channelling all his energy into survival. He had been moving around the courtyard to avoid getting trapped and had snapped off a short branch from one of the bushes. Pathetic though the weapon was, he held it out in front of him with both hands as if it were a sword.

But now he *was* cornered, with two of the serpents closing in on him and two more lurking behind them. Their eyes resembled dull grey marbles and were fixed on the interloper. The smaller of the first two kept its head off the ground as its coils propelled it forward to within five feet of its prey.

Ulixes swatted at it with the branch. 'Gods save me!'

The tortuous advance suddenly seemed too much for him and he kicked out.

'Bad move,' said Kushara. His mother stepped forward, fingers gripping the grille of the window.

The snake had retreated momentarily. But as Ulixes threw himself backwards into the corner, the coiled body suddenly unwound. Cassius glimpsed a pair of long white teeth as the snake lunged.

Zaara-Kitar craned her head to see into the corner. 'Did it get him? Did it get him?'

Once it had struck, the snake withdrew.

Cassius and the brothers moved closer to the window. Ulixes gripped his stomach and looked down. All the remaining colour had drained from his face. But then he touched the thick, military-style belt he wore and a slight grin appeared.

'Lucky bastard,' said one of the younger brothers.

Reinvigorated by his close escape, Ulixes lashed out with the branch once more. This was enough to deter the smaller snake but the larger one showed no fear as it raised its head and slithered across the stone. Still stuck in the corner, Ulixes had nowhere to go.

'Don't think he'll get that lucky again,' observed Kushara.

Zaara-Kitar pressed her face against the window grille, desperate to see the next attack.

'This is barbaric,' said Cassius. 'And stupid.'

'Careful, Master Crispian,' said the moneylender.

'My friends will be here within minutes. What will you have gained?'

She kept her eyes on the garden. 'As you can see from my home, I want for nothing. This is really about the principle. Oh look – I think your friend's time has come.'

Ulixes seemed to be trying to push his way back through the wall. He had turned side-on to the snake, which was just inches from his feet. Hissing loudly, it continued to sway and bob its head, apparently choosing the best place to bite.

Cassius heard shouts from outside, then quick, heavy footsteps.

'Sir! Sir! I'm here!'

'That's Simo,' said Cassius. 'That's your money. Let Ulixes out of there. Do it!'

Simo ran in, satchel jangling.

Zaara-Kitar made no attempt to hide her disappointment. She waved at Hyakinthos, who handed over the dog again, then unbolted and opened the door. He took the stone off the pail and deposited several small rats onto the ground. They scurried off in different directions, closely followed by the snakes. All except the one in front of Ulixes.

Hyakinthos picked up the cane and struck the ground as he walked confidently towards the snake. Once he'd driven it off, Ulixes scrambled along the wall and threw himself into the atrium. He tripped and landed face down on the floor.

Cassius turned to Simo. 'Where's Indavara? And what kept you?'

The attendant didn't have the breath to reply; he was doubled over, sweat pouring from his face.

Cassius took the satchel from him and looked inside. 'It's all here.'

Zaara-Kitar told Kushara to count it. He took the bag from Cassius and deposited it on the table.

The lady was twirling her hair again. She looked down at Ulixes as he got to his knees. 'You're a very fortunate man.'

'Why can't you just break people's fingers like a normal moneylender?'

Kushara stopped counting. Cassius and the others looked at Zaara-Kitar.

But she smiled. 'Nobody remembers broken fingers. I imagine you will remember the garden until the day you die.'

Indavara reached the top of the roof then slid down the other side, knocking off yet more tiles. By moving across to the right he was able to lower himself onto the wall enclosing the rear courtyard. This too was covered with glass and he had to step carefully as he tiptoed along it. He had almost reached the rear wall when a door banged open.

'You! You!'

An elderly woman came across the courtyard at surprising speed, a broom in her hand. Indavara had to negotiate the last few feet of the wall with the sharp bristles raking his calves. He jumped down into the adjacent alley with the old woman still yelling. He could hear the labourers too; they weren't far away.

He ran in the opposite direction.

Zaara-Kitar looked up at Cassius. 'What did you say you do, Master Crispian?'

Her perfume was excessive and up close he could see the wrinkles under the powder. But even though the woman's behaviour disgusted him, Cassius conceded to himself that – in the right circumstances – those smoky green eyes might be hard to resist.

'Merchant.'

'Really? Most of the merchants I know are fat and old and easily panicked.'

Kushara turned from the table, where he had stacked the coins in neat piles of ten. 'It's all here. Thirty aurei.'

Zaara-Kitar was still looking up at Cassius. 'I must admit, you intrigue me, Master Crispian. Perhaps if your friends leave us I can put back my appointment and we can take lunch together.'

Cassius had recently altered his views on the merits of older women but, whatever her other attributes, he felt sure that Zaara-Kitar was quite mad.

'What's on the menu?' he asked, tilting his head towards the garden. 'Fresh rat?'

'Whatever you want – my chef can prepare anything.'

Kushara observed this exchange with a neutral expression; presumably it wasn't unusual for his mother to throw herself at men younger than her sons.

'Thank you for the invitation, but I'm afraid I've rather lost my appetite and it appears our business is concluded. However, before we leave I expect you to return our weapons.'

'A bold demand.'

'Your sons didn't even give me a chance to speak. It's hardly a surprise that my friends and I defended ourselves.'

Kushara's hand drifted towards his knife. 'You—'

'Oh, calm yourself, Kush,' said his mother. 'Master Crispian has a point. You're just angry because that bodyguard got the better of you. Fetch the weapons.'

Kushara departed, fists clenched.

Cassius reclaimed his satchel.

'You're not a merchant,' said Zaara-Kitar with a final smile.

'All right, I admit it, I'm not a merchant,' said Cassius. 'But sometimes – days like today, for example – I rather wish I was.'

◄ 8 ►

After Indavara had recounted his misadventures back at the inn, Cassius slumped down on his bed. 'Gods, the sooner we get out of Petra the better.'

'Fine by me.' Indavara looked down at his hands; they were heavily grazed and coated with orange dust from the tiles.

'We should clean you up,' said Simo, who was at last recovering from his exertions.

Indavara was more interested in grabbing figs from a bowl and washing them down with wine. 'Don't fuss, Simo.'

The pair of them were also resting on the beds, while Ulixes sat against the wall by the window. The ex-legionary had barely

199

said a word on the way back but now nodded at the jug of wine. 'Servant, pour me some of that.'

'He is not *your* servant,' said Cassius. 'But go ahead, Simo. And fill mine up too.'

'So when do I get my coin?' asked Ulixes.

'We'll see.'

'What's that supposed to mean? I had an agreement with Pitface. One hundred aurei.'

'You're getting fifty,' Cassius told him. 'Minus thirty now.'

'Twenty? A measly twenty – after what I've been through?'

'That's your own stupid fault – what about what you put *us* through?'

Still chewing on a fig, Indavara glowered at Ulixes, who pretended not to notice.

'So you want to know where this stone is, then?'

'Keep your voice down.' Cassius sat up to check that the sentry Mercator had left behind was nowhere near the window. 'Go on.'

'Town called Galanaq – about a hundred and twenty miles south of here.'

Cassius reached for his map.

'It won't be on there,' said Ulixes. 'Very remote. Deep in the Hejaz mountains.'

'How long to get there?'

'A week, maybe.'

'And what about this chief? This religious sect?'

'I don't know. My contact was just passing through. I already told Pitface everything. Anyway, that's your problem now. I've done my bit – where's my coin?'

'You're not getting it now.'

'What?'

Ulixes was halfway to his feet when a fig bounced off his nose.

'Stay there,' said Indavara.

'Yes,' added Cassius. 'Stay there and drink your wine.'

Ulixes reluctantly sat down and took the mug from Simo.

'You've given a location, yes,' Cassius continued. 'But as I pointed out to Abascantius, that doesn't prove a damned thing. You'll get your money when I see the stone.'

'When you . . .' Ulixes gulped down some wine before continuing. 'I'm not going down there, you lot are liable to get yourselves killed messing with the desert folk.'

'I don't expect you to accompany us for nothing,' said Cassius. 'Taking into account your time and the factor of risk, I shall double your fee to forty aurei.'

'Fifty.'

'It's forty. Take it or leave it.'

'And if I leave it?'

'I'll still have the name of the town and you'll have nothing. And judging by the state of your clothes I'd say you've had nothing for quite a while. No offence.'

Ulixes drank more, then gaped thoughtfully at the wall. 'Don't really have much choice, do I?'

'Glad you're seeing sense. There's not much space but you're welcome to stay here tonight. Do you have a mount?'

'Sold it.'

'You'll need one – Simo will give you the money. And you'd better go now – there'll be no time tomorrow.'

───■8■───

Later, Cassius and Mercator left the men eating dinner outside the inn and took a walk. Fires glowed inside the cavern-houses and liquid ran down to the ground from channels worn in the rock face. Hoping it was water, Cassius listened as Mercator briefed him on the condition of the men. Though still perturbed by what awaited them farther south, they had avoided any trouble and bought some provisions for the next stage of the journey.

'It would help if we at least knew where we're going,' said the optio.

Cassius could see no reason to disclose the name of the town yet. 'We're continuing South on the Via Traiana, then taking the Incense Road. From there we will enter the Hejaz mountains. Do you know the area at all?'

'No. I think Andal visited Arabia Felix once but no one else has been that far.'

'Well, we do have a guide.'

'The man who was leaving when we came back?'

'Yes. His name's Ulixes. Ex-legionary.'

'Really?'

'I know. Unfortunately we need him but we'll be keeping a close eye on him and I suggest you do the same.'

In the distance a bell clanged, announcing some ceremony at one of the city's innumerable temples. They turned back towards the inn.

'Are you prepared to tell me what all this is about yet?' asked Mercator.

'Once we're out of the city.'

'But this Ulixes – he knows?'

'Yes.'

'And your bodyguard, and your servant—'

'Mercator, listen, it's certainly not that I don't trust you. Quite the opposite. But the fewer people who know the better. I will tell you as soon as I can.'

'The men heard some talk today – about the desert, about the Incense Road. Some of the locals say the Tanukh are no longer the allies of Rome. That it's impossible to know friend from foe in the southern lands.'

'The situation does seem dangerous, it's true. Which makes it all the more important that we maintain the cover. Obviously the story must change now. I have been checking the map. Do you know of this place Hegra?'

'Only the name.'

'If asked, we will say we are journeying there to sample trade goods.'

'I'll pass it on to the men.'

'Good. We leave at dawn.'

XVI

The Via Traiana stretched away across a plain littered with rocks ranging from pebbles to boulders the size of a cart. In the distance were the remarkably bright buildings of Humeima, a town where a particular type of local white stone was used. The largest structure there was the fortress manned by two centuries of the ninth cohort.

'What do you make of that?' said Cassius, reining in. A mile or so ahead was a tall plume of dust.

'Not sure,' said Mercator, raising a hand to stop the others.

'A fast-moving column; horses or camels,' suggested Ulixes. He was riding alone, between Indavara and Simo and the first pair of auxiliaries.

'Where's the turn?' asked Cassius. It was the ninth hour; they'd made good time since leaving Petra and were now approaching the Incense Road.

Ulixes ran a finger and thumb down his chin. 'About where they are.'

'We have time, then. Let's get out of their way and give the horses a break.'

He led the way off the road. Once they'd all dismounted, Ulixes looked to the south-east. 'This wind's getting up. See the clouds over there?'

Cassius wiped some of the day's grime off his face. 'Yes.'

'If they break over us we'll get a drenching – could be a thunderstorm.'

'We have tents.'

'If they *don't* break, there might be a haboob.'

'A what?'

'A sandstorm,' interjected Mercator. 'Isn't it too early in the season?'

'I've seen them this time of year,' replied the gambler.

'We've already had one windy night,' said Cassius. 'The tents held up well.'

Ulixes's brow furrowed. 'It's not just a wind, it's a storm. These things can uproot trees, suffocate animals, bury whole villages.'

'And I thought sea storms were bad. What do you suggest?'

'We need shelter for the night. Proper shelter.'

'Are there no villages, inns?'

'On the Incense Road? Not many. Settlements are few and far between, only at springs or oases.'

'But it's a trade route,' said Cassius. 'Surely there must be stopping points for the caravans.'

'The Saracens don't need stopping points. They make their own camps and they always know how to find water or shelter if they need it. The Incense Road is not a Roman road – it twists and turns and in parts almost disappears. Anyway, there's a tower used as a tax post where we leave the Via Traiana. We may be able to get some information there.'

Indavara and Simo had tied their reins around a nearby rock. Cassius wandered over and looked on as they ignored their horses in favour of Patch.

'How's your friend?'

'Not himself today, sir,' said Simo.

'How can you tell?'

'He's off his food. Staying clear of the horses.'

'Inferiority complex?'

Indavara frowned. Simo took a bowl from a saddlebag and filled it with water for the mule.

'Difficult life, I suppose,' added Cassius as he sat down on a conveniently smooth boulder. 'Carrying things around all day, getting hit if you don't do as you're bid.'

'Pretty similar to a slave,' said Indavara.

Ulixes sat on another stone close by and took off his boots. Cassius noted that they were in as poor condition as the rest of his kit, with barely any tread left on the sole.

Simo put the water down in front of the mule. It sniffed it, looked up at him, then turned away. Indavara offered some dried apple but Patch wasn't interested in that either. Cassius thought it all rather strange; their attachment to this lowly animal. He could just about understand it with horses – they were noble, impressive creatures. But a mule? They really were a simple-minded pair.

'Why not try a prayer or offering to Epona?'

Indavara brightened. 'The goddess of horses.'

'Yes,' said Cassius. 'Not sure if she watches over mules.'

'What about them?' said Ulixes, pointing south.

—❈—

The camels weren't actually on the road; they were on the opposite side, lolloping across the softer ground in ranks of three. The column stretched back such a long way that Cassius at first thought it was a caravan. Only when they were closer did he spy the imperial standard being carried by the central rider in the first rank. The camels were lightly loaded and many of the men carried spears and bows instead of swords.

Having ensured all the horses and mules were under control, Mercator loped over to Cassius. He had to shout to be heard. 'I've seen them a few times in the north but they spend most of their time down here. See the big fellow closest to us?'

On the right side of the standard-bearer was a broad, bearded character on a similarly sturdy camel. His robes were the same as the other riders. His scarlet cape was not.

'Decurion Viridio – his men are known throughout the province. They're based at Sadaqa, probably on their way back there now.'

Viridio raised an arm. His steed and the other two in the front rank broke into a run and the rest of the riders immediately followed. Cassius almost laughed: the manic, arrhythmic gait of the camels looked bizarre. But the column was soon up to full speed and galloping away at an impressive rate. He and the others turned away as the dust rolled up from the ground.

Yorvah strode up to Mercator with a beaming smile. 'Never thought I'd see Viridio in the flesh. I'd heard he was big.'

'See his men?' replied Mercator. 'Not one of them yapping, not one camel out of line.'

'Quite a sight, I must admit,' said Cassius.

'You know what they did during the Palmyran attack, sir?' asked Yorvah.

'No.'

'They fought one battle in the morning – killed scores of Palmyrans and lost a quarter of their number. Then they rode twenty miles and fought another battle in the afternoon. Brilliant bowmen. Very hard to bring down, camels.'

Cassius looked at the distant sky. The clouds showed no sign of breaking up. 'Rest's over. On we go.'

—◆8◆—

The tower was situated within the apex of the two routes (the Incense Road led south, the Via Traiana continued south-west to Aila) and constructed of the same white rock used at Humeima. Ten yards high and five wide, it was square in shape with a flat, open roof. To the rear was a timber shelter housing several horses and a water channel running to an outcrop of rock and some unseen cistern.

Half a dozen legionaries sat or lay close to the doorway. One was dozing, several were playing a game that involved throwing pebbles into a jug. A few yards away was a table where a young clerk sat hunched over a leather-bound book.

Resisting the temptation to admonish the soldiers for their slovenly manner, Cassius told Mercator to halt the men and guided his horse towards the tower. He had found the mare to be an obedient beast, so once on the ground let it stand untended.

'Good day.'

The legionaries ignored him but the young clerk looked up.

'Good day.'

The party had passed several way-stations while on the Via Traiana but Cassius recognised this as something different. Any goods coming up the Incense Road would be liable to pay import tax – the twenty-five per cent levy on products entering the Empire.

The clerk looked barely out of his teens. He had a few spots on his chin and several tufts of wispy hair that in no way constituted a beard. 'Heading south?'

'Yes. Hegra.'

'You do know there are only three army posts beyond this point? Well, two now.'

'Two?' asked Mercator as he arrived. Cassius rather wished he had stayed with the others.

'The fort at Ruwaffa was attacked,' said the clerk. 'Almost an entire century wiped out.'

Cassius tried to look as surpised as the optio.

'Must be more than a week ago now,' added the youth.

'Who did it?' asked Mercator.

'Bloody Saracens. Always trying to get out of paying their taxes. Now this.'

Mercator looked along the road.

'Did you see the camel-riders?' asked the clerk. 'Extra security. Usually it's just me and a couple of sentries.'

Cassius asked, 'Is there anywhere we might find shelter for the night?'

The clerk seemed to enjoy dispensing bad news. 'Just desert between here and the Wadi Rum.'

One of the legionaries sauntered over, tapping his belt with his thumbs. He was a portly man with a heavy jaw and little hair. He nodded at Cassius's bracelets. 'If I were you, I'd be careful showing off that gold. Especially if you've got more tucked away somewhere.'

'Just this.'

'You told them about Ruwaffa?' the soldier asked the clerk.
'I did.'

The legionary glanced at the men. 'At least you've got a few swords with you. After somewhere for the night?'

'Yes.'

'You've left it a bit late. There're some decent inns in Humeima.'

'Too much of a detour,' said Cassius. 'There's nowhere else?'

'Depends how you feel about the quality of your accommodation.'

'Go on.'

'This end of the road has a few watchtowers like this. See there?'

The legionary pointed south. Two or three miles away was an upright shape beside the road. 'That's the next one. Hasn't been used for years but it'll be a roof over your heads. There's even a little stable though you won't get all your mounts in.'

Cassius turned to the tower only a few yards away. 'I don't suppose we could use this.'

'Sorry,' said the legionary. 'Regulations. We'll be locking up before we leave.'

'Fair enough.'

The legionary turned and shouted at the men. 'You lot, get the horses. We're off.'

'At last,' muttered one of them.

The clerk closed the book and tidied away some papers.

'One other thing,' said the legionary. 'Those storm clouds. When they bubble up slowly like that you're never sure when it's coming. Be careful tomorrow. You don't want to be stuck out on the road when it hits.'

'Thanks for the advice,' said Cassius before ushering Mercator away from the tower. 'Not sure we should mention this Ruwaffa business to the men.'

'We only left five days ago,' said the optio thoughtfully. 'Time enough for the news to reach Bostra.'

Cassius could see where this was leading.

'Did you know?'

After their conversation of the previous evening, Cassius felt it inadvisable to keep anything more from him. 'Yes.'

'By Mars.' Mercator looked south again.

'I was told to keep it—'

'From me?'

'From everyone.'

'Almost a whole century. I've not heard of such an attack in all Arabia.'

'We'd have more to worry about if we were in uniform.'

Mercator didn't seem reassured. 'Is it connected to our mission?'

'Not as far as I know.'

'Sir, with respect, I think it's time you told me what we're doing here.'

Cassius knew he had to do something to retain the optio's confidence, even though a full disclosure of the operation was unlikely to improve his spirits. Perhaps now was the time.

'Very well. I'll tell you everything once we're at the tower.'

Cassius reached the top rung of the ladder and opened the trap-door. It clattered onto the roof and he pulled himself up. Staying clear of a large, ragged hole in the timbers, he walked up to the surround. In one corner was an abandoned bird's nest containing two shattered eggs.

Hearing noise from below, he looked down at the men. Andal and a few others were putting horses in the shelter while the remaining animals were being watered and fed. The mules had been unloaded and roped together. Indavara was squatting next to Patch, stroking the mule's neck. His mouth was moving.

'Gods, he's talking to it now.'

Cassius thought of one of his uncles: a tough, taciturn farmer who lavished more care on his hunting dogs than on his wife and children.

'You all right up there, sir?' said Simo. 'Do watch out for that hole.'

'I'm watching. Ask Mercator and Ulixes to come up.'

Ulixes arrived first, looking no happier than he had for the rest of the day. Despite the increasingly strong breeze, Cassius could smell the man. In keeping with his wolf-like face, he gave off a rather bestial odour.

Even so, Cassius forced himself to be pleasant. 'Find a place to bed down?'

'Oh yes. Your friends left me a lovely space – right next to the door. Except there is no door.'

'A man of your means is used to the most luxurious inns, I suppose?'

'I've had a bad run is all. Thought I'd be heading north with heavy pockets, not holed up in this shithole with a bunch of second-rate soldiers.'

'Watch your mouth.'

Mercator climbed up and did a circuit of the roof.

Cassius walked over to the trapdoor. 'Simo, anyone else on that floor with you?'

'No, sir.'

Cassius retreated to a solid-looking section of wall and leaned back against it. 'Have you heard of the Black Stone of Emesa?'

'Of course,' said the optio.

'Several weeks ago it was stolen. The Emperor wants it back. We have good reason to believe it's being kept at or near the town of Galanaq. Ulixes is going to guide us there.'

'Who has it?'

'We're not sure.'

'Any ideas why they took it?'

'Presumably for worship. There is some talk of a religious sect in the town.'

Mercator turned to the gambler. 'You know the way?'

Ulixes pointed south. 'Tomorrow we cross the Wadi Rum, continue down the Incense Road then turn west into the mountains.'

'I heard you're an ex-legionary,' said Mercator. 'Why'd you leave the army?'

'None of your business. And by the way, I'd rather be an ex-legionary than a serving auxiliary.'

Cassius was about to intervene but Mercator didn't rise to the bait. 'How come you know this area?'

'I know every mile of this province.'

'Our horses are going to get through a lot of water out here. We've no more than three or four days' worth.'

'There's enough water in those mountains for a legion. You've just got to know where to look. Any half-decent soldier should know that – especially an Arabian.'

Mercator took a step towards him.

'Perhaps you would excuse us, Ulixes,' said Cassius, gesturing towards the ladder.

With a sly grin for Mercator, the gambler climbed down. Cassius shut the trapdoor behind him.

'You sure you want to put our lives in his hands?' asked the optio.

'Once we locate the stone I'll cut him loose.'

'Isn't it quite large?'

'Apparently.'

'How are we going to move it?'

'We'll cross that bridge if we get to it. We've got to find the bloody thing first. Listen, you can tell Yorvah and Andal where we're going if you wish, but nothing about the stone. There's no need yet.'

'Understood.'

Mercator looked over the surround. 'Indavara really likes that mule.'

'What can I tell you? Similar level of intellect.'

<hr>

Cassius sat on a blanket in one corner, his thickest cloak wrapped around him. Judging by the way the wind seemed to blow straight through the tower, he doubted there was much cement left in the walls. On the floor next to him, a little clay oil lamp flickered. He had been checking the map but it was now virtually useless. Only two towns in the area were marked – Hegra and Ruwaffa.

Planks squeaked above as the rooftop sentry paced around, presumably trying to keep himself warm. Cassius had considered attempting to sleep but the auxiliaries on the ground floor were making too much noise. Several were to bed down on the first floor with him, Mercator, Indavara and Simo but for now they were all gathered below playing dice. From the sounds of it, Ulixes was teaching them some new game.

Cassius might have used the spare time to offer a prayer to Jupiter but Simo and Indavara were sitting only a few yards away, on either side of another lamp. The Gaul had a needle and thread out and was attending to a split hem on Cassius's sleeping tunic. Indavara was cleaning out the interior of his scabbard. The pair were sharing almonds from a bowl and discussing Patch; they were worried how he would fare during the cold night.

Sometimes Cassius envied them their easy way with each other. They were usually both involved in some sort of practical labour and since Simo had largely given up trying to indoctrinate Indavara with his Christian teachings, they always seemed happy in each other's company.

'Almond, sir?' asked Simo.

'No, no. I'm fine.'

'A snack before bed, perhaps?'

'I said I'm fine, Simo.'

As the attendant went back to his sewing, someone gave a great shout from below. The other men laughed.

'How's Indavara's riding?' asked Cassius. 'I don't see much with you two behind me all day.'

'Better, sir, I think.'

'Good.' Cassius looked at Indavara. 'Though your galloping still leaves a lot to be desired. You were lucky not to come off when you went to help Usrana.'

'Still waiting for more lessons.'

'Yes, yes. Well, could be worse – at least you don't have to learn on a camel.'

'Strange creatures,' said Indavara. 'Very strange.'

'But useful at times, eh, Simo?'

'Oh. Yes, sir.'

'What?' said Indavara.

'Long story.'

More shouts and laughter from below.

'I think I'll go and see what all the excitement's about.' Cassius took off the cloak and started down the steep wooden staircase, mug of wine in hand.

Mercator was sitting at the bottom. He was about to make way but Cassius motioned for him to stay put and sat a few steps above him. Most of the men were sitting in a loose circle on the floor. In one corner was the only item of furniture: an old bed, which the veteran Andal had commandeered.

Ulixes seemed to be enjoying himself. Cassius knew he wouldn't have had much change left over from what he'd been allocated in Petra but he seemed to have turned it into quite a pile of sesterces.

One of the other gamblers shook his head. 'I don't like this game.'

'I think it's good,' said another.

Cassius watched the game progress and saw that the men were playing not with six-sided dice but 'knucklebones' – oblongs with rounded ends and four sides showing one, three, four and six. The players first took turns to throw three knucklebones. Whoever rolled the lowest total had to put two sesterces in the middle. The players then completed a second round of rolls. Whoever got the highest took the money.

As the game continued, so did Ulixes's good luck. Many of his morose competitors were obviously running out of funds. After only three more rounds, he scooped up his coins.

'What are you doing?' asked one of the men. Cassius knew every name now: this was Apollinaris, a tall, long-limbed fellow who'd seen a lot of action in the Palmyran war.

'Going to bed.'

Apollinaris had only a few coins left. 'You've got to give us a chance to win some back.'

'Who says? We did rules at the start – no one mentioned time or number of rounds.'

'The luck's all gone with you, it'll swing back later.'

'Probably. Which is why I'm finishing now.'

As Ulixes stood up, Mercator weighed in. 'The men usually play for longer. You've taken quite a bit off them – perhaps you can put in for the next round.'

'Perhaps you should mind your own business.'

The usually cheerful Yorvah eyeballed the ex-legionary. 'And you should mind your manners.'

'Enjoy the rest of the game.' Carrying the coins in two hands, Ulixes picked his way through the men towards his bed. Apollinaris was about to follow but Yorvah put a hand on the taller man's arm. Apollinaris reluctantly stayed where he was but he and the other auxiliaries turned towards Mercator.

The stocky optio stood. 'Ulixes. How much have you got there?'

The ex-legionary rolled his eyes, then looked at the coins. 'I don't know – forty-five, fifty.'

'Put ten in for the next round.'

'*Ten?*'

'Or I can come over and take them.'

Cassius felt eyes on him but he kept his expression neutral. He'd seen enough to know Mercator was a capable leader and he wasn't about to intervene and undermine him now. The gambler was probably entitled to his winnings but he'd been stupid to annoy the men and Cassius certainly wasn't going to stand up for him.

Ulixes glared at the optio. 'You think because I don't have a sword I won't defend myself?' He pulled a money bag from his pack and dropped the coins into it.

'I don't need a sword to deal with you,' said Mercator calmly.

Ulixes glanced up at Cassius. 'You should tell your auxiliary friend to calm down. Fair's fair.'

Cassius sipped at his wine.

Mercator hadn't taken his eyes off Ulixes. 'Ten for the next round. Or you and I can settle it outside.'

Grinning, Ulixes looked around the room. 'You know, the truth is I just wanted to get out while I was ahead. It's a weakness of mine – staying in too long.'

He reached into the bag, counted out some coins, then offered them to Yorvah.

'There's fifteen there – in the interests of maintaining good relations with you noble auxiliaries.'

Mercator sat back down on the step.

Once the game was under way again, Cassius returned upstairs.

XVII

Gutha was concerned. When Ilaha had summoned him the previous night he had been dressed in his priestly robes, having just concluded some ceremony involving the stone. He seemed troubled and distracted. The old crone had been there too, of course, lurking in the shadows, listening in.

But she was now absent and Ilaha looked his old, commanding self as he swept into the cavern. Gutha was relieved to see he had followed his advice – he was wearing a plain tunic and was armed with his sword.

'Mushannaf. It has been too long.'

The older man and his two sons stood and the chiefs exchanged a slight bow. In contrast to his host, Mushannaf was wearing a rich blue cloak striped with green thread. The fingers of his left hand were weighed down with several bulky gold rings. His right hand was bare, the arm thin; he had suffered a stroke years earlier and was weak on that side. He kept his hair dyed black, as if to compensate by suggesting a youthful vigour.

'Ilaha. Isn't that what we're supposed to call you these days?'

'If you don't mind. Please, sit, we have much to discuss. Can I offer you anything more?'

The table was covered with a remarkable array of food and drink, none of which had been touched.

'No, but we thank you for your hospitality.'

The sons sat down on either side of their father.

Gutha – standing a few yards away by the wall – had let them keep their swords. He didn't want to cause offence and knew it wouldn't make much difference if things turned nasty. Both sons were known for an indulgent lifestyle funded by their father's wealth. Neither was a swordsman of renown.

Ilaha sat at the other end of the table. 'How was your journey?'

'Annoying,' said Mushannaf as he dragged his weak arm onto his lap. 'I intended to continue south and check my caravans coming up from Thoma. I have lost three days coming here.'

'The gesture is appreciated.'

'I came out of respect for your past achievements. We fought together and we fought well. As equals. The Tanukh has always been a loose alliance – we chiefs work together when it suits us. It was never intended to provide an army for one man.'

'Mushannaf, let me be clear: however the situation develops, you will retain complete control of your trade interests and tactical command of your warriors.'

'"However the situation develops". That sounds disturbingly vague. Do you expect me to blindly pledge myself to your cause? Risk my treasure, my blood?'

Ilaha held up both hands. 'You need wait only a matter of days to hear my proposal. I simply need to know that you will be here with the others – that the Confederation will meet as one.'

'Your request seems reasonable but your actions do not. This senseless attack on Ruwaffa – your work, I presume? Or more likely his?'

With his good hand Mushannaf gestured towards Gutha, who did not react. It would be better for all concerned if Ilaha could win the obstinate chief round, though that was looking increasingly unlikely.

'You mentioned your treasure,' said Ilaha. 'Is it right that a quarter of all your profits should go to Bostra, and from there to Rome?'

'It has always been this way.'

'Not always. They exploit us and our trade only because we haven't the backbone to stand up to them. And what do we get in return? Our lands pillaged by the Palmyrans, occupied for almost two years. And now they've allowed them to rebel *again*.'

'If you expect me to defend Roman policy, you are talking to the wrong man. But I am a realist. This Aurelian is a soldier. He will deal with the Palmyrans and the Egyptians and if we take up arms against him he will deal with us.'

'You fought with me, Mushannaf. You know that I would never be stupid enough to be drawn into an engagement with the legions. But now is the time to push for a stronger position. I have a way for us to secure our own lands in perpetuity and exist as equals, not lackeys.'

Gutha was beginning to think Ilaha might be making progress. It was a while since he'd heard him speak with such clarity and force.

'You are talking about betraying Calvinus,' replied Mushannaf. 'I have no great affinity for the man but at least he respects us and our ways.'

'So your loyalty lies with him, not your own people?'

Mushannaf raised his voice. 'My loyalty *is* to my own people. My own tribe. And I will act – as I have always acted – in their best interest.'

Ilaha was silent for a moment.

'There cannot be one leader,' added the older man. 'Or one god.'

'Choose your next words wisely, Mushannaf.'

'It appears we will have to agree to disagree. Pursue this course if you will, but you will do so without me and without my men.'

Mushannaf had his good hand on the side of his chair, ready to get up.

'A final offer,' said Ilaha.

'I'm listening.'

'A thousand golds.'

'A considerable sum. But I am not for sale.'

Gutha strode over to their end of the table. Mushannaf and his sons looked at him, then at the huge axe hanging from his shoulder. Gutha tapped the handle as he spoke for the first time. 'With respect, I suggest you reconsider.'

'I suggest you stay out of it, northerner.'

Mushannaf stood. The sons were already on their way up when Gutha reached inside his tunic and threw a little leather bag onto the table.

'What's that?' asked the chief.

'Open it and find out,' said Gutha.

Ilaha watched dispassionately as Mushannaf untied the top of the bag and turned it over. A lock of dark brown hair fell onto the table. He picked it up and examined it.

'Father?' said one of the sons.

'Ellari,' breathed Mushannaf.

Gutha took another step towards him. 'I hear she's quite a beauty, your new wife.'

Mushannaf's mouth twisted into a snarl.

The closest son sprang to his feet. As he reached for his sword, Gutha gripped the axe handle.

'I wouldn't bother. We need your father – we don't particularly need you.'

The son moved his hand away from the sword. His brother was still sitting down.

Mushannaf turned his glare on Ilaha. 'You evil little . . .'

'Now now,' warned Gutha. 'There's no need for that. You were given the chance to cooperate but you've left us no choice.' He nodded at the lock of hair still in Mushannaf's hand. 'If I order it, my man can get that close again. He's very good. She won't even see him or hear him. The first she'll know of it is cold metal on her skin, then—'

'All right,' said Mushannaf. 'All right, curse you.'

At last, Ilaha spoke again. 'All I am asking is that you come with the others and hear me out. That is all.'

Mushannaf was still looking at the hair. He answered in a whisper. 'Very well.'

XVIII

By the afternoon they were past the Wadi Rum and facing the bleakest terrain yet. There seemed to be no traces of life at all, just the dusty wastes and the austere bulk of the mountains. Dark cloud still shadowed the sky to the south-east and now seemed to be on the move.

Earlier, they had encountered several caravans heading north. The largest had been of at least a hundred men, with three times that number of pack animals. They passed the occasional way-station too: all were ruined and stripped of timber and anything else of value. The watchtowers were similarly ancient and empty – all except one that had been appropriated by a local family eking out a living by selling water and dried fruit.

Cassius's attention alternated between the gathering storm and the mountains. Despite the heat, he felt a chill feather his back when he thought of what the next few days might hold. Ulixes had told him that the Hejaz peaks were part of an enormous range fifty miles across and a thousand long that stretched all the way to the southern tip of the Arabian peninsula. Somewhere inside that formidable maze of rock was Galanaq and the mysterious enemy who had orchestrated this daring strike against Rome.

At the tenth hour, he was forced to call a halt. The eastern horizon had disappeared and now distant formations were being subsumed by the long-feared haboob. While the rest of the sky remained an unsullied blue, the seething mass of dust seemed to be growing higher and wider with every passing minute.

'We need shelter,' he said. 'But where?'

The western edge of the mountains was at least five miles away; to the east was an isolated formation.

'That's closer,' said Mercator.

'But it means riding into it,' replied Cassius. 'We'll reach the storm sooner.'

Mercator called up Andal. The veteran scratched his chin then nodded at the formation. 'I'd say there.'

'Ground's not good,' observed Ulixes. 'The sand will slow us down and there's all those nasty little rocks – difficult for the mounts.'

A flock of birds flew overhead, squawking as if warning the stranded humans below.

'We can walk,' said Andal. 'Lead the horses.'

'Tell the men,' said Cassius. As Mercator began barking orders, he dismounted and led the way off the road.

———◆8◆———

They almost made it in time. As the storm rolled towards them, tendrils of dust swirled high into the air. Then came waves of wind that rippled across the sand, surging then dying like water upon a shore. As the great cloud loomed, the sun disappeared and visibility dropped to little more than a hundred yards. Soon everything was cloaked by an opaque, yellow hue.

Though the soft sand had slowed them, it was – as Ulixes had warned – the treacherous shards of rock that really caused problems. Cassius's horse had already stumbled twice and – despite its compliant nature – was now resisting. He was sure this was at least partly because of the other animals fleeing the haboob: a small herd of ibex trotting west, hares bolting across the ground, high-flying vultures and eagles trying to outrun the storm.

Glad to see some clear terrain ahead, Cassius looked back. Most of the auxiliaries were in a straight line but one man towards the rear was off to the side, examining his horse's hoof. Cassius gave not a moment's thought to stopping. The auxiliary would just have to keep up as best he could.

The formation seemed to have been dropped from the heavens: a colossal lump of dark grey rock half a mile long. Cassius had been aiming for a hollow at the base of the western face but now saw it was an illusion created by a variance in colour.

Even so, he quickened his pace, tugging the horse after him. The dust had coated his tunic, his skin, his hair. He could feel it on his eyelids and taste it in his mouth. He snatched another look back but couldn't even make out the middle of the column, let alone the rear. He ploughed on.

Nearing the formation, he heard what at first he thought was someone whistling. Then he realised it was the wind, howling through the voids in the rock. He towed his horse right up to the face and tied the reins around one of the numerous boulders scattered along the base.

Simo arrived, leading horse and mule. The Gaul's dark hair had been made fair by several layers of sand.

'Rope them to mine,' Cassius told him.

'Yes, sir.'

Cassius waved Indavara past too and then saw Mercator, who offered him his reins. 'Here, I'll go back and check the others.'

'I'll do it. Tie the horses in a line along the formation.'

With his cloak whipping around his legs and sand peppering his face, Cassius guided the others in. Having passed Ulixes, Yorvah and most of the men, he looked for the next auxiliary but there was no one there.

Visibility was down to a few yards now. He was about to give up when a shape emerged from the storm. It was Andal.

'Straight ahead!' Cassius shouted. 'You're almost there.'

'Not sure who's still with me.'

'Just keep going.'

Behind the veteran were only three more men. Cassius had counted a total of sixteen. Two more were out there somewhere.

Hood flapping, wind blasting his back, he waited for the missing pair. Three times he thought a man was about to materialise, but they turned out to be imaginary spectres, like those glimpsed in a sea of cloud.

Fearing he would completely lose his bearings, Cassius retraced his steps and found the rest of the party in good order. The closely packed horses stood with heads bowed and eyes closed. Many of the men stayed beside them, a comforting hand on a shoulder or flank. Ulixes was sitting on a boulder, pouring water into his eyes. Mercator was with the guard officers.

'Two missing, yes?' said Cassius.

'Plus some of the mules. A rope must have come loose. Andal suggests tying a long line on someone and sending them out. What do you think?'

'Let's try it.'

Simo appeared. 'Sir – we saw them. We saw the men.'

Cassius followed him back to the end of the line. 'Where's Indavara?'

'I think he went to find them.'

Cassius looked out into the swirling, orange fog. For more than a minute he saw no one but then he spied a single figure walking parallel to the formation, no more than twenty feet away.

He shouted.

The figure turned and walked towards him. The broad shoulders, bulky legs and shaggy hair made identification easy.

'See them?'

'I thought so,' replied Indavara as he brushed sand from his eyes. 'Lost them, though.'

'Just stay here or we'll lose you too.'

One of the mounts was unsettled and the movement on the line was upsetting the others. As Indavara and Simo went to calm their horses down, Cassius noted an absentee.

'Where's the mule?'

Simo looked around. 'I'm not sure. I thought—'

'Indavara. Where's the mule?'

He didn't reply.

Knowing the hearing in his disfigured ear sometimes failed him, Cassius shouted.

'Indavara. The mule?'

The bodyguard looked at the empty space between his and Cassius's horse. 'He was there. I thought he'd feel safe between the horses.'

'Tied on?'

'No, but he wouldn't go off on his own.'

'Gods' blood – the money.'

Cassius jogged all the way along the line. Having come across several other mules but not the one he was looking for, he sprinted back to the others and found Indavara still holding up his hands in dismay.

'He was right there.'

'*He?* By Jupiter – your precious Patch. Well, *he* is a lot less valuable than what he's carrying on his back.' Cassius kicked the ground.

It wasn't just the money. If the worst came to the worst, a sight of the spearhead would give second thought to anyone with hostile intent, even in these lands beyond Roman rule.

'The men,' he asked Indavara. 'You're sure you saw them?'

'Fairly sure, yes. You don't think—'

'I don't know what to think. Let's just hope that bloody mule hasn't gone far.'

———◼8▶———

The missing pair were named Actis and Corydon. Cassius knew both faces but had barely spoken a word to either of them. Andal was first to take his turn with the rope. He walked along the base of the formation to the south then out in an arc before eventually reappearing from the north. He had seen nothing. While another man took his turn, Cassius spoke to Mercator. He didn't want to tell him about the money or impugn his men, but there was still no sign of the mule and time was passing.

'Actis and Corydon. Neither of them given to panic, I trust?'

'Not at all. I think they just got separated at the back. Four mules gone too. Got yours?'

'No.'

There was nothing to do but wait for the storm to pass. Every object and being was now bathed in an ethereal golden glow. The horses pressed themselves close to the rock face and the men sat in twos or threes, clasping their hoods over their faces.

Indavara and Simo, however, stayed on their feet, still looking for any sign of the mule. Cassius decided he would leave them to it; they had lost the beast, after all.

Sitting between two boulders, he took a drink from his flask then poured the remainder over his face. His eyes still stung so he kept them shut. Despite the storm raging around him, he suddenly felt very tired. He uttered three lines of a prayer to the weather gods but never finished it.

━━■8■━➤

Simo shook him awake.

'What? What is it?'

'We think the worst of the storm has passed, sir.'

Cassius pulled down his hood and looked around. He could see some way along the formation and much of the ground ahead. The sky to the west was dark.

'The mule?'

Indavara – who had appeared from behind one of the horses – shook his head.

'The men?'

'No, sir,' said Simo.

As he went in search of Mercator, Cassius found most of the auxiliaries up on their feet. Some were eating and drinking; others were brushing down their horses or washing out their eyes. Mercator and Yorvah were with Andal, who had just returned with one of the mules. There was no barrel on its back nor white mark upon its fur.

Over the next half-hour, the haboob moved farther away. The storm clouds seemed to dissipate as they met the higher ground and soon the mountains were visible once more.

Mercator ordered the men to prepare themselves then spoke to Cassius. 'Hopefully they found shelter somewhere else on the formation.'

Cassius didn't think that was the only explanation but there was no sense airing such a suspicion yet. 'I'll take one half of the men around to the north, you take the others around to the south.'

'Good idea.'

Cassius then noticed Ulixes talking to two of the auxiliaries. The gambler had his knucklebones ready.

'Forget that,' Cassius told him. 'We're moving out.'

—8—

Within another half an hour, they were riding along in sunshine with clear skies in every direction. Rounding the formation, they saw a variety of wildlife warily leaving the safety of the natural shelter: lizards scampering out from behind boulders, birds flitting from high crevices, even a family of gazelle that bolted from a cave then loped away to the north. No man or mule appeared, however, and Cassius's fears only grew. Upon reaching the far side they were surprised by a distant sight. Two miles to the east was a cluster of high, healthy-looking date palms.

Cassius halted his horse. 'An oasis.'

'A what?' asked Indavara.

'An underground spring – provides water, allows trees to grow where there's no other vegetation for miles.'

They heard shouts and saw Mercator coming the other way. Before the two groups met, Cassius had counted up and realised the missing men were with them. Actis and Corydon came forward with their optio.

'They sheltered in a cave,' explained Mercator. 'Actis has lost his horse so we've given him one of the spares. No sign of the other mules, though.'

While some of the auxiliaries aimed light-hearted insults at the unfortunate pair, Ulixes pointed at the oasis. 'They're probably there. Drawn to the water.'

Andal had dismounted. 'There are some tracks leading that way. Fresh. Too small for a horse.'

Indavara and Simo went to investigate.

Mercator looked west towards the road. 'We've already lost three hours.'

'Let's replenish our water while we have the chance,' said Cassius.

'You really want to lose more time out here?'

Cassius nodded at Indavara and Simo. 'If we don't at least try and find their precious Patch I'll never hear the end of it.'

— 8 —

As they neared the oasis, Cassius realised there was a narrow path leading through the ridge of sand that surrounded the depression. He then saw light sparking off water.

'Could be people here,' said Mercator.

'Could be.'

Considering what they'd heard about hostile tribesmen, Cassius wouldn't have minded dropping back but, in the interests of maintaining appearances, he stayed alongside the optio as they approached the path.

It soon became obvious that the oasis *was* occupied, or at least had been until very recently. The pool was on the far side, a glittering oval mirror ringed by reeds and palms. The trees could not have looked healthier; vibrant green branches proudly sticking out at every angle. Close to the pool were about a dozen tents, some of which appeared to have been damaged in the storm.

They halted. Mercator offered a speculative look. Cassius shrugged and nudged his horse on to the path.

It was hard to work out where the shout came from but the result was clear enough.

Men rose smoothly and silently up from behind the ridge. More appeared among the tents, and yet more who had been hiding in the trees. There were at least sixty of them, all in pale, flowing robes and clutching either bows or swords. The Arabians were already converging on the path.

Cassius raised a hand and tried to sound calm. 'Everyone dismount. Don't go anywhere near your weapons.'

As the men complied, the warriors closed in. Each archer picked a target and Cassius found himself looking at the iron head of an arrow only ten feet away. The bow was held by a lean, gnarled Saracen with a dead-eyed stare and a remarkably steady hand.

One of the auxiliaries muttered something.

'Quiet there,' ordered Mercator.

The group that had been hiding behind the tents ran up to the path. Leading the way was a short, squat man; the only one whose sword remained undrawn. His angular face seemed at odds with his body; a narrow blade of a nose and a sharp chin accentuated by the most immaculately maintained beard Cassius had ever seen. The leader appeared to be in his forties yet there was no grey in his coal-black hair. He did not look happy.

After inspecting Cassius and Mercator, he gave an order and the archers lowered their bows.

'Do you speak Greek?' he asked in a deep, rich voice.

'Yes.'

'What are you doing here?'

Cassius offered what he hoped was his most engaging smile. 'Looking for our mule.'

XIX

Though aware there were far more important matters to concern him, Cassius couldn't stop looking at Khalima's beard. (He was relieved to have been given the Saracen's name; surely a man was less likely to kill you if he'd bothered to introduce himself.) But that beard – the hair was as thick as an animal's pelt, the moustache shaped as perfectly as the square wedge running from chin to bottom lip. That lip was now turned down as the Saracen surveyed the three men in front of him. Cassius glanced back at Mercator and Indavara. The optio looked anxious; the bodyguard looked bored.

Having been summoned to the largest of the tents, Cassius had insisted on bringing the other two and was glad he'd done so, even though they'd had to leave their weapons outide. Simo, Ulixes and the auxiliaries remained at the edge of the oasis, watched by Khalima's tribesmen.

Three of his warriors were behind Indavara and Mercator. Two others – sons by the looks of them – were talking to the chief.

The tent reminded Cassius of a similarly spacious and well-appointed example used by Prefect Venator of the Fourth Legion. The floor was reed matting covered with rugs and cushions decorated with colourful oriental designs. The Saracen owned several pieces of furniture, including a small desk equipped with an abacus and writing equipment. Next to it was a cupboard with a metal grille at the front. Inside were half a dozen objects made from silver and gold.

The tent's entrance had been left open. Outside, dozens of women and children had appeared. None dared get too close but a group of young boys was staring inside and talking excitedly.

'What was the name again?' asked Khalima in his faultless Greek.

'Cassius Oranius Crispian.'

'Remind me why you were on the Incense Road.'

'I am a merchant, looking to buy goods in Hegra.'

'You don't look like any merchant I've ever seen – even one from Raetia. And what kind of merchant travels without anything to trade?'

'It is my first trip to Arabia – more of a fact-finding visit really.'

Khalima looked past him. 'And these two?'

'My bodyguard, Indavara. And the leader of my hired men, Mertan. He and the others are locals. They joined me in Bostra.'

'What are you looking to buy in Hegra?'

'I'm not sure yet. Certainly some frankincense.'

'Really? Well then, tell me – what would you expect to pay for top-quality Sabaean? Per pound.'

Cassius had done a little research in Bostra and Petra in case of such situations but was already wishing he'd done a little more. 'I believe twelve denarii is the going rate.'

Khalima gave no indication of whether this was correct. 'And nard – small leaf, per pound?'

Cassius considered his answer. Was nard the really expensive one or was that myrrh? Hesitation might cost him as much as a wrong answer. 'That would be expensive. Very expensive.'

'Indeed it would.'

Cassius scratched his chin to cover a gulp.

Khalima fingered the bangles on his left wrist. 'You shouldn't have any problems with this last question – it concerns a product from your homeland. Raetian honey is considered the best and sells well in the markets of Antioch. They charge five times what it would cost back in Raetia. What would a native merchant pay?'

'Er . . . honey . . . you see food's not really my area.'

'But you are from Raetia. You could certainly make an educated guess.'

'Per pound?'

'Yes.'

'Er . . . three denarii? I'd say about three.'

Khalima drew his sword and walked up to Cassius, who sensed Indavara poised to move.

'Don't,' Cassius told him, even though Khalima had now raised the sword.

The Saracen's unblinking eyes were a pale orange. He brought the finely honed tip of the blade up until Cassius felt it against his throat. 'Liar. They don't even export honey from Raetia. The good stuff comes from Dacia. Who are you?'

'Now, don't go casting aspersions on our fine Raetian honey,' Cassius stuttered. 'Highly underrated – why, it's lovely on a piece of—'

'Who – are – you?'

'I told you.'

Cassius felt the sword pressing into his skin. On balance, he didn't think Khalima would kill him, but he wasn't about to take the risk.

'All right. I'm not a Raetian merchant. I'm Roman. I'm a Roman soldier.'

Khalima lowered the blade.

'An officer, in fact,' added Cassius.

'You're not old enough.'

'It's true.'

'Prove it.'

'Er, the thing is, at this particular moment . . . I can't.'

Indavara spoke up. 'Actually, I think you can.' He pointed outside.

A mule had appeared on the far side of the oasis and was walking towards the pool. The barrel and the saddlebags were still attached.

Indavara was grinning. 'That's Patch.'

The spearhead lay on a rug: three feet of steel topped by a blade kept safe by a piece of cork. Welded to the middle of the shaft was the square badge bearing the SPQR legend and the (recently inscribed) emblem of the Governor's Office of Arabia.

Khalima was lying against a pile of cushions, eyeing it. A young girl had just brought him some wine in a fine glass which he hadn't yet touched. He picked up the spearhead – which took two hands to lift – and peered closely at the inscriptions.

'Would you like me to translate?' asked Cassius.

'Are you *trying* to offend me, Roman? I've been speaking Latin since before you were a glint in your father's eye.'

'Apologies.'

'I saw such a thing once before. During the Palmyran war.'

Cassius hadn't been offered any cushions. He was sitting cross-legged on a reed mat.

The Saracen put down the spearhead, then took a drink. 'You, Mertan.'

Mercator and Indavara were standing outside with Khalima's sons. All four turned round.

'Your men may take what water they need. Stay on the far side of the pool, away from my people.'

After a nod from Cassius, Mercator left.

'I would speak with you alone, Roman.'

'Very well,' said Cassius. He looked at Indavara. Though the others' weapons had been returned, Cassius was unarmed and wouldn't stand a chance against Khalima. But he could not afford to offend this man.

'It's all right.'

Indavara followed Mercator. At a word from the Saracen, his sons lowered the flap of canvas so that no one could see inside.

The Arabian leaned forward and offered his forearm. 'I believe this is how you people greet each other.'

Cassius was ready for the strong grip, but not for the way Khalima held on and locked eyes with him. 'This means only that we can speak as equals. I have not decided yet whether you are enemy or friend.'

Cassius pretended he hadn't noticed the marks Khalima's fingers had left on his arm. 'Is there no position between those two extremes?'

'These days – not much.' The Saracen looked at the spearhead. 'The other officer I saw with one of those was a scout. Is that what you are doing this far south?'

'I suppose you could say that.'

Cassius was unsure how to proceed. Having admitted his true identity, he would now have to reassure Khalima without revealing too much. He resolved to handle it one point at a time. 'The governor is interested in what is going on beyond the reach of our conventional forces.'

'I'm sure. This incident at Ruwaffa must be of great concern to him.'

'Indeed.'

'To be honest, I'm surprised he hasn't taken action already. Calvinus always seemed to be a decisive man. Perhaps it is his age.'

'You know the governor?'

'Not to speak to. I've heard him address the Confederation several times over the years.'

'You belong to the Tanukh?'

'I do. Though it now seems a long time since the tribes last fought together.'

Cassius almost asked another question but he held back.

Khalima grinned, those amber eyes glinting like some wise old lion. Cassius found him frightening and engaging in equal measure.

'You would like to press me, wouldn't you, Roman? See what you can find out? But you're not sure of me yet.'

'This is a delicate situation for us both.'

'You are lucky it was me you blundered into. Many of those you'll meet south of Humeima would happily kill a Roman spy and his men – slit their throats and bury them in the Sea of Sand where they'd never be found.'

Cassius didn't want to dwell on that thought. 'The governor

wishes only to understand why the Confederation has turned its back on Rome.'

'Is it really such a complicated question?'

'Educate me.'

Khalima threw up a hand. 'Why? Why should I tell you anything? I am a businessman, not an informer. I trade – something for something.'

'Perhaps I can help you. I am a member of the governor's staff. I have influence. How is business?'

'I think you already know the answer to that question. Business is bad. Rebellions in both neighbouring provinces, brigandage on the rise and the producers down south squeezing our profits.'

'Perhaps we can discuss money.'

'I certainly hope so. But before you make me an offer, you should know that you are already worth a great deal to me. A certain individual would pay handsomely if I were to deliver you and your men to him.'

'Yet you don't seem overly keen on doing so.'

'I am not particularly keen on the said individual – what he stands for or what he has done. But be in no doubt, I will serve you up to him on a golden platter if you cannot offer me something of substance.'

Cassius wasn't sure the bribe money would be enough; fortunately that wasn't all he could offer. He touched the spearhead. 'This gives me the power to act with the authority of the governor. Tell me what I can do for you.'

Khalima ran his tongue around his mouth while he considered his reply. 'As I said, business is not good. Most of those people outside are members of my family: I have to provide for them all. We have with us seven hundred pounds of incense, ready for the markets of the Red City. As usual, I have already paid out to the three kings and two priestly clans whose lands I have passed through in the south. Then there are my other costs: water, fodder, materials, breakage – the list goes on. And before I can even sell in Petra I must pay a quarter to your administrators. When my margins were better, I could just about live with the import tax. Now it's wiping out all my profit. On this trip, I'll be lucky to break even.'

'I think I can help. But what can you offer in return?'

Khalima straightened his robes while he considered his reply. 'You seem to be lacking information. I am prepared to tell you what I know. We are in an isolated spot. My men can be trusted. As long as yours can too, no one else need even know we ever met.'

'My thoughts precisely. Now, this tax situation. I am sure that exceptions can be – and are – made. A letter to the governor from me and we can have a written agreement in Petra within days. It would explain that Calvinus himself has awarded you a special exemption regarding import tax – reduced rates for a certain period of time.'

'What rate? What period?'

'That depends on the value of what you tell me. As a starting point, let us say that you will pay no more than twenty per cent for the next two years.'

Khalima didn't look impressed.

Cassius held up his hands. 'A starting point. No more.'

'Very well. What do you want to know?'

'You mentioned a certain individual who would be interested to know of my presence here. Is this the same individual responsible for Ruwaffa?'

'Nobody knows for sure who attacked Ruwaffa. Just as nobody knows for sure who has been raiding the temples. But nobody is mentioning any other names.'

'And what is his?'

'I am told he goes by Ilaha these days. He is a warrior who fought the Persians and the Palmyrans under Charaz, a great ethnarch of the Tanukh.'

'Ethnarch?'

'That is what we call the leaders of the thirteen tribal clans. Mine is named Uruwat. Charaz was killed during the Palmyran war and – in the absence of any male heir – succeeded by Ilaha. He had a reputation for being more interested in fighting than trade and was generally considered one of the less powerful ethnarchs. But a year or so ago we began to hear that he had styled himself as a warrior-priest and devoted himself to the sun god Elagabal.'

Cassius maintained a neutral expression as Khalima continued.

'It is said that he can perform magical acts – that he can summon the voice of the god and see into the future. No one took him particularly seriously to begin with, but his warband has grown rapidly and his warriors are fiercely loyal. It is said he now has more men than any of the other ethnarchs.'

Cassius remembered Calvinus mentioning the name but it seemed odd that news of Ilaha's rise had not reached Bostra.

'His ascent seems swift indeed.'

'That in itself is exceptional; and some say further evidence of a divine hand at work.'

'You don't agree?'

'Unrest breeds unrest. The chiefs all know what is happening to the north and south of us. This Ilaha thinks his time has come, and it seems some of the other ethnarchs agree with him.'

'But not all?'

'Far from it. My chief, Uruwat, believes in the old ways. The Tanukh has never fought against Rome and has always spoken with one voice when negotiating with the governor. It seems that Ilaha prefers to hear his voice alone.' Khalima smiled. 'I see from your face that this is all useful to you.'

'Most useful,' admitted Cassius. 'Useful enough for us to make considerable modifications to our starting point. What else do you know about this Ilaha?'

'I saw him once. He is very handsome.'

Now Cassius smiled. 'Anything else?'

'I met Uruwat's son while passing through Dumata. Ilaha has called a meeting for the last day of this month. All the ethnarchs have been asked to attend. Uruwat will be there.'

'Where is this meeting to be held?'

'He operates from a base deep in the Hejaz mountains. That too might explain why his rise has not been fully appreciated by you and your colleagues in Bostra.'

'This base – a town named Galanaq?'

'You are not as ignorant as you claimed, Roman. Now, tell me what "modifications" to your original offer I can expect.'

'We can discuss that if you wish but I have a further request. There is considerable risk attached for you so let me first disclose what I will offer in return. You will pay *no* import tax. For five years.'

Khalima tried not to show too much but his eyes shone. 'You can really make that happen?'

Cassius felt sure Calvinus would consider it a small price to pay. 'Absolutely.'

'What must I do?'

'I and my men need to get to Galanaq. If we journey there alone, as strangers, I doubt we'll get within ten miles of the place. I want you to get us into the town. Nothing more, but you must get us inside.'

Khalima looked away. 'Information is one thing. That is something else.'

'But in five years you'll be a very, very rich man.'

'Such a risk might expose not only me but my entire family. I must consider it.'

'I want to be there before that meeting. Which would give us only four days.'

'We would need to leave tomorrow.' Khalima fiddled with one of his bracelets for a while then looked up. 'If I decline—'

'We will discuss appropriate recompense for the information you have already provided. You have my word.'

'I will give you an answer by sundown.'

——8——

Cassius felt numerous eyes upon him as he walked across the oasis. Khalima's men were repairing the tents, the women preparing a fire. Perhaps still upset by the storm, the children were being allowed to play. To Cassius they seemed a healthy, harmonious group and every single one of Khalima's clan wore clean, well-cut clothing and at least one piece of jewellery. The best clothes, however – soft, lustrous red robes – were reserved for a trio of lovely young women cleaning their hands in the pool. They were the only adults not working.

'Well?' said Indavara when Cassius reached him, Mercator and Ulixes.

'Possibly an improvement in our fortunes.'

'Better than having a sword stuck in your neck, you mean?'

'Oh, certainly.'

Mercator had stationed the horses by the edge of the oasis so there was no risk of them fouling the water. They had been roped together and were being watched by a few of the auxiliaries. The rest of the men were washing and refilling their water skins.

'You were in there a long time,' said the optio.

'Worth every minute, I assure you. Khalima has already provided me with some useful information and now we must wait to see if he will help us into Galanaq.'

'Isn't that what I'm supposed to be doing?' asked Ulixes.

'You may be able to find the place but getting inside might be difficult.'

'You seem very trusting of a man who seemed about ready to chop off your head an hour ago. What have you offered him in return?'

'That's between him and me,' said Cassius. 'But given what he's revealed about the man who may have the stone, I doubt we have much of a chance without him.'

'All right if I send Yorvah to try and find those two last mules?' asked Mercator.

'Not yet. No one has witnessed this meeting and Khalima would prefer it to stay that way. Until we have a decision let's keep our heads down and try not to annoy him.'

'Very well.' The optio walked away.

Ulixes was still glaring at Cassius. 'You *must* have asked him about the stone.'

'No. And I don't intend to unless I have to. As far as he's concerned I need intelligence for the governor, nothing more.

You'll get the money when I see the stone. But until then keep your mouth shut about it. Say nothing to anyone.'

'What about giving me *half* now?'

'No chance.'

Indavara stepped in front of him. 'You heard the man.'

As Ulixes sloped off, Simo walked up from the pool. He was leading Patch, who was licking water off his snout.

'Are you all right, sir?' asked the attendant. 'I was starting to wonder if you'd ever come out of that tent.'

'Fine, Simo. And our furry friend?'

'Better now, sir. He must have been so frightened during the sandstorm – he was still shaking.'

'Well, he couldn't have timed his return any better. And if we hadn't gone after him, I would not have met Khalima.'

Cassius stepped forward and tried to stroke the mule but it veered away towards Indavara, who ruffled one of its ears.

'You know who really likes you and who doesn't, don't you, Patch? Very good judges of character, mules.'

'Ha bloody ha.'

XX

Cassius sat against a knobbly date palm, idly watching insects buzz around the pool. On the other side of the water, the fire was heating a steaming pot into which the women were dropping a seemingly endless series of ingredients. Most of the tents were now back up but the men continued with their repairs. Cassius guessed their horses had earlier been taken somewhere to shelter from the storm; a group of lads had just brought them back.

A few yards away, an old woman was supervising two young boys as they nimbly scaled another palm using belts. Given the season, Cassius knew they wouldn't be collecting the dates but thinning them out to produce a better harvest later in the year. Their ascent had disturbed a small flock of colourful birds, some of which were now hunting in the reeds. According to Simo, they were bee-eaters: pretty little things with sky-blue chests, yellow throats and vicious-looking bills. Cassius knew of the breed; his grandfather had kept bees and once told him how they killed their prey. Once a bee was lodged in their bill, the birds would hammer it against something hard until the stinger fell out, then swallow their meal. Cassius was yet to see a single assassination.

The sun was currently veiled by cloud and, with the cooling effect of the water, the temperature was perfect. He might have dozed off had it not been for the anxious wait. Whatever Khalima's decision, he at least knew something of his foe now: this warrior-priest Ilaha, who apparently wished to lead the Tanukh against Rome.

One thing was certain; the governor would have to know. A message wouldn't reach him for at least three or four days and it would be two weeks before he could take any significant action in the area. So whatever Calvinus did, it would not interfere with the operation. But Cassius felt sure now that the nature of that operation had to change.

With what Khalima had revealed about the size of Ilaha's force, it seemed doubtful they would be able to recover the stone. Even Abascantius wouldn't expect him and the auxiliaries to mount a raid with no chance of success. Surely it made more sense to gather intelligence about Ilaha and the location of the stone, then return to Bostra. Perhaps Tribune Pontius would get his wish: march an army to Galanaq, reclaim the Emperor's prize and regain control of the province.

Cassius was thinking how to word his letter to Calvinus when he noticed Mercator waving to him. The optio then pointed towards the camp. Khalima was striding across the sand.

— 8 —

Cassius felt even more eyes upon him this time and he wiped his clammy hands on his tunic. Sometimes he hated being in charge, making decisions, having such influence over the lives of others. Sometimes he wished he was a gardener or a scribe with no responsibility for anyone else. Just for a day, of course.

He met Khalima between the two camps.

'I and a detachment of my men will escort you to Galanaq and get you inside the gates. The rest of my family will continue on to Petra.'

'Excellent.'

'I have some conditions.'

'Go on.'

'Firstly, our agreement must be laid down in writing and a copy despatched immediately to Governor Calvinus.'

'Agreed.'

'Secondly, we will add a clause that it remains valid even in the event of my death.'

'Agreed.'

'Thirdly, I am in charge until we reach Galanaq. Once there you must do what you have to without endangering me or my men.'

'Of course. As you know, I simply wish to gather intelligence.'

'If you or any of your men are caught or identified, I will deny all knowledge.'

'Fair enough.'

'Then we have an agreement. Can you have it drawn up in Greek tonight?'

'Certainly.'

'We will leave at first light,' added Khalima. 'But there are some practicalities to attend to.' He looked past Cassius at the auxiliaries. 'I have employed numerous sword-hands over the years. That should not arouse suspicion. Do they speak Nabatean?'

'Every one.'

'Who's that fellow losing his hair?'

'Ulixes. An associate.'

'And the fat one?'

'My attendant.'

Khalima scratched his chin. 'They don't look much like warriors but as least they're dark enough. Not for Arabians but there are plenty of Syrians around these parts. Which leaves us with one remaining problem.'

'Yes?' said Cassius.

'You.'

———8———

Dusk was close by the time they found the mule. Andal had located the other missing animal an hour earlier; it had been sighted wandering towards the formation where they'd sheltered. Bored by inactivity, Indavara had offered to help Mercator look for the last one. They found it south of the oasis at a smaller, angular outcrop of rock that resembled a fin.

The mule was drinking water that had collected in a hollow. The pair dismounted and closed in from either side but the beast showed no inclination to resist. In fact, it seemed happy to be in company once more and nuzzled Mercator's horse. The optio roped it to his mount and they set off back towards the oasis on foot.

'Might be dangerous down here, but there are some amazing sights.'

'There are,' replied Indavara.

Even his dislike of the dry, hot lands couldn't blind him to the stark beauty of the place. The sunset had divided everything into layers. The closest flank of the Hejaz mountains was black, the distant peaks shrouded by grey. Above was a hazy band of orange, then the sun itself, a perfect yellow disc.

'What do you think of this Khalima, then?' said Mercator. 'These desert folk can be tricky.'

'Corbulo usually knows what he's doing.'

'And Ulixes?'

'The sooner we get rid of him the better.'

'Right,' said Mercator. 'Slimy bastard, that one.'

'I wanted to ask – what's it like in the army?'

'Can't really remember anything else. Been in since I was seventeen. Almost half my life.'

'Have you been in many battles?'

'Not many. One against the Persians, two against the Palmyrans.'

'Corbulo fought the Palmyrans. At a fort.'

'He told me. Doesn't really seem the soldier type.'

Indavara would have put it in stronger terms than that but knew he shouldn't criticise Corbulo too much in front of the optio. 'He says we all have our strengths and weaknesses.'

'Considering his job, I imagine he's glad to have you by his side.'

Indavara didn't reply.

'And you?' continued Mercator. 'I assume you've been in more *fights* than battles.'

Indavara nodded.

'How many?'

'Enough.'

'Don't like talking much, do you?'

'Doesn't it annoy you? Being told what to do every hour of the day?'

'I'm an optio. Once you reach that rank you spend more time giving orders than taking them.'

'But you often have to do things you don't want to.'

'That's life.'

'Like what?'

'Beating a man who won't tow the line. Being sent out with a tax collector and having to get money off some poor bugger who doesn't have two coins to rub together.'

'All for Rome,' said Indavara, kicking away a pebble.

'Rome is not perfect,' acknowledged Mercator. 'I know both sides. But the army has given me a good life and the Empire brings order. And – for the most part – peace. Honestly, most of the time it's just about looking after the men, getting them through.'

Indavara couldn't imagine that. Having never had to look out for anyone other than himself, keeping an eye on Corbulo and Simo was more than enough for him. 'Must be difficult.'

To Indavara's surprise, Mercator laughed. 'Gods, I remember my first few years. I'd get out of any job I could. I hated to be put in charge of anything.'

'What changed?'

'I'm not sure. But I remember one time when we'd chased a band of Palmyrans into the hills west of Apamea. Bloody diehards they were – dug themselves into these tunnels. Centurion needed volunteers. I was just a guard officer back then.'

'You went in?'

'Just me, a dagger and a lantern. By Mars, I've never been so scared.'

'But you did it.'

'I just realised I'd rather go myself than watch someone else do it.'

'That took courage,' said Indavara.

'Or stupidity,' replied Mercator with a smile. 'Sometimes there's a pretty thin line between the two.'

'Is this really necessary?'

Khalima had his arm over Cassius's shoulder as he led him into one of the smaller tents. Standing inside were the three young women he'd seen earlier.

'Let me put it this way,' replied the Saracen. 'When we reach Galanaq are you keen to be the first one pulled out of line by Ilaha's guards?'

'Er, no.'

'Well then, let me introduce Farrai, Elymaris and Golpari.'

'Your daughters?'

Khalima roared with laughter, answering only when he'd recovered himself. 'No, Roman. My wives. Well, some of them.'

Though surprised, Cassius was aware of this tradition among certain peoples of the East.

'Is it really so shocking?' asked Khalima, eyes twinkling.

'I suppose not,' said Cassius. 'In fact I think it's an excellent idea.'

'Quite so.'

Khalima spoke a few words of Nabatean and the oldest of the girls came forward. She looked about Cassius's age.

'Golpari is Persian. She was an actress and what she doesn't know about altering one's appearance isn't worth knowing.'

Golpari examined Cassius's face and hair, then pointed at the freckles on his forearms. The two other girls giggled.

'Where are you from originally?' asked Khalima. 'Gaul or Germany, I imagine.'

'The north of Italy.'

'Ah. Well, by the time Golpari's finished with you, you'll look like one of us.'

'What? How?'

'You'll see. Shouldn't take more than an hour or so. You'll join me later?'

'By all means.'

Khalima left.

Cassius stood there for a moment, not quite sure what to do with himself. 'Do you speak Greek?'

'And a little Latin,' said Golpari. Her voice was almost as enticing as her face. 'Which would you prefer?'

'Greek is fine.'

Golpari gestured to a large cushion below a lantern. 'Could you kneel there, please?'

'Happy to.'

Farrai and Elymaris went to the back of the tent, where there were several wooden chests and some mixing bowls. Golpari brought over a stool and sat in front of Cassius. Unable to see much of the rest of her body because of her robes, he found himself staring at her face – and what a face it was. Her skin was flawless and surprisingly pale, though more surprising still were her eyes. They were an entrancing light blue, brilliant amidst the dark kohl and beneath the sweep of black hair.

'You are fair,' she said. 'But I'm sure we can do something.'

As she spoke, Cassius's gaze drifted to her plump, sensuous lips. It took him a while to remember what she'd said and formulate a reply.

'Er . . . what exactly?'

The girls returned with two bowls. One contained a watery brown liquid, the other a thicker black substance.

'Yuk.'

'The brown is for your skin. It is a mix of plant dyes and oils. Usually we use it for decoration, like a tattoo. It will stain the skin temporarily.'

'How temporarily?'

'It will wash off gradually over a period of weeks.'

'And the other one?'

'That's for your hair. It contains many ingredients including vinegar, nut extract and . . .' She gave a little smile and consulted the other girls for a translation. '. . . and leeches.'

'Leeches? By the gods.'

The three girls laughed.

'It's harmless,' said Golpari. 'It too will wash out after a while.'

'Very well. I suppose I shall just have to trust you.'

'What will you be wearing? How much of your skin will be visible?'

'I can keep my riding breeches on, I suppose. Face and hands should be enough.'

Golpari took a dark cotton sheet from Elymaris. 'It will be easier if you take off your tunic. I'll have to do some of your neck.'

'I'm sure you know best.'

Cassius removed his boots and socks, then his belt. Farrai and Elymaris took them and put them to one side. Cassius couldn't actually stand up straight in the tent so he bent over and Golpari helped him take his tunic off over his head, leaving him in just his loincloth. He had spent enough time naked around both men and women not to feel self-conscious, though he imagined his newly acquired tan lines looked rather unattractive.

Golpari gestured at the cushions and he knelt down again. She had to lean forward to wrap the sheet around him and Cassius breathed in the heavenly scent she was wearing. After a week on the road with the men, being alone with these three was really quite delightful.

Once the sheet was tied, Golpari took a brush and put it into the liquid. 'Now, Master Cassius, close your eyes.'

8

An hour later, the transformation was complete. Golpari held up a mirror.

'By Jupiter.'

Cassius watched the new him frown. He really did look like an easterner. His hair and skin were as dark as Indavara and Simo's and looked convincingly natural. Golpari had even tinted his eyebrows with an appropriate tone.

'Did we do well?' she asked.

'Exceptionally well.'

'You must not wash – tonight *or* tomorrow.'

'Oh, really?' said Cassius. 'But it smells a bit.'

'That will wear off too.'

Golpari removed the sheet and picked up his tunic.

'Shall I put it on for you?'

'Please.'

Cassius used every last moment to examine that wonderful face and commit it to memory.

'Come on, then, who's going to crack the first joke?'

The men had gathered around their own fire. Cassius came close enough to the flames so that they could see him. Their reaction confirmed the quality of Golpari's work.

'Remarkable, sir,' said Yorvah. 'Just like one of us now.'

Simo peered at him. 'Amazing, sir. Amazing.'

Indavara was sitting against some sacks of fodder, nibbling a piece of lamb stuck to the end of his dagger.

'Well?' said Cassius.

'You look the same,' said Indavara, 'but darker.'

'Insightful as ever.' Cassius sat down next to him. 'Get me a plate of something, would you, Simo, I'm starving. Oh, have you finished the agreement?'

'Yes, sir. Both copies.'

'What's that smell?' asked Indavara.

'Me. Apparently it will wear off.'

Indavara downed the rest of the meat then let out a satisfied belch. 'Delicious. That Censorinus knows his lamb.'

'Fancy a few drinks to wash it down?' asked Cassius. 'Khalima has invited me for an evening drink with my senior men. That means you and Mercator.'

'If you like.'

'Best behaviour. We will be relying on these people.'

'Ha!' cried Khalima when they arrived at his tent. 'Look at our new Arabian friend! Did I not tell you that wife of mine has a talent?'

'Indeed she does,' said Cassius.

The Saracen appeared the picture of contentment, again leaning back on a mountain of cushions with his two sons beside him. A teenage girl was kneeling to one side.

'Please, sit.'

More cushions had been put down at the guests' end of the tent. Dividing them from their host was a line of bowls containing various foods. Khalima clapped his hands and the girl poured wine from an ornate silver jug into equally expensive goblets. She placed one in the hand of each of the three guests then left. Nothing was said while this was going on and Cassius felt himself growing rather nervous. After their earlier meeting, he felt he had some measure of the Saracen but he doubted Mercator would feel much more comfortable than Indavara.

The chief gestured to his left. 'My oldest son, Miraz. He will take my family and the caravan on to Petra.'

Miraz looked like a younger version of his father, though he clearly preferred a more natural look for his beard. He offered a vague nod.

Khalima gestured to the right. 'Adayyid, my youngest. He will accompany us.'

Adayyid was slimmer than his father and brother. He was slumped languidly against the cushions.

'A pleasure,' said Cassius.

'Please, eat,' said Khalima.

Mercator selected some dates and seeds. Though full after the lamb, Cassius took a handful of raisins. Indavara grabbed a selection of everything and noisily devoured it all.

Cassius gave an apologetic grin and aimed a thumb at him. 'Never needs a second invitation.'

'A body such as that needs feeding,' said Khalima. 'Were I a few years younger I might challenge your friend to an arm wrestle, but I fear I might embarrass myself.' He turned to Mercator and spoke in Nabatean. The exchange was brief but – to Cassius's relief – friendly.

'I asked Mertan if he likes our little oasis,' continued Khalima in Greek. 'It is good that your men will enjoy a pleasant night's rest. We have far to go tomorrow.'

'Khalima, I wonder if you could tell us a little more about your business. We can pass it on to the men; and will be prepared if any of us are questioned.'

'Of course.'

Khalima did precisely that, outlining the basics of his work and the incense trade. Cassius had to nudge Indavara several times when he seemed not be listening. After Khalima had finished, Cassius supplemented his knowledge with a few precise questions.

The chief then told Adayyid to refill everyone's goblet and asked Indavara how he had acquired such a remarkable number of scars. Fearing an awkward exchange, Cassius intervened, joking that Indavara was 'accident prone'. Fortunately, Khalima pressed him no further.

'My people have a tradition of telling stories,' said the Saracen. 'Miraz will start us off. But you three had better start thinking of a good one – we consider it rude not to contribute.'

Miraz's tale involved an unfortunate merchant who became rather too close to his camel and met a sticky end. Cassius wasn't really one for jokes or humorous tales but Indavara and Mercator seemed to enjoy it and he made himself laugh along.

'And now it is the turn of our guests,' said Khalima.

'Do they have to be funny?' asked Mercator.

'No, not at all. We just like a good story. Anything interesting or entertaining. As long as you keep the listeners listening.'

'I have a few,' said Indavara, who had already finished his second goblet of wine.

As the bodyguard usually struggled to string more than a few sentences together, Cassius couldn't imagine what he would come up with. 'Why don't I go first?'

'Please,' said Khalima.

Despite his reticence about comic offerings, Cassius retained a bank of amusing tales for social occasions and he chose one guaranteed to elicit a few laughs. Rejecting any of the more subtle anecdotes, he instead opted for one from his teenage years.

Having successfully wooed a neighbour's daughter back in Ravenna, he'd had to escape her room via a tree. His toga had got caught on a branch and he'd eventually found himself hanging several feet from the ground with his nether regions exposed. When the girl's father arrived he'd expected a beating at the very least. However, it turned out the man was in desperate financial straits and eager to marry off his daughter as soon as possible. He not only helped Cassius down from the tree but made his wife repair the tunic.

'Did you see the girl again?' asked Adayyid.

'No,' said Cassius. 'But I still have the tunic.'

Khalima laughed until his whole broad frame was shaking. He then took his turn; a scatological tale about an inept doctor and his bizarre prescriptions.

To Indavara's dismay, Mercator weighed in next with a spectacularly dull anecdote; something about a mix-up with some signal flags. Adayyid then offered his contribution – a short but engaging tale about a remarkable coincidence. Then it was Indavara's turn.

Cassius couldn't help feeling apprehensive on his behalf but the bodyguard was by now onto his fourth goblet of wine and seemed keen.

'I was a fighter,' he said. 'It's true.'

He was holding the goblet at a dangerous angle. To avoid any wine spilling on the rug beneath them, Cassius took it from him and put it down. Indavara didn't seem to notice.

'There was this trainer, Derkylos. He fought with sword and shield. Big tall sod. He didn't believe in taking your time, softening the man up. With him it was always: "The head! The head!" That was all he ever said: "The head! The head!" Anyway, somehow he got into debt so he decided to return to the arena – a one-off contest for the money. He was in a pair, up against these two

Africans. I wasn't fighting until the next day so I was watching with this other fellow, Krantor. Towards the end of the bout Derkylos lost his shield. Can you guess what happened?'

'No,' said Khalima.

'Can you?' he asked Miraz.

'No.'

The bodyguard reached for his goblet.

Cassius moved it away. 'Just finish the story.'

'So anyway, this African got Derkylos against the wall. The first swing shattered his blade, the second one took his head clean off. Clean off.'

Indavara made a cutting motion with his hand. 'Krantor started laughing and I couldn't work out why because I liked Derkylos and although it was quick I didn't like seeing him go.'

'Yes,' said Khalima. 'And?'

'Krantor was still laughing. He pointed at Derkylos and said: "The head, the head!"'

Indavara looked around at the blank faces and chuckled to himself. 'Ah, it was funny. Very, very funny.'

XXI

As the tents were taken down and the two groups prepared to leave, Cassius returned to the quiet cool of the date palms. He walked up to the water and looked at his reflection. The bright dawn light showed the full extent of his new colouring.

'By the great and honoured gods.'

Of all the turns his life had taken since joining the Service, this was surely the most bizarre. Yet he was grateful for Khalima's help; infiltrating Galanaq sounded hard enough – he certainly didn't want any extra attention coming his way.

He looked across the pool. While the auxiliaries packed their gear away, Ulixes stood alone with his horse. The previous evening, while Cassius had checked that all the money was still in the barrel, Indavara had queried why he didn't just pay the man off and cut him loose.

It was a fair question. Khalima had corroborated the significance of Galanaq and it seemed likely this man Ilaha would keep the stone there. Ulixes himself was desperate to leave and Indavara, Mercator and the others would be glad to see him go. But – after some consideration – Cassius had decided to keep him around.

He could not be certain of Khalima. The Saracen didn't seem like a man to renege on a deal but he was in effect turning against his own, and who knew what they would find at Galanaq? With this meeting of chiefs – Khalima's clan leader included – the situation would be complicated, fluid and dangerous. If the chief's nerve failed him, there was no one else but Ulixes who knew the area; no one else to help them escape.

And there was another reason. Even if Cassius did give the gambler his money and let him go, what was to stop *him* betraying them to Ilaha? Unlikely perhaps, but Ulixes clearly wasn't happy with his cut and – unlike Khalima – he knew exactly why they were headed to Galanaq.

Cassius nodded to himself, satisfied with his original decision. When – and if – they located the stone, the gambler could leave.

He snapped off a dead reed and flicked it into the water, shattering his reflection.

As well as Ulixes, he now held another man's fate in his hands. He looked at the busy auxiliaries; twenty had become eighteen, and now he had to lose another.

—8—

Most of the horses were loaded and some of the men had already mounted up but Indavara and Simo seemed to be lagging behind.

'Hurry up, you two,' said Cassius as he trotted past them up to the ridge.

In his hand was a cloth bag containing two encoded letters – one for Abascantius, one for Calvinus – each detailing what he had learned about Ilaha (including the attack on Ruwaffa) and the assistance secured from Khalima. Accompanying Calvinus's letter was a copy of the agreement which Cassius and the Saracen had both signed.

Cassius had disclosed little about his intentions; merely that the party would proceed to Galanaq and he would report back at the next available opportunity. How his superiors reacted to what he'd discovered was up to them; by the time they knew of it, Cassius's party would be deep in the mountains.

Mercator was with Andal and Yorvah. Cassius would gladly have entrusted either man with the task of delivering the letters but he couldn't spare them.

The optio looked at the bag. 'So who are we sending?'

'Apollinaris.'

The big auxiliary did not welcome the news. When Cassius and Mercator went to tell him, he screwed his eyes shut and shook his head.

253

'Sorry,' said Mercator. 'But Officer Corbulo here needs a reliable man.'

'Quite so.' Cassius also needed someone who people would think twice about taking on. 'I appreciate that you don't want to leave the others but these letters are extremely important. One is bound for the governor himself.'

Apollinaris cheered up a bit. 'To Humeima, sir?'

'Yes. Report to the senior officer at the fortress and tell him these are for the imperial post – utmost urgency.'

Apollinaris took the bag and tucked it into his tunic.

A shout went up behind them and Khalima's people set off to the north, with Miraz in the lead. Some of the older children rode mules while the younger ones sat behind their mothers and sisters. Khalima, Adayyid and ten of his warriors watched the rest of their clan leave.

'You'd better go,' Mercator told Apollinaris.

'With them?'

'No,' said Cassius. 'Too slow. I suggest you head straight for the road, leaving the formation to the south. You should make Humeima by nightfall. Stop for nothing and no one. Those letters *must* arrive. Wait for us at the fort.'

'Understood, sir. Can I say farewell to the men?'

'Go ahead.'

Mercator was looking at the Saracens. 'I'm not sure Khalima's warriors are as happy with this new alliance as he is.'

'Possibly not. But I gather they're mostly nephews and cousins. I doubt we need concern ourselves with their loyalty.'

Mercator inspected Cassius's clothes – he had changed into his dullest tunic and riding trousers. 'So no more pretty colours and bracelets, eh? Sure you're ready to rough it with the rest of us?'

'A rather sudden demotion, but I think I'll manage.'

In fact, Cassius found it rather pleasant to be temporarily free of the travails of command. He and Mercator stayed at the rear while Khalima returned them to the Incense Road in good time. With the sky patched with white cloud and the temperature warm rather than hot, they continued southward. The road was marked only by intermittent lines of pebbles and took occasional diversions around rock formations both large and small.

Later in the morning, Cassius moved up to give Indavara more guidance on his riding. He was not at all bad now when walking, so Cassius asked him what problems he had at speed and offered advice. Despite his obvious hangover, Indavara seemed to appreciate the help.

Just after midday they passed a caravan heading north, each of the fifty men towing a packhorse or camel heavily laden with the usual jars of incense. Once they were past, Khalima dropped back to speak to Cassius.

'Their leader is named Anzarekk. I have met him before but I thought a conversation best avoided.'

'Quite so. He belongs to your tribe?'

'No. That was the other reason I ignored him; his ethnarch is Kalderon – one of our more fiery chiefs. I'm sure he will already have allied himself to Ilaha. Like many, he has harboured ill will towards Rome since the Palmyran war.'

'Do Kalderon and Ilaha and their like not appreciate the fact that Rome has never even tried to conquer their lands? There are many other provincials with a good deal more to complain about.'

'That is only because your masters know they would fail,' said Khalima. 'And don't forget, Rome has repeatedly called on us to lay down our lives in the defence of the province.'

'Surely you would have done so anyway?'

'Certainly, but on our own terms. No offence, but we would have stood more chance against Zenobia's horde without the Roman commanders. They do not understand how to use the desert as we do. People were hopeful about Aurelian but now it seems not even he can bring peace.'

Cassius didn't want to argue with the man so he changed the subject. 'The Saracens don't actually harvest the incense, correct?'

'We never have. It grows best in the coastal areas near the Arabian Sea, almost a thousand miles south of here.'

'What is the ocean like?'

'Like any other. But on a clear day you can see what your people call Dioscorides' Island.'

'I vaguely recall the name.'

'Great winged beasts dwell there, guarding a distant land far over the sea. We have our own term for the creatures in Nabatean. You Romans use the northern word. Dragon.'

'You have seen these beasts, I presume?'

Khalima stroked his beard. 'Not personally. But then I don't suppose you've seen Jupiter either. Does that mean he doesn't exist?'

Cassius had no desire to get into that one. 'Back to the incense – so the south Arabians grow it, you Saracens move it?'

'For centuries it has worked this way. Of course, your antecedent Aelius Gallus tried to take the lands of both peoples but he didn't fare very well.'

'Strabo tells us he was betrayed by the locals,' replied Cassius.

'He failed for the same reason that an invasion would fail now. You Romans cannot build one of your big roads through there. You will never govern the Sea of Sand. That is why you need us.'

'I daresay you're right.'

'They came through this area,' continued Khalima. 'Gallus and his men. I have seen markings on the rocks at Ruwaffa – dedicated to the emperor Augustus.'

'How far is Ruwaffa from here?'

'A couple of days' ride west. In my grandfather's time there was an entire legionary cohort split between there and Hegra. Calvinus should have known that leaving a single century so far from help was a risk.'

'And a tempting target for Ilaha.'

'Indeed.'

Khalima looked forward and cursed in Nabatean. 'My son is a wonderful boy; brave and bright – but he always rides too slowly!'

The Saracen galloped away.

For the rest of the day they saw only the occasional trace of humanity; refuse left by the road, the scorched skeleton of a cart, some distant riders visible only by their dust trails. The quiet worsened Cassius's sense of unease as they traversed the edge of the desert, hemmed in by the lifeless wastes to the east, the forbidding mountains to the west. With every passing mile, they were farther from help and deeper inside this foreign land.

At dusk they made camp by the road. Khalima seemed confident the weather was set fair and with sentries drawn from both his men and the auxiliaries on guard, the night passed without incident.

As evening approached on the following day, the Incense Road began to veer east, at which point they left it. Khalima picked up a westbound track even less clearly marked than the road and within a few hours they came to a pass between two imposing peaks, each at least a thousand feet high. Scree lined the pale grey slopes and lay close to the track.

Khalima insisted they were still too far from Galanaq to be concerned about Ilaha's men, but brigands were known to operate in the area and he advanced warily through the pass. Twice they stopped because of noises from above but it was nothing more than sliding scree.

Beyond the pass, they found themselves in a landscape unlike any Cassius had seen or could ever have imagined. Separating them from the next group of mountains was a plain perhaps three miles across. The ground was unremarkable – sand dotted with thin shrubbery – but the shapes of the scattered rock formations were surreal. Sandy brown in colour, some resembled pyramids and towers, others enormous logs or beehives. Dead ahead was one so weathered and striated that it looked like a giant mushroom – a broad, curved head standing on a narrow body.

Adayyid had ridden at the rear for most of the day. 'Good shelter and a spring,' he told Cassius and Mercator. 'We will spend the night there.'

Cassius looked south and spotted a distant line of camel-riders also heading west. 'What about them?'

The Saracen seemed unconcerned. 'Could be a caravan headed for the coast. Or going to Galanaq like us.'

Khalima opted for the northern end of the 'mushroom' and the entire party was able to shelter under the enormous overhang. As he dismounted, Cassius noted Indavara glancing warily upward.

'Feels like it could fall at any moment, eh?'

'I don't want to sleep under that.'

'Calm yourself, it's probably been there for thousands of years.'

'At least,' said Khalima, stretching his arms as he walked over to them. He pointed at the base of the formation. 'There are ancient drawings there. People have been stopping at this place since the beginning of time.'

'You saw the riders?' asked Cassius, taking off the sword Mercator had lent him.

'I did. Tomorrow we will join the road to Galanaq – I'd be surprised if we didn't see many others converging on the town.'

'These ethnarchs,' said Cassius, lowering his voice. 'How many men will they have with them?'

'Usually they travel with an honour guard of their finest warriors. Perhaps fifty or a hundred swords. Although Ilaha has organised the meeting alone, it is not unlike a gathering of the Tanukh. These occasions can be a chance for the chiefs to show off their riches and their strength.'

'And Ilaha?'

'He has a hand in the caravan trade himself and has gathered around him the single largest force of warriors. Probably two or three thousand men, though there won't be that many at Galanaq. The town is small and there is little fertile land close by.'

Cassius would have liked to grill Khalima about every last detail of the place but that risked betraying his true purpose.

'How long are you intending to stay there?' asked the Saracen.

'Until this meeting of the ethnarchs at least. In case I can glean any information about the result and their future intentions.'

'As long as you don't expect me to provide it.'

'Of course not.'

The pair moved aside to let the auxiliaries lay out their bags and bedding.

'By the way,' said Khalima, 'there are only two ways in and out. One is the road we will pick up tomorrow. The other is what they call the Goat Trail. Horses and camels can just about get through. It runs west all the way to the coast and comes out not far from the port at Leuke Kome.'

The Saracen moved off. 'We shall get a fire going. The nights can be very chilly under all this cold rock.'

Cassius hurried over to Mercator. 'Sounds like we'll be encountering more tribesmen tomorrow; others headed for Galanaq, perhaps even Ilaha's guards. I want the men to mix with Khalima's people; get to know each other, practise your Nabatean.'

'Very well.'

Cassius picked his way through the auxiliaries over to Ulixes. The ex-legionary had grown even more reticent since their arrival at the oasis and had barely spoken to anyone for two days. Forcing himself to ignore the odour of the man, Cassius asked whether he was all right.

'Wonderful,' he replied, not looking up as he unrolled a blanket.

'Do you know Galanaq well?'

'Surely you don't need my advice any more.'

'Actually I do.'

'Can't you get what you need from your Saracen friend?'

'You can only get what *you* need from me, so I suggest you cooperate.'

Ulixes dropped his blanket in the dust. 'I've been there a couple of times. Why?'

'What are the ways in and out?'

'The main road and the coast road, which ends up at Leuke Kome.'

Cassius was relieved to discover Ulixes did indeed know something.

Looking past him, he saw the pictures Khalima had mentioned. Carved into the rock were images of numerous creatures drawn at unlikely angles. Amongst them were lions, hyenas and cheetahs.

'Those animals once roamed these lands?'

'So they say. There are images like that all over these mountains. They come from the ancient times.' Ulixes smiled slyly. 'It seems a new predator rules here now. One who defies Rome and takes what he wants from the Emperor.'

'Keep your voice down.'

'This operation is suicidal. What chance do you few have of getting away with that rock? What are you planning to do – roll it all the way back to Bostra?'

Despite the smell, Cassius stepped closer to him. 'You just want your money, correct? Well, in a couple of days you just might get it, and then you can roll *yourself* back to Damascus or wherever it is you come from.'

'Even assuming we get into Galanaq, there's not much chance we'll get out.'

'No wonder you're a poor gambler,' countered Cassius. 'You seem averse to any kind of risk.'

'Actually I am a very good gambler – mainly because I know when the odds are against me.'

––◆8◆––

By nightfall the men were settled. Khalima had assured Cassius they could do without the tents but advised him to wrap up well. The temperature had already dropped sharply and almost the entire party was gathered around a large fire of wood drawn from both supplies. Even though the auxiliaries and the tribesmen were sitting in distinct groups, Cassius had been glad to see a good deal of chatter amongst them and some exchanging of food; Yorvah had offered Khalima's men the last of Censorinus's lamb, and in return the auxiliaries had dined on spiced goat.

Ulixes had already taken himself off to bed. Cassius glanced over his shoulder at the prone figure lying next to the rock wall. He had instructed Indavara and Simo to place their gear close by; he wanted Ulixes where he could see him.

Unlike the Romans, Khalima and his men left their horses loose and the animals wandered around the edge of the camp. Some of the auxiliaries had the dice out again but didn't look particularly involved in their game; after the incident at the tower, Mercator had insisted that they not play for coin. The ever-conscientious optio was checking their supplies. The ever-sociable Yorvah, meanwhile, was sitting with Adayyid and some of the other Saracens, one of whom was demonstrating his juggling skills with four stones.

'Good for the reflexes,' observed Indavara. 'Might take it up myself.'

'Did you see the pictures on the rock?' asked Cassius.

'The locals probably hunted those animals. Maybe that's why they're not here any more.'

'There are pictures like that in many parts of the world,' said Cassius. 'They come from before Rome, before everything.'

'Did the gods make animals as well as men?' asked Indavara.

'Most people think so.' Cassius looked around; no one else was paying any attention to their conversation. 'Though Simo would tell you it was *a* god, of course.'

The attendant – who was sitting between them – continued to eat his allocation of spiced goat.

'Did the gods make the animals for us to eat?' asked Indavara.

'Yes,' said Cassius.

'But not all animals can be eaten.'

'True. In fact, some like to eat *us* – as you well know from our outing in Cyrenaica.'

Indavara grinned.

Cassius turned to Simo. 'Never seen anything like it.' He'd recounted the tale to the Gaul before but couldn't resist telling it again. 'They threw him into a pit to face this big old lion called Chief, which they'd given a taste for human meat. I thought he'd had it but what did he do? Pulled off his belt and used it to whip the beast across the nose. Poor thing jumped back twenty feet.'

Cassius reached over and clapped Indavara on the shoulder. 'Ha! By Jupiter, that shut Carnifex and his cronies up.'

'Lions are also used in the arena,' said Simo. 'To kill.'

Cassius kept his voice down. 'To kill your people. Yes.'

'I heard of that,' said Indavara. 'It used to happen in Pietas Julia.'

Simo said, 'It used to happen everywhere.'

'Barbarism,' added Cassius. 'Nothing more. Though I have to say, they could have been spared. All they had to do was offer a simple prayer to the Emperor.'

'Why not just do it?' said Indavara. 'Better than dying.'

'My thoughts precisely,' said Cassius. 'But like some of Simo's friends in Antioch, they actually wished for death.'

'Strange,' said Indavara.

'Not if you believe you are going to a better place,' replied Simo quietly, his face at peace.

'Death is death, Simo. The end. You may believe that your Christ returned to life but I certainly don't.'

'Excuse me, sir. I need to find your sleeping tunic.' Simo got up and walked away.

'He always does that when the questions get too difficult,' said Cassius.

'Why did the gods make us?' asked Indavara.

'I've said it before and I'll say it again. You have a remarkable gift for irony.'

——8——

A pleasant peace enveloped the camp as the men lay down under their blankets. The fire burned to grey, giving off a good deal of heat for those closest to it. Cassius, Indavara and Simo were too far away but the Gaul had employed every last cover and cloak to ensure his master was well insulated.

Cassius lay on his side, staring out at the night sky beyond the overhang. There was a tinge of purple splashed across the firmament, where thousands of stars shone. It was quite beautiful and he wondered, not for the first time, why so many – the new Emperor and this man Ilaha included – devoted themselves to the sun, when as much time was spent under the stars and the moon. Cassius preferred them; they seemed tranquil and benevolent.

Shortly after he drifted off to sleep, he was woken by the sound of Indavara quietly cursing. He turned over and watched the bodyguard disentangle himself from his blankets.

'What are you doing?'

'It's no good. I can't sleep under this bloody thing.'

Indavara picked up his covers, stepped over Simo and relocated to a spot beyond the overhang. Annoyed by the disruption, Cassius feared he would struggle to get back to sleep. He needn't have worried.

—◆8◆—

At first he thought it was a dream. Whispering voices, then a cry, then the sounds of a scuffle.

'What—'

'You thieving piece of shit.'

'Let go of me, you arsehole!'

Cassius sat up and turned round. Just behind his bed, two dark figures were grappling in the darkness. Still half-asleep, he couldn't work out who they were.

Flames flashed past him. Mercator was holding a torch in one hand, his sword in the other.

Indavara and Ulixes were standing over the wine barrel. The bodyguard had a firm grip on Ulixes's tunic; the ex-legionary was trying to get free.

'What's going on here?' demanded Mercator as Cassius got up.

'Nothing,' said Ulixes.

'Liar.' Indavara turned to Cassius. 'He was snooping around our stuff.' Indavara nodded down at the barrel, then pushed Ulixes away. 'Saw his opportunity when I moved.'

263

'Gods, man, you're paranoid,' said the gambler. 'I was after a drink from the barrel is all.' He raised the mug in his hand.

Some of the men were stirring, asking each other what was going on.

'You don't have any water?' demanded Indavara.

'I wanted a proper drink. Can't sleep.'

'Horseshit.'

Mercator turned to Cassius. 'Well?'

Cassius took the torch from him. 'I'll deal with this.'

Mercator withdrew and told the auxiliaries to go back to sleep.

Indavara whispered to Cassius. 'He knows what's in there. He meant to take it and escape.'

'Calm down or *everyone* will know what's in there.'

Cassius gestured for the gambler to return to his bed. 'Please.'

After a bitter glance at Indavara, Ulixes walked away. The bodyguard looked about ready to punch him.

'All right,' whispered Cassius. 'I believe you – he was up to something. But we can't prove he was trying to steal the money.'

Indavara muttered a curse. 'Do you really want to go into this enemy town worrying about what that sneaky bastard's going to do next?'

'Not particularly but the decision has been made.'

'Fine. But I'm not sleeping over here. You're on guard duty now.'

XXII

The rest of the night passed peacefully, as did the first hours of the day; and they saw no other travellers until they reached the Galanaq road.

Resting in the shadow of a towering rock face, they watched another group headed for the town. There were two dozen of them: a well-armed, grim-looking bunch who didn't seem interested in exchanging pleasantries. Once they were past, Cassius asked Khalima whether he knew them.

'No. But they were from one of the eastern tribes judging by those swords. Long and curved like the Persians use.'

Cassius gazed along the road. 'You're sure we won't make Galanaq by nightfall?'

'No, the road is too difficult. Also, I suggest that tomorrow we bide our time, perhaps wait for another – preferably larger – group to enter the town.'

'Less attention for us?'

'Precisely.'

They rode on, deeper into the mountains, eventually reaching the jagged peaks they'd been approaching since dawn. The range ran from east to west and from a distance seemed impassable, the tallest reaches at least a mile high. But now the road ran upward, winding its way over several interlocking spurs beneath the largest of the crags: a vast, dark pyramid.

'The Black Tooth,' said Adayyid, who was again riding close to the rear with Cassius. 'The rest of the going will be slow.'

265

Even though the Saracen was soon proved right, Cassius drew encouragement from the quality of the road: it zigzagged sharply to negotiate the steeper slopes and seemed well maintained. He saw numerous wheel marks and evidence that some areas had been cleared and flattened. If Ilaha's men had brought the stone in this way it would be no more difficult to bring it out.

As they passed the Black Tooth, Cassius observed eagles or vultures circling close to the summit. He also saw the huge hollows and ravines high on the mountain's flanks. It occurred to him that if the gods resided anywhere other than the sky, they might choose such a lofty, lonely place.

Later that afternoon, the road straightened and followed a fissure that tapered eventually to a gap no more than twenty feet across.

'The Scorpion Pass,' announced Adayyid as the party funnelled into pairs. 'And it's well named, so don't get off your horse.'

The tightest section of the pass was enclosed by a pair of almost vertical cliffs.

'It's the only way through for ten miles,' added the Saracen.

'Man-made?' asked Cassius.

'Nobody knows who carved it out – probably the same people that did the paintings.'

Etched upon the cliffs were scrawled writing and a collage of images in white and yellow: coiled snakes and prancing horses; suns, moons and stars; gods, kings and stick-men. But it was the faces that struck Cassius. Formed of only a few lines, they nonetheless captured something real, something human. He couldn't decide whether they were supposed to be frightened or frightening.

As the gap widened out again, he looked down at the stony ground. 'Haven't seen a scorpion yet.'

'You never see the one that kills you,' said Adayyid. 'My cousin was bitten not far from here. By the end he was begging for death.'

'Lovely part of the world,' said Cassius.

'There are spirits,' said Indavara. 'I can feel it.'

'I know what you mean. There's a chill about the place.'

'This is a forsaken land,' observed Simo. 'Nothing grows here.'

'At least the road's in good condition,' said Cassius, trying to sound optimistic.

'And easy to follow,' added Indavara.

'Just as well,' replied Cassius. 'Whatever happens in Galanaq, we'll be coming back this way.'

━■8■━

Once past the Black Tooth, the landscape opened up and they eventually found themselves above a steep valley. Like the line of mountains, it ran at right angles to the road, east to west. Beyond was an apparently endless maze of peaks and ridges.

With dusk close, Khalima called a halt at a broad, diamond-shaped slab of stone overlooking the valley. On the right side of it was a rock face, to the left the road descended along the side of the cliff. In the distance – just rounding a bend – were the horsemen from earlier.

Numerous sighs of relief and curses of exhaustion filled the air as the men dismounted. Khalima found Cassius and pointed along the road.

'It follows the cliff down to Galanaq at the eastern end of the valley. This is the best place for the night. It's called "the Step".'

'Just "the Step"? Seems a tad dull after the other place names round here. Sure there's enough space?'

'It's a well-known stop.'

Between the Step and the rock face to the right was a strip of sand and the remains of several fires.

'In any case,' added Khalima, 'there's nowhere else.'

'What about them?' asked Cassius, pointing at the easterners.

'There are some caves which they'll just about reach by night-fall. It's only a few hours from there to Galanaq.'

'Good. Ugh, what the . . .'

Cassius looked down at his boot. He had just trodden in a large black turd.

'One of the advantages of the site,' said the Saracen.

'How is that an advantage?'

'There are always a few ibex around.' Khalima nodded approvingly at the turd. 'That looks fresh.'

Adayyid handed his father a short bow and a quiver.

'Will you join us for a hunt?' asked the chief. He jabbed the bow at the valley floor. 'The ibex like to climb the ravines looking for food. If the gods smile, we'll bag one before sundown. Cunning creatures, tremendous sport. Well?'

'No, thank you.'

Cassius walked over to Mercator, who didn't seem impressed by their home for the night.

'Hardly enough room to swing a cat here.'

'I know,' replied Cassius. 'Let's sort the horses out.'

Khalima's men had already gathered their mounts in the corner of the Step, by the road. Cassius and Mercator helped the soldiers rope theirs in a single line along the strip of sand. Once plenty of water and fodder had been provided they moved away to give the animals space and time to calm down. Patch and the other mules were put between them and the Saracens' mounts.

Khalima led his men in a ceremony before the hunt. They knelt in a circle, took out charms and hurried through a chant. Once this was done, they followed their leader to the rear of the Step where there was a tiny gully Cassius hadn't even noticed. Khalima had to breathe in and hold his bow up as he squeezed through. In moments, the Saracens were gone, leaving only two men behind to watch their horses.

Once Ulixes's mount was tied to the others he took his gear and went to sit alone close to the cliff-edge. As Indavara and Simo started unpacking, Cassius looked at his hands. His reins had worn away a little of the dye but for the most part Golpari's work remained intact. He wished he had a mirror but Simo had assured him that the colouring still looked convincing.

Golpari. Cassius had seen only her face but had spent much of the last two days imagining what the rest of her looked like. Though he had never seen the Palmyran Queen Zenobia, he guessed she might be similarly sultry and exotic. There was an equally gorgeous Persian bar girl in one of the taverns back in Bostra. She earned enough to be picky but had propositioned Cassius a number of times. He couldn't really spare the money but now promised himself he would visit the tavern when – if? – they returned to the capital.

Around him, the men pulled off their boots and lay out their aching bodies. Ulixes threw pebbles off the cliff. Mercator stood with Yorvah and Andal, sharing a flask of wine. Indavara was scraping dirt off his boots with a stick. Simo was rummaging through a saddlebag.

'Ha. Look!'

One of the auxiliaries pointed upwards. Fifty feet above, an eagle was swooping past the cliff. Pinned in its talons was a struggling rabbit. The eagle stalled in midair, thrashing its wings.

'Go on,' cried one of the men. 'Rip it to shreds!'

'He got greedy – it's too heavy.'

'Nah – the eagle always triumphs.'

'He'll have to drop it.'

By now, every last man was watching.

The eagle suddenly let go. The rabbit fell, bounced off one of the auxiliaries' horses then landed on the ground.

Some of the men laughed and cheered.

Though bloodied, the rabbit was still alive. Panicked by the noise, it ran straight under the legs of another horse. The horse reared and fell to one side, striking the animal next to it. The others whinnied and shuffled away.

Mercator was the first to see the danger. 'Grab that one at the end!'

He ran across the Step but had to dodge around the auxiliories and their bags.

Khalima's men grabbed two of their mounts and pulled their animals towards the road.

Cassius looked at the other side of the step. The horse closest to the edge was bucking against the others, desperate to get clear of the cliff.

'Cut the rope!' yelled Indavara.

Mercator had made it through. He jumped down onto the sand and drew his dagger.

The horse fell onto its front knees, then was struck by another. It slid off the edge and disappeared.

As he tried to barge his way through the auxiliaries, Cassius saw another horse fall, eyes bulging as it slipped over the cliff.

'Cut it!'

'Cut the rope!'

Each of the mounts had a line looped around their neck which was attached to the main rope. Braving the lashing hooves of the third horse, Mercator darted forward and clamped one hand over the rope.

Cassius glimpsed Indavara and Andal at the other end, vainly attempting to pull the mounts back the other way. As the horse tottered on the edge, mouth foaming, Mercator slashed the blade down, severing the rope. As both ends flew away, he fell back.

It was too late for the horse. Something close to quiet briefly returned and Cassius heard the animal bumping against the rocks as it fell the hundreds of feet to the valley floor. He joined the others as they grabbed the mounts, helping Indavara and Andal steady them.

'Try to stay still,' ordered Andal. 'Calm them down.'

Though some were still whinnying and scraping the ground with their hooves, the wide-eyed horses gradually quietened again. The mules had been on a different rope; Patch and the others had remained safe throughout.

After a time, some of the men walked up to the cliff-edge and looked over it.

'Oh dear Lord,' breathed Simo.

The auxiliaries were cursing and shaking their heads.

'An eagle of all things,' said one.

'A terrible omen,' said another.

'A terrible *accident*,' affirmed Cassius.

Mercator's hands were still shaking as he fitted his dagger back into the sheath. 'We cannot leave the mounts like this.'

'Agreed.'

Cassius also wanted to keep the auxiliaries busy, knowing how quickly this talk of an omen would take hold: 'You men, listen. We're going to move the horses out back along the road – give ourselves more space. Andal, Yorvah, quickly now.'

In fact it was Cassius who took charge, chivvying the men along, giving anyone unoccupied something to do. Within a quarter-hour they had the horses spread out opposite Khalima's animals, with the best of the fodder to occupy them.

But the murmurings continued. When even Yorvah was heard to mention the 'omen', Cassius ordered Mercator to assemble the men. Given the effect of the accident and the fact that this was their last day before trying to enter Galanaq, he reckoned the time was right for a very specific concession, especially as Khalima and most of his men were absent.

While the auxiliaries gathered, he delved into the grain sack containing the satchel and pulled out the other item he had secreted there, which was wrapped in cloth. He walked over to a small outcrop of rock at the rear of the Step, the top of which was at head height. He waved Mercator and the men over and they formed a loose semicircle facing him. With Ulixes and the Saracens looking on, Cassius waited for silence before speaking.

'Well done, all of you. We shouldn't have any further problems here tonight. This was an unpleasant incident, but do not get drawn into fantastical talk. We all saw the bird drop the rabbit. The rabbit startled the horses. Simple cause and effect.'

'But an eagle, sir,' said one of the men. 'I've never seen such a thing.'

'Why now?' said another. 'It *has* to be a sign.'

'Accidents happen,' replied Cassius quickly. 'We've dealt with it. It's over. Do you think Jupiter would abandon his loyal followers because a bird drops its dinner? In any case, I wanted to take a moment together as a group. I realise that you men have had no proper opportunity to worship since we left Bostra. I don't think we will have another chance to do so. We shall pray to the god of gods.'

Cassius carefully unwrapped the bronze figurine of Jupiter, which he had liberated from the villa in Bostra. It was no more than six inches high, the metal dull and marked, but it would suffice. Cassius placed it on the outcrop and wedged it between two stones (the last thing he needed was another bout of superstitious rambling).

Mercator got down on one knee and the others swiftly followed. Cassius was grateful that Indavara and Simo did so too, though he knew neither would say the words. He checked the figurine a final time, then turned and knelt beside Mercator. He thought briefly about what to say, then began, allowing time for the men to repeat each line.

'Great and honoured Jupiter, king of kings, god of gods. We – your children, your followers, your warriors – are gathered here in the service of Rome and the Emperor. Pray favour us. Pray watch over us and deliver us from harm. In return we offer our ever-lasting love and fidelity. Great Jupiter, watch over us.'

———◄8►———

A welcome distraction arrived an hour later in the form of Khalima and his hunting party. Two of the warriors were carrying slain ibex over their shoulders, each with a single arrow wound to the neck. They were large animals – one male, one female – and caused a good bit of interest fom the auxiliaries.

Upon hearing what had happened, Khalima apologised for not seeing the danger and posted some of his warriors to watch all the horses. As his other men built up a fire farther down the road, he promised a good cut of meat for everyone.

By the time the meal arrived, the auxiliaries had settled down for the night but they tucked in with enthusiasm, all pronouncing it at least as good as Censorinus's lamb. Cassius allowed Adayyid to drop a portion on his plate to avoid causing offence but later gave it to Indavara. He couldn't face a thing.

XXIII

Cassius hardly slept. The valley below and the surrounding rock seemed to amplify every sound; every fall of scree, every bird's cry, every wolf's howl. But worst of all was the horses. Cassius lost count of the times he and various others sat up at the slightest noise from them, dreading a repetition of the earlier disaster. Simo seemed equally unsettled; Indavara snored through it all.

Grateful for the dawn, Cassius was one of the first up, walking a respectful distance down the road to relieve himself. On the way back he exchanged a greeting with Khalima, who was already breakfasting on more of the stringy ibex meat. Ulixes was still asleep, wrapped up in his blankets just feet from the cliff.

Brushing away thoughts of the fallen horses below, Cassius went to the outcrop and recovered the figurine. As he replaced it in his satchel, he noticed his papers and thought of Apollinaris. If all had gone to plan, both letters were now speeding north to Calvinus and Abascantius.

The men were beginning to stir. Cassius gave Simo and Indavara a gentle kick. 'Come on, you two, we're leaving within the hour.'

Mercator was already up. Belching and rubbing his stomach, he ambled over to Cassius. 'Not the most restful night I've ever had.'

'Me neither. I shall be glad to leave this place.'

Mercator looked along the road. 'Though at least here we only have ourselves to worry about.'

'For now our main aim is to just get through the gates. Remind the men: nothing but Nabatean. If anyone questions them, they must stick to the story and keep it simple.'

'Will do. So you three are supposed to be Syrian, yes?'

Cassius indicated himself, then Indavara, then Ulixes. 'Castor, Imbrasus and Ucalgen. Simo will stay as he is. I've come up with some details and a backstory. We'll go through it with everyone on the ride down.'

'Sir, what if we are discovered?'

'If we do have to escape or if we get split up, I suggest two rally points – here and the mushroom. Everyone should be able to find their way to those. And from there to Humeima.'

Mercator scratched his flattened, lumpen nose. He lowered his voice. 'And the rock? We'll need a big cart to get it back along this road.'

'If it is at Galanaq, then they brought it here all the way from Emesa, so there's no reason why we can't take it back.'

'You make it sound easy.'

Cassius bent his head towards the shorter man. 'Mercator, listen. I'll follow orders, but only up to a point. If there's no chance of recovering the stone, we'll withdraw. I'm not about to throw our lives away on some suicide mission, regardless of how much the Emperor wants the bloody thing. Establishing its location will still represent considerable progress. We can always just get the lie of the land and report back to Abascantius; let the top brass take it from there.'

'I'm glad to hear you say that.'

'All this for a rock, eh?'

———◆8◆———

The road clung to the side of the cliff and descended past precipitous drops and around perilous corners. Even though there was sufficient space, the party moved in single file; everyone seemed to prefer it that way. Around the third hour they passed a merchant heading a column of six carts. Cassius was relieved to see the vehicles negotiating one of the steeper slopes with little difficulty; the main preoccupation for the drivers seemed to be staying away from the edge.

Still bringing up the rear, he was one of the last to hear from the front that armed men were approaching. Khalima issued a few orders to his warriors; Mercator and the guard officers did the same. The party moved to the left side of the road as the first of the warriors rode into view.

The Arabian was moving quickly, his horse taking the slope at a trot. In his attire, he looked little different to Khalima's men or the auxiliaries. He was, however, armed to the teeth, with a sword at his belt, a long spear over his shoulder, and a circular shield hanging from his saddle. With no more than a cursory glance at the strangers, he continued on, followed by a dozen more warriors. Other than their heavy armament, the men displayed one other common feature: each had a bright yellow circle sewn onto their tunics over their hearts.

— ◾8◾ —

At midday they stopped to water the horses. An anonymous crack in the cliff turned out to be the top of a cistern; one of Khalima's men collected water via a roped pail and two others distributed it. Every last man seemed conscious of the previous evening's events and all took care to keep close control of their mounts.

Grateful that his horse continued to display a calm temperament, Cassius passed his reins to Simo and walked to the edge. The valley had narrowed to a canyon perhaps half a mile across. Directly below was the road; a few hundred yards ahead it turned back on itself then zigzagged down to the ground. From there it crossed a short causeway across a marsh – the first sign of fertile ground for days. Beyond the causeway, the road bent around to the left and finally reached the town.

Galanaq was protected by a massive, ancient-looking wall: row upon row of colossal grey stone blocks. A pair of masons were at work and, using them for scale, Cassius estimated the wall's height to be at least twenty feet. The arched gateway was secured by two huge timber doors, now slightly ajar. The only high structure within the town was a circular stone tower set just back and to the left of the gate. A large standard flew from a pole but Cassius could see nothing of the design. Gathered in front of the gate was a handful of guards. Two other groups of riders were waiting outside – one of about a dozen, the other twice that.

Inside the wall were around a hundred small, rock-built dwellings squeezed in between the broad central street and the sheer sides of the canyon. Galanaq seemed an arcane, primitive place. There were no large buildings, little use of timber or in fact any material other than the grey and black basalt.

Past the last of the houses was a stretch of open ground. On the left side scores of tents had been erected to form a large encampment. To the right was a walled complex with several buildings plus a corral and stables. It looked to Cassius very much like a military compound.

At the end of the road was a second, inner wall that ran for perhaps two hundred yards across the width of the canyon. The only way through was another arched gateway; here the doors were closed. Over the top of the wall, Cassius could see the dark mouths of numerous caverns hewn from the rock. A quarter-mile to the east was the end of the canyon; another vertiginous face at least three hundred feet high.

Cassius's stomach turned over as he at last saw the overwhelming obstacles that stood in their way. Locating the rock in this small town might prove the easy part. But getting it out? There was only one road, a pair of huge walls, and then the small matter of a three-day journey out of the mountains and two more to reach the safety of Humeima. And how many hundred warriors were down there, ready to protect the stone or give chase if it was taken?

Indavara and some of the auxiliaries were drifting across the road to join him but Cassius waved them back. As Simo returned his reins, he forced himself not to dwell on thoughts of the stone. It seemed likely that intelligence was the best they could hope to retrieve from Galanaq. First they had to get inside.

Once over the causeway, Khalima led the party off the road and sent Adayyid up to the gate. The large group had been allowed into the town but the smaller group remained outside.

Cassius looked at the tower. It was far more impressive up close; thirty foot high and twelve wide, with a high surround and several arrow slits. The two sentries on duty each had a bow over their shoulder and were surveying the new arrivals below. Cassius could also now see the detail on the big standard; another golden circle upon a square of purple.

'Fancy flag,' said Indavara.

'Hundreds of denarii's worth.'

'So this Ilaha's got lots of money and lots of men.'

'Looks that way.'

Cassius turned his attention to Adayyid. The Saracen had spoken to the guards at the gate and was now returning. Behind him, the smaller group were trudging towards the causeway, towing their horses. They didn't look happy.

Mercator walked over to Cassius as the departing swordsmen passed by. 'That's not good.'

'Possibly not. Go and tell the men to loosen up and mix in with Khalima's lot. They look apprehensive.'

'What's that mean?' asked Indavara. 'Apprehensive?'

Cassius didn't answer; he was watching Adayyid and Khalima, who were deep in discussion.

'Worried,' explained Simo.

Indavara grinned at Cassius. 'No one looks more . . . apprehensive than you.'

Cassius never ceased to be amazed at how Indavara could make japes on such occasions; then again, a man who'd fought for his life twenty times in the arena – and survived – was unlikely to be given to nerves.

'I'm fine.'

'Well, maybe Simo,' added the bodyguard.

Cassius had insisted the Gaul wore his seldom-used dagger and Khalima had lent him a sword, but he remained a rather unconvincing Syrian mercenary. Cassius was still wearing the spare blade Mercator had given him; a well-used piece with several chips out of the blade and a smooth bone handle.

'Simo, try and look a bit more like a fighting man. Also – you have a tendency to smile when you're nervous. Do not smile.'

Cassius moved subtly through the men to Khalima and Adayyid, wary of suspicious eyes at the gate.

Khalima turned his back to the guards and nodded at the warriors who had been sent away. 'They wanted to join Ilaha's force but weren't allowed in – no one here to vouch for them. Adayyid told the guards that we belong to Uruwat's tribe. He is already here so they will try to find someone to vouch for us. Shouldn't be a problem.'

'Shouldn't be?'

They had to wait for a quarter of an hour, though to Cassius it seemed twice that. He had retreated to the rear of the group once more, but looked on as the guards parted and two of their number appeared accompanying a third man with a piece of green cloth tied around his arm. The Saracen was wearing more gold than Khalima, and the pair met with an embrace and two kisses. The guards seemed satisfied and one of them handed Khalima a small woven basket. He passed it to Adayyid, who worked his way through the party, handing each man a piece of the green cloth.

'The man with my father is named Urunike,' he explained. 'Uruwat's son. Ilaha's men are concerned about all the new arrivals so we have to wear these to mark our tribe.'

Cassius took his piece of cloth and tried to tie it around his upper arm one-handed. As he struggled, Simo reached over to help him.

'Get off, you dolt,' snapped Cassius. 'You're a mercenary, remember? Not an attendant.'

'Sir, everyone's doing the same. It's impossible to tie it yourself.'

Cassius looked around and realised Simo was right. 'Ah. Very well, go ahead.'

Indavara grinned.

They walked the horses up to the gate and formed a line. Khalima went through first with Urunike, his performance an exemplar of jocular relaxation. The other Saracens also appeared at ease as they walked under the arch and past the guards, most of whom seemed uninterested.

Mercator had done a good job of mixing the auxiliaries with Khalima's men. Cassius was in the middle with Adayyid while Simo and Indavara were towards the back, with only Andal behind them. As Cassius passed the tower, his horse slowed and he gave it a tug to keep it moving. Glancing left, he saw an aged warrior sitting on the steps that led up to the tower's first floor. He was a rangy fellow with little hair and a white beard. He was wearing a sleeveless tunic and had a long, curved sword hanging from his belt. The veteran eyed Cassius from below a pair of remarkably bushy eyebrows.

Cassius kept his head down and quickened his pace. But after only a few yards he had to stop – there was some delay up ahead and the line had halted. Throat tight, he pulled up the collar of his tunic; even though the dye reached down as far as his chest, he was fearful someone might notice.

He heard a voice and turned to see the old warrior right behind him. The man spoke again in Nabatean.

Adayyid replied. The warrior listened but kept his eyes on Cassius.

'You with Khalima?' he asked in Greek.

'I am,' Cassius replied gruffly.

'Where you from?' The Arabian was chewing something that had stained his teeth green.

'Syria.'

'You a hired man?'

'Yes.'

The veteran pointed at his sword. 'Ever used that?'

'Many times,' said Cassius.

The warrior looked at his face, then his hands. 'Barely a mark on you. Never been caught with a blade?'

'I thought that was the idea.'

The Arabian considered this. When he started smiling, Cassius could see the dark leaf he was munching. The veteran chuckled, then returned to the tower.

The line got under way and Cassius walked on, swallowing back the lump in his throat. He looked ahead and saw that a column of mules were now were filtering onto the main street and holding up the new arrivals. Several men – Urunike and Khalima included – were shouting at them to move.

The line stopped again. Cursing under his breath, Cassius looked over his shoulder. The veteran had disappeared but two other guards were inspecting the strangers and seemed interested in Simo. Conscious of other eyes on him, Cassius turned back. *Don't smile. Just don't smile.*

Indavara watched the guards circle Simo and his horse. They exchanged a few comments then stood in front of the big Gaul, glaring at him. Simo responded with a warm smile.

The larger of the two men said something, his voice angry. Andal came forward to intervene but the guard waved him away with his spear. Indavara counted a dozen notches close to the iron head. From what he could see of the man, he suspected the Arabian had enjoyed carving every one.

'Hired sword?' asked the guard in Greek.

Simo nodded.

'Been with this lot long?'

Simo nodded again.

'Don't say much, do you? You simple or something?'

'He is actually,' said Indavara, dropping his mount's reins and walking forward.

The large man inspected him, then jutted his jaw towards Simo. 'What use is a cretin as a fighting man?'

'You haven't seen him in a fight. We're brothers. Normally he's as gentle as a lamb but in a scrap . . . well, you'd have to see it. Only fights when I tell him to. And *who* I tell him to.'

The guard tapped his fingers against the spear. 'That sounded a little like a threat.'

Indavara shrugged. 'Only a little.'

The big man came up close; close enough for Indavara to smell him. 'Best remember where you are, friend. This is Galanaq.' He planted a big, dirty finger on the sun emblem on his tunic. 'We're Lord Ilaha's guards and what we say goes. You got that?'

Indavara forced himself to appear compliant. 'Got it.'

Once clear of the gate, Cassius hoped his nerves might recede, but what he saw of the rest of the town did little to ease his mind. Judging by the smell, whatever sewage system they had in place was failing to cope. All the houses and inns seemed full and dozens of warriors – bearing eight different colours at the last count – had spilled out onto the street. They leaned against walls and gathered around benches and tables, watched by scores of guards. Women and children were outnumbered ten to one and those few Cassius saw seemed as unsettled as he was by the oppressive, febrile atmosphere.

One man lurched out of an inn, slurping from a flask and barely able to stand. A group of guards descended on him and in moments the wine had been knocked out of his hand and half a dozen kicks sent him sprawling to the ground. The guards left the drunk groaning with his face in a puddle, then barked at others from his tribe to deal with him.

Cassius followed Adayyid as they approached the track that led left and up a slight slope to the encampment. He glanced to the right, over the low walls of the compound. In contrast to the rest of the town, this area seemed highly organised, with only local warriors visible inside. As well as the stables and the corral there was also a small archery range and some wooden posts for sword practice. Smiths could also be seen at work, one hammering something on an anvil, the other adding coal to a forge. Closer to the road, scores of warriors were stacking boxes and barrels

281

under an awning. Also stored there were spears, shields and arrows.

Cassius's first few minutes in the town had already changed his view of this man Ilaha. Having previously thought of him as a more powerful version of Khalima – a tribal leader commanding desert warriors – he was now beginning to think of him as rather more like a general.

The only available space in the encampment was close to the side of the canyon. The base of the wall was dotted with small, shadowy entrances to what Cassius guessed were tombs. The free area had been marked out with twine and sticks and was close to the rest of Uruwat's tribe. The other Saracens looked on, each gathered with fellows bearing the same colour cloth upon their arms.

The impression of order was reinforced by the arrival of a middle-aged man bearing the solar symbol. He welcomed Khalima then pointed along the track towards the middle of the encampment and two larger tents. Cassius understood via Mercator that these were a latrine and a food tent, both of which they were free to use.

Cassius continued to play his role, unloading his horse like the others and resisting the temptation to approach Khalima and Adayyid, even when Urunike and the local man left.

'Nice welcome,' said Mercator as they helped the auxiliaries put up one of the tents.

'This Ilaha is clearly keen to keep the other ethnarchs onside.'

'But also leave them in no doubt about who is in charge,' added the optio, nodding at the distant compound.

'He has a small army here. And perhaps the other tribes are to be his auxiliaries.'

Adayyid was proving to be as competent a performer as his father. He yelled instructions at the men, then walked up to Cassius and spoke quietly. 'Uruwat and the other ethnarchs have been given quarters in the caverns beyond the inner gate. My father will go there shortly to pay his respects and talk to you when he returns. Until then, he suggests we keep ourselves to ourselves.'

'We'll pass it on to the men,' said Cassius. 'By the way, where's this Goat Trail?'

'Above the compound – you can't see it from here. What did you say to the old warrior?'

'Not much.'

'He is best avoided.'

'Isn't he a bit old for the rough stuff?'

'I wouldn't advise testing him out. His name's Theomestor.'

'*The* Theomestor?' said Mercator.

'You've heard of him?' asked Cassius.

'Of course.'

'He has fought for Ilaha's tribe since the older Charaz was in charge,' explained Adayyid. 'In his prime, he was one of the most lethal swordsmen in all Arabia.'

Cassius let out a breath. 'Lucky for me he has a sense of humour.'

XXIV

Gutha had to admit the cavern looked impressive. He hadn't actually been there before but knew it was the largest in Galanaq, larger even than the temple. On one side of the curved roof was a shaft that admitted a square beam of sunlight. In the middle of the chamber was a circular table around which were thirteen ornately carved chairs. Surrounding these were ten tall silver candelabra. None of the candles had been lit, nor was there any food or drink – that would come later.

Ilaha strode in, cloak flowing gaudily behind him. He placed both hands on the back of a chair and smiled. 'Suitably grand, don't you think? There'll be wine brought in from Gaza, a dozen different meats, fish fresh from the coast.'

'I have no doubt the ethnarchs will enjoy their meal,' replied Gutha. 'I just hope no stomachs are turned by what they hear afterwards.'

Ilaha tutted. 'You worry unnecessarily. When I have spoken they will understand that my plan is both equitable and achievable. Mother read the shadows and the offerings this morning. All the signs favour us.'

Gutha acceded with a nod.

'Anyway,' said Ilaha, 'why are you up here?'

'I saw Reyazz. He told me the stone is being moved outside later. Are you sure that's wise?'

'Not only wise but essential.'

'You will reveal it to all?'

'Of course. Tonight the chiefs will be persuaded, tomorrow the men.' Ilaha walked over to Gutha and gripped his shoulder. 'Have faith, my friend.'

'There's something else. Two new groups arrived today. One is of no concern – Yemanek's uncle and his men. The others are with a chief named Khalima – part of Uruwat's tribe.'

'I don't remember the name.'

'Commander Oblachus just notified me. I've done a little asking around and there is a certain amount of surprise that he's here. Apparently this Khalima is rather similar to our friend Mushannaf – his interest in coin usually outweighs other considerations.'

'Except perhaps loyalty to his chief. Nobody expected Uruwat to attend either but he is here and he is ready to listen. Maybe this Khalima simply wishes to be part of our great endeavour.'

'Possibly. But I have ordered an inspection all the same. Ilaha, you must appreciate the possibility that in amongst all these new arrivals there might be a Roman spy.'

Ilaha waved the suggestion away. 'Even if Calvinus were to hear of what is happening here he would be powerless to do anything about it. I told you – our time has come.'

'I have asked Oblachus to pay them a visit.'

'As you wish.'

Ilaha turned to leave but then paused. 'One more thing, Gutha. You should really address me as *Lord* Ilaha from now on.'

——8——

Cassius sat on his saddle just inside the tent, looking out at the track. Dusk was near but there was still enough light for him to see when Khalima returned from the meeting with Uruwat.

While Simo continued to unpack around him, he switched his gaze to the formidable inner wall. When he also considered the overwhelming number of guards and other warriors present, the whole concept of retaking the black stone now seemed almost laughable. How easy it must have been for Abascantius to concoct this scheme with no concept of the realities on the ground.

No, best to find out what they could, then slip away and make for Humeima. Galanaq's defences were impressive, but nothing compared to the colossal walls of the Roman fortress. Cassius wished he were already behind them.

'Starting to think you've bitten off more than you can chew?'

Cassius had almost forgotten Ulixes was in the tent. He turned. The gambler was lying on his side, a lamp flickering in front of him, that wolfish face grinning.

'Well, you're young,' he continued. 'Naive. Just another puppet for old Pitface. He must have been through dozens like you over the years.'

'I daresay,' replied Cassius, doing his best to affect nonchalance.

'I don't rate normal soldiering much,' said Ulixes. 'But at least you know where you are. A spy never knows who he can trust, how to tell friend from foe. And the bastards in charge are just as likely to get you killed as the enemy. After a while I couldn't take it any more.'

'So you chose to become a gambler and mix with upstanding citizens such as Zaara-Kitar. Spare me the lecture, Ulixes, you are most unconvincing.'

'I didn't choose the dice. The dice chose me. And like I said before, I know how to read the odds. Aren't looking too favourable now, are they?'

Determined to ignore him, Cassius looked out again and saw a dozen guards marching up the track. The large, limping figure at the front seemed to be staring right at him.

Mercator suddenly appeared outside. 'You see them? Adayyid says that's one of Ilaha's commanders. Looks like he's coming our way.'

'All right, calm down.'

'I'll warn the men.'

Cassius got up, and in his haste knocked over an unlit lantern. As Simo righted it, Ulixes chuckled.

'Perhaps it's you who needs to calm down.'

Cassius glanced towards the wine barrel and the grain sack, which had been purposefully buried under some other baggage.

'Outside,' he said. 'Let's not look like we're hiding.'

Ulixes got up and came forward.

'Sir.' Simo nodded at the gambler.

He was wearing a sleeveless tunic. Visible upon his upper right arm was a tattoo detailed in green ink. *SPQR.*

'Oh, sorry. I forgot.'

Cassius grabbed him by the collar. 'You stupid prick. You dare betray us and I'll—'

Ulixes swatted his hand away. 'You'll what? Don't forget I saw your performance at the spice market. Your bodyguard's not here now. Do you really think I'm scared of you?'

Cassius could hear the guards speaking as they approached. 'They see that tattoo, you won't see another sunrise.'

'Possibly. Unless I have something to offer them.'

Indavara ducked into the tent. 'You should come outside.'

Cassius was still looking at Ulixes. 'Cover it.'

The gambler picked up a sleeved tunic.

'Problem?' said Indavara

'Not any more. Everyone outside.'

As they joined Mercator, Adayyid and the men by their newly lit fire, the commander led his men off the track. He was an imposing figure, his broad frame heavy with muscle and fat. Like the others, his tunic bore the solar symbol, yet it was of notably higher quality. The commander was bald and clean shaven but this was a face crying out for hair and a beard: not a single feature was unmarked, symmetrical or in any way appealing. He carried a gnarled stick in one hand to help him walk. Cassius reminded himself to fade into the background as the commander spoke to Adayyid in Nabatean.

Mercator whispered a translation. 'His name's Oblachus, chief of guards. Wants to look around, check our gear. Adayyid told him we have nothing to hide but he's insisting. We must stay here while they carry out the search.'

Oblachus directed one man towards the horses, another to the supplies piled up close to the fire. The rest – some of whom were carrying lanterns – went into the tents. Oblachus limped over to the watching auxiliaries and tribesmen. He spoke to one of Khalima's men briefly, then moved on to Mercator.

With the chief guard occupied, Cassius looked at the tent. He could see the lanterns moving within and the guards' backs pressing against the covers. He doubted the barrel would arouse any suspicion, and even if it did the money could be explained away. The contents of the grain sack were another matter.

Please, Jupiter. Please.

Oblachus continued to examine the new arrivals. He switched to Greek. 'So where are these Syrians?'

Cassius stepped forward, along with Indavara, Simo and Ulixes.

'My grandfather was Syrian,' said Oblachus. 'He was a miserly prick but I'll try not to hold it against you.'

Like the others, Cassius manafactured a grin.

'Where are you from?' asked Oblachus, resting both hands on the top of his stick.

Cassius continued to affect a rough Syrian accent based on one of his father's gardeners. 'Antioch.'

'Who'd you fight for in the Palmyran war?'

'Wasn't here. We were in Thrace. We go where the work is.'

'Ever fight for the Romans?'

'Nah.'

Oblachus turned his gaze upon Ulixes. 'What about you?'

'Same.'

Oblachus nodded at Adayyid. 'How long you been with this lot?'

'Must be about a year now.'

Cassius tried not to show his relief. Ulixes *had* been listening.

Oblachus waved Indavara forward. 'What's your name?'

'Imbrasus.' Indavara didn't have to try to affect a rough accent; Cassius imagined he'd picked it up from his fellow gladiators.

'Why you carrying a Roman sword, Imbrasus?'

'I could ask you the same,' said Indavara.

'Just testing. Can't say a lot else for the arseholes but they know how to make a blade. So if you've been with Khalima's lot all these months, you must have been down the Incense Road?'

Cassius cringed. They had been over all this but Indavara wasn't the best when it came to remembering details.

'We have,' said the bodyguard. 'Twice.'

'Tell me – heading south from Sa'ada, what's the next stop?'

'Er, Yathul, is it?'

'It is.' Oblachus moved on. 'Now here's the fat lad. My friends down at the gate told me you're quite the swordsman. That true?'

Cassius didn't dare look.

Simo was staying quiet.

'You don't look like much of a fighter to me,' added Oblachus. 'Draw your blade.'

Adayyid walked over. 'Commander, I must protest. If my father were here—'

'If your father were here, he would be sensible enough to hold his tongue.'

'We were invited to Galanaq by Lord Ilaha,' continued Adayyid. 'This interrogation is—'

Oblachus aimed his stick at him. 'Shut your mouth, pup, or I will shove this so far up your arse you'll think you're a tree.'

Adayyid retreated. Simo was frozen to the spot, eyes wide, sweat glistening on his face.

'Draw your blade,' repeated Oblachus.

One of the guards called out. For a horrifying moment, Cassius thought they'd emptied the grain sack, but the man came out of one of the auxiliaries' tents. He hurried over to Oblachus and gave him a small object.

The commander limped over to the fire and held it up. 'Well, well. An interesting find.'

It was a small wooden figurine; a god holding a spear.

'Mars,' said Oblachus distastefully. 'Tell me, who has dared to enter Galanaq as a devotee of the Roman god of war?'

Mercator had reddened with rage. Andal looked almost as angry as the optio. Yorvah was chewing the inside of his mouth.

'It is mine.'

One of the younger auxiliaries stepped forward. Khiran – an excellent rider who often volunteered to do the cooking and had struck up a friendship with Simo.

Oblachus gave Adayyid a triumphant smirk. 'I knew something didn't smell right about you lot.'

The rest of the guards had finished their search. At Oblachus's order, they readied their weapons and gathered behind him.

Cassius could feel Mercator's eyes on him but he was still looking at the figurine. He decided to act quickly.

'Ha.'

Oblachus glared at him. 'Something funny, Syrian?'

'Not really. But if you want to have a go at our mate, you might want to take another look at that.'

Oblachus did so.

'No beard, right?' added Cassius, maintaining the low-born accent.

'So?'

'Mars is one of the Roman *father* gods. He has a beard. That ain't Mars.'

To Cassius's surprise, Ulixes spoke up. 'He's right.'

Now Oblachus was looking confused.

'That there is Ares,' said Cassius. 'Greek war god. Ares is young – no beard.'

Oblachus turned to the man who'd found the figurine. The guard shrugged. Two other, older men nodded. Oblachus aimed his stick at Khiran. 'That right?'

'Yes.'

'Well, Greek's better than Roman, I suppose, but as you can see' – Oblachus tapped the solar emblem on his tunic – 'we're of one mind in these parts when it comes to worship. You lot better get that message pretty quick if you want to stick around.'

He tossed the figurine into the fire.

To Cassius's amazement, Khiran ran at him. Fortunately, Andal and Yorvah blocked his path and grabbed him before he got very far.

Oblachus found this very amusing. 'Just trying to help you lads fit in, is all. Best watch yourselves. '

After a last look around, the commander addressed his men in Nabatean. They sheathed their swords and followed him back along the track.

Mercator ran up to Khiran, grabbed him round the throat and shoved him towards one of the tents. Andal and Yorvah followed. The others – auxiliaries and Saracens alike – remained where they were.

Cassius caught Indavara's eye. The bodyguard hurried after Mercator.

Cassius watched the guards disappearing into the darkness. 'By the gods.'

'Lucky,' said Ulixes. 'Very, very lucky.'

Simo was holding his chest and drawing in deep breaths. 'Is that true, sir? About the figurine?'

'Not entirely,' said Ulixes. 'Most images of Mars are of him as an older man, but some – like that one – show him as a youth.'

'So it wasn't Ares?' asked Simo.

'It was Mars,' said Ulixes. 'But your master here guessed that ignorant nomad wouldn't know the difference.' He offered Cassius an approving grin. 'Nicely done, grain man. It seems that you are not averse to the odd calculated gamble yourself.'

Having prevented Mercator from beating Khiran to a pulp, Indavara waited for the optio and the guard officers to leave the tent. Khiran lay in a corner, groaning, having been struck half a dozen times by his superiors. Indavara threw him a flask of water, then left. He reckoned Mercator and the others would have been justified; the idiot had risked all their lives. But they might need every last man fit and able to fight.

Realising the state Simo was in after his encounter with Oblachus, Indavara decided to keep him busy. They hadn't eaten yet so he asked the Gaul if he wanted to investigate the food tent. Simo agreed and they set off.

Some of the Saracens were working but most were sitting around their fires. Indavara had noticed how sociable these desert men were but there was little singing or laughter tonight.

'I don't like this place,' said Simo, staying close to the middle of the track.

'Me neither. But I've a feeling we won't be here too long.'

'Master Cassius hasn't told me much about what we're doing here but I'm not sure I really want to know.'

'It may not even happen,' said Indavara. 'I don't think he and Abascantius realised what it would be like here. These bloody guards – there's hundreds of them.'

Simo reached inside his tunic. 'That horrible limping man. I thought he was going to hit me with that stick of his.'

'Fortunate timing with them finding that figurine,' said Indavara. 'I bet you were praying. Perhaps your god answered you.'

'The good Lord has always watched over me, even in the darkest places and times.'

'If you really want to avoid dark places and times, you should find a new master.'

Indavara had often tried to draw Simo into criticising Corbulo, never with much success.

As they passed a group of Saracens coming the other way, Simo kept his head down. Indavara looked at them only to check the colour of cloth on their arms but it was too dark to tell.

'You should have seen him back in Bostra, Simo. He was in a right mess without you. We were starting to think you weren't coming back. He practically pleaded with me to come along.'

'As long as I can be of service to Master Cassius, I will remain by his side,' said the Gaul stiffly. 'I am not a freedman. I do not have the choices some others have.'

'Good point. And yet I'm here too. Which probably makes us as stupid as each other.'

They passed the latrine and reached the food tent. Simo slowed when he saw a pair of sentries outside but Indavara gave him a nudge. Just as they arrived, a trio of tribesmen left, each carrying a wicker basket full of food.

The sentries ignored the pair as they entered the tent. Several lanterns were hanging from the walls, illuminating a large and varied array of food in barrels, boxes and amphoras. Two serving women came forward. One said something in Nabatean and the other gave both of them a wicker basket then gestured at the food.

Given Galanaq's location there weren't a lot of fresh fruit or vegetables but Indavara was almost drooling as he ran his eyes over the rolls and loaves, the strips of dried meat and the wheels of cheese.

He beat Simo to the nearest basket of bread. 'Maybe this Lord Ilaha isn't so bad after all.'

⬤8⬤

Khalima returned to the camp at the third hour of night, by which time the other tribesmen and soldiers were inside their tents. Cassius had asked Indavara to keep an eye on Ulixes while he waited by the fire with Mercator. The temperature in the canyon had dropped sharply; both men wore their thickest cloaks.

Khalima fetched Adayyid then came and sat with them. The Saracen looked preoccupied and refused the offer of a drink.

'Well?' said Cassius.

'An interesting meeting.' Khalima rubbed a thumb and forefinger down his chin.

'Will your chief join Ilaha?' asked Cassius.

'The ethnarchs are meeting this night. I believe Uruwat, and many of the others, are waiting to hear what Ilaha has to say before making any decision.'

'Any idea what the general feeling is?'

'No. Only that nothing has been agreed upon yet.'

'Did you learn anything else?'

'There will be a ceremony inside the inner wall tomorrow. Everyone is to attend.'

'What kind of ceremony?'

'I'm not sure.'

'What does it look like over there?' asked Mercator.

'Well guarded. Dozens of men on either side of the gate. The chiefs are being housed on the right side of the canyon, Ilaha's

293

headquarters are to the left. Something's going on; there were men working by torchlight.'

'Working?' asked Cassius.

'They were operating some kind of crane.'

Cassius resisted the urge to look at Mercator. 'A crane? For lifting something?'

'What else would one do with a crane?'

'Fair point.'

'Adayyid told me what happened earlier with Oblachus. I hadn't anticipated this amount of attention.'

Cassius held up a calming hand. 'We dealt with it.'

'Can we speak alone?'

After Adayyid and Mercator had left, Khalima stood up and gazed thoughtfully down at the flames for some time. Cassius stood too and waited for the Saracen to speak.

'Roman, if you and your people are found here my position will be very difficult – Uruwat's too. I am an acquisitive man but not even I will forever tarnish the name of my family by bringing my ethnarch down with me. Every hour we remain here we risk discovery. I will glean what further I can about the meeting and its results. But once this ceremony is concluded we will have little opportunity to learn anything more. We must leave tomorrow. You agree?'

Cassius looked down at the inner wall. 'I agree.'

XXV

Ilaha and Mother walked down the passageway, arm in arm.

Gutha knew what they had been doing. According to Oblachus, dozens of goats and calves had been taken up to the temple during the evening. Apparently the animal screams had gone on for so long that one guard had vomited and another had fled outside.

Gutha saw they had washed but the pink stains remained on their fingers, the blood in the lines of the old crone's skin. He wondered – how strong could their faith really be if they felt such excessive offerings were necessary? Perhaps they just enjoyed it.

After a wary glance at Gutha, Mother spoke some quiet words to Ilaha then walked back the way they'd come, stick tapping on the rock.

Ilaha ran his fingers through his hair. He had forgone his priestly garb once more and was wearing his sword. He touched the hilt then looked along the passageway. 'Are they all here?'

'All twelve. They have eaten, the table has been cleared. We will not be disturbed.'

Around them, a breath of air made the torches flicker.

'I have waited a long time for this moment.'

'I know. Lord Ilaha, I advise caution.'

'Yes you do, Gutha. Persistently.'

'Having at last gathered the ethnarchs it would be . . . regrettable if some were put off by—'

'By what?'

'By going too far too fast.'

Gutha was relieved to see his employer remain calm, despite the provocation.

'Mighty Elagabal has spoken to me. Now is the moment.'

Ilaha composed himself, then walked on.

Gutha fell in behind him, holding his axe handle to stop it swinging. One way or another, he reckoned what happened in the next hour might affect not only his destiny but that of every man gathered in Galanaq.

Commanders Oblachus and Theomestor stood on either side of the doorway, a dozen guards lined up beside them. They all bowed as Ilaha and Gutha strode into the cavern. The twelve other ethnarchs were already sitting. Several men stood but Ilaha waved them back down with a genial smile. As dictated by tradition, each chief was accompanied by another man. Some were sons or trusted advisers, others bodyguards. All were well armed and several glanced curiously at Gutha's axe.

The heavy door boomed shut. Gutha waited for Ilaha to sit down then took up a position by his right shoulder. Some of the ethnarchs looked attentive and keen; others would clearly be harder to win round. Mushannaf made little attempt to hide his contempt as Ilaha poured himself a drink with a remarkably steady hand.

'Welcome, all, to Galanaq. A toast – to your safe arrival and the favour of Mighty Elagabal.'

Ilaha raised his goblet and drank. The others matched the gesture.

'More than a year has passed since the Tanukh last met, since we ethnarchs sat together. At the meeting before that we were addressed by the Romans Marcellinus and Calvinus.'

Ilaha spoke clearly and precisely, the cavern amplifying his soft, earnest tones.

'They thanked us for our efforts and sacrifices and told us we would now reap the rewards of fighting alongside them against the Palmyrans. We, the Saracens, were told our losses would be worthwhile, that we were still better off with Rome.'

Some of the other chiefs were nodding.

'I admit I believed it,' continued Ilaha. 'This Aurelian seemed capable. He defeated Zenobia, after all. And yet what do we find now? Chaos to our south and north. Trade down, profits down – for all of us. Yet again the Romans are in disarray.'

'Rome is dying,' said Kalderon, a loyalist who'd lost two of his brothers fighting the Palmyrans. He was a small but muscular man who loved leading his men into battle and enjoyed his reputation for taking on – and beating – larger foes.

Ilaha leaned forward. 'The Empire remains divided, the west a separate domain. As ever, there is trouble from the Goths and another clash with Persia probably not far away. Rome is incapable of governing its own lands, too weak to destroy its enemies—'

'Ilaha.' Yemanek had raised his hand. Gutha had always found him impressive. He was one of the older ethnarchs, a burly man with a wild beard and a blotchy, red face. His appearance belied his temperament. He was moderate, pragmatic and respected by all at the table.

'Every man here knows the situation. We have come to hear what you propose to do about it.'

Gutha half-expected Ilaha to berate him for the interruption but he simply nodded.

'I would ask for a little patience, Yemanek. I shall tell you in due course. But first I shall tell you what I *do not* want. I do not want war. I do not want bloodshed – our people suffered enough under the Palmyrans. What I want is peace, and freedom – freedom to live and trade as we see fit. Not just for us, but for our sons and our sons' sons.'

Gutha felt himself relax. This was the old Ilaha; assured, compelling, reasonable.

'Let us consider what we give – and what we have given for two centuries – to Rome. We guard the eastern frontier and fight alongside them when the time comes. We journey to places they've never even seen, brave dangerous lands and barren deserts to bring them the incense and the spices they cannot get enough of. And what is our reward for all this? We must *give them* one quarter of all we earn. *One quarter.* What if the first Rabbel and our forefathers were here now? They would laugh – mock us for allowing ourselves to be so enslaved.'

'It's true,' said one of the chiefs thoughtfully.

'So someone tell me, then,' continued Ilaha, 'what they have given us in return?'

'The road?' offered another of the ethnarchs. Gutha thought he was about to take Ilaha on but then the man smiled: 'Except of course that the forefathers you spoke of used an almost identical route.'

'Indeed they did,' said Ilaha. 'Anyone else?'

No one responded.

'I see that Yemanek is still eager to hear my proposal,' added Ilaha. 'It can be summarised as simply as this: what I want is a fair deal for the Tanukh, for our families, for our future.'

Gutha had to acknowledge it had been a masterful performance so far, especially as he had barely mentioned his sun god.

Ilaha picked up the leather folder sitting on the table in front of him and took out a piece of papyrus. The edges were ragged, the papyrus holed and yellowed. Ilaha held it up. 'Any guesses?'

'The treaty,' said Yemanek.

'The treaty. Well, a contemporary copy.' Ilaha placed the sheet on the table. 'The thirteen ethnarchs signed this not long after the Roman annexation. It is not an agreement in the true sense of the word – more a list of obligations for us to fulfil. I suggest a new arrangement, a real treaty. It will be simple, consisting of only three clauses. Firstly, we will retain and control the traditional tribal areas east and south of the Roman road. We also undertake to protect those lands.'

'You are describing the situation as it is,' said another ethnarch. 'What's new?'

'At present, the Romans believe that they *allow* us that territory. This would enshrine our right to our own land in law.'

The ethnarch chose not to press him further.

'The second clause: we will agree to defend any part of Arabia against any hostile force or invader. The third and final clause: import tax on all products coming into the Empire from or through our lands – and therefore subject to Roman tolls – will be taxed not at one quarter, but at one *sixth*.'

Silence returned as the chiefs absorbed this concept. After a while, a new speaker made his contribution. 'The import tax has been at a quarter for more than a century.'

'Things change,' replied Ilaha sharply. 'I doubt the Romans expected they would lose half their empire, or that a woman would almost take the other half.'

'Calvinus will not negotiate on that point,' said another of the chiefs. 'We tried before when we began losing profits to the sea trade. His hands are tied. The quarter rate is universal.'

'Not true,' countered another man. 'Reductions have been negotiated in the past.'

Three others spoke simultaneously and suddenly the ordered debate began to unravel. Ilaha raised a hand. 'Please.'

After a while, his fellow ethnarchs quietened.

'I do not expect Calvinus to accede simply because we ask him to. It is we who must change his mind. With your agreement, I will send an emissary to Bostra with a copy of the new treaty for him to sign. At the same time, we will leave here and I will ask each of you to gather every last swordsman you can spare. We will make camp, tens of thousands of us, within sight of the fortress at Humeima. We will be close to the Via Traiana and only two days' ride from Aila. We will leave Calvinus in no doubt about the seriousness of his position.'

'A sixth *is* reasonable,' said one of the chiefs before glancing around at his compatriots. 'And for us, it would turn loss into profit.'

'But if he refuses?' asked Uruwat. Gutha looked at the old ethnarch; only his fine blue tunic and silver rings marked him out as a man of means.

'We will block the road until he concedes,' said Ilaha. 'Trade will grind to a halt, the Roman coffers in Bostra will empty.'

'They will attack,' said Uruwat.

'Good,' replied Kalderon, who was sitting beside him. 'We have been lapdogs long enough. Shame upon all of us that Zenobia could push the legions out of the east, yet we won't even stand up for ourselves on our own soil.'

'Remind me,' said a deep voice. 'What happened to Zenobia in the end?'

It was Enzarri. Gutha was surprised it had taken him so long. Of all the ethnarchs he was generally considered the most loyal to Rome. Ilaha – and everyone else – had been taken aback that he'd even agreed to attend the meeting. But had he done so only to foil Ilaha's plans in person? Use the occasion to advance his own cause?

Enzarri was a tall, handsome man with a mane of black hair. A notorious drinker and womaniser, he was nonetheless immensely popular amongst his own tribe and with many other Arabians. His reputation had been enhanced during the Palmyran wars and the Romans had decorated him many times. Even now – even here – he wore the golden bands on his wrists.

'Tell me, Ilaha,' he continued. 'Are you also keen on being dragged to Rome in chains?'

Almost imperceptibly, Ilaha's jaw trembled.

Enzarri continued. 'My point is, the Romans may be on the back foot and their response may be slow, but there *will be* a response. Aurelian is marching eastward with tens of thousands of men.'

'You probably wish you were with him.'

Enzarri glared at Kalderon. 'Unlike you, I respect my fellow chiefs and the traditions of this Confederation. I meant no insult to Ethnarch Ilaha. I simply wish to remind him of certain realities.' Enzarri turned back to his host. 'The Romans will wipe Palmyra out in weeks, days even. The Emperor will show them no mercy this time. And you would choose this moment to provoke him?'

Ilaha had calmed himself down. 'As direct as ever, Ethnarch Enzarri. I thank you for your contribution. But there is one crucial difference between us and the Palmyrans. Zenobia attacked Rome, took territory that had never been hers. I – we – are asking for no such thing; merely control over our own lands and the right to provide for ourselves.'

Kalderon was still eyeballing his fellow ethnarch. 'Your lack of insight surprises me, Enzarri. The Romans could never do to us what they did to Palmyra. We have no cities to raze, no standing armies to meet in battle. If it came to it, we would strike when and where we wanted to then disappear into the desert. They would get lost or die of thirst. They couldn't defeat us with ten legions!'

Three other men cheered and banged their fists on the table.

Ilaha smiled. 'Kalderon is right. We do not want war, but we must show our strength to get what we want. The Romans know they need us. They *will* negotiate.'

Enzarri looked at Mushannaf, then Uruwat. It was obvious to Gutha that while perhaps half were onside, these three were not the only ones to harbour doubts.

Ilaha seemed sure he would never get a better opportunity to bend the Confederation to his will. He leaned forward once more. 'The Tanukh must speak as one. If I am to communicate our demands to Calvinus he must see that we are in agreement.' Ilaha tapped the treaty. 'Shall I burn this, free us from enslavement?'

'Do it,' demanded Kalderon.

Ilaha took out a second, newer sheet. 'I have here the agreement, written up with the three clauses I described. Shall we all sign it and despatch it to Bostra at dawn? A show of hands, perhaps?'

Of the twelve other ethnarchs, six raised their hands immediately. Several others appeared to be wavering.

Enzarri spoke up. 'I believe there are some other issues worthy of discussion.'

'You have spoken enough,' said Kalderon.

'What is it, Enzarri?' asked another of the chiefs impatiently.

'The raid on Ruwaffa. An unprovoked attack that the Romans might easily interpret as an act of war. Does our host deny responsibility?'

'I do not know who was responsible,' said Ilaha flatly. 'If you do, please share the information with us.'

Enzarri glanced up at Gutha. 'Perhaps he knows?'

Gutha resisted the temptation to meet his stare.

'You should be wary of making unfounded accusations,' said Ilaha.

'It's true I have no proof,' conceded Enzarri. 'Though the same cannot be said of the two raids on temples within my territory. Men were killed, treasures taken.'

'You would blame me for brigandage within your own lands?' asked Ilaha.

'Witnesses I trust recognised some of the warriors,' continued Enzarri. 'They were your men.'

'That is idle rumour,' countered Ilaha. 'Not proof.'

'You have spoken today of enslavement,' said the older ethnarch. 'My people worship a dozen different gods.' He gestured around the table. 'And how many within all our lands? A hundred or more. Tell me, Ilaha, under your leadership will they – will we – be able to worship freely? Or will you demand that we all prostrate ourselves before *your* sun god?'

Ilaha had put his hands under the table so no one could see them shaking.

Yemanek was about to speak but Enzarri wasn't finished yet.

'Today you carry a sword and appear to be one of us. But it is said here, among your own people, that you consider yourself more priest than warrior these days, that you spend most of your time engaged in religious ritual with your . . . elderly friend.'

'Watch yourself,' warned Kalderon.

Despite the tension, it was clear to Gutha that even the more sympathetic of the chiefs wanted to hear a response.

Ilaha seemed to be fighting to control himself. He eventually took a breath and leaned back, the tension gone from his arms.

'I could answer you now, Enzarri. I could. But I should prefer to wait until after the ceremony tomorrow. I think what you see will give you all the answers you need.'

After a long silence, Yemanek spoke. 'My friends, it is perhaps better in any case that we all take time to consider Ilaha's proposal. I suggest that we reconvene tomorrow to make a final decision.'

'As ever, you speak with great wisdom, Yemanek,' said Ilaha. 'Shall we meet here at the same time?'

Yemanek and the other ethnarchs gave their assent, Enzarri included.

As the chiefs rose and left, Ilaha stood by the door, maintaining his composure until the door was shut.

Then, fists clenched, he stalked back to the table.

Gutha took his axe from his shoulder and put it on one of the chairs. 'Overall I think that went fairly—'

Ilaha swept a hand down, sending a goblet clattering into a corner. 'That piece of shit Enzarri. I'll bleed him white and feed him his own innards.'

Ilaha grabbed the sheet outlining the new treaty and crushed it into a ball. 'They almost signed it. I almost had them.'

'You may still,' said Gutha, electing not to mention his previous warning about the temple raids. 'Perhaps if you told me what you have in mind for tomorrow.'

The door opened. Mother walked in and one of the guards shut the door behind her. She looked at Ilaha, who was leaning against the table. He didn't even move when she walked up to him and placed her hand upon his shoulder. Gutha took a step backwards. He could smell her.

Ilaha turned to him. 'Enzarri has no more than fifty men here. Take Oblachus and Theomestor and as many warriors as you need. With him dead, the others will fall into line.'

'That would be a terrible mistake,' said Gutha.

To his surprise, the old woman agreed. 'He is right.'

'I want him dead,' said Ilaha, his eyes wet and bright.

'What happened?'

Ilaha told her; and the process of repeating it all seemed to calm him down.

'Enzarri's time will come,' said Mother, stroking Ilaha's back. 'You can rest easy tonight, my son, for tomorrow they will see. They will see the true power of Mighty Elagabal. They will kneel before him and they will kneel before you.'

Ilaha closed his eyes.

'I wish I was so certain,' said Gutha.

The crone smiled; a joyless smile that cracked her wrinkled face. 'You will kneel too.'

XXVI

The ceremony began at midday. For an hour beforehand the beat of drums and the clanging of bells rang out from beyond the inner wall. When the noise stopped, the doors opened and the guards lined the road all the way to the town. Once the men of Galanaq had entered, the ethnarchs came out to lead their warriors inside.

Uruwat was one of the last to appear, accompanied by a retinue of senior men, his son Urunike included. Cassius guessed the ethnarch was at least sixty. He was small in stature and wore modest attire, but had a stately manner about him and was clearly revered by his tribesmen. Once he reached the camp and collected them, Cassius and the others followed Khalima and started down the track. As a mark of respect, only daggers were to be carried. Each man still wore the green cloth upon his arm.

Two things led Cassius to believe that they wouldn't particularly stand out. The first was the air of tense expectation that seemed to focus all discussion and attention on Ilaha and the upcoming ceremony. The second was the weather. The sun was blisteringly hot and many – Cassius included – were wearing their hoods.

Where the track met the road they waited for another tribe to pass, then joined the throng heading for the inner gate. The guards stood in silence and good order. Unlike the other Saracens, they had kept their swords. The compound – like most of the rest of Galanaq – was empty.

Cassius grimaced at the harsh odour in amongst the men. Beside him, Simo plucked a handkerchief from his belt and wiped his face and neck. Even Indavara seemed unnerved by the sheer size of the crowd. Cassius was glad to be surrounded by friendly faces; just ahead were Khalima and Adayyid, behind were Mercator and the guard officers.

The doors of the inner gate looked new; the huge slabs of timber pale, the nails and bolts free of rust. The wall had clearly been improved too, with rubble and cement inserted to plug weak points.

As they passed through, the first thing Cassius noticed was the crane. It had been erected at the base of a rocky slope on the left side of the canyon. The main arm was a reinforced triangle of timber, hanging from which was a rope connected to the triple pulley system that gave the crane much of its lifting power. The rope ran down to the base of the arm and from there around the winch, which was turned by two spindle wheels. Iron weights at the rear stabilised the machine.

As the column shuffled on, Cassius also saw that a level platform had been carved from the slope next to the crane. The platform was about ten feet above the canyon floor and the front three sides of it were protected by dozens of closely packed guards. Steps had been cut up to the platform, and from there to the narrow path where the slope met the cliff face. Upon the steps stood nine priests of varying ages, all clothed in red cloaks and each holding drums or bells.

Above them, lining the path all the way back to a large cavern, were dozens more guards. Outside the cavern was a group of older men. Cassius recognised only one: the shiny head and unpleasant visage of Commander Oblachus.

The lemony, woody aroma of incense had reached the encampment hours earlier but now the grey smoke seemed to be everywhere. Wafting it away from his nose, Cassius waited for his eyes to clear then realised there were great smoking bowls of the stuff lining the canyon.

Indavara was coughing. Once he'd drunk from his flask and recovered, he croaked a whisper to Cassius. 'I feel like a smoked fish.'

'It's supposed to purify you. These easterners love it.'

Cassius didn't mention his suspicion that their host might also be trying to intoxicate his guests; make them more susceptible to suggestions of the fantastical or the divine. He was in little doubt about what the guards on the platform were protecting.

Some of the tribes had already stopped but Uruwat kept moving. As they drew level with the platform, Cassius noticed a youthful warrior supervising a large crew of guards moving the crane to create more space. When four of them thumped one of the weights down upon another, the young man loudly berated them.

Uruwat led his men beyond a tribe of warriors wearing red cloths. Cassius and the others followed Khalima to the rear of their group and they turned to face the platform. Not long after, a clan wearing white cloths lined up beside them, farthest from the gate.

Ulixes sidled up to Cassius. Despite their situation, he was grinning. 'I think we both know what's up on that platform,' he whispered. 'Hope you've got that coin ready.'

Once the doors were shut an uneasy quiet settled over the mass of men. Cassius estimated there were a thousand of Ilaha's warriors, five hundred visiting tribesmen and a similar number of locals. The rock walls seemed to magnify the heat and suck any remaining moisture out of air already thickened by sweat and smoke. Cassius had downed half his flask of water but was relieved to find that others were faring no better. One of Uruwat's men was vomiting and another from a neighbouring tribe actually passed out.

The drums and bells began again; a simple, repetitive beat that further dulled the senses. After a time, heads began to turn towards the cavern. Oblachus and the other senior men moved away from the entrance and three figures emerged from the shadows. The first of them was a slight man wearing a voluminous purple cloak embroidered with gold. Little of his face could be seen under the hood but Cassius noted the sword swinging from his belt. He thought of another man clad in purple whom he'd faced in battle three years ago; a nerveless warrior who'd led from the front and given his life fighting Rome.

But surely this was Ilaha. Five paces behind him was an old woman who was moving surprisingly swiftly. The third individual was a giant of a man with blond hair and a freakishly thick neck. He was wearing a plain tunic and was armed with some weapon hanging from a strap on his shoulder.

Adayyid had subtly edged back through the men to stand beside Cassius. Indavara joined them.

'Lord Ilaha,' breathed the Saracen contemptuously.

The guards on the path bowed as their leader passed. The low drums and high-pitched bells echoed around the canyon.

'Who's the big fellow?' asked Cassius.

He could now see that the northener's weapon was an enormous double-bladed axe. Even at that distance, the man looked like a different species to everyone else present.

'Name's Gutha,' replied Adayyid. 'German mercenary. My father remembers him from the Palmyran war. He killed scores of them. They say he's the only living descendant of hired men who came east to fight the Goths under your emperor Severus. He's been with Ilaha for some years.'

Cassius exchanged a speculative glance with Indavara, not only because of what they had heard in Bostra about the big, fair-haired warrior who'd taken the stone.

'What?' asked Adayyid.

'Big Germans are his speciality,' said Cassius

Indavara ignored him.

'And the hag?'

'She's always been with him,' replied Addayid. 'A sorceress, if rumour is to be believed.'

As the trio neared the platform, the priests ceased their music and knelt down, prompting all Ilaha's warriors to do the same. The other tribesmen, however, merely looked on in respectful silence. Cassius was encouraged to see that they and their ethnarchs were not yet in thrall to their host.

In fact, most of the Saracens seemed more interested in their first sight of what the guards had been protecting. Cassius heard dozens of whispered comments as the men peered up at the object. It didn't seem particularly large and was covered by a dark sheet.

While Gutha and the old woman remained on the path, Ilaha strode down the steps. The priests and the guards withdrew to the rear of the platform.

Suddenly alone, Ilaha walked to the front and pulled down his hood. Cassius was surprised to see a youthful face, though even at that distance he could see grey bags under his eyes. His dark hair was cropped short like a military man but his body appeared thin, almost wasted.

Adayyid moved closer to Cassius, ready to translate.

Ilaha clasped his hands together then spoke. 'Welcome, great chiefs and brother warriors of the Tanukh.'

He spoke loudly but did not shout, aware that the quiet and the amplifying effects of the canyon would do the rest.

'I thank each and every one of you for journeying to Galanaq. Last night, I and the other twelve ethnarchs met. What I have asked of them I will ask of you. I believe you have come here because you realise that the Tanukh must stand up for our people. Rome has yet again shown itself incapable of ruling its vast empire. Rome takes; and gives nothing back. Rome is divided and weak. Now is the time to find a new path for we Saracens of Arabia.'

Other than a few quiet comments and nods, there was no significant reaction.

'But there is another reason why we must act now,' continued Ilaha. 'Mighty Elagabal has chosen this moment to favour us. You are privileged to be here this day. You will see him, you will hear him, you will *feel* him among us. And with him at our side, you will know – as I know – that we *cannot* fail!'

Ilaha held up a hand.

A priest came forward and pulled the sheet away.

Though black, the strange surface of the conical rock seemed to glitter and gleam. After a collective intake of breath, a third of the Saracens dropped to their knees and bowed their heads. Cassius looked around. None of Khalima's men had prostrated themselves but a few of their tribesmen had.

'Fear it not!' cried Ilaha. 'For this is the earthly dwelling-place of Almighty Elagabal, god of the sun.'

Though he had expected it to be bigger, Cassius had to admit there was something uncanny about the sacred stone. He had never seen a substance that so embodied both light and dark. Ilaha stood in front of it.

'The Roman emperor wanted this – the Black Stone of Emesa – for himself, but I have reclaimed it for the true followers of Elagabal.'

Ilaha changed the tone of his voice. 'I know that this is difficult for some of you. You worship other gods. Elagabal does not hold this against you. He knows you are good, that you seek only freedom – to live under your own governance, to provide for your tribes and families. Mighty Elagabal welcomes you to the light.'

The sun's rays seemed to dance off the stone, creating a shimmering haze behind the small figure upon the platform. More of the Saracens dropped to their knees. A few cried out.

'Pray silence, brother warriors,' said Ilaha. 'Listen now, to Mighty Elagabal.'

He knelt down and bowed his head.

Then came the voice.

A low, unearthly rumble that seemed to emanate directly from the stone.

A chill prickled Cassius's spine. At first he could make nothing out of the slow, growling hisses, but then he realised the voice was uttering words.

More than half the warriors were now on their knees. Simo dropped to the ground and covered his ears. Indavara was muttering to himself. The auxiliaries and the Saracens looked terrified. But they listened.

Trying to ignore the voice, Cassius recalled a discovery made during the affair of the imperial banner. He had witnessed an underhand method used by priests to influence their followers, and now he looked for some sign that trickery was afoot here. But the voice was so loud, so powerful, so . . . godlike.

Now some of Khalima's men prostrated themselves, though the chief and his son remained on their feet. Cassius could see from the warriors' faces that they weren't doing so merely to conform.

The voice grew louder. Though Cassius didn't understand the words, they seemed to penetrate his head. As others dropped down around him, the halo of light around the rock became almost blinding.

Everything around him seemed to fade away. There was only the light and the voice.

He saw a vast black figure, a colossal warrior, striding across mountains, the sun blazing behind him.

— 8 —

Gutha saw a gaping mouth with jagged rocks for teeth and fire for a tongue. The god's words were irresistible.

Ilaha is the chosen one. Follow him and you will get all you desire. Ilaha is the chosen one. Follow him and you will get all you desire.

Gutha opened his eyes. The first thing he saw was the amulet, hanging out of his tunic on the chain. He had worn it only to appease Ilaha but now felt an urge to touch it. As incense smoke drifted past, he held it in his hand. It felt warm.

Gutha had never cared much for the gods. His family had forgotten theirs and shown little interest in those of their adopted homeland. He knew some said they heard voices from above but he'd never quite believed it.

Yet it was real. Ilaha had been right all along and now Gutha felt stupid for ever doubting him. As the voice continued its insistent refrain, he looked down at the warriors gathered in the canyon. Twice as many were now kneeling as standing. Some were covering their ears or shaking their heads or gaping up at the stone, open mouthed.

The priests were on their knees too but their heads were tilted to the heavens, faces serene. Gutha saw Reyazz, down by the crane. He too was looking up – but at Ilaha.

Gutha turned to his left. The old woman stood with both hands planted on her cane, gazing triumphantly at the scene below.

Suddenly the voice stopped.

— 8 —

Cassius shook his head to clear his mind of the vision. His throat was so dry he thought he might choke. He grabbed his flask and gulped down the remaining water.

Ilaha was back on his feet, arms raised high. He spoke once more.

Adayyid looked in no fit state to translate. Cassius moved closer to Mercator. It took a moment for the optio to gather himself.

'His voice has not been heard for hundreds of years but now Mighty Elagabal has spoken. I ask you now to join me when the sun rises tomorrow. We will ride out from this place. We will show Rome our numbers, our strength, and with the unconquered god of the sun to guide us we shall reclaim our lands and our freedom. With Elagabal beside us we shall be victorious!'

A cheer went up from the guards and some of the tribesmen. But many of the Saracens did not join in; many had not yet yielded to the warrior-priest and the black stone.

'It seems that some are not with us,' said Ilaha. 'That does not concern me. These brothers mean us no harm, they are simply taking a little longer to see the light.'

Ilaha prowled along the front of the platform, the calmest man present. 'But there is another here who *does* mean us harm. A traitor.'

Cassius was still trying to absorb what he had seen, but now his stomach began to churn. He reached up and pulled the hood tighter around his face.

Ilaha continued: 'A man who serves not I, nor any of the ethnarchs, but our enemies.'

Khalima turned, then thought better of it.

There was a noise from over to the left. Commander Oblachus was limping down the wide path from the cavern, a dozen guards behind him. All the Saracens began to look warily around.

'On occasion Mighty Elagabal speaks only to me,' said Ilaha, stopping in front of the stone. 'He told me this man would be here today; that he would show him to us.'

Oblachus and the guards were walking along the front of the crowd. The Saracens were backing away.

Ilaha threw up his hands. 'Mighty Elagabal, show us this traitor. Where is he?'

Ilaha moved aside and from the centre of the rock came a shaft of red light. Certain it was pointing directly at him, Cassius turned away, eyes stinging.

This is it. You're a dead man. Dead.

He had always doubted the power of the gods. Only now – when it was too late – did he realise his error. As dread washed over him, he spun around, looking for help from Indavara, Simo, Mercator. Anyone.

But neither they nor anyone else were looking at him. They were all staring at the centre of the crowd.

The light now seemed to be a faint, narrow beam, projecting from the middle of the rock. A space had appeared amidst a group of Saracens wearing grey cloths. They had all moved away from a man who looked just like the rest of them except that the red light was sparking off the metal of his belt and playing over his face.

The warrior looked around desperately and cried out in Nabatean. He stepped out of the light and reached for his fellows but they fled from him. He ran up to an older man dressed in the fine robes of an ethnarch, but other warriors pushed him back.

By the time Oblachus and the guards arrived, the light had disappeared. The man appeared too stunned to resist as the commander's men dragged him away.

As the noise died down, the ethnarch ordered his men back down to their knees.

The effect spread out like a wave, until all the Saracens – Khalima and his men included – were on the ground too. Ilaha raised his hands high and spoke once more.

The only word Cassius could make out was Elagabal. What he had just witnessed seemed incontrovertible, yet doubt still tugged at him. Surely there was some sort of deception at work here? Clearly, nobody else thought so. Now Mercator and the auxiliaries were on their knees as were Indavara and Simo. Only Ulixes was still on his feet. He cast a speculative glance at Cassius then followed the others.

Quite possibly the last man standing, Cassius dropped down too. Beside him, Indavara was staring blankly at the ground, shaking his head. Simo was mouthing prayers to himself, hand inside his tunic.

Staying low, Cassius moved over to Adayyid. Like the others, the Saracen was listening intently.

'Who was he?' asked Cassius. 'The man they took.'

Adayyid did not respond.

'That tribe wearing grey, who are they?'

Adayyid remained silent. Khalima turned around and raised a finger to his mouth. Cassius moved back to Mercator. Though clearly shaken, the optio managed to translate.

'Mighty Elagabal has helped us. With this traitor unmasked, we are now united as one people. The Tanukh will march tomorrow. Stand now, brothers. Join with me. Join me in praise.'

The priests stood and tapped out a swift beat with the bells and drums. Ilaha began the chant.

'Ela – ga – bal! Ela – ga – bal!'

The guards took it up immediately, then the cry rippled through the crowd. Cassius watched Khalima, his warriors and most of the auxiliaries stand and join in too; and he had no idea whether their cries were genuine or they were playing along. Mercator, Indavara and Simo were still on their knees, watching.

'Ela – ga – bal, Ela – ga – bal!'

Ilaha took up a position beside the stone, arms stretched skyward, eyes closed, soaking up the noise. Some of the Saracens drew their swords and jabbed them in the air. Cassius looked at them; their pale, wet faces, their bulging, bloodshot eyes. Some bawled at the stone, others threw their hands up to the sun, yelling invocations in Nabatean. Their cries reverberated around the canyon.

'Ela – ga – bal! Ela – ga – bal!'

Ilaha opened his eyes and smiled. As the chant continued, he walked away up the steps.

Despite the chaos and confusion without and within, Cassius was struck by a single question. Why hadn't the light shone on him?

It was hard to tell who was more terrified, Khalima's men or the auxiliaries, and their mood seemed little different to the other tribesmen gathered in the encampment. Though the fire wasn't lit, they sat around it; a few talking, most still taking in what they'd seen beyond the inner gate. Mercator sat with his elbows resting on his knees, fingers interlocked, staring at the ashes. Indavara and Simo stood together, deep in discussion. Cassius was in front of the tent, waiting while Ulixes counted his money.

Once the gambler was finished, he came outside. 'Quite a show, eh?'

Cassius looked at the men. 'I'd say it had the desired effect. You don't believe it either, do you?'

'People believe what they want to believe. Just all seems a bit convenient to me.'

'But how? That voice, the light . . .'

'I don't know.' Ulixes turned towards the men. 'But I do know you haven't a hope of getting them anywhere near that stone.'

'We never had a chance of getting it out of here anyway.' Cassius shifted his gaze to the outer gate. 'In fact, now we can't even get ourselves out. Everyone will be expected to ride together tomorrow.'

Ulixes checked the bag of coins was secure inside his tunic. 'My suggestion? We wait until nightfall then make a run for it.'

'To Humeima?'

'Where you go is up to you. I'll be heading out of the province. Seems to me there's a storm coming.'

Just as Ulixes walked away, Khalima – who had been speaking with Adayyid by the corral – strode over. Ignoring his men, he pointed at the tent.

'Can we talk?'

'Of course.' Cassius followed him inside.

'You knew about the stone, didn't you, Roman?'

'No.'

'You're a poor liar.'

'It's true I knew it had been taken. But I did not know it was here.'

314

Khalima rubbed his brow. 'My men are scared. They fear we will be found out too.'

'And you?' said Cassius. 'Were you convinced by that charade?'

'I saw your face, young man. You were as afraid as anyone.'

'For a moment perhaps.'

'You cannot deny the power of that stone.'

'This supposed traitor – I'd be very surprised if his tribe isn't loyal to Ilaha. Am I right?'

Khalima looked away.

'Am I right?' demanded Cassius.

'The ethnarch is named Kalderon. He is an ally of Ilaha, yes.'

'Because Ilaha needed to take someone whose chief wouldn't protest. Let me guess: he was a known man but not close to this Kalderon.'

'A distant cousin, apparently. Leader of a group of villages. Not one of his favoured men.'

'Ilaha and Kalderon used the poor bastard – a convenient scapegoat to show the god's power and unite the warriors. Yet not one of us was identified. Not even *me* – a Roman officer right under his nose. This Ilaha is no great leader, he is a charlatan.'

'Your words ring true, but the light—'

'I've been thinking about that. The beam came directly from the rock. Kalderon could have positioned himself there on purpose.'

'But that voice—'

'That too was a trick. I'm sure of it.'

'I saw the god. I saw—'

'I saw something too. But think about what he did to us in there. The heat, the incense, then these tricks to tip us over the edge.'

Khalima took a breath. 'It hardly matters what you or I think. The men believe it. All of them. No one will be able to stand up to Ilaha now. Not Uruwat nor anyone else.'

'That is precisely what this "ceremony" was designed to achieve.'

Khalima looked out of the tent. 'We will not get out of these mountains alive. My own stupid greed has blinded me. If we are discovered my men and I will be torn apart.'

315

Adayyid appeared outside the tent. Cassius beckoned him inside and he spoke to his father. Khalima listened then covered his eyes with his hands and cursed in his own language.

'What is it?' asked Cassius.

'Uruwat wants to see me. I must go now.'

Without thinking about it, Cassius gripped the Saracen's arm. 'Do not lose your nerve. We can still get out of here.'

Khalima shook him off and left. The chief and his son walked away down the track.

Cassius's tunic was sticking to his back and his head was buzzing. He felt as if he were trapped under a pile of rocks and someone kept adding new ones.

He sat down, located a wine flask and took a long drink. He could not escape the fact that there was now a very real possibility that Khalima would betray them. The Saracen would have difficulty doing so without implicating himself but he might see it as the only way to save he and his men. There was nothing Cassius could do about that. If it came to it, he would take out the spearhead and try to negotiate. They hadn't actually done anything yet except infiltrate Galanaq. Perhaps moderate voices might prevail.

But all things considered, he didn't fancy their chances. In fact, now that Ilaha had so effectively tightened his grip, he reckoned the warrior-priest wouldn't hesitate to interrogate then dispose of every last one of them.

Simo approached, and bent over to look inside the tent.

'Leave me alone for a bit.'

'Yes, sir.'

Cassius drank more wine.

What if Khalima didn't betray them? They could try to survive the next day or two in amongst the Saracens, then make their escape; or perhaps try to flee that night. Whatever they did, considerable nerve and composure would be required and the auxiliaries were currently showing little of either. Cassius knew then exactly what he had to do; it certainly beat waiting around to find out if he was going to die.

The tomb was musty but cool. Carved into the walls were dozens of niches but every one was empty. The burial spaces were identified by metal plaques or – for the poorer inhabitants – names scratched into the stone. Upon the floor were bits of candle and the skeleton of a bird.

Cassius had noticed tribesmen wandering up to the shady caverns from time to time to escape the heat and was relieved to see the men trooping up the slope attract little attention. He had told Simo and Indavara to attend and they arrived first.

'What's this about?' asked Indavara as he entered the tomb.

'You'll see. And take those bloody stupid looks off your faces. If you can't get hold of yourselves, how do you expect me to have any influence on the men?'

'We should leave this place,' said Indavara

'Some hard man, you. I'd forgotten how easily you fall for conjurer's tricks.'

'What tricks? Didn't you see the power of this god? We cannot fight this thing with blades.'

Cassius turned his ire on Simo. 'And what about you? Ready to give up your precious lord for a new one?'

'No, sir. It must have been the work of a demon. It *must* have been.'

Mercator and others had reached the top of the slope.

'Make way,' Cassius told Indavara and Simo. The entrance to the tomb was a long, narrow passageway. Farther on it twisted and turned some distance into the canyon wall. Cassius waved the men along until they were in a row well away from the door.

'This won't take long,' he said. 'Nobody need talk but me.'

He looked along the line, meeting every soldier's gaze before continuing. 'I'm not in the habit of telling people what to believe but unless you men stay calm we're not going to get out of this. So I shall not tell you what I believe, but three things I *know*.'

He waited until he was sure they were all listening. 'Number one: I can't tell you exactly where that voice was coming from but I do know of another group whose god told them to follow one man. If you think that's how it should be, why not forget Lord Ilaha and worship Jesus Christ? Any takers?'

Cassius made sure he didn't look at Simo.

'Number two: I know – and you know – that we are without question enemies of this man Ilaha, yet no light shone upon us.'

Cassius let that one hang in the air a while.

'Number three: Each and every one of you has sworn an oath not only to the Empire and the Emperor, but to the god of gods, great Jupiter – a god who does not *tell* his people what to do, but a god who *listens*. I know, *I know*, that even here, in this dark place, in this dark time, you will *not* forsake him.'

One of the men dropped to his knees. It was Yorvah; and for once the cheerful guard officer could not have looked more earnest. 'All praise Jupiter. God of gods.'

Cassius knelt too. Next was Andal, then about two-thirds of the men. Mercator briefly glanced outside, then followed. The remaining auxiliaries did so too.

Cassius continued: 'All praise Jupiter, god of gods. Please watch over us and deliver us from this place. Protect us from those who wish us harm. All praise Jupiter, god of gods.'

The men repeated the prayer.

Cassius stood up. 'Wait down at the camp. I'll brief you all later.'

The men filed out. Cassius gave a nod of appreciation to Yorvah. Mercator hung back. 'I'm sorry. I—'

'Don't worry. Just get them ready to move – without looking like they're getting ready to move.'

'Will do.' Mercator followed the others down the slope.

'You're a clever bastard, I'll give you that,' said Indavara. 'But I know what *I* believe, and I'm not going anywhere near that rock.'

'Forget the rock,' replied Cassius. 'Let's just get out of this bloody place alive.'

XXVII

Gutha wasn't sure what to believe. He stood alone on the path, still gazing down at the platform. The stone had been covered once more and only half a dozen guards remained. The men stood in pious silence, facing outward. Judging by their faces, they would have preferred another duty.

Other than them, and the guards at the inner gate, the previously packed canyon was now deserted. Ilaha had retreated into the caverns – to rest, he said – before a later meeting with his commanders.

In the moment of the vision, Gutha had felt so convinced, so sure; and he could not forget that voice. At the end, when every last warrior had knelt before him, Ilaha had walked past with a victorious look upon his face. Was it aimed at Gutha himself – the satisfaction of showing him the true power of the sun god? Or was it solely because he knew now the other ethnarchs could not resist him?

It was then that the doubts struck. Amongst all the hundreds of men serving the likes of the hostile Enzarri and Mushannaf, the traitor had come from Kalderon's ranks? And Kalderon himself had abandoned his man almost automatically, without pause or question.

And yet that light, that voice.

Some ill-defined thought lurked at the back of his mind, yet to fully form and offer itself. Something was wrong.

He heard a shout from the gate. A waving guard pointed to a lad running along the path. As he got closer, Gutha recognised him as one of the boys who delivered messages around the town. When he took the note, he saw his name written in one corner. The handwriting was familiar.

Qattif's horse was tied up outside the inn. Judging by the state of it, he'd not been there long. The parlour was empty apart from Alome, who was sweeping up behind the counter.

'Wine?'

Gutha shook his head.

Qattif was sitting alone on a stool by the unlit hearth, a mug on the table in front of him. On the floor were his sword and saddlebags.

'Afternoon,' said the nomad. 'Sounds like I missed all the excitement.'

'What do you have for me?'

'I had to spend a lot.'

'You'll get it back,' growled Gutha as he sat down.

Qattif reached inside his tunic and pulled out a worn sheet of paper. He laid it out on the table between them. 'It's all a bit complicated so I took some notes.' He ran a finger down his bony nose. 'You really wouldn't believe how much I had to spend.'

Gutha's hand thumped down onto the table. One of the legs cracked but it stayed upright. Qattif's mug, however, had landed on his saddlebags, spilling wine all over them. He would have grabbed it if not for the look on Gutha's face. 'I suppose I can clean that up later.'

He coughed, straightened the page and began. 'I eventually found the only man still in the village who knew anything about the old girl. Like everyone else he was reluctant to talk about it so I had to give him . . . well, anyway, here's what he told me. It turns out one of his aunts had lived quite close to this "queen"'s family – this would be about fifty years ago now. Her name was Kara Julia. Apparently she was quite a beauty in her day and she caught the eye of a young local priest. Rumour had it they were lovers. A few years later this priest became popular with the local legion. It was a time of great unrest for the Romans and he also happened to have certain influential family connections. You're not going to believe this next bit.'

'He became Emperor of Rome. Elagabalus of Emesa.'

'You know the story, then?'

'The basics. Continue.'

'When Elagabalus journeyed to Rome he insisted that this Kara Julia accompany him. He never married her but kept her as a consort through most of his four-year reign. As you will know, things didn't go well for him. He lost his mind before the end and rejected her. She was cast out with not a coin to her name and returned to Syria, to this village. Even so, she told everyone that she had been his "queen". A few weeks later Elagabalus was assassinated. Talk of his insanity and depravity had spread even to Syria and she was shunned by what remained of her family and the other villagers. So she was cast out again, and went to live alone in this house I mentioned before.

'Except she wasn't alone for long. She had been with child before her return. When anyone saw her, she would rant and rave about how her son would be a great man, a leader, a king. But she bore a daughter. It was said that she had inherited her mother's beauty but that she was simple; because Kara Julia had tried to strangle her for not being a boy. When the child was older she would offer her to the men of the village but none of them would go near the place, or the girl.

'Apparently Kara Julia began to study lore and magic and eventually tempted a traveller to the house. He stayed – and when it became known that the daughter was with child, lived with them as a family. A boy was born but the mother and father disappeared not long after. The villagers were sure Kara Julia had poisoned them. When the boy was fully grown, the pair of them left.'

'Ilaha joined Charaz's tribe—'

'And eventually became the leader his "mother" wanted. Quite a tale, eh?'

Gutha sat back and stared at the floor. Ilaha – grandson of a mad Roman emperor; raised by Elagabalus's murderous mistress. And he wasn't even Arabian.

Qattif at last felt safe to retrieve the mug and wipe down his bags. 'Er, Commander, if it's all right with you, I was thinking of taking a few days off. Done a lot of riding of late.'

Gutha was preoccupied. 'What did you say?'

Qattif repeated himself.

'You have done well. But I have one last job for you. Come.'

Up in the bedroom, Gutha counted out one hundred aurei and placed them inside a tatty sack. 'Here. Deliver that to my man in Gaza and you can take a tenth.'

Qattif's eyes lit up. 'Very generous. Thank you. Should I come back here after? I mean, will you—'

'You've got your orders.'

'Very well. The Goat Trail will be quickest. I shall try and get away tomo—'

'Today.'

'I shall leave today.'

'Qattif – that *was* quite a tale. Don't be tempted to tell it to anyone else. Not here. Not anywhere.'

'As you wish. One more thing, Commander. Ilaha – the name. I asked around up in Syria. People had only heard of it as the first part of a longer name – Ilaha Gabal – the ancient version of Elagabal.'

━8━

'You're quiet, Gutha.' Oblachus was sitting on the other side of the table. 'Still hearing that voice in your head? Me too. I must admit I had my doubts when he took up these priestly ways. Nor did I understand why he was so determined to take the stone. Now I see it is the will of Mighty Elagabal that we embark on this struggle. What a sight it will be – thousands of us riding together. Those legionaries at Humeima won't believe their eyes.'

'But will it be enough to force concessions from Calvinus?' said Theomestor.

'I hope the old drunk does make a fight of it,' replied Oblachus. 'The light of Elagabal will blind the legions as we fall upon them.'

322

Theomestor didn't appear excited by the prospect. 'I would have thought a man of your age had seen enough bloodshed.'

'Depends on whose blood is being shed.' Oblachus turned his attention back to Gutha. 'Come, man, drink with us.'

Reminding himself to keep up appearances, Gutha downed the wine and raised his mug with the other two. He wasn't particularly keen on either man. Oblachus was as arrogant as he was ugly, Theomestor conservative and parochial. But the pair were capable and – more importantly – loyal. Gutha wondered how long they would remain so if they knew what he did.

The door opened and Ilaha entered, once more in simple robes. Like the others, Gutha stood and bowed.

Ilaha smiled as they all sat down. 'Since the ceremony I have received messages from Enzarri, Uruwat and Mushannaf. They have pledged themselves unconditionally to our cause.'

'Every last swordsman will fight for you, Lord Ilaha,' said Oblachus.

'How are the preparations proceeding?'

'More mounts have arrived and more will be brought up from the valley in the morning. There will be one for every man and a hundred spare. We have also sent word to our patrols – those men will join us on the Incense Road. By the time we reach Humeima, there will be two thousand behind you bearing the sun upon their chest. Each warrior will carry extra supplies of fodder and the baggage will follow in a few days. We can use the springs in the northern Hejaz if necessary. We can make camp wherever you need us to, for as long as you need us to.'

'Excellent. Commander Theomestor?'

The aged warrior delivered his report in a rather more sober manner. 'If the other ethnarchs and their men do indeed ride out with us tomorrow, we can count on at least another six hundred warriors from their honour guards. Kalderon and our other long-standing allies have already sent messages to their homelands. If they all produce the numbers they have promised, our total force will number somewhere between eight and nine thousand men.'

'More than a legion,' said Ilaha.

'With many more in reserve, if required,' added Theomestor.

Oblachus turned to Gutha. 'And only two centuries at Humeima? You're sure of the intelligence?'

'Yes.'

'What about the standards?' asked Ilaha.

'All ready, sir,' said Oblachus. 'The largest is twenty feet by fifteen, bigger even than the tower flag. It must be borne on poles and by two riders. The purple and gold cloth looks spectacular in sunlight.'

Theomestor spoke up again. 'Lord Ilaha, as I mentioned before, the use of a standard could be seen as very provocative.'

'That's the idea,' said Oblachus.

Theomestor continued: 'All of us here have ridden under Roman standards alongside Roman soldiers. This new flag suggests not only that we reject Roman rule but also that we have raised an army to *fight* Rome. It may be a step too far. And if the Emperor hears of it—'

'As ever, you make a reasoned point, Theomestor,' said Ilaha. 'But the flag is merely to show our unity and our connection to Mighty Elagabal. Surely you wouldn't deny the men such a symbol; such encouragement?'

Theomestor conceded with silence.

'An army we are,' said Oblachus proudly. 'An army to rival Rome. And if it comes to a war, then—'

'Let's not get ahead of ourselves,' said Ilaha. 'The mere sight of us will be enough. We need only be there long enough for Calvinus to begin negotiations.'

There were numerous other details to be discussed. Gutha made only a few contributions and once Ilaha was satisfied with the arrangements he dismissed Oblachus and Theomestor.

'What's wrong?' he asked, standing up and walking over to him.

Gutha was tired of playing along. 'I was just wondering how you're going to do it.'

Ilaha leaned back against the table. 'Do what?'

'Make sure the Romans fight. The show of strength at Humeima might do it, the flags might do it, but how will you make sure?'

Ilaha gave a thin smile. 'If I am to answer that honestly, I first need to know I can be absolutely certain of you. You knelt, you bowed, but I wonder – even now – if you truly believe.'

'I think we both know I didn't before. But when that voice spoke . . . I saw . . . something. I think I saw *him*.'

Ilaha touched his arm. 'Elagabal reveals himself to each of us in different ways.'

'He *is* with us. I am sure of that now.'

In truth, Gutha wasn't sure of anything. Yet he could see he had done enough to convince Ilaha.

'I am so glad. Mother still has her doubts but I see the change in you.'

'If we are to fight the Romans – and if you still wish me to be of use to you – I must know what you intend. I must be able to look ahead, to plan and prepare.'

'You are right, of course.'

Gutha had leaned his axe up against a table leg. Ilaha ran a finger along the honed edge and waited for the blood to appear. 'I do want to fight them. Now. While they are weak; while we are strong. Arabia will be mine before they can even react.'

Ilaha licked off the blood then laughed. 'It was Mother's idea. The treaty. Once all the ethnarchs have signed it, we will simply alter the text before despatching it to Bostra. Calvinus will see a demand not for import tax of one sixth, but one *eighth*.'

'He will refuse.'

'Of course.'

'The ethnarchs and the men will be angry.'

'Angry enough to storm Humeima,' said Ilaha. 'We will have the legionaries make crosses for themselves and leave them to die slowly under the glare of Mighty Elagabal.'

'And then?'

'And then Bostra, and then the rest of the province. And then Aurelian.'

Gutha tried to react to this as if it were a plausible course of action.

You mad bastard. You mad, mad bastard. Although . . . there is a kind of reckless genius to it. I wonder how far you might get?

Gutha was sure of one thing. The day he saw a legion marching towards him was the day he and Ilaha parted company. Until then?

He did pay well. Unusually well.

'You will stand beside me, won't you, Gutha?'

'Lord Ilaha, I shall.'

XXVIII

Though tempted by a third mug of unwatered wine, Cassius resisted. While the men subtly went about their preparations to escape if need be, he circled the camp, glancing at the road every few minutes. Though he was looking for Khalima and Adayyid, he knew they might not return. It was perhaps just as likely that he might see that ugly bastard Oblachus and his guards coming for them.

Indavara had a standing order to stay by his side but they'd barely exchanged a word. Cassius halted by the corral. His horse trotted over and he stroked its muzzle, happy the beast had recognised him.

'I – I saw something,' said Indavara. 'I saw a man rise up out of a lake of fire. He spoke those words. I can still hear them.'

'It's your imagination,' said Cassius. 'You created that vision.'

'Me? No. It was him – Elagabal.'

Cassius slapped a fence post in frustration. 'Tell me this: how does an artist create a picture? How do we dream? The images come from within, not without.'

'What about the voice?'

'That I'm still not sure about, but—'

'Corbulo, you don't know everything.'

'True, but I do know more than you. So listen to me. Remember those vicious bloody mercenaries in Antioch? Carnifex and his murdering mates? Who got us out of those holes? It wasn't any god.' Cassius prodded Indavara's arm then pointed at himself. 'It was *you* and *me*.'

While Indavara considered this, Cassius noted movement at the inner wall. The gate had opened to admit a column of horses.

Once they were through, a group of guards came out, heading for the town. Two figures hurried past them. There was no mistaking the broad Khalima and his lean son.

Cassius gripped Indavara's shoulder. 'Pray to your Fortuna if you must. Do whatever you have to do. But get hold of yourself. I don't know who I can trust. I don't know how Mercator and the others will fare. I need you at your best.'

Indavara nodded.

'By the gods,' said Cassius. Fifty feet left of the gate, a body had appeared at the top of the wall. It was hanging from a rope, the face swollen and red. As word spread, faces turned.

'The spy,' said Indavara.

'Poor bastard.'

Indavara then pointed at Khalima and Adayyid. 'They're alone. That's a good sign, isn't it?'

'Be ready for anything.'

By the time the Saracens reached them, Khalima looked almost as anxious as when he'd left.

'You won't like what I have to tell you.'

Cassius had prepared himself for the worst. 'Go on.'

'Once he realised Ilaha had stolen the stone from Emesa, Uruwat had second thoughts about the new faces in my group. He questioned me, demanded I tell the truth.'

Cassius didn't really want to hear any more but Khalima continued.

'I did so. They wish to see you.'

'They?'

'It's complicated.'

'Enlighten me.'

'I have been forbidden to say any more. You must come with me – to a meeting place in the town. You may bring Indavara but no one else.'

'How do I know it's safe?'

'You don't. But unless you cooperate there's nothing stopping them turning you over to Ilaha.' Khalima gestured towards the road. 'I must accompany you. Shall we?'

The centre of the town seemed even more crowded. Men gathered outside every house and hostelry but few were drinking; most were packing up or cleaning weapons or loading carts. The initial shock and awe generated by the unveiling of the stone seemed to have been replaced by the earlier atmosphere of excited anticipation. Yet more horses had been brought into Galanaq and the road was slick with manure.

Cassius slipped in some of it and stumbled. Indavara grabbed his elbow and helped him avoid a particularly unpleasant-looking guard. Cassius thanked him and they hurried after Khalima. As they neared the gatehouse, he saw that the doors had been shut and that dozens of warriors were on duty. There were now five archers at the top of the tower.

'See that?' said Indavara.

'I know.'

Khalima turned left down a side street, which was also overflowing with Saracen warriors. Two tribesmen were arguing with a middle-aged couple outside an inn. As Cassius and the others passed them, a group of guards arrived and intervened. Fortunately, the day had remained hot; the trio's hoods drew little attention.

On either side of Galanaq's central road there was space only for one parallel street. Khalima led them across it and into an alleyway. A hundred paces beyond was the shallow slope that led up to the side of the canyon. The only people nearby were an elderly man lying on a bench, apparently asleep; and two children playing with a kitten.

At the end of the alleyway, Khalima turned right. The third house they came to was a ruin. The roof had collapsed into the first floor and a cascade of blocks covered the doorway. Khalima took a brief look around, then stepped through a low window. Cassius and Indavara followed.

The ground floor of the dwelling was intact and surprisingly large. Above them was a wooden roof, ahead a staircase almost filled by another pile of blocks. As usual, Cassius could not stand up straight. As they removed their hoods, he looked over Khalima's shoulder at the other side of the room.

Two figures stood by the rear door, barely visible in the shadows. One was notably bigger than the other. Cassius felt sure they were looking at him.

Khalima asked a question in Nabatean. The smaller man replied with a single word.

'We wait,' said the Saracen.

Cassius looked at Indavara. The bodyguard inspected the hooded duo, then checked outside to make sure no one had come around behind them. He kept his hand on his sword.

While they waited, Khalima sipped wine from a flask and started at every noise from outside. At one point they heard voices close by but soon realised it was just the children with the kitten. After a time they moved away.

A little later four more men arrived at the rear door in quick succession; one pair followed by another. Three of them conferred, then gestured for Khalima and his companions to approach.

Cassius followed the Saracen but stayed closer to Indavara. When they stopped, he realised that the large, well-armed men hanging back were bodyguards. One of the others was the elderly Uruwat; the other two ethnarchs Cassius had seen leading their tribesmen earlier in the day. They inspected him. The bodyguards inspected Indavara.

Then the tallest of the ethnarchs spoke to Cassius in Greek. 'Are you brave or stupid?'

'Probably a bit of both, but I'd err towards the latter.'

Only the tall Saracen smiled. 'I could hardly believe my ears when Uruwat told us. Romans – here. I must admit I'm rather impressed. Are you a spy?'

'Of sorts, I suppose.'

'Except you're not *just* here to spy, are you? If you were here to spy you'd be alone. You're here to reclaim the stone for the Emperor. That's why you have twenty men with you.'

At this point, Cassius couldn't find a decent reason to lie. 'An objective rather easier said than done.'

'Certainly. But we're sure that won't stop you trying.'

Cassius turned to look at Khalima, who did not react.

'We want you to go ahead with it,' said Uruwat.

'You will try?' asked the tall man.

'I don't even—'

The third ethnarch spoke up. 'You must make the attempt at the third hour of night.'

'What? Why?'

'Because that is the time at which we intend to strike,' said the tall man. 'The ensuing confusion will aid both groups.'

'Strike? Groups? Sorry, I know Uruwat but—'

The tall man gestured to his right. 'He is Mushannaf. I am Enzarri. At the third hour of night we are to attend a meeting with Ilaha and the other ethnarchs. After today, he will be expecting us to do his bidding and ride out with him tomorrow. Until tonight we will give him every possible signal that that is exactly what we intend to do.'

'And your true intention?'

Enzarri glanced at each of his compatriots before answering. 'We will kill him. We will kill him, and you will take the stone, and the Tanukh will be free of this madman.'

'What makes you think Kalderon and the other ethnarchs will stand for it? Or the men? You were there today.'

At first, none of the ethnarchs spoke. Cassius wondered; did they believe in the power of the stone?

'Cut the head off a snake, the body dies swiftly,' said Uruwat.

'And if you fail?'

'We will not,' said Mushannaf.

Uruwat held up a hand. 'We cannot guarantee that.' He turned to Cassius. 'Even if Ilaha remains alive, with the stone gone, all will see him for what he truly is.'

'And if I refuse?'

'You could, of course,' said Mushannaf. 'But now that you know of our . . . treacherous intentions we couldn't possibly let you leave this place alive.' He nodded at Indavara. 'Khalima tells me you've a good man there but I assure you he won't fare well against our three.'

The bodyguards each took a step forward.

Enzarri looked around the ruined building in which they stood. 'Dirty. Smelly. No man wants a sordid death.'

'You will have some help,' said Uruwat. 'Khalima and his men will do all they can.'

Enzarri offered his forearm. 'I believe this is how your people seal an agreement.'

Cassius could see no workable alternative.

Enzarri had a strong grip. 'The third hour.'

'The third hour.'

No one spoke until they reached the edge of the encampment.

'By the great gods,' said Cassius. 'I did not expect that.'

'Neither did I,' replied Khalima. 'By the way, I trust that this in no way affects our earlier agreement.'

Had it not been for the events of the last hour, Cassius might have laughed. 'No.'

The Saracen scratched at his beard. 'Now I'm even more glad I added that clause in the event of my death.'

'*Will* your men help?' asked Cassius. 'Will they dare act against Ilaha after what they've seen today?'

'They can no more refuse our ethnarch than I can. They are bound by the same blood-oath that ties them to me. And yours?'

'They will do as they are ordered.'

Cassius looked back across the road at the compound. Hundreds of guards were at work loading carts with weapons and supplies.

Khalima glanced up at the sky and whispered something in Nabatean.

'What's the hour?' asked Indavara.

'About the ninth,' said Cassius.

'Six hours?' Indavara stopped in the middle of the track. 'It's just not possible.'

'But a talking rock is?' Cassius walked past him. 'Hurry up. We're wasting time.'

◄—8—►

Back at the camp, Khalima gathered his men inside one of the tents while Cassius briefly addressed the auxiliaries. 'You will receive precise orders within the hour. In the meantime, check and double-check your weapons. And no more wine.'

He despatched Simo and another man to the town to purchase several essential items, then summoned Indavara, Mercator and the two guard officers to the smaller tent.

Ulixes intercepted him. He had a pack on his back and looked ready to leave. 'What's going on? Where have you been with the Saracen?'

Cassius ushered him to one side. 'Not your concern.'

'When are we leaving?'

'Tonight. But our plans have changed.'

'How?'

'As I said, not your concern.'

'You're not going after the stone? You'll get us all killed.'

'A third time – not your concern. If I want your advice, I'll ask for it. Go and sit by the fire. Do not speak to the others. Do not move.'

Ulixes muttered oaths as he walked away. Cassius asked Mercator to assign two men to watch him, then the five of them assembled in the tent.

He spoke to Andal and Yorvah first. 'I daresay you may already have worked this out but we were sent here to recover the black stone. I had abandoned all thoughts of trying it but we now have no choice. Certain elements within the other tribes want rid of Ilaha. There is to be a meeting tonight – at the third hour. They will try to kill him. They are doing their part. We must do ours.'

Andal gazed out of the tent down at the inner wall. Yorvah looked at Mercator, who turned to Cassius.

'How?' demanded the optio.

333

'That's what we're here to discuss. We at least have Khalima and his men to help us.'

'Take the stone from its place, sir?' said Yorvah.

'Its place is in Emesa,' said Cassius, not feeling it necessary to disclose the Emperor's ultimate intentions for it. 'This Ilaha had it stolen from a temple. We're stealing it back.'

'Transportation?' asked Indavara wearily.

Cassius pointed at the compound. 'One of those big lumber carts will do. We'll have to liberate one.'

'But the gates?' said Mercator. 'The tower?'

'The way I see it, we will need two groups. One to get the rock, one to secure the outer gate and the tower.'

'I'll take the gate and tower,' offered Indavara. 'As long as it keeps me away from that stone.'

'What's your plan?' asked Cassius.

'Leave it to me. All I need is a few strong daggers.'

'How do we get inside the inner gate?' asked Yorvah.

This elicited a series of suggestions from Mercator and Andal.

Cassius was only half-listening because he'd noticed one particular individual walking towards the town – the young warrior in charge of the crane.

'What is it?' asked Indavara.

'We're going to recruit someone else to help – someone who can get us through those gates and get the stone into the cart.'

'Who?'

Cassius pointed down at the road. 'Him.'

XXIX

'What happened?' asked Cassius. 'I told your men to watch the sneaky son of a bitch.'

Mercator looked mortified. 'They went with him to the latrine but he somehow got away.'

'Don't forget he was a spy,' said Indavara. 'Maybe he got to that Goat Trail or found another way out of here.'

The three of them were standing by the track. After his discussion with the others, Cassius had met with Khalima. The Saracen and his men were out gathering information – the first stage of the operation.

'Did you pay him off?' asked Mercator.

'Yes.'

'So he wouldn't have gone to Ilaha's men? He wouldn't have betrayed us?'

'How in Hades should I know?' said Cassius. 'Even if he has, there is absolutely nothing we can do about it. We shall continue the preparations as planned.'

'Can I brief the men now?' asked Mercator.

'Go ahead. Make sure each and every one understands his task. We cannot afford any more mistakes.'

'Well,' said Cassius to Indavara once Mercator had left. 'Do you think we have a chance?'

'There are a hundred things that might go wrong.'

'I was thinking more like a thousand.'

As sunset neared, the air cooled and shadows crept out from the walls. Torches and lanterns were lit. The road was a little quieter but dozens of men were still on the move; buying supplies, loading carts, checking their horses.

Khalima still hadn't returned. Mercator and the auxiliaries quietly attended to their personal gear, each readying himself for the perilous night ahead. Each man was to carry his weapons and a single pack containing essentials and enough provisions for a few days.

In the smallest tent, Cassius had nothing to do. Simo had filled his pack for him and he sat by the open flap, once again awaiting Khalima. Ever fastidious, Indavara was repeatedly checking every weapon and piece of equipment. He had already retied his boot laces three times. Simo had purchased all the items on Cassius's list: most of them were still in a large box outside the tent. Now the attendant was completing the extensive sewing job his master had given him.

Cassius looked down at the sword lying between his legs. It was standard legionary issue, a lot easier to wield than his own. He gripped the handle, imagined drawing it, swinging it at some faceless guard. He felt almost faint as he thought of the last time he'd seen blades used on men; the battle between the legionaries and the tribesmen in Cyrenaica. Though he'd now witnessed it many times, nothing sickened him more than the sight of human flesh pierced and sliced by sharpened metal.

Next to him was his pack; and buried at the bottom was his satchel, the money and the spearhead. He had been given his share of food, wine and water too. He almost laughed at the thought of watching Simo put in his favourite snack of bread, goat's cheese and olives. As if it mattered. And yet somehow it did.

The Gaul finished his work then packed away his needle and thread. 'There, sir. All done.'

'Good. Don't forget your own gear.'

'Or your sword,' said Indavara.

'I daresay you wish you'd been another day late back to Bostra,' said Cassius.

Simo said nothing.

'And both of you keep close to Khalima and his men,' added Indavara.

Cassius brushed sand off his knees. 'I must admit I'd prefer it if we stayed together.'

'You didn't say anything earlier.'

'Mercator needs you more than I do.'

'Mercator will do his best,' said Indavara firmly. 'Andal and Yorvah and the others too.'

'Just make sure you get that outer gate open.'

'I will, but . . .'

'But what?'

Indavara pushed his pack aside. 'Part of me hopes we don't get the stone.'

'What do you mean?'

'The god lives within it. He speaks, shines out his light. He could kill us. Or curse us for the rest of our lives.'

'I thought we'd been through this,' said Cassius. 'Forget that nonsense. A god who can't sniff out twenty enemies right under his nose doesn't worry me.'

'You were as scared as anyone.'

'That may be so, but then I thought about it – logically. And I made up my own mind. You should try it sometime.'

Simo was buckling the straps of his pack. 'It *was* the voice of a demon. Hell is revealing itself. War is coming. Bloodshed and suffering. I think the time of judgement is close.'

'Simo.'

'I am ready, sir. I have prayed for you both. But you must know that God will judge us all.'

'It's a bit late for me,' said Indavara. 'All the killing I've done.'

He tapped his belt. Cassius didn't need to see across the tent to know his figurine would be tucked in there.

'I've got my Fortuna. She'll see me through. Is she stronger than Elagabal, do you think?'

'Jupiter is,' said Cassius. 'I know that much.'

'Will you pray to him?'

'Already have. And for you two.'

His companions looked at him.

'Back in Bostra I was desperate for both of you to come with me. And I am grateful you are here, now more than ever. But once again I have led you into great danger. If we don't get out of here alive, then I am truly sorry.'

—◆8◆—

Khalima returned just as the last vestiges of red were fading from the sky. Cassius, Indavara and Mercator spoke to him outside.

'Apparently our young friend is an engineer,' explained the Saracen. 'He is currently eating his dinner at an inn. Adayyid will lure him up here.'

'What about a cart?' asked Cassius.

'Those lumber vehicles in the compound are big enough but it's too well guarded. We could try a bribe but I doubt they'd take it – more likely they'd go straight to Oblachus or Theomestor.'

'Any other ideas?'

'A couple of the other tribes have one big enough but they're all loaded and ready to go. We could offer a very high price but it might draw suspicion.'

While Cassius tried to think of an alternative, Mercator spoke up.

'What about the inner gate?'

'Good news and bad,' replied Khalima. 'Because the chiefs are being housed inside there is a bit of traffic, so we may be able to get through – especially if Adayyid can get us some help.'

'The bad?' asked Cassius.

'I heard from one of Mushannaf's men that there is still a small detachment of guards protecting the stone.'

'At least the crane and the platform are quite a way from the gate,' said Cassius.

'My men can kill quietly,' said Khalima. 'But even then, we've still got to get the rock onto the cart and get back out again.'

'And what about what happens inside that cavern?' said Mercator. 'We can't know *exactly* when the ethnarchs will strike or how it will affect what we're doing.'

'We need some kind of distraction,' said Khalima. 'Something to occupy the guards.'

'We'll see what we can come up with,' said Cassius. 'What about the outer gate?'

'Never less than six by the doors and old Theomestor seldom strays far. Then there are those accursed archers in the tower.'

'You can leave them to me,' said Indavara.

'Ulixes?' asked Cassius.

'We didn't see him,' said Khalima.

'But I saw you.' Ulixes appeared suddenly out of the darkness. The four others stared at him, dumbstruck.

The gambler winked at Khalima. 'I wouldn't advise a career in espionage. If those guards had anything about them they would have seen you scouting the place.'

'Where were you?' asked the Saracen.

'Good question,' added Cassius.

'Around. Stupid though they are, Ilaha's men aren't opening that gate for anyone but their own. The Goat Trail is well guarded too. So it looks like I'm stuck with you lot. I assume you're going for the stone after all, correct?'

Nobody said anything.

'I'll take that as a yes. From what I can tell there at least seems to be no system of alarm. So the men at the inner gate can't communicate with the men at the outer gate; which is good. Got transportation?'

'That's proving rather problematic,' admitted Cassius.

'Not any more. If you can spare a hundred denarii, there's an innkeeper down there will sell you his wine-cart. He's been doing a roaring trade since all the warriors arrived but he'll part with it if the price is right. Those things are strong because they have to carry a huge weight of liquid – the wine's all in one big leather bag in the back of the cart. Once all the wine's out you can cut a hole in it and use it to cover the stone. I had a look at it. It'll do the job.'

'Very resourceful,' said Cassius. He looked down at the sack Ulixes was holding. 'What do you have there?'

'A few bits and bobs. Seems to me we're going to need some kind of distraction.'

➤8➤

Half an hour later, they had the cart.

'That'll do nicely,' said Cassius as he walked along the side of it, checking the sturdy wheels and solid construction. At the rear was a hinged plank of wood that could be lowered for loading. Mercator was already in the back, cutting up the huge wine skin. Yorvah had just brought out two of the calmest horses from the corral to draw the vehicle. Andal, meanwhile, was getting the other mounts ready to move. He was to lead a third group, which would bring the horses down to the outer gate at the last moment.

Cassius looked out at the rest of the encampment. Although the canyon was now dark, many of the other tribesmen were still making their own preparations and were too busy to notice theirs.

'Sir.' From the top of the cart, Mercator nodded down at Adayyid, who had just appeared out of the gloom.

'We have him.'

Cassius followed the Saracen back to their tent. Inside, he found the young engineer on his knees and surrounded. One man was binding his hands, while another had an arm around his throat and a knife against his neck. Khalima ruffled his hair and grinned. The Arabian spat curses.

'Adayyid told him we needed help with a damaged cart,' explained Khalima. 'Paid him up front for his help.'

Adayyid plucked a silver coin from the money bag on the captive's belt.

'Sure he'll cooperate?' asked Cassius.

'Never,' said the young man in Greek.

The Saracen with the knife pressed the blade in harder.

'What's the name?' asked Khalima.

'Reyazz,' said Adayyid.

'So you're an engineer, eh, Reyazz? Good with your hands, then?'

340

Khalima drew his own curved dagger and took hold of the younger man's wrist. 'Not so easy with missing fingers though, eh? Tell me, which one can you most easily do without?'

Khalima gently ran the blade across the digits. 'This one? This one? Come on, you choose.'

Reyazz gaped at the knife, not daring to move an inch.

'Very well, I shall choose.' Khalima gripped the middle finger and lined up the dagger. 'Ah. I almost forgot. The scream. Somebody gag him.'

Another of the Saracens located a cloth and came forward. It was close to Reyazz's mouth when he gave in.

'All right. All right. I'll do as you tell me.'

'Good lad.'

——●8●——

On the way back to his tent, Cassius passed Ulixes. The gambler was sitting alone, cracking a striker against a flint.

'You have two, I take it. To be sure?'

'Relax, grain man. I was doing this shit when you were just doing shit.'

Cassius was too busy laughing to feel insulted.

Ulixes put the equipment back into the sack. Next to it was a lantern and an hourglass which he peered at before packing it away. 'Three-quarters of an hour. I'll leave now, get in position.'

'Where exactly are you—'

'Haven't decided yet. Just keep a look out – it'll be big, orange and smoky.'

'Sure you don't want some help? I can probably spare a man.'

'I'll work better alone. This will help, though.'

Ulixes touched the tunic beneath his cloak. Simo's task had been to sew a yellow solar emblem onto one for every man. 'Looks like I'm not the only one with good ideas.'

Ulixes stood and patted down the usual errant strands of hair.

'Be careful,' said Cassius.

341

'Don't worry about me,' replied the ex-legionary as he picked up the lantern. 'Just make sure there's a horse for me at that gate.'

They gripped forearms. Ulixes shuttered the lantern, walked towards the track and disappeared into the night.

━━■8▶━━

As soon as Cassius entered their tent for the last time, Simo approached him.

'Sir.'

'What is it?'

'I understand that a third group led by Master Andal is to watch the horses and bring them down to the road for the others.'

'That's right.'

'I wondered, sir – if it's agreeable to you – could I stay with them?'

Behind him, Indavara had just pulled his mail-shirt on and was now adjusting his belt.

Cassius looked at Simo. His broad, kind face was tight with nerves.

'Don't want to get caught up in any fighting, eh? Well, why not? To be honest, I wish I could join you.'

'Thank you, sir. When are we leaving?'

'As soon as I've got *my* mail-shirt on.'

Cassius removed his belt and knelt down, then pulled his tunic off. Simo took the padded undershirt from where it had been lying on his pack and put it on him. Once it was tightened, Simo picked up the mail-shirt. The rings jangled as he lowered it over Cassius's head.

'At least you're getting your money's worth out of that thing at last,' said Indavara.

Cassius tugged at the leather collar of the shirt. 'By Mars, I'd forgotten how bloody heavy these things are.'

'Not as heavy as mine,' said Indavara. 'We can't all afford copper alloy.' He pulled a long-sleeved tunic on over it, complete with the solar symbol.

342

Simo was tugging the bottom of the mail-shirt.

'What's wrong?' asked Cassius.

Simo let go. 'Sorry, sir. It's been a while.'

Indavara came over, shaking his head. 'How many times do I have to tell you two? Practise, practise, practise. Check, check and check again. If either of you had ever bothered to listen to me you would know what you're doing.'

Simo moved aside.

'Look here,' said Indavara. 'The double layer at the shoulder – it's tangled.' He pulled at the shoulders and sleeves until the mail was even against the undershirt. 'There.'

Simo put one of Cassius's long-sleeved tunics on over the top – also complete with the symbol.

Indavara had more advice as Simo put on his master's belt. 'Higher and tighter than usual – you don't want the mail riding up.'

Once this was done, Simo reached for the sword belt but Indavara grabbed it and chucked it at Cassius. 'He's not a child. Let him do it himself, get a feel for it.'

Cassius hung it over his shoulder, then got to his feet.

'Good height?' asked Indavara.

Cassius reached down for the hilt. 'It's fine.'

'Better than that big thing, but you're not used to a smaller blade now, so if you get in a scrap remember to keep moving.' Indavara tapped Cassius's chest. 'Fortunately, not much will go through that.'

'Feels good. Safe.'

'Safe? If anyone works out you've got armour on they'll go for your head or groin.'

'I take it back.'

◄─■8■─►

When Cassius's hourglass showed that the third hour was close, the entire group gathered for a final time by the unlit fire. Quiet farewells were said then they pulled on their packs and went their separate ways. Indavara and his team left first; they were to edge around the camp and the town before approaching the outer wall. With him were Mercator, Yorvah and eleven of the auxiliaries. The other five men – along with Andal and Simo – headed over to the corral. Both groups would do nothing until they saw a signal from the third group.

Cassius walked up to the cart. Khalima was holding a shuttered lantern and sitting in the rear of the vehicle along with most of his men. Between the driver and Adayyid on the bench at the front sat Reyazz. No longer bound, he nonetheless had to contend with the blade Adayyid was holding against his back.

Cassius climbed up and saw that the box containing the purchased items was lying next to the wine skin. Once he'd taken his pack off and got settled, Khalima gave a quiet word to the driver, who set the horses away at a gentle walk. The only noise was the rattling of the wheels and the occasional shout from the compound. Cassius was certain Ulixes would be over there somewhere.

The cart trundled to a stop about halfway down the track. There were a few lights moving along the road but no one close by. Cassius looked up at the sky. Again, purple daubed the countless stars amid the black. The light of the half-moon was enough for him to see those around him but not much farther. There was nothing to do now but wait for the first sight of smoke and flames.

8

Gutha watched the ethnarchs arrive. Little was said as they sat around the table once more, bodyguards and advisers behind them. The mood was hard to judge but it was now Kalderon who seemed most preoccupied. Despite what Ilaha had told him about the newly receptive mood of Enzarri and the others, Gutha still wondered if he would get the twelve signatures he needed.

Yemanek was the last in. As he and his bodyguard reached the table, they hesitated. Gutha realised this was because some of the ethnarchs had taken a different chair from the previous day. Amongst those who had moved were Enzarri and Mushannaf. They were now sitting side by side, Enzarri only one away from Ilaha's empty seat.

As Yemanek took another chair, Gutha tucked his thumbs into his belt and sauntered around the table so he could get a good look at Enzarri and Mushannaf without attracting their attention. He decided they didn't look any more anxious then he would expect.

Hearing Ilaha's voice outside, he returned to his position. He dropped his right hand to his side, fingers against the smooth wooden handle of the axe.

Probably nothing.

Even so, he kept his hand there.

XXX

Hunched over, hoods up, Indavara and Mercator crept along the narrow path between the buildings and the outer wall. The dwellings and inns to their left gave out little light or noise. Dead ahead were the torches at the gate and a larger one at the top of the tower. Three archers prowled below the bloom of flame, bows over their shoulders. Indavara slowed and drifted into the welcome gloom of the wall.

They had left the men in a courtyard hiding behind a stack of firewood – all except Yorvah, who remained on the slope above the town, watching the inner gate, waiting for the signal.

Indavara stopped by the staircase that led up to the first floor of the tower. The door was shut, the interior dark.

'Just the bottom and the top to worry about,' whispered Mercator.

'Looks that way. Let's check the gate.'

They edged around the staircase and along the tower. On either side of the doors was a torch mounted on a bracket, providing enough light to see the six guards on duty. The locking arrangement on the doors was as simple as Indavara remembered: a sturdy plank slotted across the middle.

They retreated along the path.

'Those six we can handle,' whispered Mercator. 'But what about those bloody archers?'

'I told you. Leave them to me.'

'There,' said one of the Saracens. Cassius followed the line of his outstretched arm and spied the flickering flame at the rear of the compound.

'The stables,' said Khalima. 'Good choice.'

Horses began to whinny, then came a shout. After a while, more flames appeared in two other locations. The shouts multiplied and got louder.

'Now?' asked Khalima.

'Wait a moment,' said Cassius.

Inside the compound, torches and lanterns bobbed in the darkness as guards converged on the stables.

'Look there,' said Khalima. 'Your friend has been busy.'

Fire and black smoke were also spewing from the door of a house on the edge of the town. A woman clambered out of a ground-floor window and fell to her knees, coughing.

'All right,' said Cassius. 'Let's go.'

The driver urged the horses down the track at a trot, then turned onto the road towards the gate. Cassius looked back at the town and saw two more figures fleeing the burning house. Some others arrived with pails of water but the fire had already taken hold and smoke was rising from the higher windows.

Cassius felt that familiar churning in his guts as they neared the gate. Khalima pulled back the shutter on his lantern and spoke calmly to his men. They shifted towards the sides of the cart, ready to move if necessary. As the driver halted the horses, one of the sentries called out in Nabatean. With a prod from Adayyid, Reyazz answered.

A guard holding a spear walked past them. He didn't even look at Cassius and the others; he was staring at the flaming house.

Reyazz kept talking. Two of the guards lifted the locking plank and pulled back the doors. The slabs of timber were so huge it took a while to get them moving. Once there was enough space, the driver got the cart under way again.

When they were safely through, Cassius spoke to Khalima. 'What did he say?'

'That we're under attack – that Commander Oblachus has ordered him to take the stone to a safe place.'

Cassius looked back at the gate. The guards had left the doors open. Every last one of them was watching the fire.

Gutha was beginning to relax. Ilaha had arrived, the door was closed and the other ethnarchs sat patiently waiting for their host to speak. Ilaha had once again forgone his priestly attire and was wisely avoiding the trap of appearing arrogant or overconfident. He spoke softly.

'I do not blame anyone for not believing before. There are hundreds of gods and prophets and oracles. All I can hope for is that what you saw today has opened your eyes to the true power of Mighty Elagabal. It is his will that his earthly dwelling-place come to us. The stone has been in my possession for weeks yet the Romans have no idea where it is and have made no attempt to retrieve it. Their impotence is plain for all to see. There can be no question; now *is* our time. Your warriors know it, and I hope that each of you do too.'

Ilaha picked up a new copy of the treaty. 'By signing our names, we show that we are united in seeking a better future for the thirteen tribes, for this great Confederation. Is there anyone still unwilling to do so?'

Yemanek raised his hand. 'You spoke of victory today, Ilaha. I – and many of us here – hope it is to be of the bloodless kind; and that you meant what you told us yesterday. You do not want a war?'

'Yemanek, only a madman would want a war.'

'Then let us proceed.'

Ilaha took a silver pen from a writing box. He tested the nib then signed his name halfway down the page, under the three clauses of the proposed agreement. Once it was done, he passed it to his left, to Dasharean, ethnarch of one of the northern tribes. Dasharean signed, then passed the paper to the next ethnarch. Just as Enzarri took the pen, someone hammered on the door.

Everyone turned.

'Commander.'

Gutha didn't recognise the voice but whoever it was sounded

anxious. He had taken only three steps when chairs scraped on stone and shouts erupted behind him.

He turned, fingers already tight on the axe handle.

Enzarri and Mushannaf were up and moving, daggers drawn. Enzarri darted around Dasharean and jabbed his gleaming blade down at the still-sitting Ilaha. With nowhere else to go, Ilaha drove himself back, tipping the chair over. Enzarri ran straight into his flailing feet. As they – and the chair – crashed to the floor, Enzarri's knife slapped harmlessly against Ilaha's chest.

But the older ethnarch recovered quickly and – before Ilaha could get a hand on him – raised his dagger again. He seemed to have forgotten Gutha.

With a soft chop like a knife through an apple, the axe severed Enzarri's arm at the wrist.

The dagger clattered against a table leg. The hand flew into the air then flopped down by another ethnarch's foot, squirting blood.

Aware that Kalderon and some of the others were also moving, Gutha stepped in front of Ilaha and turned to meet the next attack. Mushannaf was just feet away but Gutha was more concerned about the big bodyguard behind him.

Seemingly unperturbed by Enzarri's fate, Mushannaf tried to outfox the northerner with a sly slice at his groin. Gutha batted it away with an axe blade, then jabbed the top of the shaft up into the ethnarch's chin.

Teeth shattered noisily. Mushannaf dropped like a stone.

'Guards!' someone shouted. 'Fetch the guards!'

Gutha wanted a moment to check behind him but the bodyguard wasn't about to let him have it. Stepping over his fallen master, he pivoted sharply as he swung the sword at his foe's head.

Gutha centred his weapon and set himself for the impact. He doubted the Saracen would have encountered a war axe. Especially not one with a three-inch elm shaft reinforced by tempered bronze and blades of Noric steel.

The bodyguard's sword was broad and long and well made, but not well made enough.

As it broke in two, Gutha felt something strike his head. Ignoring it, he took a step to his left and swung low into the defenceless Saracen's belly, slicing him open from hip to hip. The warrior fell on top of his master, bloody innards sliding out over his tunic.

Gutha looked to his right. Kalderon was struggling with Uruwat while their bodyguards traded sword blows. Gutha only glimpsed them because Enzarri's bodyguard had just pushed past another of the ethnarchs and was coming at him. Gutha backed towards the door to give himself space to fight.

Ilaha had pushed Enzarri off and was now lashing at him with his feet.

The second bodyguard wasn't stupid. He kept his distance and used the sword's range, jabbing at Gutha's head. Wishing he had his armour on, Gutha was nonetheless unwilling to let the fight drag on, even though he'd just heard the door open at last.

As another straight thrust came at him, he lowered the axe then drove it up, jamming the sword between one blade and the handle. He wrenched both weapons to the right, stepped forward and head-butted the bodyguard. The stunned Saracen dropped his sword and slumped to the floor. As soon as he was down, Kalderon and his bodyguard arrived and stuck their blades into him, one in the gut, another in the throat.

The guards flew into the room, then stopped to survey the carnage.

Ilaha was dragging himself clear of Enzarri, who lay staring at his bleeding stump, long hair plastered to his brow. Mushannaf was rolling around, pawing at his ruined mouth. Uruwat was lying motionless, a gory wound in his neck. His bodyguard was dead too and the man who'd had his guts sliced out of him looked like he'd be joining him soon.

Kalderon and his man stood side by side, blades bloodied, breathing hard.

Ilaha hauled himself to his feet. His unblinking eyes ran over the dead and injured.

One of the ethnarchs put a hand on his shoulder. 'Lord Ilaha, are you—'

Ilaha appeared not to have noticed him. 'They . . . they . . .'

Mushannaf was groaning, now holding a handful of broken teeth. Enzarri was on his back, still entranced by his mutilated arm.

Ilaha drew his sword.

'Yes,' hissed Kalderon. 'Finish the traitors.'

Yemanek held up his hand. 'Wait. Perhaps—'

'Now is not the time for mercy,' said another of the ethnarchs. 'You would do the same.'

Ilaha still hadn't blinked. He extended his arm and put the tip of his sword against Enzarri's heart.

'We should question them,' said Gutha. 'Identify any other conspirators.'

Ilaha drove the blade in.

As blood coloured his tunic, Enzarri's head fell back and his body shook. Satisfied that he'd done enough to kill him, Ilaha turned his attention to Mushannaf.

Gutha tried again. 'Lord Ilaha, we must question him.'

This time, Ilaha struck the heart through the back. He seemed to enjoy skewering Mushannaf and moving the blade around until the ethnarch stopped screaming and trying to reach back and pull out the sword. When it was over, Ilaha retracted the blade, then dropped it.

'Commander.'

Gutha turned to the guard. 'What is it?'

'Sir, there's a fire in the compound and another in the town. It seems it was done deliberately. Theomestor and Oblachus have gone to investigate.'

Gutha hung his axe from his shoulder and walked over to Ilaha. 'You must come with me. Somewhere safe.'

◄8►

Cassius didn't know why he was arguing. They had halted the cart halfway between the gate and the platform and it was surely only a matter of time before the guards came forward to investigate.

Khalima was in no doubt about the wisdom of the prearranged strategy. 'We will drop my warriors here, then distract the guards long enough for them to strike.'

'But the men at the gate simply did as Reyazz told them,' countered Cassius. 'These men might cooperate too.'

'This is no time for half-measures, Roman. All it takes is one troublemaker and we're finished. We stick to the plan.'

Cassius belatedly realised he was arguing with himself. His protest wasn't based on logic; just the messy business of killing.

'Do what you must.'

After a few brief orders, the men dropped quietly to the ground and slipped away into the darkness. Khalima moved up behind Reyazz and said something in his ear. He then waited for the men to get in position before ordering the cart forward.

There were two lanterns: one hanging from the crane, one up on the platform. Cassius saw three guards in front of the covered stone, three more on the ground. One called out as the cart approached. Prompted by Khalima, Reyazz replied. The guards watched warily as the driver reined in.

As Khalima jumped down, the same guard spoke to him. The Saracen laughed and pointed at the sun on his tunic. As the guard peered at it, he swung the lantern at his head, knocking him to the ground.

Dark figures leaped out from behind the crane, the first of them driving a blade into the second guard's neck. Before the third man could even reach for his sword, he'd been struck too.

Reyazz could no longer contain himself and tried to intervene but Adayyid grabbed him round the neck and used the knife to change his mind.

Cassius heard blow after blow from the Saracens' blades. He looked up at the platform; the other three guards seemed to have lasted no longer than their compatriots. As he jumped down, Khalima's men were already dragging the dead men out of the way. Cassius covered his mouth as the tang of freshly spilled blood reached him.

Khalima spoke to Adayyid, who prodded Reyazz along the

bench. As soon as the young man's feet were close enough, Khalima grabbed an ankle and pulled. Reyazz fell five feet straight onto his back. Cassius actually heard the air knocked out of him but Khalima wasn't finished. He grabbed him round the throat and spat more vicious words into his ear before letting Adayyid pick him up.

'Don't worry,' the Saracen told Cassius. 'He won't try anything again.'

Cassius looked back at the gate. None of the guards were on the move.

Unsurprisingly, the lantern Khalima had used as a weapon had gone out. He took the one hanging from the crane and handed it to Cassius. 'Your turn. I know nothing about these devices.'

'I used to watch them down at the docks in Ravenna. Simple mechanics. You'd better bring our friend, though.'

Cassius looked up at the crane, which was still facing the platform. Below the pulley were two straps forming a cradle to be placed under the stone. There wasn't enough slack to reach the platform so Cassius ran to the rear of the machine, opened the locking clamp and took the rope off the winch. He then grabbed the straps and hurried up the steps.

The dead guards were nowhere to be seen, though there was a wide puddle of blood next to the lantern. The Saracens had withdrawn to the edges of the platform, as far from the stone as they could get. Cassius whipped the cover off, then took the straps and fitted each one under the rounded base. As he walked back across the front of the platform he heard a hollow sound underneath him.

He tapped downwards with his boot and realised he was standing not on rock but on wood. With no time to investigate further, he hurried down to the crane.

'Back the cart up to the platform,' he told Khalima. 'We only have to lift it an inch or two, swing it forward, then lower it.'

Grabbing the thick rope once more, Cassius ran it back around the winch then fed the end through the locking clamp.

'I'll need two men on the rope and the others pulling.'

Khalima gave the orders and the Saracens took their places. Cassius joined the men on one of the spindles. 'Ready? Heave.'

——8——

Simo watched the bleary-eyed tribesmen staggering out of their tents to look across the road at the burning compound. Thick tongues of flame could now be seen in at least five different places, and speeding lanterns and torches left orange streaks in the darkness. Shouts drifted across the canyon as the warriors tried to organise themselves.

Andal and the auxiliaries also looked on while doing their best to calm the mounts. Like them, Simo had four horses roped to his own. They were standing in the corral, waiting for the signal. The Gaul spoke soothing words to his horse but it and the other animals were growing increasingly agitated by the fire and the noise.

Of all the dangerous, hateful places he had found himself while in the service of Master Cassius, he reckoned this to be the worst. Though he knew little comfort lay beyond the outer gate, he longed for the moment when they would ride out onto the road.

None of the men saw or heard him pray. 'Deliver us from this hellish place. Please, Lord, deliver us.'

——8——

Leaving the others in cover, Indavara peered around the courtyard arch. The guards were still in place by the gate but were now looking along the road. The earlier quiet was long gone but there was little attention on this end of the town. It was the perfect time to strike.

Indavara looked up the slope but there was no sign of Yorvah returning to confirm the signal had been given.

Come on, Corbulo. Has to be now.

Cassius couldn't work out what was wrong. They had tried twice but the stone hadn't moved even an inch.

'Shit.' He grabbed a lantern and inspected the locking clamp, the winch, the arm and the rope. Everything seemed to be in order.

'I don't know. I don't know.'

Adayyid was guarding Reyazz. He pushed him towards the crane. 'You – help him.'

The engineer did nothing but curse at his captors in Nabatean.

Still holding the lantern, Cassius sprinted up the steps and leaned across the rock. He examined the complicated workings of the pulleys, checking the blocks and each individual rope. Everything seemed to be running freely.

'What is it?' he whispered to himself. 'What in Hades is wrong?'

He arrived back at the crane to find Reyazz spreadeagled on the ground, Khalima on his back. The Saracen was holding the young man by the hair and waving his dagger in his face.

'He won't help,' explained Adayyid.

'Yes he will,' said Khalima.

Reyazz started laughing.

Khalima pushed the tip of the knife into his cheek.

'Wait,' said Cassius.

'We don't have time to wait!' snapped Khalima. 'He said we're so stupid we'll never work out what we're doing wrong.'

'Just give me a minute,' pleaded Cassius.

He looked at the crane. He knew the answer was right in front of him but he couldn't see it. Focusing on the winch, he thought of the *Fortuna Redux*, the ship he'd sailed on during their last assignment.

'Tell the men to try again.'

Cassius kept his eyes on the winch. As the men heaved on the spindles, he realised the rope was slipping. That was it. He'd seen it on the winches aboard the *Fortuna* – the rope had to be wrapped around four or more times to gain sufficient grip.

'Let go.'

He took the rope from the men manning the locking clamp and ran it around the winch an additional two times. 'Let's try it now.'

With those at the rear anchoring the rope, Cassius lent his efforts to one of the spindles. The crane creaked and groaned as the rope pulled tight. The men on the platform called out. The rope moved three or four inches.

'That'll do.' He returned to the men at the rear. 'Lock it off.'

This was done by jamming the rope between two wooden wheels with triangular teeth.

Cassius noted the sour look on Reyazz's face.

'Ha!' Khalima pushed his head down as he got off him.

'Now we have to swing it over to the edge and lower it.'

Cassius fetched a coil of rope from the cart and ran back up to the platform, where he found the stone now off the ground. He ran the rope around the lifting line then dropped both ends over the edge of the platform. On his way back down he grabbed Khalima and two others. The four of them took hold of the rope and walked backwards, pulling until the stone was close enough to the edge.

With prompting from Cassius, Khalima's men released the lock and let out the lifting line. The stone scraped down the rock beneath the platform then a gentle thud confirmed it was down.

'We're there – Adayyid, give the signal!'

The Saracen grabbed a bow from the cart. Another man used a lantern to light an arrow topped with a wrapping of oiled skin. Adayyid nocked it and aimed the bow skyward.

■8►

Gutha sat Ilaha down in a chair. 'You must stay here.'

Ilaha gazed vacantly at his hands, which were grazed and spotted with blood.

Mother appeared from an antechamber, arms outstretched, robes trailing on the floor. 'My son, what happened? What happened?'

Gutha hurried out into the passageway and shut the door behind him. A pair of guards were waiting outside.

'Stay with him. Let no one approach.'

'Yes, sir.'

Steadying the axe with one hand, Gutha ran back to the meeting room. He heard the shouts long before he saw anyone. The bodies had been laid out in the passageway and covered with blankets. A dozen guards had gathered outside the door. Kalderon was remonstrating with the senior men, trying to get past. As usual, Yemanek was playing peacemaker.

'Gutha, thank the gods,' said Kalderon. 'Get these cretins out of my way.'

'Sir, it might be better if you remain here for now.'

'What? If we are under attack you must allow me to help.'

'Please,' said Gutha. 'Galanaq is our territory. I need to establish what's going on. I will keep you informed.'

'Our men are out there,' said another of the ethnarchs.

'Just give me a little time.'

'He is right,' Yemanek told Kalderon. 'This is Lord Ilaha's domain.' He turned to Gutha. 'Tell us immediately you know more.'

The ethnarch waved the others back into the room.

Kalderon gripped Gutha's arm. 'I'm coming with you.'

Gutha spoke into the older man's ear. 'Somebody must watch the other ethnarchs – any one of them might be involved in this plot. Lord Ilaha will be most grateful.'

Kalderon glanced back into the room and made his decision swiftly. 'Very well.'

Gutha addressed the guards. 'Half of you stay here. The rest with me.'

He sprinted off down the passageway.

XXXI

The flaming arrow was still in the air when Andal ordered Simo's group to move out. The men immediately mounted up but there was a long wait while they each led their horses clear of the corral. Simo was last to leave and by the time he reached the track, there were numerous riders and men in the way. Some were still watching the burning compound, some were running to help, others were moving their horses away in case the fire spread. Though the sheer weight of numbers slowed them down, Simo realised the chaos was undoubtedly working to their advantage: no one had given them so much as a second glance.

------8------

Indavara heard Yorvah running down the path. 'Here he comes.'

Mercator and the other auxiliaries gathered around him as the guard officer arrived.

'I saw the arrow. It's time.'

Mercator nodded at his tunic; there were drops of blood across the front. 'What happened?'

'There was a man posted up where the slope meets the wall. I . . . dealt with it.'

Andal clapped the younger guard officer on the shoulder.

Indavara turned to Mercator. 'Get as close as you can to the gate then wait.'

'How will we know when you've taken the archers out?'

'You'll know.'

Indavara ran past the buildings and up the slope. As he neared the side of the canyon, the outer wall became low enough for him to climb up. Once there, he looked east and was surprised to see the extent of the fire – no wonder the guards were staring. He retrieved a heavy bag from his pack then set off.

The uneven surface was awkward but the moonlight allowed him to make out the edges and stay in the middle. He kept low, so low that the fingers of his free hand dragged across the stone. He ignored the lights and the noise to his left, the black nothingness to his right; and he didn't look at the tower until he was twenty feet away.

Had there been one or two archers, he might have considered taking them out from a distance, but once alerted they would have the upper hand. With the surround for protection and such a height advantage, even one man could keep firing and control the gate. This way would be better – as long as they didn't hear him coming.

His next steps were careful and slow. The top of the tower was about ten feet higher than the wall and he halted again when he had a good view of the men. The three were together on the town side of the tower, still preoccupied by the fire. They weren't wearing helmets or armour.

Knowing the auxiliaries were waiting somewhere below, Indavara continued on until he was within touching distance of the tower. As he had previously noticed, there was only a three-foot gap between it and the wall.

He untied the twine that held the bag shut and tied it to his belt. He then planted his feet on the inner edge of the wall and let himself fall forward onto the tower. Now stretched across the gap, he checked the surface, hoping the top of the structure was similar to the bottom. He soon found a suitable crack between two bricks where the cement had dried out. He reached into the bag, took out one of the daggers and pushed the blade into the gap. He then located another void and placed a dagger there to form his second foothold.

Indavara whispered: 'I beg for Fortuna's favour.'

He put his left boot on one handle and tried his weight. It held. Then he brought across his right boot. The second dagger held too. He reached up to find the next gap.

Cassius hadn't realised he was touching the black stone. While he crouched at the rear, Khalima and his men stayed at the front as the cart rumbled away from the crane. One of the Saracens suddenly pointed at the stone; a red light was shimmering across the honeycomb surface. Fearing some divine manifestation, Cassius let go and shrank backwards. Only then did he realise the effect had been caused by the lantern in his hand.

Then he noticed something twinkling within the stone itself. He moved the lantern and discovered a small hollow. Something inside was reflecting the light. Curious, he reached inside.

Khalima cried a warning but Cassius's fingers had already found a smooth, circular shape. He gripped the edge and pulled it out.

In his hand was a highly polished mirror of red-tinged glass mounted in a wire frame. Thinking instantly of the mysterious light, he circled the rock, looking for another hollow. Despite the juddering of the cart, he persisted and eventually found a second hole – and a second mirror – in the opposite side of the stone. Khalima looked no less stunned than the other Saracens. Even though he knew they were nearing the gate, Cassius couldn't stop himself. He found the third mirror embedded in the conical top of the stone, mounted at an angle.

'I knew it.'

With the midday sun above, the light would have bounced off the three mirrors and projected the beam directly out of the rock. Ilaha had been standing right in front of it just before the light had appeared. All he would have needed was a cover of some kind to remove at the desired moment.

'And there was a secret compartment on that platform. I'll wager he had a man in there doing the voice. I knew it.'

'Roman,' said Khalima. 'Sit down. We're close.'

Cassius did so and put the mirrors inside his pack.

Khalima and his men drew their swords but kept them low and out of sight. Cassius wedged himself in place and put down the lantern. Reyazz was at the front once more, again with Adayyid's knife pressed against his back.

The guards were still watching the fire but they turned as the cart stopped. One man steadied the nearest horse and spoke to Reyazz. Instead of replying, Reyazz threw himself forward off the bench. He slid down the horse's side and landed on all fours, already yelling.

The driver tried to set the horses away but the guard had already jumped up and grabbed his belt. As the tribesman was hauled to the ground, Adayyid leaped after him, dagger at the ready.

Khalima gave a shout. Despite his size, he leaped nimbly out of the cart and came down beside his son. The closest guard still hadn't drawn his sword when a slash from Khalima's blade carved a diagonal line across his face. As he fell, the Saracens piled out of the cart and past their leader to take on the guards. Khalima shouted at Cassius without turning round. 'Go! We'll catch up.'

Cassius scrambled past the stone and climbed onto the bench. The startled horses were already on the move but he grabbed the reins.

Suddenly one of the guards appeared to his right, sword swinging up at him. Cassius threw himself to the left and the blade clanged harmlessly against his flank, the tough copper alloy doing its job.

The horses pulled away, veering dangerously close to the side of the gate. Cassius winced as the cart scraped along the door.

Once they were clear, he recovered the reins and yanked them to the left, guiding the horses into the middle of the road. He looked back in time to see the last of the guards' lanterns smash upon the ground.

➤8➤

Gutha had collected six more guards on the way out. As he reached the top of the path, he knew instantly that the fire wasn't their only problem. There were no lights by the platform or at the gate. Then he heard the cries.

'Help us here!'

'Guards to the gate!'

'With me.' Still wishing he had his armour on, Gutha charged down the slope. As his eyes adjusted, he spied the clashing figures close to the gate. He slowed as he neared them; with only the moonlight to see by, it was hard to make out who was fighting who.

'Careful,' he told the guards behind him. 'Mark your man.'

The closest combatants were a pair swinging wildly at each other. Gutha couldn't tell friend from foe.

'Snake's tongue,' he shouted.

'Vulture's claw.'

Relieved that the man had the presence of mind to recall the previous week's watchword, Gutha circled around to his opponent. The warrior never saw him or the weapon that almost took his head off. Gutha needed both hands to dislodge the blade from the lifeless lump of flesh at his feet.

As the guards came past him yelling the watchword, he skirted around the melee along the wall. Such a chaotic scrap robbed him of his advantages and – as the guards seemed to have the numbers – his priority was to get through the gate and find out what was going on. As he neared the doors, a figure tottered out of the fight and fell in front of him.

This warrior hadn't seen him either. He leaped to his feet, panting like a dog.

Gutha knew it might be one of the guards but if he called out he would alert him. Better not to take the chance. He raised the axe.

The warrior twitched, sensing danger.

Just before Gutha brought the blade down, something hit him hard in the back. The pain dropped him to his knees and it took a moment for him to realise he hadn't been cut. He swung the axe at where he thought his foe was but missed. Sand splattered into his face.

Someone ran past. Someone else said 'this way' in Nabatean. Fearing he would be struck before he could see again, Gutha got to his feet and withdrew to the wall. He stayed there until he'd managed to blink and paw most of the sand out of his eyes.

'Commander Gutha? Commander?'

'Reyazz? Over here!'

The engineer could barely get his words out. 'They – they have the stone. I'm sorry, sir. I'm so sorry.'

Indavara was down to one dagger – his own – so was therefore relieved when his fingers found the edge of the surround. He paused to make sure none of the archers had noticed then hauled himself up. His left boot found half a hold on a protruding brick; enough to help him get his elbows over the surround.

Beyond the flaming torch – which was mounted to one side – were the backs of the three archers, each man still entranced by the unfolding chaos below. Indavara almost grinned. The hard part was over.

He swung his right leg over the surround, not seeing the mug until he kicked it – straight across the tower and into the backside of one of the archers. The mug clattered to the ground and the three Arabians turned. As Indavara dropped over the surround he was glad to see none of them had swords.

One man gave a shout and charged straight at him. Indavara didn't have enough time to draw his blade, only enough for two thoughts. First, the guard was brave. Second, the guard was small.

They met in the middle of the tower. Indavara drove in low, his shoulder audibly cracking a rib or two as he sent the lighter man flying back through the air. Eyes bulging, arms clutching at the others, the archer bounced off the surround then disappeared into the darkness.

'Is Indavara going to give a signal or what?' asked Yorvah.

The body thumped into the ground three yards away.

363

'Offhand, I'd say that's it,' replied Mercator. He pointed at the town side of the path. 'Archers there, swords with me. I want every one of those guards down and cold inside a minute.'

——8——

To Indavara, they weren't really men now: just two dangerous shapes he had to get rid of. One had just drawn his dagger, the other was pulling his bow from his back and hammering on the wooden floor with his boot.

Sword now drawn, Indavara came at the dagger-man from the left, forcing him towards his compatriot. He feinted a sweep then thrust straight into him. The blade bounced off the guard's breast-bone but froze him. The second thrust went in close to his heart. As Indavara pulled the blade out, the archer collapsed against the surround, wheezing.

The last man's bow came down hard on his arm but met only the unyielding metal of the mail-shirt. Realising he was in trouble, the archer sidestepped away, fending off his pursuer with the bow.

As Indavara went for him, his left foot landed on nothing and he fell onto his right knee. Someone grabbed his leg. He peered down through the trapdoor and saw a head of greasy black curls. As the Arabian looked up, Indavara brought the sword hilt down on his skull. The guard blinked once then fell. He grunted as his groin landed on a lower rung, then tumbled all the way to the bottom.

Indavara was more concerned with the archer, who was coming at him with the bow again. Still stuck, he stretched out his sword arm and hacked at his assailant's legs. The blade connected with both of them.

Shrieking, the archer dropped his bow and fell head first through the trapdoor. He landed next to the other guard with a crushing thud.

Tasting blood, Indavara realised the leg wounds had splashed him on the way past. He wiped his mouth, then sheathed his sword and started down the ladder.

Cassius was all set to drive past the figure waving at him. But then the hood came down and he saw the distinctive features of Ulixes. The gambler was holding his lantern in one hand, the sack in the other. As Cassius stopped the horses, Ulixes nodded at the rear of the cart. 'You might want to cover that up.'

'There wasn't much time.'

'Allow me. Before you attract some unwanted attention.'

Ulixes climbed on, put the lantern down and lifted the wine skin. Cassius turned and watched him spread it over the top of the stone. Ulixes nodded at the compound. The fiercest of the flames were now higher than the buildings.

'Distracting enough?'

'I'd say so.'

Two warriors ran across the road, heading for the compound. Ulixes waited for them to pass, then pulled the skin down over the other side of the black stone.

'Where are Khalima and the others?'

'Got caught up in a fight.' Cassius peered at the track to the right of the road. 'I think I can see Andal and the horses.'

'Then let's get them and head for the gate.'

'We wait for Khalima.'

Ulixes thumped down onto the bench. 'We have one chance to get out of here, grain man. It won't last long.'

Cassius couldn't deny the logic; he at last had the stone, his job now was to get it out of Galanaq.

He took up the reins. 'Yah!'

Indavara reached the first floor and ran to an arrow slit facing the gate. Below, Mercator and the auxiliaries were already in control; while the optio and Yorvah stood guard, the others were dragging bodies away into the shadows.

But suddenly they all stopped what they were doing and looked along the street. Mercator led them forward, sword high.

Indavara ran across the tower to the door. He grabbed the latch and pulled it up but the door was locked. There was a torch in a bracket nearby but the light was weak, the twigs and oil almost burned out.

He blundered around in the gloom, searching for a key. From outside came shouts and the clash of blades. Fearing he might have to go back up and check the guards, he at last found a hook. The key was hanging from it on a string. He grabbed it and fitted it into the lock.

'Come on!'

He had to shake both the door and the key to get it to turn. Once it was open he drew his sword and sped down the stairs.

The auxiliaries had been attacked by a group of Ilaha's guards. Two figures moved clear of the melee. Indavara recognised Khiran, the auxiliary who had brought the Mars figurine. Clearly wounded, he seemed unable to lift his arms and defend himself. Indavara was already running but he knew he'd be too late.

Khiran's opponent thrust in low. The auxiliary's head flew up, exposing his throat. A moment later, the guard's blade slashed across it. Even before Khiran hit the ground, the man who'd killed him heard the new threat and turned.

Indavara found himself face to face with Theomestor.

—8—

'By Jupiter,' said Ulixes as Cassius halted the cart. 'What a mess.'

The junction of the track and the road was a morass of men and horses. Most of the men were carrying pails of water towards the compound. Others were leading horses away from the fire. Cassius waved at Andal and pointed towards the town. The guard officer waved back.

Cassius guided the horses to the left where there was more space, but it was slow going until they got well away from the junction.

'Damn. Out already,' said Ulixes as they passed the house he'd set aflame. A man outside was reaching through a window, recovering blackened clothes.

'Are they behind us?' yelled Cassius.

'Andal is. Can't see the others.'

Driving the cart through the town was a nightmare. Despite the dozens of lanterns and torches alight, Cassius couldn't keep track of all the people crossing the road ahead of him. Suddenly a woman and a girl shot out of an alley and disappeared in front of the mounts. He hauled back on the reins and horses skidded to a stop.

'What are you doing?' bawled Ulixes.

The pair reappeared, the girl wide eyed and gripping her mother's thigh.

'By the great gods.' Cassius wiped his slick hands on his tunic. He was about to move off when he noticed a large figure standing outside a doorway. Commander Oblachus was leaning on his stick, bellowing orders and directing any guard he saw towards the compound. He looked up at Cassius and Ulixes, then at the rear of the cart. Confusion became comprehension. Disbelief became anger.

Before the Arabian could react, Cassius drove the horses onward. He could see the outer wall up ahead.

— 8 —

Indavara hated fighting the old ones. Crafty, patient, controlled – that was how the bastards stayed alive so long. A flurry of well-aimed jabs and sweeps from Theomestor's long, curved blade had already driven him back towards the tower.

The old warrior's movements were unerringly fluid. He came in at odd angles, used unusual combinations. Indavara had no idea what was coming next.

He parried a high sweep then stumbled as he retreated, wondering how close he was to the tower. Once he hit the stone, the Arabian would have him at his mercy.

Indavara tried to stand his ground but a sly flick caught his wrist. The mail held firm but it could easily have been his hand. He blocked another blow, evaded another flick and continued to back away.

They were well into the shadows now.

Cursing in Nabatean, Theomestor thrust at him two-handed. Indavara deflected the blow with the base of his blade, then chopped quickly at the Arabian's face. To his amazement, the veteran made no attempt to avoid it.

The blade cut across his chin. Theomestor staggered backwards as blood seeped from the wound. He centred his sword and peered forward. Only then did Indavara realise. The dark was even worse for his old eyes. He couldn't see.

Indavara just rushed him. Theomestor swung clumsily and far too early. Indavara had time to pick his strike – an arrow-straight thrust into his opponent's throat.

The Arabian somehow held on to his sword as he stood there, impaled by the blade, trembling and gasping.

Indavara didn't want him to suffer. He retracted the sword.

As the veteran's limp form fell, he wished he hadn't had to kill him.

Sorry, old boy. You had a good run.

━━●8●━━

Cassius was surprised to see the gate still shut. He stopped the horses and looked down at the chaotic scene.

Mercator was standing alone, staring at the ground. He was surrounded by fallen men, only a few of whom were still moving. It was hard to tell which were auxiliaries and which were guards. Yorvah was helping another soldier up while two more were attending to a man lying on his back.

Ulixes spoke before Cassius could summon any words. 'Mercator, the doors.'

The optio didn't respond.

Cassius threw the reins at Ulixes and climbed down. 'Mercator!'

The optio managed to look at him but his eyes were glassy and wide.

Yorvah grabbed his arm and shook him. 'Sir, Optio Mercator, sir!'

'What? What is it?' He looked at Cassius. 'Corbulo.'

'We have to go. Now. Where's Indavara?'

'Right here.' He ran past them, sheathing his blade once more. 'I'll get the doors.'

Cassius spoke to Mercator and Yorvah. 'Any injured that can move – get them in the cart.'

He looked back along the road. Andal and another man were arriving with their horses.

The three other auxiliaries were on foot. 'Sir, we just couldn't get through,' said one. 'We had to leave ours.'

'Looks like we're not going to need them all anyway,' said Cassius. 'Everyone mount up. Where's Simo?'

'Not sure, sir. We lost sight of him back there.'

'Damn it.'

Cassius turned back towards the gate. Indavara seemed to be having trouble with the locking plank. Cassius dodged through the men and drew his sword. Using the pommel, he knocked the plank upwards. Indavara pulled it free and threw it aside. They each grabbed one of the doors and heaved them open.

Simo was stuck. In front of his horse was a hand cart stacked with barrels. The cart had lost a wheel and wouldn't be moving any time soon. Next to it was a woman trying to round up a gaggle of crying children.

Simo heard an angry cry from behind him and spun around.

Oblachus. Not a name he was likely to ever forget. The commander was limping past the line of horses, stick in one hand, lantern in the other.

Simo had seen the other men abandon their charges and

decided he didn't have much choice. He dropped the reins and slid off the horse, stumbling on an unsteady flagstone. He looked back. Oblachus had collared a guard and was pointing at him.

Simo checked his pack was secure then ran.

■8■

'What about Khalima?' asked Indavara.

'They got caught at the inner gate,' said Cassius. 'We can't wait any longer.'

An injured man had been put in the cart. Mercator and the others were on their horses and ready to move.

'What are we waiting for?' yelled Ulixes.

Cassius slapped Indavara on the shoulder. 'Go. Get moving.'

'Where's Simo?'

Cassius looked back along the road again. All of Andal's group was there apart from the Gaul. 'I'll find him. Just get that bloody stone out of here.'

Indavara hesitated. 'Corbulo—'

'That's an order. You're an army man now, remember?'

Indavara climbed up beside Ulixes. As the ex-legionary got the cart under way, the others followed.

Andal was the last in line. He was holding Cassius's grey mare by the reins. 'Here, sir.'

Cassius took them and swung up into the saddle. 'Go!'

As Andal set off through the gate, Cassius wheeled his mount around and trotted back into the town. Several of the unused horses were now free and running loose, adding to the confusion. He had just rounded one when he heard a familiar voice.

'Sir! Sir, I'm here!'

Simo had just emerged from behind a pair of mules being towed across the road.

'Here, Simo, jump up with me.'

A less composed animal might have protested at such an added weight but the mare remained still as the big attendant hauled

370

himself up behind his master. Cassius was already turning when he heard another voice in Greek.

'You!'

Oblachus was pointing at him. In his other hand was a long spear.

But of more immediate concern was the guard just feet away. Cassius kicked out with his right boot but delivered only a glancing blow to the shoulder. The guard tried to grab his leg but Cassius urged the horse back and freed himself. His second kick cracked the Arabian's chin and sent him tottering away.

Wrenching the reins to his left, Cassius was about to charge for the gate when he spotted a boy of no more than five standing directly in front of him. The child was not crying or screaming, just staring up at the animal towering over him.

'Damn it!' Cassius guided the horse around the boy and was about to straighten up again when something thudded into the animal's neck. The mare shrieked and staggered, then toppled to the left. Fearing it would land on top of him, Cassius threw himself to the right. He came down awkwardly, almost horizontal.

His right foot hit first and twisted under him. His cry was cut short as his face smashed into the stone.

He lay still, listening to the desperate whinnies of the horse, the shouts of people nearby. Shards of pain shot up his leg. Blood welled in his mouth and ran between his teeth. He looked up and saw the long spear still stuck in the horse's neck, swaying back and forth.

Two big hands grabbed him under the arms and lifted him. Cassius cried out again as his weight came down on the ankle. He thought he was about to faint but Simo took hold of his belt to keep him up.

'Left hand over my shoulder,' instructed the Gaul.

Cassius did so and, with Simo's help, hobbled to the side of the street. He spat out a mouthful of blood and turned. Oblachus was knocking people aside with his stick as he pursued them.

Cassius nodded at a nearby alley. 'There, Simo.'

After a few steps, he discovered that he could actually put a little weight on the foot and he hopped and stumbled along as best he could. There wasn't much light in the alley and the darkness suddenly became their ally.

'You!' came the enraged shout from behind them. 'I'm coming for you!'

They reached the next street and turned right. A woman ran past, holding up her robes. Cassius's injured leg caught something on the ground. He barely stifled the cry.

'Blood of the gods.'

'Sir, we won't get far. We must hide somewhere.'

They struggled on, looking for shelter, not daring to open a door or enter a courtyard. They heard Oblachus shout again then turned right down another side street.

'There,' said Cassius.

Between two dwellings was a small outhouse. Simo found the bolt and opened the low door. Tied up inside was a calf which let out a moan but seemed otherwise unconcerned. Once in, they moved along to an empty second stall hidden from the street by a wooden divide. At the far end was a big pile of straw. Cassius spat out more blood as Simo took his pack off then laid him down. The attendant sat against the timber wall and took several deep breaths before speaking.

'Sir, your leg?'

'I can just about move my foot.'

'Can you feel your toes?'

'Yes.'

'Then it may not be broken.'

'Doesn't matter. The others are gone.' Cassius slumped back into the straw. 'We'll never get out of here on our own. We're as good as dead.'

— 8 —

'Where are they?'

Indavara was facing backwards, holding on tight as the cart sped across the causeway and up the slope. He could see more lights at the gate now but no sign of any riders.

'Stop. We have to go back.'

'Are you insane?' said Ulixes.

'They should be out by now. *Where are they?*'

Ulixes was more interested in Mercator and the other riders ahead. 'This cart isn't that bloody slow! Ride on!'

Mercator – who seemed to have recovered – dropped back so that he was trotting alongside. 'No sign of Corbulo?'

'I'm going back for them,' said Indavara.

'Talk some sense into him,' yelled Ulixes.

'He's right, Indavara,' said Mercator. 'Look at the lights. You'd never even get back through the gate.'

Ulixes weighed in again. 'There's maybe one chance in ten we'll make it out of these mountains alive. You go back, you've no chance at all. That master of yours is no fool. If he does find a way out of that accursed place it won't be by fighting. You can't do anything more for them now except pray.'

'Corbulo told us to get the stone out,' added Mercator. 'We need you here.'

Indavara let go of the side of the cart. Even before the others had spoken he'd known there was no sense in it.

As Mercator rode on ahead, he closed his eyes and followed Ulixes's advice.

Dear Fortuna, goddess most high. Please watch over them. Please keep them alive.

XXXII

Gutha was sure he'd spotted Oblachus but the commander had disappeared by the time he reached the outer wall. A handful of guards were standing at the gate, staring uselessly towards the road. Others were checking the numerous bodies strewn across the ground.

He slowed to a walk, axe still in his hand. He had run all the way from the inner wall and somehow lost Reyazz. One of the guards turned towards him, his expression a blend of confusion and fear. Gutha recognised him but couldn't recall his name; a hulking thug who could just about follow orders.

'Sir.'

'Were you here?'

'No, sir. Just arrived.' The guard pointed at the tower. 'There are more dead there. Some of them are wearing our tunics but they're not ours. A cart was seen leaving, men on horseback too.'

'Who saw them?'

The guard shrugged.

'What was in the cart?'

The guard shrugged again.

Gutha felt like chopping him in half but instead he strode past the others and beyond the gate. There were no lights on the road but just about enough moonlight to ride by. He couldn't be sure because of the noise from the town but was that the distant rumble of hooves?

Gutha gazed despairingly at the sky and unleashed a stream of bitter curses in his own language. It seemed almost beyond belief that these people had been able to steal the stone just weeks after he had brought it to Galanaq.

As he stalked back inside, a trio of tribesmen rode up, each towing a number of horses. Two guards blocked their path.

'Let us through,' demanded one of the men. 'We need to move the horses out where there's space.'

'No one is leaving,' Gutha told him.

'But the fire, we need to—'

Gutha reached up, gripped his belt and yanked him off his horse.

The tribesman landed heavily on his side, then rolled onto his back. 'Aaaagh! What in the name of the gods?'

Gutha turned to the big guard. 'Man the gate. Anyone else gets out of Galanaq without my say-so and I'll cut your ears off for failing to listen to orders.'

'Yes, Commander.'

Gutha used his axe to slice through the rope leading from the tribesman's saddle, then mounted his horse. He aimed the weapon at another guard. 'You there. Find Oblachus and Theomestor. Tell them to meet me here.'

'Sir, I'm . . . I'm afraid Commander Theomestor is dead.'

'Dead?'

'He's lying just over there, sir.'

Gutha cursed once more. Clearly these people were not to be underestimated.

'Oblachus, then.'

Reyazz arrived, coughing and holding his chest.

'Round up as many men as you can,' Gutha told him. 'They'll need weapons and mounts. We'll leave as soon as I return.'

'Yes, sir.'

'You have failed Lord Ilaha once this night. Do so again and you'll not see the dawn.'

Gutha kicked down hard and galloped away along the road. He made no attempt to avoid anyone on foot or on horseback and roared at anything that got in his way. The compound fire at least seemed to be under control. The flames hadn't spread and the two buildings still alight were in any case past saving. He looked for any further sign of the enemy but saw only groups of confused guards and tribesmen.

The men he had left to fight had stationed themselves at the inner gate. As they parted to let him through, Kalderon came running up with his bodyguard and a few warriors.

'Where is Lord Ilaha?' asked the ethnarch.

'He's safe.'

'No. He left the caverns. What about the fire?'

'The worst has passed. Please gather the loyal ethnarchs and your men. If the tribes of the traitors hear what happened to their chiefs there may be trouble.'

'Of course.' Kalderon started doling out orders.

Another guard carrying a lantern approached from the direction of the platform. He was one of the pair Gutha had left to protect Ilaha. 'Commander.'

'Where is he?'

'Just sitting there. With her.' The guard came closer and whispered. 'Sir, the stone has gone.'

'Tell no one.'

Gutha rode on.

Once at the crane, he dismounted and ran up the steps. Ilaha and Mother were kneeling beside each other on either side of an oil lamp.

'How dare you show your face?' snarled the crone. 'You have let them take the stone.'

Ilaha's eyes were bloodshot. 'How could Mighty Elagabal allow this?' he wailed. 'How?'

Gutha crouched close to him and was surprised to feel the platform wobble. He felt it with his hand and realised it was made of wood. He examined the surface near the lamp – it had been cleverly painted to resemble the natural colours and contours of the rock. He tapped it with a knuckle; it sounded hollow.

'What . . .?'

He found the edge of the compartment and saw that it formed the whole front section of the platform. He noticed a small hole, then saw several more.

He thought of the priests. Usually there were ten of them but there had only been nine present at the ceremony. Suddenly everything was clear.

Gutha laughed. 'The voice of a god, eh? What about the light – some other trick, I suppose? And Kalderon was happy to play along.'

Ilaha bent forward and pressed his face into his arms.

Mother pushed her long white hair away from her face and glared at Gutha, still defiant. 'What do you care, mercenary? Sometimes it takes a little persuasion for the weak-minded to see the truth.'

'I know you.'

'You know nothing.'

'I know who you are. Kara Julia.'

Her wizened features froze.

'I know who you are,' repeated Gutha. 'And I know what you are capable of. Was this deceit your idea? Or has everything been your idea from the beginning? Is there anything you wouldn't do to see him rule? He is not his grandfather. He is not Elagabalus.'

'I am Elagabalus. I am.' Ilaha turned to the old woman. 'Aren't I, Mother?'

Gutha shook his head. The hag disgusted him; more than ever he'd have happily run her through. Though Ilaha evidently didn't know it, he had spent his whole life as a plaything for this deluded, murderous creature.

She placed a hand on his shoulder. 'You are. You are, my son.'

'Then why has the god of the sun betrayed me?'

'He has not,' she said softly. 'Others have done that. You *will* rule, my love. The traitors are dead and their thieving accomplices will not escape these mountains alive.'

'Oh?' said Gutha. 'And who is going to stop them?'

'You,' said Mother. 'To atone for your failures this night.'

'No.' Gutha got to his feet. 'I have stayed here far too long as it is. I should have listened to my instincts.'

'He *will* rule,' repeated the old woman. 'And there can still be a place for you at his side.'

'Next to you? No thank you.'

Ilaha looked up. 'Remember that golden mask, Gutha? The one you couldn't take your eyes off? I know you want it. Bring the stone back and it's yours.'

Gutha hesitated; he wasn't about to reject that offer out of hand. Looking at it logically, he had plenty of men at his disposal and the thieves had had less than an hour's start. They were also burdened by the cart and limited to a single escape route. The old bitch was probably right – they didn't have much of a chance.

That Gerrhan mask was worth twenty gold ingots at least.

'Very well. A fair trade. But then I leave. All ties are severed. We never see each other again.'

'Whatever you want,' cried Ilaha. 'Just get the stone.'

'You must be quick,' said Mother. 'Bring it back before the others even know it is gone.'

Gutha ran back down the steps. He had a stop to make before leaving.

■8►

Cassius was almost glad of the pain; it gave him something else to thing about other than their predicament. He lay on the dirty straw, the smell of manure thick in the air, his ankle throbbing, his cheek aching. He had no idea how long he and Simo had been there, waiting for the inevitable moment when a guard entered the outhouse and discovered them. And yet undiscovered they remained.

'We must try and move. Oblachus is bound to have this area searched before too long.'

Simo was no more than a bulky shape to his left. 'Where to, sir?'

'I don't know – the camp? Perhaps someone made it back there. Help me.'

Once up on his left foot, Cassius lowered the right once more. By putting the weight on his toes, he could just about move unaided. 'By the gods, that hurts.'

'With a little time and some light I can strap it, sir.'

They put their packs on and walked around the divide into the other stall. With some calming whispers from Simo, the calf remained quiet. He left Cassius against the wall, then edged forward. He looked over the top of the door but hurried back straight away.

'Guards. They're working their way along the street.'

'Is there time to . . .'

Cassius could hear them chattering in Nabatean. 'Back where we were. Now.'

The voices got louder as they returned to their hiding place. Cassius hobbled over to the wall that divided the outhouse from the dwelling next door. He ran his hands over the stones – some of the lower layers felt less than solid.

'This wall's roughly made, Simo,' he whispered. 'Come here, see if you can find a gap to work on. Quietly, though.'

The Gaul crouched down. Cassius moved back to the wooden divide and peered around it. The calf shuffled its hooves and snorted.

The black figure was framed by the entrance and silhouetted by the lights beyond. The bolt snapped back. The guard spoke to another passing by who gave him a lantern. Cassius glimpsed a young face and heard a blade slide out of its sheath.

He retreated as carefully as he could, gritting his teeth with every spark of pain from his ankle. Simo was standing still. Cassius leaned in close and whispered in his ear. 'One man. We have to deal with him.'

'There are a couple of missing stones down low near the corner. We can make a space.'

'There's no time. You have to help me.'

'Sir, I cannot.'

'You . . .'

Cassius could hear the guard's feet sliding across the straw. He moved back to the divide and put his hand on his dagger. The yellow glow of the guard's lantern illuminated the back of the outhouse – a rotten length of rope, half a candle, the stones of the wall. Cassius gripped the dagger handle and held the sheath. He pulled the blade out inch by inch, wincing at every inkling of noise. When it was finally free, it felt as heavy as a sword.

The guard took two more steps.

Cassius closed his eyes. *Please, Jupiter. Stop him. Turn him back.*

The guard spoke in Nabatean. It sounded like a question.

All Cassius could think of was what Indavara always told him. *Him or me. Him or me.*

The guard asked the question again. He sounded young. Frightened. He took another step. Cassius saw a foot in a poorly made sandal and the end of his sword.

Another step. Cassius saw the hand holding the sword. A small, undamaged hand. He *was* young.

Cassius drew back the dagger. He would go for the throat – stop him crying out.

Him or me. Him or me.

He had forgotten the pain in his ankle.

Another step. Cassius saw his arm, his shoulder.

He drove the dagger handle down onto the guard's skull. It connected with a dull crack and the man staggered into the wall. He dropped his sword then the lantern, the straw softening the noise.

The guard slid down the wall, then onto his knees. Cassius picked up the lantern. Simo came forward and they watched as the guard's entire body began to shake. He looked to be no more than twenty, a slender man with delicate features and a mop of hair. His eyes were still half open as his head twitched and his fingers tapped against the floor. White froth dripped from his mouth and ran down his chin.

Cassius looked at his head – there wasn't even any blood. 'What in . . .'

The guard pitched forward. Simo caught him and lowered him onto his side. The paroxysms grew stronger, his feet kicking up the straw.

'I didn't hit him that hard,' breathed Cassius. 'What's wrong with him?'

'I – I don't know.' Simo was trying to hold the man still. 'Some sort of fit.'

Cassius looked around the divide towards the street. There were no lights close by.

'Do something, Simo.'

'I don't know what I can do.'

Simo held the man by his arms but the shaking continued. He lifted his head onto his lap.

'Simo, do something, please.'

'Dear Lord help me,' said the attendant. 'Help this man.'

Cassius heard voices outside again. His hands were trembling so badly it took him three attempts to sheathe the dagger. Still holding the lantern, he limped to the back of the stall.

He took off his pack, sat down and put his hands on the wall. Forcing himself to ignore what was going on just feet away, he located the largest gap and began levering out one of the adjacent stones. Once it was out, several above fell to the floor.

Cassius stuck his head through the hole. Beyond was a small, dark room with a single window. He reached for the lantern and pushed it through ahead of him. Apart from a pile of animal hides and some cobweb-covered amphoras, the room was empty.

He slid backwards and continued removing stones. Before long he had cleared quite a space but he knew the wall might easily collapse. He slid his pack under it as a support, leaving just enough of a gap to squeeze through.

He hobbled back to the divide and checked outside. He could no longer hear the voices but the lights were close. Only then did he look down at Simo and the guard. The man's eyes were closed and he was no longer shaking. His head was still in the Gaul's lap.

'Simo.'

He was whispering prayers.

'We have to go. The shaking's stopped. He'll be all right.'

Simo seemed not to have heard him.

'He'll be all right. Come now. I am your master and I order it.'

Simo ceased his prayers and gently lowered the guard's head to the floor. He stood up.

'You go through first.'

Simo took a last look at the guard.

Cassius coaxed him towards the rear of the stall. 'He'll be all right. We have to go. He'll be all right.'

━━8━━

Having donned his armour and grabbed a few other essentials, Gutha swapped the tribesman's horse for his own and rode swiftly to the outer gate. Waiting there were Reyazz and several dozen men.

'Gutha.' Oblachus appeared from somewhere, waving his stick. 'Do they have the stone?'

'Quiet.'

'It's true, then,' replied the older man softly. 'Two of the thieving bastards are still here. I have men searching for them now. They killed Theomestor too – those Syrian mercenaries who were with Uruwat's lot.'

Gutha leaned down towards him. 'Uruwat, Enzarri and Mushannaf are dead. They tried to assassinate Ilaha.'

Oblachus cursed and wiped sweat from his hairless head.

'Now listen to me,' added Gutha. 'You must gather all our men and work with Kalderon. Once the warriors from their tribes hear their ethnarchs are dead, we may have a problem. And the last thing we need is for them to find out the stone has gone. Keep it quiet. You may search for the traitors but do nothing to spark an incident. We must maintain calm.'

'Understood.' Oblachus limped away.

Reyazz hurried over, towing his mount.

'You saw them up close,' said Gutha. 'How many?'

'They had around thirty but most of them were killed at the inner gate and here. No more than ten left.'

'Who do you think they are? These so-called mercenaries?'

'I don't know, sir. I think I heard some Latin but it may have been Greek.'

Gutha waved the young engineer closer. 'All your work with

382

the rock, moving it to the platform. You must have known of Ilaha's deception.'

Guilt flashed across Reyazz's face. 'Commander, I – I just wanted to serve him and Mighty Elagabal as best I could.'

'Is that right?'

Reyazz looked away, then pointed at the men gathered behind him. 'We have forty warriors, sir. I can get more but—'

'There's no time; and I don't want some great mob. Food and water?'

'Yes, sir – enough for several days if we need it.'

'We won't.'

—8—

Cassius sat back against the rock wall. Despite the cold of the night, his tunic was sodden with sweat. Simo took a flask of water from his pack and handed it to him. Cassius drank too quickly and had to stifle a cough. Only when the discomfort had passed could he finish drinking. He loosened his belt and leaned sideways against his pack.

Once into the storeroom they had entered a kitchen. They had unbolted the door then crept out into the side street. By using the darkness and timing their movements, they had evaded the guards and made their way up to the canyon wall.

'How is your ankle, sir?'

It was the first thing Simo had said since the outhouse.

'I had to do something.'

The Gaul didn't reply.

'He would have raised the alarm. It was him or us.'

Simo remained silent.

'Speak, damn you.'

When no reply came, Cassius turned and slapped Simo across the face. He had never hit him before.

'Speak. I command it.'

'What would like me to say, sir?' Even then, he somehow managed not to sound insolent.

383

'I had to do it. I had to do it or we'd both be dead.'

'I am ready for death, sir. I am ready for the Kingdom.'

Cassius almost laughed. 'You are a fool, Simo. And a coward. And you are no use to me here.'

'Because I will not help you kill?' Simo took no care with his tone this time.

'Address me correctly, damn you, or I'll keep striking you until you do.'

'Sorry. Sir.'

Cassius took a while to reply. 'Your faith has blinded you, Simo. Tell me – where is the sense in valuing the lives of others if you do not value your own?'

Simo was praying again.

'Ah, waste your breath if you must. It saves me having to talk to you.'

Cassius looked down at the town. The lights told the story. Lanterns, lamps and torches were clustered together and moving slowly. Order had been restored. Though bitter smoke still drifted across Galanaq, all the fires were out. As for the encampment, he could see many lights there too and a lot of movement.

Now information was everything; and he needed to know more. If the assassination attempt had succeeded, he could make contact with Uruwat, Enzarri or Mushannaf. If it had failed, he might be turned over to Ilaha. He could not risk entering the camp yet.

Cassius used the wall to get to his feet, shrugging off Simo's helping hand. 'We shall shelter in that tomb we used yesterday. If they haven't found us by daylight, at least we'll be able to see what's going on.'

He pulled on his pack and managed two steps before stumbling. Simo grabbed his belt and kept him on his feet.

'Please allow me to help you, sir. Just let me put my pack on.'

Cassius said nothing, but he waited and put his hand over Simo's shoulder once more. As they struggled on along the canyon wall, he continued to look down at the camp, but they were too far away to tell who were guards and who were tribesmen, let alone to which clan they might belong.

At last they reached the tomb. The interior was darker than the sky, darker even than the rock face itself. Cassius knew Simo had his fire-striker and candles with him but they couldn't risk it outside.

'There was a turn to the right after about twenty feet. We shall go in as far as we can. You first.'

Simo helped his master up the high step then advanced slowly into the tomb.

One hand flat against the cool, rough rock, Cassius limped after him. He had counted eight paces when Simo cried out.

Something struck Cassius in the face. As he tottered backwards, his ankle gave way and he fell onto his backside.

'Where are you?' demanded a voice in the darkness. 'Where are you?'

'Simo, what—'

Something heavy landed on Cassius's chest. Scrabbling fingers reached for him. He lashed out and caught his assailant on the head but the fingers were now around his neck and tightening. Spit landed on his face.

'Why are *you* alive? Why *you*?'

Cassius recognised the voice but more pressing concerns prevented him from working out who it was. He gripped the man's wrists and tried to wrench them away but the attacker was heavy and strong; stronger than him.

He heard movement, then an impact. The assailant groaned and suddenly the weight was gone.

'Sir.'

Simo reached down and took his hand. Cassius got to his knees then Simo helped him to his feet. They retreated side by side.

'You,' cried the voice, more desperate than angry now. 'Why you and not him?'

Cassius drew his dagger. 'I have a blade. Come near us and I'll cut you.'

The man groaned again.

Cassius stopped. 'Wait, Simo.' He could hear crying.

'Why him?' implored the voice.

'Gods. Khalima?'

He had been hiding deep within the tomb, and led Cassius and Simo around three more turns to a small chamber. They sat there in silence while the attendant took out his fire-starting kit. Cassius knew from experience that despite his other deficiencies, Simo could carry out the whole procedure even in this utter darkness. Before long the striker was clashing against the flint. At the second attempt, Simo lit some kindling, then a candle.

Khalima was in a bad way. A gash across his forehead was oozing blood and he had several more cuts on his hands and arms. His tunic had been torn down the middle, exposing his muscled chest and considerable paunch. His face was paler than the rest of him.

'What the . . .?'

Cassius felt a presence close by, as if someone had crept up next to him. He turned and saw a body lying not two yards away. He scrabbled backwards until he was pressed against the wall beside Simo.

'Oh my Lord,' said the Gaul.

Khalima was gazing at the candle. 'My boy. He came to my aid but he'd been cut close to the heart. He died just after we got here.'

Adayyid was lying on his back at the far end of the chamber, his head turned away from them.

Cassius could find no adequate words.

'The others?' he said eventually.

Khalima seemed entranced by the flower of light. Blood trickled between his eyes and onto his nose. 'My stupidity, my greed, has cost them all their lives.'

'What about Uruwat? Enzarri?'

'I have seen no sign of them. The German and his men remain in control. I believe the ethnarchs must have failed. I believe Ilaha is still alive.'

Cassius squeezed his eyes shut and bowed his head. In what was looking like an increasingly hopeless situation for him, his allies and the entire bloody province for that matter, he had been allowed one small blessing: time to think. He resolved to do exactly that.

'How did you get up here?' Simo asked Khalima after a while.

'Reinforcements came from the cavern, led by the German. Adayyid and I got past him and through the gate. There were guards everywhere but they were occupied by the fire. We followed the inner wall up to the side of the canyon then came here. After Adayyid took his last breath I wept awhile. And then I heard you.'

Khalima looked at his son's body. 'Can you cover him with something?'

'Of course.'

Simo took a blanket from his pack and gently laid it over Adayyid's head and lean frame.

'That is a deep cut,' he told Khalima. 'May I treat you?'

'It matters not.'

'Please.'

'There is no point.'

'Let him help you, Khalima,' said Cassius.

'They will come for us, Roman. You know they will.'

'They're not here yet.'

Khalima gave in.

Simo wetted a cloth and cleaned the wound. 'There is dirt and hair in there. I shall have to pick it out.'

Cassius wasn't watching. He had his eyes shut again, and by the time he opened them, Simo had treated and dressed the wound.

'Sir, I should check your ankle.'

'Not now.'

'Look at the state of us,' said Khalima. 'We won't even be able to put up a fight.'

'Fighting can't save us now anyway,' replied Cassius.

'Nothing can.'

'Having given the matter some consideration, I'm not entirely sure that's true.'

'What do you mean?'

'I think you're correct to surmise that the assassination attempt failed. Which almost certainly means that Uruwat, Mushannaf and Enzarri are dead. Their warriors will want to know what happened and there's no real reason for Ilaha to keep it secret. Even if the men of their three tribes want revenge, there aren't enough of them to take on Ilaha's men and the warriors of the loyal ethnarchs – who will probably be even more loyal now.'

Khalima shook his head. 'This was madness. We have made his position even stronger.'

'But he has lost his precious stone. That he *will* try and keep quiet as long as possible. Some of the guards will know already, of course, but he can keep that contained. But the other tribes? All that talk of the sun god favouring him, of their fates being tied together . . .'

Khalima was starting to look a little more hopeful.

'Uruwat's men,' said Cassius. 'Would they betray you?'

'That depends on Urunike – he is in charge now.'

'Might he be persuaded to help us?'

'His father has just been killed. I imagine he might.'

Cassius leaned forward. 'Then we may still have a chance of ridding this province of Ilaha and escaping this place alive.'

'Go on.'

'It's simple. You just tell Urunike and the men of your tribe that the black stone has been taken. And you ask them to pass it on into every inn and every house and every tent until by dawn there isn't a single person in Galanaq who doesn't know.'

'And then?'

'It's hard to predict what will happen. But one thing's certain: Lord Ilaha, we and everyone else will discover if Mighty Elagabal really is on his side.'

XXXIII

It was Ulixes who finally called a halt. They hadn't stopped once and the weary horses pulling the cart were beginning to falter and drift alarmingly close to the cliff-edge. The auxiliaries were so intent on escaping that Indavara had to bellow at them to stop. Ulixes threw down the reins then dropped to the ground. Mercator trotted back to the cart with Yorvah and Andal, who had opened the shutter of the lantern he was carrying. Mercator saw the condition of the horses and instructed the guard officers to swap them. Three of the men were leading fresh mounts for this very purpose.

'Third one's for me,' said Ulixes as he checked his money bag was still secure inside his tunic. 'I've done more than my bit – this is where we part company.'

'You're bloody handy with that cart,' said Mercator. 'Why not stay with us?'

'How about an angry German giant and however many hundred warriors he has with him?' Ulixes pointed down the trail. The dots of lights were quite clear. 'I doubt we've more than half an hour on them now. Unless you leave the cart, of course. Then we can all make it.'

Indavara jumped down beside the ex-legionary. 'We came here for the stone.'

'And Khalima and his men probably gave their lives to help us get it out,' added Mercator.

'Eager to join them?' said Ulixes.

Mercator called out to one of the auxiliaries, who brought over the last spare horse.

Ulixes briefly checked the animal over then mounted up. 'Go on for now if you must, but if they get close, ride for your lives.'

He nodded at the back of the cart. 'That thing's not worth dying for.'

'You still here?' said Indavara.

With a final shake of his head, Ulixes set off up the slope.

While Mercator took charge, Indavara grabbed one of the lanterns and climbed into the back of the cart. Trying his best to ignore all thoughts of the stone, he stepped over the injured man and knelt beside the wooden box. Corbulo had said it contained some 'surprises' for anyone that pursued them. Indavara opened it and examined the contents, then called out to Mercator. 'How long to the Step?'

'Maybe half an hour.'

'We'll stop there. Briefly.'

'Why?'

'You'll see.'

———8———

Khalima survived his covert trip to the encampment unscathed.

'Well?' Cassius asked as the Saracen sat down in the chamber. He had regained a little colour but the bandage upon his forehead was red with blood. He took a long drink of water before answering.

'Fortunately for us the guards seem wary of searching the camp and provoking the tribesmen. There's a lot of confusion – no one knows what's happening or who they can trust.'

'And Urunike?'

'He'd already been told of his father's death but not about the loss of the stone. He and Mushannaf and Enzarri's tribes are biding their time. They have assured Oblachus they knew nothing of the plot – which is largely true – and will not act against Ilaha.'

'But did—'

'Yes, he has agreed to help. He has sent out men to do as you asked.'

'Subtly, I trust.'

'Urunike is no fool,' replied Khalima sharply. 'And we have

good cause to be thankful to him. He would even help us escape if there was a way out. But Oblachus has stationed a hundred men at both gates and is guarding the Goat Trail too. Rumour has it the German has gone after the stone.'

'Not much we can do about that,' said Cassius, wondering how far Indavara and the others might have got.

'But he may return with it,' said Khalima. 'And it's only a matter of time until they search up here.'

'True. It had already occurred to me that we might have to . . . move things along.'

'How?'

'We will need not only Urunike's help but the men of the other two tribes as well.'

'What do you have in mind?'

'Lord Ilaha has shown himself to be rather adept at manipulating the masses. Let's see how he responds to a taste of his own medicine.'

Ideally, Gutha would not have hurried. Ideally, he would have run down the thieves in his own time, arriving with the men fresh and ready to fight. But – as was invariably the case – things were far from ideal and he needed to get back to Galanaq as soon as possible.

Ilaha didn't seem in any fit state to lead and though Kalderon and several of the other ethnarchs were firmly onside, it was hard to predict what the others might do, especially if they learned the stone had been taken. The situation was a mess; but restoring order was no longer Gutha's problem. What he would need, however, was enough time to exchange the stone for the mask and safely make his escape. Once that was done, the travails of the Tanukh, Ilaha and that insane old bitch would soon be nothing but a memory.

As the horses ahead slowed, Reyazz dropped back to speak to him.

'We are nearing the Step, Commander. A suitable spot for an ambush. Shall we dismount – send scouts?'

'There is no time for that. We must press on.'

'Yes, sir.' Reyazz moved up the column and shouted instructions.

Despite the orders, the men slowed again to negotiate the narrow turn beside the Step. Gutha was four ranks behind the torch-holders at the front and allowed his mount to proceed at its own pace amongst the closely packed horses. As the road bent around to the right he heard a cry from ahead.

'Wait, there's something—'

'Halt! Halt!'

Others shouted but the noise was drowned out by the agonised shrieks of the lead horses. Gutha reined in but collided with the mount ahead of him. He was sent sprawling forward and held on only by gripping tight with his legs.

Other horses bucked backwards and one man was thrown. The torch he was holding just missed another warrior's head, bounced off Gutha's leg then hit the ground. He ordered the men back, stopping them before they got too close to the edge. Half a dozen of the lead riders had not retreated.

'What's going on up there?'

One warrior appeared on foot, leading his mount. The horse's head was jerking up and down and it was hobbling badly.

'Glass, Commander. There's glass everywhere.'

Gutha dismounted and threw his reins to the man next to him. He passed a warrior clutching his elbow, two more lame horses and two more animals lying on their side.

A man with a torch was peering down at the ground. Gutha joined him and examined the shards of clear and green glass littering the smooth rock. They appeared to have come from broken bottles.

'What are you waiting for?' Gutha bellowed. 'Clear it. Clear all of it!'

◆—8—◆

Indavara turned and looked back into the darkness – as he had for every minute of the last half-hour.

'Still nothing?' asked Andal, who was now driving the cart.

'Not yet.'

Ahead, Mercator and the others trotted on in single file, still using only the moonlight to guide them.

'Should have slowed them down at least,' said the veteran.

'Not for long. We'll need to stop again soon.'

'Why?'

'To give them their next surprise.'

— 8 —

Gutha had lost eight men, which left him with thirty-two. Three had been too injured to fight; five others had lost their mounts. One of the horses was so badly cut they'd had to put it down. The eight warriors were now leading the other horses back to Galanaq.

Gutha had rearranged the column into pairs and ordered that the front rank go no faster than a swift walk; they would still be moving quicker than the cart. He had also – subtly, he hoped – moved most of the best warriors towards the rear. Now they were on a section of the road that ran along a gully with walls twenty to thirty feet high; another area well suited to ambush.

He reckoned they'd been on the move for three hours. Riding at night was always taxing, and the incident with the glass had sapped the men's early enthusiasm. Like him, they clearly just wanted to catch their enemies, deal with them and return home. Gutha doubted it would be that easy.

The thrumming of the horses' hooves was amplified by the rock around them and the relentless noise eventually lulled him into a numb stupor. He shook his head, trying to stay alert. The men were taking turns to hold the lanterns and torches. Around him, the swirling flames picked out hunched, grim-faced figures peering into the darkness, fingers white on their reins.

A man of regular habits, Gutha often awoke in the last moments before the sun rose. The next attack came like that; he felt it just before it actually happened.

First came the heavy impact of another horse going down, then a cry, then a dozen voices calling a halt. As he stopped, some dolt rode into the back of him, almost knocking him out of his saddle once more.

'What is it?' he yelled.

'Ropes! Ropes across the path.'

Gutha jumped down. 'Make way, make way.'

Upon reaching the front of the column, he found that both of the front pair had been felled. The horses had recovered but one man was nursing a crushed arm. The ropes had been fixed a foot above the ground and ran right across the road. Reyazz was already there. As he stepped over the first rope, his lantern picked up another one several yards beyond it.

'There can't be too many, sir. We can cut through these in no time.'

'That's not it,' said Gutha.

'Sir?'

'The ropes are just there to stop us.'

The wail that went up from behind him was that of a man who'd been hit by a weapon that was either sharp, heavy or both. Gutha turned and saw another warrior fall from his mount.

'They're behind us,' shouted someone.

'Javelins. Javelins from behind us!'

'Leave the horses,' thundered Gutha. 'Cover! Move to the sides!'

— 8 —

Indavara reached down and gripped the cold metal. He set his feet, aimed at a torch and let fly.

Disappointingly, no cry went up.

Beside him, Yorvah and two other auxiliaries launched the remaining projectiles. They were standing just below the top of the formation that made up one side of the gully. At about a

394

hundred feet from the first of the ropes, it was the perfect position from which to attack the rear of the column.

Indavara picked up another javelin. Like the others, it was shorter than standard army issue but well balanced and lethal enough. Most of the Arabians had been bright enough to drop their lanterns or torches but he could just make out a group heading for the opposite side of the road. He waited for them to reach it, then launched his remaining three javelins in quick succession. At least one found its target.

———※———

Gutha made sure he was well away from the lights. He already had his helmet on and was crouching behind a rocky outcrop. He supposed it might have appeared rather cowardly to any of the watching men, but if they were sensible they would be doing exactly the same thing.

One of the javelins struck the outcrop. A fragment hit Gutha's cheek and he ducked lower. Another of the projectiles hit a man close by. From the sounds of it the javelin had gone through his throat – he seemed to be choking.

'Commander?' Reyazz dropped down next to him. 'Sir, they're definitely behind us – on the other side, I think.'

'They'll run out before too long,' said Gutha. 'They must have horses waiting ahead of us. Take five men and see what you can find.'

'Yes, Commander.'

———※———

The last javelin had already been thrown. While Indavara had seen to the ropes, Yorvah had worked out the easiest route back over the lump of rock and he now led the way. Once down on the ground, they ran along the edge of the formation towards a ravine that cut through to the road. Waiting there were the horses and the man they'd left to guard them.

The sentry had been holding a lantern but, as they approached, they instead saw three flaming torches.

'Looks like a few of them,' said Yorvah. 'How did they get ahead of us?'

'What about Sergius?' asked one of the other men.

'Probably dead,' said Indavara. 'We have to be quick, before more of them arrive. You three go in from the left – and make plenty of noise. I'll come in around the horses where they won't expect it.'

The three auxiliaries moved off. Indavara continued forward. As he got closer, he could see enough below the torches to count six men. He climbed a few yards up the rocky slope, then carefully rounded the horses until he had a clear run at the Saracens.

Yorvah and the others had taken the long way round and were now heading for the ravine; feet scuffing the ground, voices loud. One of Ilaha's men gave an order and they turned towards the auxiliaries, swords at the ready.

Padding softly towards their backs, Indavara at last drew his own blade.

The Saracens were whispering – they seemed confused as to why their enemies were announcing their presence. Then Yorvah gave a cry and the three auxiliaries charged out of the gloom.

Indavara had never particularly enjoyed sneaking up on a man but there was no sense using surprise if you didn't make it tell. The first warrior never knew what hit him. Indavara swept the blade into the back of his neck, cutting deep.

Hearing the blow, the next man turned. He hadn't even brought his sword up when the tip of Indavara's blade sliced across his throat. He tried to fight but by then blood was spraying out of him and he was unable to make his arms work. He fell beside his compatriot.

Three of the Saracens were now battling the auxiliaries.

The last man had just enough time to parry Indavara's first strike. Even so, the weighty blow knocked the flat of the blade back onto his nose. Momentarily stunned, he dropped his guard, seemingly unaware that he'd lost his one chance at survival.

The thrust tore in under his ribs. Indavara wrenched the sword free and cursed as the poor bastard hit the ground. The trio hadn't died well. He picked up a still-burning torch and moved forward but he could see only four men. The two men standing had no symbols on their tunics (the auxiliaries had torn them off) but the pair lying motionless did.

'Good work,' said Indavara. 'Where's Yorvah?'

The two auxiliaries were still looking down at the men they had killed. Indavara heard something hit the ground a few yards away. He hurried over and found the guard officer and the last Arabian. The dead Saracen was lying face down. Yorvah was sprawled next to him on his back. His tunic had been sliced apart and his wounds were bleeding badly.

'Did I get him?' he spluttered.

Indavara knelt down as the other two arrived. 'You got him.'

One of the auxiliaries grabbed the dead man's hair and turned his face towards him. 'The engineer.'

'Others?' asked Yorvah.

'Got them too,' replied the second auxiliary.

Indavara couldn't help wishing it was one of them with his chest cut up. He had taken to the popular guard officer who always seemed to have a smile on his face.

Yorvah touched one of his wounds. 'Not good. Not good.'

One of the auxiliaries offered him some water but he couldn't keep it down.

'Can you ride?' asked the other man.

Yorvah summoned what Indavara suspected would be his last smile.

'Come on, sir,' said the auxiliary. 'We can help you. Indavara, can't we get him onto one of the horses?'

Blood bubbled from the worst of the wounds. Yorvah had already lost pints. Indavara didn't reply.

'He's right,' said the guard officer, jaw now shaking. He gripped Indavara's wrist. 'How many did you get?'

'Three,' said one of the auxiliaries.

'Ha.' Yorvah slapped his arm. 'Hard bastard, I knew it. You lot better get going. I'll be all right here.'

The three men stood.

'Marcella,' said Yorvah. 'You make sure she's cared for. My money's to go to her. Make sure they know in Bostra. Every last coin.'

'I'll do it, sir, don't you worry,' said one of the men, wiping his sleeve across his eyes. 'By the gods I pledge it.'

'Just get that accursed rock to the Emperor. If not, all this is for naught.'

Indavara knew the auxiliaries wouldn't move of their own accord. He turned both men round and shoved them in the other direction. 'Fetch the horses. All of them.'

As they reluctantly departed, Indavara knelt down once more. 'Ilaha's men will want information. You're in enough pain as it is. Do you want me to—'

'I won't last that long,' said Yorvah, letting his head drop back on the ground.

When Indavara looked at the wounds again, he realised the guard officer was right. Yorvah tried to speak but could manage only a whisper. He beckoned Indavara closer.

'Sixteen aurei sounded like a lot,' he croaked. 'It's not.'

Indavara placed a hand on his shoulder. 'Farewell, friend.'

Yorvah tried to reply but no words would come.

———◄8►———

Gutha looked along the road but could see no trace of a light.

Two warriors came up behind him; one holding a lantern, one several coils of rope. 'That's the last of them, Commander.'

'Mount up. We're moving out.'

On the way back to his horse, he passed the injured. The choking man had been struck by a javelin that had pierced the right side of his neck and gone all the way through to his left armpit. He hadn't lasted long. Two other men were dying and nine others were too badly wounded to ride. They had been put together by the side of the road with what supplies could be spared. One of them was leading the others in a prayer to Elagabal. Knowing most of them would be lucky to make it back to Galanaq, Gutha quietly cursed Ilaha.

They found Reyazz face down next to a dead enemy, his arm twisted under him. When they turned him over, they saw he was still clutching a golden solar symbol on a chain around his neck.

As they rode on, Gutha realised he had lost another twelve men. Only twenty left. Still enough, though, and more of the night had passed than was to come. Dawn – and a final reckoning – was not far away.

XXXIV

Sunlight filled the canyon, swiftly vanquishing the cold night. A baby's cries grew louder and louder, despite its mother's desperate entreaties. Two old men wandered along the main street, stopping to examine bloody puddles where warriors had fallen. A dog trotted towards the outer gate, then stopped to sniff a dead horse.

Before long, dozens of the townspeople had left their dwellings to speak with their neighbours and survey the damage. Over in the compound, guards picked their way through the ruined buildings, sorting through the remains and clearing rubble. Scores of other warriors were still gathered at both gates; others had been stationed along the road.

At the encampment, some of the Saracens were also up. A few set about everyday duties, most stood in small groups, talking. The camps of Uruwat, Mushannaf and Enzarri's tribes seemed empty but then the men quietly filed out of their tents. Following the fallen ethnarchs' sons, they met on the track then marched down towards the road, two hundred strong. Every man bore his sword but not the coloured cloths.

Cassius looked on. Despite the blanket over his back, he couldn't stop shivering. He and Simo were lying just inside the tomb entrance. It had been impossible to sleep inside the icy chamber but they had at least eaten. Simo had also bandaged Cassius's swollen ankle and re-dressed Khalima's head. Cassius looked for him, but the Saracen had successfully hidden himself amongst his fellow tribesmen.

'Look there, sir,' said Simo, pointing at the compound.

Oblachus was not a difficult person to spot. He had seen the tribesmen on the move and was now hurrying away from the compound towards the inner gate, accompanied by a dozen men.

'Still can't believe he didn't send anyone to check the tombs,' said Cassius. 'Someone must have been listening last night.' At various points, all three of them had made requests to their gods, Khalima pleading with the supreme Nabatean deity, Dushara. 'I just hope their favour continues for the next hour or so.'

By the time the tribesmen reached the road, other curious warriors were following in their wake – some from the camp, others who had been billeted in the town. Oblachus was now at the gate and yelling orders.

Cassius dragged himself a yard closer to the light and watched as the guards swung the doors open. Without breaking his awkward stride, Oblachus went straight through. At another sweep of his stick, the guards immediately shut the doors behind him. The fifty or so of them left outside turned towards the advancing warriors and formed a line in front of the gate.

The tribesmen stopped about ten yards short. Those that had followed them drifted into the rear of the group. A shout went up and hundreds of voices repeated a single line of Nabatean – the precise phrase Cassius had suggested.

'Show us the stone! Show us the stone! Show us the stone!'

Cassius hoped things would move quickly. Despite Khalima's prompting and the determination of the three tribes to see Ilaha discredited, the impact of the crowd would not last long. Their demand had to reach the ears of the other ethnarchs if it was to have the desired effect.

'Look, sir,' said Simo.

More warriors from the other tribes were now gravitating towards the gate.

After a few minutes the guards parted and the doors opened once more. Cassius half-expected to see Oblachus but it was in fact the richly attired ethnarchs who appeared, each on horseback and with a handful of their senior men. Only Kalderon was missing.

Their arrival drew virtually every last warrior to the inner wall. While the tribes of the three dead ethnarchs remained by the gate, the others congregated around their leaders, who stayed on their horses. Judging by their behaviour, Cassius gathered they were trying to calm their men down.

'What is it, sir?' asked Simo, noting his master's grimace.

'The ethnarchs. Either Ilaha's convinced them he still has the stone or they know it's gone but are remaining loyal. Either way, they don't seem keen on a confrontation. But unless they turn against him, Khalima and the three tribes are heavily outnumbered. Which means we have no chance of getting out of here.'

'And Ilaha will continue with the revolt.'

'Precisely.'

The crowd had quietened, even though hundreds more guards and townspeople had arrived. The ethnarchs were no longer speaking and attention had shifted to the gate, where the doors remained open.

Oblachus reappeared, surrounded by a mass of guards holding heavy spears. With him were Kalderon and his men, each bearing the grey cloth upon their arms. The combined force moved up until they were only feet from the warriors of the three rebel tribes.

Behind them was a small cart being pulled along by four men. When it stopped between the doors, a slight figure climbed onto the back. Clad once more in the purple cloak, Ilaha strode confidently to the front of the vehicle.

Cassius grabbed his satchel. 'Help me up, Simo.'

'Sir?'

'We're going down there.'

'Really, sir?'

'Believe me, I'd prefer not to but there's no other way.'

'What if someone sees us?'

'That is why we must go now,' said Cassius as he pulled the hood up over his head. 'Everyone is watching him.'

━━8━►

Indavara and Mercator looked on as Andal inspected the auxiliary's shoulder. As exhausted as the rest of them, the soldier – who was named Damon – had strayed too close to the rear of the cart. The wheel had shaved one of his mount's front legs, causing the horse to stumble and throw him. The horse seemed unhurt but Damon had landed awkwardly on the rocky ground. The shoulder was badly cut and bruising was already coming through.

Mercator looked back along the road. 'How far ahead do you think we are?'

'An hour if we're lucky,' said Indavara.

'And they have the whole bloody day to run us down.'

Mercator turned back the other way. Less than a mile ahead were the soaring walls of the Scorpion Pass.

'You thinking what I'm thinking?' asked Indavara.

'We're still a long way from open ground. We keep riding, we'll just get more and more tired and they hit us when they choose.'

'We've taken out quite a few already. At least we'll get time to prepare; choose our own ground.'

'I'll tell the men.'

Indavara almost felt relieved. They could stop looking over their shoulders at last; the pursuit would come down to a simple, stand-up fight.

His thoughts turned to the others. Though he knew it would be light at Galanaq too, he somehow still imagined Corbulo and Simo being pursued through the darkened streets. Corbulo was a crafty sod – and perhaps Khalima or some of the others would help them – but however he looked at it, he couldn't find much hope that he would see his friends again.

The soldiers broke up and hurried towards their horses. Indavara ran over to join them. If they couldn't prevail, he, Mercator and the auxiliaries would never see *anyone* else again.

Cassius felt barely in control of his bowels as he hobbled across the sandy ground towards the crowd. There were, however, more new arrivals and no one took any notice of the two hooded men joining the throng. Cassius supposed it might have been wise to put his mail-shirt back on but it was unlikely to make much difference now.

Just as on the previous day, every pair of eyes was fixed on the compelling figure standing before them. Though pale and drawn, Ilaha stood proudly, chin held high as he addressed the crowd in a conciliatory tone. The Saracens listened respectfully.

Cassius was looking for Khalima but many of the warriors also had their hoods up and he didn't want to draw attention to himself. Someone tugged on his sleeve. He turned and saw a familiar face: Urunike. The young chief nodded towards the gate and Cassius spied a squat figure ahead.

When he arrived next to the Saracen and drew back his hood, Khalima shook his head in disbelief. 'By all the gods, I didn't think you'd actually come down here.'

Cassius whispered, 'What's Ilaha saying?'

'He has spoken about the assassination attempt and the death of the ethnarchs. He holds no grudge against the sons or the tribesmen and hopes they will now join him and the rest of the Tanukh in the struggle against Rome. He denies that the black stone has gone.'

Khalima paused to listen before continuing. 'He says there is no time for a ceremony now, that we must put all our energies into finding the saboteurs who set the fire. Gutha is pursuing some but others may be hiding here.'

When Ilaha briefly paused, a big warrior from Mushannaf's tribe shouted out.

Khalima translated. 'He claims one of the guards admitted to him that the stone has been stolen.'

Ilaha offered an appeasing smile before replying. Khalima waited until he'd finished.

'He told Mushannaf's man to be careful with his words. He risks offending Mighty Elagabal and should pay no heed to these lies.'

Cassius glanced around. No one else seemed keen to persist, not even the ethnarchs. The eight men remained easily identifiable – they were the only ones on horseback.

'Are you ready?' Cassius asked Khalima.

'Yes, I have it. But are you sure about this?'

'If he wins this crowd over, all is lost. It's now or never, I'm afraid.'

The Saracen closed his eyes and muttered a quiet prayer.

'Khalima, if this goes badly – kill me.'

'What?'

'Torture – I can't face it. Slit my throat. Promise me you'll do it.'

Those amber eyes searched Cassius's and saw that he could not have been more serious. 'Very well. And I shall slit my own a moment later.' He pulled his hood forward to ensure it still covered his bandaged head.

Cassius looked up at the sky. The sun had reappeared from behind a cloud, once more bathing the valley in light.

He nudged Simo. 'You remember what to do?'

Simo wiped his brow, took two paces forward, then turned towards his master.

Ilaha was speaking again.

Cassius whispered a prayer to Jupiter then pulled down his hood and shouted in Greek: 'There is a traitor here!'

Ilaha stopped mid-sentence, then shielded his eyes and peered at the figure twenty yards away in the middle of the crowd. 'Who are you?'

All those close by turned to look.

Cassius's throat felt as dry as sand but he got his words out. 'Nobody special. But I can identify the traitor.'

Ilaha hesitated, then gestured towards him. 'Show us.'

'I do not need to. Mighty Elagabal will show us all.'

'What do you mean?'

At a nod from Cassius, Simo and Khalima held up the small, circular mirrors of red-tinged glass each had just taken from their tunics. Khalima angled his so that the sunlight from above was reflected onto Simo's.

Several of the nearby warriors moved away.

Despite his trembling hand, Cassius positioned his mirror opposite Simo's, then aimed the beam at Ilaha. In the shadows of the wall, the light could easily be seen playing over his body and face.

Ilaha held up an arm to protect his eyes. 'What . . . who are you?'

Oblachus hauled himself up onto the cart to get a better look.

Cassius let the light shine on Ilaha a little longer then lowered the mirror.

Once Oblachus caught sight of him, he bellowed at his guards to advance.

'Let him speak!' shouted Urunike, and many others took up his cry. The guards and Kalderon's men were about to try to force their way through when Ilaha raised his hands. The crowd quietened once more. Ignoring the protests of Oblachus, Ilaha stared at Cassius, fists clenched. 'Who are you?'

Cassius reached into the satchel, pulled out the spearhead and lifted it high. 'My name is Cassius Corbulo. I am a Roman soldier.'

He ignored the gasps and jeers. 'I was sent here to recover the black stone for the Emperor. My men are returning it to Emesa as we speak.'

'He lies!' thundered Ilaha.

Dozens of shouts rang out, ceasing only when Oblachus and the ethnarchs restored order amongst their men.

'No. *You* are the liar,' replied Cassius, lowering the spearhead and holding up the mirror once more. 'I found these hidden inside the stone.' He pointed up at the body hanging from the wall. 'You used them yesterday to identify that supposed spy while I and my men stood untouched. If you let us through the gates I can also show how you created that voice.'

'Kill him!' raged Ilaha. 'Kill him!'

At Oblachus's order, the guards drew their swords. Kalderon did so too and cried out to his men. The tribesmen facing them seemed unsure what to do but Urunike's warriors already had their weapons ready and had closed in around Khalima, Cassius and Simo.

Cassius glimpsed a flash of movement to the right. With scant regard for his own safety, the bearded ethnarch Yemanek was driving his horse towards the gate. Warriors and guards scattered as he forced his way between them.

Once he had separated the two factions, Yemanek wheeled his horse around. 'Lord Ilaha, we must hear this man speak.'

Ilaha seemed unable to do anything but retreat to the back of the cart, arms wrapped around himself. Oblachus attempted to speak to Yemanek but the ethnarch silenced him with a word, then turned to Cassius.

'Well, Roman?'

Cassius was surrounded by Urunike's men, their shoulders pressed against his, a forest of swords raised high. He had to cough spit into his mouth to keep talking.

'I did not come here to act against the Tanukh – only to reclaim the stone. Governor Calvinus wants peace.' He pointed at Ilaha. 'This liar wishes only to lead you into a senseless war.'

'Any man who protects him will be killed!' shrieked Ilaha.

'It is you that should be killed!' answered Urunike.

A spear flew through the air.

Ilaha threw himself to one side and fell from the cart.

Oblachus ordered the guards to attack.

But now all the other ethnarchs had reached the gate. Showing remarkable horsemanship, they lined up on either side of Yemanek, keeping the two sides apart.

As the Saracens surged past him, Cassius was almost knocked to the ground. He glimpsed Ilaha's purple cloak as Oblachus and a few others retreated, pulling the doors behind them.

Even the most committed of the remaining guards weren't prepared to challenge the ethnarchs, who maintained their position until the doors were shut. Yemanek then dismounted and spoke to Kalderon. Heavily outnumbered and facing a man who still hadn't drawn his sword, Kalderon eventually lowered his blade. His warriors and the guards followed.

Cassius turned around. There were hundreds more of Ilaha's men in the crowd but they were split into groups and didn't seem keen to take on the other tribesmen.

Yemanek remounted his horse and shouted to Urunike. 'Bring the Roman to us. He will address the Tanukh.'

They found Ulixes on the far side of the pass. He was sitting against a boulder, his horse wandering aimlessly. Once off their mounts, Indavara and the others hurried over to him. The ex-legionary's left hand had swollen to double the normal size; upon his palm was a livid red circle.

'Scorpion?' asked Andal.

The gambler let his head rest on the boulder. 'Horse threw me. Next thing I knew my hand was on fire. Never even saw it. I can feel the poison spreading through me. Anyone want this . . .?'

Ulixes took the bag of coins from his tunic and threw it. The bag landed amidst the auxiliaries and a few of the gold aurei spilled out.

'. . . because it's of no bloody use to me. All that waiting, then I finally get what's owed me and this happens.' He looked up at the sky. 'I hate the gods. Every last stinking, useless bloody one of them!'

Indavara exchanged a glance with Mercator and the optio led the men away to get organised. Andal picked up the money and dropped it at Ulixes's feet.

'What are you lot doing anyway?' asked the gambler.

'Making a stand here,' said Indavara.

'Still no sign of your master?'

'No.'

Ulixes gave a bitter smile. 'You never had a chance. That ruthless son of a bitch Abascantius should never have sent you down here. He never was one to worry about the poor sods at the sharp end.'

'Will you fight with us?' asked Indavara. 'We could use another sword.'

'I'll probably be dead by the time they turn up,' said Ulixes, wincing as he moved the afflicted hand.

'If you're not?'

'What do I care who loses or wins that stupid stone? I'm a dead man anyway. I'll sit this one out.'

Indavara wasn't about to waste any more time on him. He went over to Mercator, who was helping the injured Damon up onto the cart. The other wounded auxiliary was still in the back and it had been agreed that they would continue on with the stone. The other horses had been tethered a hundred yards along the road.

'Keep going until you reach the mushroom,' instructed Mercator. 'If we haven't caught up by tomorrow head for Humeima. Don't stop for anyone or anything.'

The pair set off.

Indavara couldn't believe how few of them were left: himself, Mercator, Andal plus four men – Bucoli, Nobus, Itys and Pelagius. All five auxiliaries were looking at the Scorpion Pass.

Indavara unbuckled his belt, pulled off the tunic with the solar symbol and threw it onto his pack. Mercator was squatting close by, checking their two bows. Indavara knelt next to him and began inspecting their meagre stash of arrows.

Mercator looked at the men then spoke quietly. 'Did we just make a big mistake?'

'We have one advantage,' said Indavara. 'We can hold our ground. They want that stone, they're going to have to come through us.'

Cassius and Simo were waiting inside a small tent close to a large one – the largest within Yemanek's camp. The nine ethnarchs – Kalderon included – were already there

With the initial sense of relief fading, Cassius knew he now faced another task of the utmost difficulty. He imagined Ulixes would have been impressed by the result of his last-ditch gamble but if what followed went badly, he, Simo and Khalima might not see out the day. The Gaul knew when to leave his master alone and hadn't spoken a word, merely finding him a barrel to sit on and some water to drink.

Cassius had no idea how the meeting would go but he was determined to strike the right balance between reverence and strength.

If he didn't appear humble before the leaders of this ancient confederation, they might easily string him up and persist with the rebellion, with or without Ilaha. On the other hand, if he didn't convince them he had the power to negotiate and the ear of the governor, they wouldn't take him seriously (and might still string him up). Nobody looked particularly favourably on spies, especially if they were also thieves; and if the ethnarchs took against him, surely Khalima and his allies would be powerless to do anything.

Simo had taken a spare tunic from Cassius's pack and replaced the smelly, filthy one he'd been wearing. He was just about able to keep his boot on over the sprained ankle if the laces were loose. He checked his belt and stood.

'Sir, perhaps a little food to settle your stomach.'

Cassius's expression gave Simo his answer. He took the spearhead from him.

'Sir, what you did was very brave.'

'It might have been if I'd had any choice.'

'I wonder what's happened to the others.'

'Who knows? But I pray they've got clear – and not only for their sakes. If that German bastard returns with the stone this situation could reverse itself very quickly.'

The tent flap opened and Khalima came in. His sword and dagger were gone. Blood was seeping through the bandage around his head and mixing with sweat upon his brow.

'They want to see you now. Leave your weapons here.'

Cassius raised his arms as Simo removed his dagger and sword. 'Will you come in with me?'

'I cannot. They will deal with me later.'

'I'll be alone?'

'They're not even allowing Urunike in – the sons are yet to be formally recognised by the Confederation. Come, you must not keep them waiting.'

'Any advice?'

'Tell the truth – or as much as you can.' Khalima lowered his voice. 'Our agreement—'

'Of course. I should speak Greek?'

'Yes.'

As they walked outside, Cassius looked around. Men bearing the yellow cloths of Yemanek's tribe had formed a cordon around the centre of the camp. Beyond them was a sea of faces, including men from every one of the other twelve clans.

Two bulky guards were standing outside the large tent. Four more swiftly appeared and surrounded Khalima. The Saracen stopped and did his best not to look concerned. 'Go on.'

Cassius hobbled to the entrance but the guards didn't move. Then, without a word, one darted forward and grabbed him. It took a moment for Cassius to realise the man was just patting him down, checking for weapons. Once he'd finished, the second man pulled two thick curtains aside and Cassius went in.

The nine ethnarchs were all standing. Most had plenty of grey in their beards and plenty of gold on their fingers and wrists. Their tunics and cloaks were of opulent reds and blues, their weapons encrusted with gems. The burly Yemanek was standing slightly ahead of the others. Kalderon – smaller but no less intimidating – was to Cassius's left, dark eyes fixed upon him.

Cassius bowed low. 'It is an honour to be summoned before the ethnarchs of the Tanukh.'

Kalderon snorted and tapped his belt impatiently. Cassius dragged his eyes off the Saracen's curved dagger.

'Do not insult our intelligence,' said Yemanek calmly. 'You are a spy and a thief.'

'Perhaps,' conceded Cassius. He held up the spearhead. 'But I am also a member of Governor Calvinus's provincial staff.'

'Show me that,' said Yemanek. Cassius gave it to him.

The ethnarch examined it then passed it to the others. 'Why are you still here if your men have escaped with the stone?'

'I was injured and had to remain behind. Fortunately, it gave me a chance to intervene and expose Ilaha.'

'Probably the only way for you to save your own skin,' said one of the other ethnarchs.

'Also true,' admitted Cassius.

'What does Calvinus know of Ilaha?' asked Yemanek.

'Very little. All we had was some intelligence that the stone was in Galanaq.'

'And it seems you had some help getting in here,' said another of the Saracens.

Only now did Cassius truly appreciate Khalima's predicament. Regardless of the outcome, he had betrayed his own to assist a Roman agent. Cassius realised he hadn't asked about their deal out of greed – but because he couldn't be sure of his own fate.

'Khalima did aid us, yes.'

'Was he paid?' asked another man.

'At no point has he acted against the interests of his tribe or the Tanukh.'

'Answer the question, Roman,' insisted the ethnarch, a broad fellow with a pale scar that ran all the way across both his chins.

Cassius aimed a slight bow at him. 'With respect, this is not a court. I am not *obliged* to disclose that. Khalima did help us but he has betrayed no one.'

'By bringing a Roman spy into our very midst?' yelled Kalderon. Another ethnarch admonished him and the meeting briefly descended into a shouting match. Cassius understood not a word of it, but retreated two steps. After a time, tempers died down and Yemanek continued.

'In trying to kill Ilaha, our three compatriots went against the traditions and spirit of the Confederation. Regardless of Ilaha's intentions, they betrayed us, as did Khalima. He will be punished.'

Despite his situation, this was not a point on which Cassius was going to concede easily; the man had already lost his son. 'Without Khalima, you and your warriors would now be setting off behind Ilaha, believing yourselves to be under the protection of "mighty" Elagabal.'

'You dare to walk in here and insult us!' spat Kalderon. 'How I would love to slit your throat and—'

Yemanek silenced him.

Cassius clenched his fists to stop his hands shaking; it didn't work.

Yemanek continued: 'Khalima's fate is neither your concern nor the most important matter we must discuss. What of the stone?'

'It will be returned to its rightful place. Ilaha stole it from the temple where it has resided for decades.'

'The Black Stone of Emesa belongs to no one,' said one of the older ethnarchs. 'Ilaha's tricks do not reverse hundreds of years of reverence nor the power of the object.'

'The Emperor agrees. He wishes to honour and celebrate the black stone, not exploit it.'

The elderly ethnarch waved a dismissive hand at him and spoke in Nabatean.

Yemanek translated. 'He says you are far too young to be a man of importance. Why should we believe that you have any influence with the governor – you will say whatever you have to to save yourself.'

'Perhaps if I show you this.' Cassius opened the satchel and took out a letter which he gave to Yemanek. He doubted the ethnarchs would know a great deal about the Imperial Security Service but he was sure they would know who led Syria's Fourth Legion. Some of the other ethnarchs read the letter over Yemanek's shoulder.

'Venator – of the Fourth?' asked one.

'Yes. Though I'm currently attached to Calvinus's staff, I am an officer of the Fourth.'

'You know him?' asked Yemanek, running his fingers through his beard.

Cassius gestured to the letter, which was written in the prefect's own hand. It described Cassius as an officer of ability and repute and requested the reader to lend him whatever assistance necessary.

'A capable warrior and a wise man,' said Yemanek before returning the letter.

'Indeed.'

Cassius decided to capitalise on the moment of calm. 'I am not a tribune or a procurator but I know the governor well and I know he would prefer an agreement to bloodshed. Whilst here, I have seen and understood the depth of feeling against Rome. I can represent your interests, arrange a meeting. Calvinus appreciates that the current situation has led to disillusionment and frustration. He is keen to make an accommodation.'

Kalderon retorted in Nabatean.

'Our compatriot argues that we can *force* an accommodation,' explained Yemanek.

'I don't believe you need to. Before I left, certain alternatives were already being discussed. Governor Calvinus recognises that your profits have fallen. There was talk of a reduction in the import tax.'

'You were in league with Uruwat and the others,' said another ethnarch. 'They told you what we discussed at our first meeting.'

'Not true,' answered Cassius honestly.

A few of the Saracens spoke amongst themselves.

Cassius pounced on the next pause. 'If I may, I should also mention that this "revolt" at Palmyra has been wildly exaggerated. Ilaha and others have used it to suggest a wider loss of control but this is simply not the case. The Emperor and his four legions will deal with it in a matter of days, then move south to crush the rebels in Egypt.'

Cassius dropped the 'four' in casually; and this too provoked a response. He in fact had no idea about the size of the Emperor's force.

'You mentioned the import tax,' said Yemanek. 'What can you offer us?'

'As you will appreciate, I cannot make the deal. But I know the governor is open to negotiation on this point.'

'That means nothing.' said the double-chinned ethnarch. 'He might simply refuse.'

'I doubt that,' replied Cassius. 'After so long without contact from his Tanukh allies, he is very keen – I might even say desperate – to re-establish relations. I can get a message to Bostra from Humeima. Perhaps we could agree now that the ethnarchs will meet with Governor Calvinus, let us say in Petra, as soon as possible. I have the utmost confidence that he will attend and that agreement can be reached.'

'You say whatever you think we wish to hear,' said another of the ethnarchs – one of the men who had not yet spoken. 'You are a spy. You will tell Calvinus that we were about to ride against him.'

'Sir, unless you know differently, I wasn't aware that you were riding to war, merely to make your point. Only Ilaha's men have drawn Roman blood. He is the enemy of Rome. What I have seen today assures me that he is the only *true* enemy of Rome here.'

'Well, he and the German,' replied Kalderon with a sly look. 'I wouldn't be surprised if he's caught up with your friends by now. If he returned here with the stone, that would rather change things, wouldn't it?'

'Perhaps. But I would remind you that my friends stole it from right under that German's nose – it would be unwise to underestimate them. And even if he did return with the stone, would it really change anything? Surely such an august body as the Confederation would not follow a leader who is now a proven liar and charlatan?'

'There is no question of Ilaha leading anything any more,' said Yemanek.

He then turned to the others and spoke for some time. At his prompting every man – Kalderon included – had their say. Cassius could glean little from their tone and at least a quarter of an hour passed until the Arabian finally addressed him again. Only Kalderon seemed unhappy with the decision.

'You and your attendant are free to leave. Send your message to Calvinus and tell him that we await his invitation to Petra. If that meeting does not take place soon, my fellow ethnarchs and I might have to pay greater attention to less moderate voices.'

'I shall of course do as you ask. I thank each of you for your time.' Cassius bowed again and made a point of aiming the gesture towards Kalderon. 'I am humbled to have stood in such esteemed company.'

One of the other ethnarchs handed him the spearhead and the letter. Cassius knew he should have left it at that, but he had to ask. 'I am sorry, but I must mention this. What is to happen to Ilaha? And Khalima?'

'I suggest you leave quickly, Roman,' said Yemanek, suddenly angry, 'and be grateful that we are about to discuss their fate, not yours.'

XXXV

Indavara watched Nobus clamber past the highest of the painted faces, already three-quarters of the way up the north side of the cliff. The young auxiliary was apparently infamous for his climbing feats and had eagerly volunteered. Indavara supposed it was possible he also felt he had a better chance of survival up there. Whenever he spied a rock suitable for throwing, Nobus dropped it into his pack.

Indavara glanced around at the others. It was all about numbers now. Only the seven of them left; it just depended how many came through the pass.

He looked down at his sword and gripped the wooden hilt. Even though he'd had it only a few months, the finger ridges were beginning to wear down. It was a basic, inexpensive weapon; just like those he had fought with in the arena. Light, well balanced and sturdy, it had already served him well.

'Here.' Mercator handed him his allocation of arrows: six.

Indavara now had an opportunity to try out a quiver and he carefully placed the arrows inside. Itys was the best archer amongst the remaining auxiliaries so he had the other bow. He, Andal and Pelagius were now stationed to the right of the road; Indavara, Mercator and Bucoli to the left. Both groups were close to the boulders and outcrops they would use for cover when Ilaha's men approached.

Ulixes was lying on a blanket a few yards behind them, working his way through a flask of wine and occasionally spitting curses.

'You think we're far back enough?' asked Mercator, brushing dirt off the javelin he'd found rolling around in the cart.

'Think so.' They were about a hundred feet from the centre

of the pass – close enough to use the bows when Nobus got things started, too far for their enemies to rush them. Ilaha's men would be vulnerable.

'Hope they haven't got too many shields,' added Indavara. 'Shields could cause us a real problem. We're lucky no one down here wears much armour.'

'Right now I'm wishing I had mine,' said Bucoli.

Mercator glanced across at the other three, who were staring anxiously at the pass. 'By the gods, I took eighteen of them into Galanaq. Not even half left alive now.'

'Yorvah told us to get the stone out,' said Indavara. 'Or else it was all for nothing. Who's Marcella? His girl?'

'Sister,' said Bucoli.

'His only relative,' added Mercator. 'Parents died years ago.'

'Optio.' Bucoli jabbed a finger up at the cliff.

Nobus had reached a natural shelf close to the top and was staring intently at something to the south.

'Gods,' breathed Bucoli. 'They're coming.'

Nobus turned and held up both hands, then repeated the gesture, then held up one finger.

'Twenty-one,' said Mercator, grimacing.

Bucoli began a prayer to Mars.

Indavara took a long last swig of water.

———8———

Once outside, Cassius found the tent still surrounded. As the ethnarchs summoned their senior men inside, Khalima and Simo hurried over to meet him. The Saracen was still being followed by the four guards.

'Well?' he asked.

'They are allowing me and Simo to leave. They have agreed to meet with Calvinus in Petra.'

'Praise to Dushara and the high gods. Something good has come of this.'

'Khalima, listen . . .'

An older warrior wearing the yellow cloth of Yemanek's tribe strode back out of the tent. He held his hands up and waited for quiet then shouted a few orders to the crowd.

'He is telling them you are not to be harmed,' explained Khalima.

To Cassius's relief, few of the tribesmen seemed overly dismayed by this instruction.

The warrior then approached Khalima and gestured inside the tent. Khalima spoke calmly to him and the warrior allowed him to call over another tribesman standing close to Urunike. Tall and broad, the warrior wore a shabby tunic and a decrepit pair of sandals. But hanging from his belt was a long and very well-maintained sword.

'This is Zebib,' said Khalima. 'I've known him since he was a child. He will watch over you and escort you to the Goat Trail. You are still in a great deal of danger – Kalderon's men, Ilaha's guards. Leave as soon as you can.'

Khalima spoke to Zebib in Nabatean.

Yemanek's man was growing impatient. He tugged on Khalima's tunic.

Cassius could find nothing to say.

'I must go.' Khalima straightened his back and walked into the tent.

Wherever Cassius looked he saw dark faces staring at him.

'What now, sir?' asked Simo.

'We need mounts. Were there any left?'

'I believe so, sir. And the mules.'

With Simo aiding him once more – and Zebib following two paces behind – they walked towards the track. The warriors moved slowly out of their way but Cassius kept his eyes on the ground. Only when they were through and approaching their tent did he turn and see the size of the crowd. There were easily a thousand of them, including hundreds of Ilaha's guards.

'Damn it.' Cassius had turned his attention to the corral. Someone had taken the horses.

'Zebib, we need two mounts.'

The big warrior looked confused.

'I don't think he speaks Greek, sir.'

Cassius had picked up the Nabatean word for horse and most of the numbers.

After the third repetition, the Arabian understood.

'Urunike.'

'Yes, ask Urunike.'

Zebib loped back towards Yemanek's camp.

With Simo's help, Cassius sat down outside the tent.

'Sir, there was some water and food left inside. I'll take what extra I can.'

Trying to ignore his aching ankle, Cassius looked across the canyon, beyond the still-smouldering compound. Somewhere over there was the Goat Trail. He could see nothing but an impenetrable wall of rock.

Indavara could hear the enemy but he couldn't see them.

He looked up at Nobus, who was perched inches from the edge, peering downward. Andal and Pelagius were sitting against a boulder, swords lying in the sand beside them. Itys had positioned himself behind an outcrop at an ideal height; he could fire from a kneeling position with good cover. Indavara wiped sweat off his fingers – he didn't want them sliding on the bowstring. Mercator and Bucoli were beside him, also staring at the pass. Thankfully, Ulixes had gone quiet.

The sound of the horses stopped.

Nobus was still watching. Indavara still couldn't see them.

Gutha looked for any sign of an ambush but all he saw was the drawings; the open-mouthed, wide-eyed faces. In the middle of the pass was a slight rise so he couldn't see the other side. But he remembered the ground – there was enough cover to conceal any number of men. Once in the narrowest section, they would have little room for manoeuvre.

'Commander?'

The warriors in front of and behind him had also stopped. They looked afraid, thoughts of the javelin attack clearly still fresh in their minds.

'We'll go through on foot.'

Once they'd all dismounted and removed their packs, Gutha assigned two men to gather and rope the horses, then picked out six others.

'You're going first. Spread out and keep your eyes open.'

The men armed themselves and pulled down their hoods, then started up the slope.

Gutha had stopped to remove his armour before dawn; his plates, greaves and arm-guards were now packed on his saddle. He hoped he wouldn't need them.

Nobus was signalling again.

'Six,' said Mercator. 'Walking.'

The optio responded with a flat hand, indicating to Nobus and the other three that no action should be taken.

Indavara picked the bow up off the hot sand and plucked an arrow from the quiver.

First he saw the heads, then the pale tunics, then the swords by their sides – except for one man, who was carrying a spear. The Arabians were well spread, moving slowly. They reached the top of the rise then stopped.

The six warriors turned around.

Gutha took the axe from his shoulder and waved them onward. Once they moved off again, he led the other fourteen after them.

Indavara was hunched over, peering between two boulders.

One of the warriors suddenly looked up.

Nobus pulled his head back just in time.

The first six were now thirty feet beyond the rise, almost at the point where the pass widened out.

Then came the huge German with his battered face and the tangle of blond hair. Behind him were more men. When he was close to the first six he gave an order and they all halted. Idly swinging the axe with one hand, he inspected the road ahead.

'Wait until they're closer?' said Indavara.

'What if we can take out Gutha?' replied Mercator. 'Knock the heart out of them.'

'You're right. But let's keep Nobus in reserve.'

Mercator moved back a little so Nobus could see him and gave the signal. The optio then looked across at Itys. He mimicked drawing the bow and raised his hand high to indicate the target. He then picked up the javelin.

Still hunched over, Indavara nocked an arrow and pulled back the string, ready to straighten up and fire.

───8──➤

Gutha shielded his eyes from the sun. The sandy ground ahead was heavily disturbed but then a lot of traffic had come this way. He could hear nothing but the men breathing. And yet he was sure.

He spoke to the warriors quietly. 'I think they're there. We shall withdraw. Do not turn.'

He took a single step backwards.

───8──➤

Itys got his shot away first. It missed Gutha and thumped into the chest of a man to his left. As the warrior shrieked and fell, the others fled back through the pass.

Indavara let fly. He'd had to adjust his aim at the last moment and cursed as he saw the bolt scratch Gutha's shoulder. The

German was moving quickly but another of the warriors collided with him and they both tumbled to the ground.

Mercator did better. He had aimed at the front rank and struck a retreating warrior between the shoulder blades. The man was now on his belly, crawling towards the rise, the javelin still in his back.

Itys's second arrow caught another man, who managed three steps before hitting the ground hard then rolling back down the slope.

Indavara's second arrow was already drawn but he couldn't get a clear shot. When he spotted the German again, the crafty bastard was holding the man with the arrow in his chest in front of him – using him as a shield. As the others ran past him, he retreated calmly.

Itys hit another man in the thigh.

Gutha was almost at the top of the slope.

Indavara steadied himself and drew the string right back. He aimed at the injured man's throat, hoping the bolt might go all the way through. He breathed out, then let go.

——=8——

Gutha felt warm blood splatter his neck and something poke into his skin. Once over the rise, he dropped the warrior and crouched down. The arrow had gone through the Saracen's neck and out the other side. The iron tip was a wet, glistening red.

——=8——

'Itys, cover me!'

Leaving the bow and drawing his sword, Indavara got to his feet and sprinted along the road. The two wounded men still moving were dragging themselves up the slope. Ignoring them, Indavara wrenched the javelin out of the dying warrior and picked up the spear, which had been abandoned. He then ran back to Mercator and dropped both weapons.

'Good thinking,' said the optio. 'Did you get him?'

'Did they get me?'

The warriors were still staring at the dead man.

Gutha touched his neck. He could feel a tear in the flesh. There didn't seem to be much blood coming out but he'd seen neck wounds turn very bad very quickly.

'You there. How bad is it?'

The closest warrior checked it. 'Bit of a slice, sir. Nothing serious.' The man then looked up at his head and frowned. 'There's something in your . . .'

Gutha bent forward. The warrior reached up then presented him with a shard of metal. It took him a while to realise it had come from the shattered sword of the bodyguard back at Galanaq.

The two injured men dragged themselves over the rise and crawled towards their compatriots. Like the others, the warrior went to help them but Gutha grabbed his arm.

'Go to my horse and take out my armour.'

━━■8■━━

Indavara and Mercator scuttled across the track to the others.

'Move back?' suggested Andal.

'Definitely,' said Mercator. 'Give ourselves more time.'

'You think they'll come straight at us now?' asked Itys.

'They know that cart's getting farther away with every passing minute,' said Indavara. 'They won't be long.'

'Four down,' said Mercator. 'That's seventeen left.'

'But the German brute counts for two,' said Pelagius.

'At least,' replied Itys morosely. 'Can't believe I missed him.'

'Let's hope they don't have much armour or many shields with them,' said Pelagius.

'We'll wait and see what comes,' said Indavara. 'Don't break cover until you have to.'

They withdrew another thirty feet from the pass. Once Andal, Pelagius and Itys had found good spots, Indavara and Mercator

423

checked no one was watching then hurried back to the other side. The best position was behind the outcrop where Ulixes was still slumped, wine flask in his hand. Bucoli was already there with the spear and the javelin.

The auxiliary suddenly stamped downward. When he took his boot away, Indavara saw the sticky, crushed carcass of a pale, almost translucent creature with some very strange-looking body parts. He guessed he'd seen his first scorpion.

'Is that the one that stung you?' Mercator asked Ulixes.

'Didn't see it,' murmured the gambler before downing more wine.

'One of Khalima's men said that most of the pale ones aren't lethal. That one's pale.'

'I'm a dead man,' muttered Ulixes. 'The pain is even worse.' He punched the ground. 'I curse the gods. I curse them all!'

'Don't say that,' hissed Bucoli.

'Think they're going to help you, lad? We're nothing but entertainment for them.'

'That's enough,' said Mercator.

Indavara briefly checked the area for any more of the creatures then crouched down close to the end of the outcrop. He ran his sword in and out of the scabbard a few times to make sure it wouldn't stick, then checked his boots. He laid the bow beside him and inspected the spear. It was crudely made but six feet long with a heavy iron head. He put it next to the bow.

◄8►

Gutha recruited another man to speed things along. Once his mail-shirt was on and the studded bronze chest and back plates attached, it was time for the greaves and arm-guards. Gutha had once weighed the entire arrangement and it had been even heavier than he'd imagined: eighty pounds, not including the helmet, which he put on last.

Six of the remaining warriors had shields; they would lead the way. Their job was to advance on the two bowmen and keep them occupied while another six came in behind them to take out the others. Gutha had selected the strongest four as his reserve. If any of the raiders were still standing, they would follow up and finish them off.

All the horses had been tied up some distance back.

Gutha checked his armour one more time; he didn't want anything coming loose at an inopportune moment.

'I doubt there are more than a few of them,' he told the Arabians. 'Just keep moving and take out those archers – then we can deal with the rest. Everyone up the slope.'

———8———

'Shit,' said Bucoli. 'They do have shields.'

'I see them,' said Indavara. 'Four. No, six.'

By crouching, the advancing men were able to cover all but their boots. The shields were circular; hide and wood with a central boss of bronze.

'Might be a job for Nobus,' said Mercator.

'Agreed.'

The optio got the auxiliary's attention, pointed at the shield-bearers and mimed a throw. Nobus waved an acknowledgement then moved up to the edge.

The six men had just reached the top of the rise. The first rock missed them. They noticed the splash of dust but continued on, apparently unaware that it had come from above.

Nobus's second throw did a lot more damage. It hit one of the men on the shoulder, the crack of bone reverberating along the pass. The unfortunate dropped his shield and retreated face contorted by pain.

———8———

Gutha ordered a man from the second rank to grab his shield. The injured warrior was told to take his place; he could still wield his sword.

As he approached the rise, Gutha looked up and saw the enemy warrior aiming his next rock. There was absolutely nothing they could do about it; they didn't have a single bow between them, not that he would have been easy to hit anyway. It was always the little things.

The next rock bounced off a shield but all six had slowed.

'Forward!' ordered Gutha.

One of the men pointed along the road and shouted back at him.

—•8•—

'He's telling them we're farther away,' explained Mercator.

'We must use the distance,' said Indavara, detaching the quiver from his belt. 'Take out as many as we can before they get close.'

Nobus's fourth throw hit a man on the head. The Arabian lurched into the wall then slumped to the ground, body inert.

From the top of the cliff came a triumphant cry.

But the five remaining men didn't lose heart. They marched down the slope to the bottom, split into two groups and continued along the edges of the road.

Nobus turned his attention to the second rank. He threw the rocks at a faster rate, forcing the warriors to look up and take evasive action.

—•8•—

Gutha watched him and the mess he was making of his advance. If he got hold of the little shit he would chop his head off. For now, he just had to get the men moving.

'Second line, get after those shields.'

—•8•—

'Here they come,' said Mercator, javelin at the ready.

Ignoring the two shield-men now only sixty feet away and

426

trotting towards his position, Indavara fired at the second rank. The arrow hit a warrior dead centre, rippling his tunic and knocking him off his feet. The men with him paused, now fearful of the bows once more.

———8———

Gutha reached the rise and shouted at the hesitant warriors. 'After the others. Charge!'

———8———

Indavara watched them speed up. He put the bow down and drew his blade.

'Itys, hit the second rank! Mercator, you too. I'm going for the shields.'

Indavara sprang to his feet and bolted towards the pair on his side of the road, who were still keeping their heads down.

Several of the second rank saw him but they were busy avoiding Mercator's javelin and Itys's arrows.

Indavara leaped over a cluster of boulders and went for the man to the left. Still covering themselves, the Arabians were caught completely by surprise. Indavara grabbed the top edge of the shield, hauled it down, then swept straight into the warrior's neck. The blade went in just above the ear. The warrior's jaw dropped and the rest of him swiftly followed.

The second man had lowered his shield to see what he faced. He got it back up just in time. Sparks flew as Indavara's blade caught the bronze boss.

With no time to tarry – and his foe again unsighted – Indavara darted forward and swung his right leg. His boot caught the Arabian just above his ankle, sending him tottering backwards.

Indavara took his chance, swinging as soon as he had something to aim at. The blade ripped across the warrior's forehead as he slammed into the sand, unused sword clattering against his shield.

Having checked that the arrows were still keeping the second rank at bay, Indavara sprinted across the road.

The other three Arabians were only yards from Andal, Pelagius and Itys.

As they suddenly noticed the new threat, one lowered his shield. Itys's arrow thudded into his face. He teetered on his heels then fell, screaming.

Andal and Pelagius rushed one of the others. The third man was already coming at Indavara in a solid defensive crouch, shield close to him, sword at the ready.

Indavara couldn't see a quick way of putting him down. Fortunately, he didn't need it.

Having dropped his bow, Itys flew past the others and stuck his knife into the warrior's back. Shock froze the Arabian's face. His legs buckled and he collapsed onto a boulder.

Pelagius cried out as the last man's blade caught his elbow but the Arabian had made his last attack. A double-handed heave from Andal almost severed his arm. The enraged Pelagius barged his shield aside and finished him off with a drive into his flank.

Indavara was already on the move. 'Cover! Back into cover!'

‒8‒

'Who is this bastard?' bawled Gutha. He had lost five more men and these determined sons of bitches still had their bows. 'Charge! Everyone charge!'

The sight of him and the last four men on the move galvanised the second rank into action.

‒8‒

Once back across the road, Indavara dropped his sword and took the bow and an arrow from Mercator. Three of the second rank were coming for them; three for the others. They were no more than forty feet away. Indavara drew and aimed at the middle man. Twenty feet. Ten.

The string suddenly broke. Indavara dropped the bow and the arrow fell harmlessly to the ground.

Seeing what had happened, Mercator darted in front of him. 'Come on!'

Bucoli followed his optio.

The first Saracen slowed but threw all his strength into a scything sweep. Mercator's blade sang as he blocked.

Indavara dared not look down as his scrabbling fingers reached for his sword. Bucoli's wild swing missed its target by a foot. Unbalanced and exposed, he was struck by both the other men, one blade going into his ribs, the other into his chest. The auxillary was dead before his body struck the sand. The larger of the two warriors grinned manically.

As the first man pushed Mercator back towards the rock wall, the others came at Indavara. The big one kicked Bucoli on the way past. He was powerfully built, with a barrel chest and arms bulging out of his tunic. The other warrior seemed content to stay behind him.

Indavara forced himself to block out the sounds of the other clashes; he knew there was again no time to tarry. He had the mail-shirt – only a heavy blow would do him serious damage. He took one step back, then rushed forward.

The Arabian obviously also knew he would need power to go through the mail. So he drew the blade back over his shoulder – nothing like quickly enough.

He had barely begun his swing when Indavara slashed up at his forearms. The blade sliced deep into one and grazed the other. The dropped sword bounced off Indavara's head as he jabbed the iron hilt of his own into the Arabian's nose, breaking bones.

Leaping past him before he'd hit the ground, Indavara's next sweep smashed into the second man's blade with such force that it flew from his grasp. Heaving back the other way, Indavara caught him under the chin, carving his neck open. The last noise he made was a whimper.

Indavara was all set to help Mercator but the optio had just driven his sword down into the prostrate warrior at his feet.

He checked the position of the German and the last four. They were twenty feet away and had just slowed to a walk.

On the other side of the road, only two men were still standing: Pelagius and one of the Arabians. They were grappling with one another, neither able to bring his sword to bear. Indavara was already on his way when Pelagius managed to get his leg behind the Arabian and trip him.

As the man hit the sand, the auxiliary swung down, slashing across his chest until the warrior stopped moving.

Indavara halted in the middle of the road.

Pelagius reached for his stomach. Only then did Indavara see the tears in his tunic. Strangely calm, the auxiliary dropped his blade then sat down and examined his wounds.

As Mercator walked over, Indavara noticed his sword was in his wrong hand. The optio was clenching his right fist, from which thick drops of blood were colouring the sand.

'Looks like you two are all that's left,' said a rumbling voice in Greek.

The German dwarfed the four men with him, though Indavara could see that they too were not be underestimated. None seemed perturbed by the demise of his fellows and each one had taken up a shield.

Indavara spied Nobus climbing down from the cliff. He was moving swiftly but would be too late to make any difference.

'Not quite,' said another voice.

Ulixes was up on his feet and holding the big spear. His left hand was now bright pink and had swollen to a freakish size.

'Thought you were sitting this one out,' said Indavara.

Ulixes nodded at the hand. 'Hurts worse than anything I've ever known. Rather get it over with. Maybe I can take a couple of these pricks with me.'

The big warrior who Indavara had just felled was trying to get up. Ulixes finished him off by jabbing the point of the spear into his chest. As the warrior spluttered his last breaths, Ulixes pulled out the tip. 'Where's your sun god now, eh? Gullible arseholes.'

Gutha gave an order, staying put while the other four advanced.

430

'Don't like getting your hands dirty, do you?' said Indavara.

'Why have a dog and bark yourself?'

One of the warriors turned round and spoke in Greek. 'I'm no dog.'

'Just a turn of phrase,' said the German. 'I'm with you.' He lifted the axe and smacked his palm into the shaft.

Indavara glanced again at the shields then spoke to Ulixes. 'Swap?'

'Why not?'

Indavara handed the gambler the sword and took the spear. The length gave him a good advantage against the swordsmen – the German too if it came to it.

Ulixes and Mercator came in close to flank Indavara. Mercator – to the left – was holding his wounded hand up but his entire forearm was now slick with blood. Indavara was glad to have both him and Ulixes alongside him, but wasn't counting on a great deal of help from either.

The four warriors strode forward, two converging on Indavara, the others towards Mercator and Ulixes. The German still hadn't moved.

Indavara put both hands on the spear and held it out in front of him. Even though he had the reach, getting through the shields wouldn't be easy. Gaze alternating between his opponents, he waited. The warriors edged forward, constantly adjusting the angle of their shields, taking no risks.

Indavara could still hear Mercator's hand dripping and he suddenly realised how much he wanted the selfless optio to live. The thought decided his next move for him, especially when he noticed that the man to the left was fractionally ahead of the others.

Three quick steps and a jab of the spear halted the pair in front, but Indavara had no intention of striking them. He turned to his left, shifted his grip and drove the spear at Mercator's man. The iron tip scraped over the top of his shield and pierced the flesh above his eye. Sensing movement from the others, Indavara pulled the spear back and retreated.

To the astonishment of all those watching, the wounded Arabian continued forward. But then he began to blink and a dark dot appeared on his skin. Next came a thin stream of blood, then a shower of red droplets. He took only two more steps.

As he sank to his knees, Mercator kicked the shield aside and swept down, slashing into the other side of his head.

As Ulixes came out to meet his man and their blades clashed, Indavara took the initiative once more. He jabbed into the shields, testing each warrior. One of them spoke and they moved slightly away from each other before coming back at him. Indavara stood his ground, looking for a way through.

Mercator provided it. Wounded hand held against his chest, the optio swung at the closest man's shield, chipping off a strip of leather. The defender was forced to turn, exposing his side.

Indavara drove at his flank.

The second man diverted the strike with his shield, knocking the spear down into the ground. He pivoted towards Indavara, sword arm swinging.

Indavara had already dropped the spear. He leaped forward and blocked with his arm. The warrior's wrist collided with his and came off worse. Barely keeping hold of the blade, the Saracen watched helplessly as Indavara plucked his dagger from its sheath and plunged it deep into his throat. The dying man grabbed at him, blood spewing from the wound.

As Indavara fought him off, a huge, gleaming shape appeared in front of him. He threw himself backward as the axe hissed through the air.

The warrior was already falling. The steel blade scalped him, excising a flap of hairy flesh.

Indavara fell onto his backside. Wiping the Arabian's blood off his face, he had time only to see that Ulixes had accounted for his man but that Mercator was on the back foot.

Gutha stepped over the dead warrior and lumbered forward. Indavara scrambled backwards looking for a weapon but there was nothing close to hand. As he got to his feet, something pinged off the back of the German's helmet. Gutha stopped and frowned.

'Uuugh!' The man fighting Mercator touched the back of his head. Eyes swimming, he dropped his sword.

Mercator took his chance and thrust his blade into the man's gut.

Gutha turned round.

'Here,' said Ulixes. He picked up his dead opponent's sword and threw it.

As he caught it, Indavara realised what had happened.

Nobus was walking along the road towards them, another rock ready in his hand. Indavara could hardly believe the auxiliary had descended the cliff in such time. But it seemed he was now done with throwing rocks. He drew his sword and stopped five yards behind the German.

Ulixes came and stood beside Indavara once more. Mercator's tunic was now sodden with his own blood but he managed to stagger over to the other two.

Indavara reckoned the axe was about the heaviest weapon he had ever seen but he had no doubt the German could wield it with ease. The combination of helmet, mail-shirt and plate armour looked damn near impenetrable and the metal only increased the bulk of the man. He was enormous, surely not far off seven feet.

Gutha took another glance back at Nobus, then the other three. He lowered the axe and wiped his marked, red face. 'Well, unfortunately for me it appears that the numbers have rather swung in your favour. I must commend you – an excellent defensive action. Romans?'

'Romans,' said Mercator.

'Thought so,' said Gutha, switching from Greek to Latin. 'I'd forgotten how resilient you bastards are – too long fighting easterners, I suppose.'

'Don't remember asking for your life story,' growled Indavara. 'Let's get it over with.'

'Oh, you don't understand. It *is* over. As you can see, I am alone; and while I think I could probably take you and your friends here, I wouldn't want to risk a serious injury. Also, I would then have to pursue your compatriots, find and recover the stone, then return it to Galanaq unaided. All in all, the risk no longer justifies the benefit.'

'You're surrendering?' asked Mercator.

'I didn't say that. I will allow you to go on your way.'

Indavara gestured at the fallen warriors who now littered the road. 'You sent them to their deaths, yet you don't have the balls to fight yourself?'

'They are true believers. I am not. By the way, if I were you, I wouldn't insult me. It isn't too late for me to change my mind.'

Ulixes was laughing. He looked down at his hand then went to sit on a boulder.

Part of Indavara wanted to take the man on but common sense and his leaden limbs persuaded him to keep his mouth shut.

'Well,' said Gutha. 'I shall leave you to it, then.' He looked Indavara up and down. 'I've not seen many men as good with a bow as they are with a sword and a spear. You're young for a centurion. Optio?'

Indavara shook his head.

'That man behind me,' said Gutha. 'Tell him not to try anything.'

Mercator ordered Nobus to come and stand beside him.

'By the way,' added Gutha, 'how did you know we had it in Galanaq – the stone?'

'We got lucky,' said Indavara.

'When we took it from Emesa, the centurion there said the army would find me. Looks like he was right.' Gutha turned and walked back towards the pass.

Ulixes was still laughing.

XXXVI

'Where in Hades is he?'

While waiting for Zebib to return with the horses, Cassius felt it wise to stay out of sight. He was lying at the front of the tent, so tired he was almost asleep. A few minutes earlier, he'd watched as Yemanek and the other chiefs led their warriors down to the road and through the inner gate. The locals had done nothing to stop them and even the guards manning the doors had stood aside when faced by the ethnarchs.

'Thank the gods.'

Seeing Zebib leading the mounts up the track, Cassius struggled to his feet.

'Sir.' Simo had also left and now returned towing Patch, who was bearing their packs. 'To spare the horses, sir.'

Cassius couldn't be bothered to argue.

'I also brought you this.' Simo handed him a strong-looking length of wood he had recovered from the fire. 'For a crutch.'

Zebib arrived with the horses. He seemed distressed about something. 'Khalima.'

'What?'

'Khalima.' Zebib made a chopping motion with one hand – into the wrist of the other.

'Oh no.'

The warrior pointed at Urunike's camp, where a few men remained. 'Khalima there.'

Cassius had given up wondering how many more horrors and trials he would have to endure in Galanaq. Part of him wanted to leave immediately but he knew he couldn't go without seeing the Saracen.

'Get the horses ready, Simo – find me a saddle if you can. Meet me down there.'

As he began removing his armour, Gutha almost changed his mind. Had there been only the three others he might have tried it, but their stocky leader looked like a hard man to put down and he'd already had enough of the bronze in this heat. He didn't much like admitting defeat but nor did he like the idea of dying in this desolate place, definitely not while there was close on five hundred aurei waiting for him in Gaza.

He could be at the port in two weeks. And then? Perhaps it was time to start spending some of that money. Ilaha had paid well. Unusually well. It was a shame about that Gerrhan mask, though.

Once the armour was off and packed, he loaded two more horses with water and food and roped them to his. As he mounted up and returned through the pass, he wondered what was happening back at Galanaq. Without the stone, Ilaha would be in trouble. Gutha hoped he would live. But not as much as he hoped Kara Julia would die.

He kept the axe in his hand as he approached the Romans. For some reason, the older one with the strange hair was smiling. The youngest soldier was bandaging the wounded man's hand.

Their leader still hadn't sheathed his sword. He had one foot up on a stone and his eyes locked on Gutha.

Gutha wasn't used to people eyeballing him.

He stopped his horse. 'I told you once not to provoke me. I won't tell you again.'

One of the others quietly advised caution but the leader just kept staring from beneath that thick fringe of dark hair, tapping his blade against his leg.

As a younger man, Gutha would have slipped off his saddle and swung at him. But there was no point getting older if you didn't get wiser. He chose his battles carefully, and his heart wasn't in this one.

He rode on.

'Arrogant prick,' said Indavara. 'Bet he never fights without that bronze suit.'

Ulixes was chuckling again. Indavara sheathed his sword and glared at him.

'Sorry, but I have good cause. Look.'

The gambler held up his hand. The livid red had faded and some of the swelling had reduced. 'It must have been one of the less poisonous ones. The pain has gone. Thank the gods.'

'You'd *better* thank them,' said Indavara, 'because you were cursing them all an hour ago.'

Ulixes looked at the bleeding, broken bodies lying all around them. 'Old Pitface must love you. How many did you take down?'

'I don't keep count.'

He never had. Everyone else had when he'd fought in the arena but he didn't want to know then and he didn't want to know now.

He looked across the road. 'Did anybody see what happened to Andal and Itys?'

The others shook their heads. Pelagius too had succumbed to his wounds, and now lay silent and still with the others. Indavara had been over to check for any signs of life but all three were gone.

'Poor Andal,' said Mercator. 'He only had two years to go.'

'Needs stitches, sir,' said Nobus as he tied the bandage off. 'A lot.'

'No problem,' said Ulixes. 'You have the kit?'

'You'd do that for a second-class soldier?' asked Mercator.

'Just this once,' answered Ulixes with a grin.

'Nobus, help me fetch the horses?' said Indavara.

'Bring plenty,' said Mercator. He nodded at Andal and the other dead men. 'For them.'

■8►

Just as Cassius and Zebib arrived, four of Urunike's men came down from the tomb carrying Adayyid's body. He was laid alongside his compatriots – those who had been killed during the fight at the inner gate. Cassius forced himself not to look at their faces.

The new chief exited a tent. Urunike was a striking man, lean but muscular, with a fine head of wavy hair. Like his father, he wore little to mark him out as a leader.

He saw Cassius. 'I'm afraid I could do nothing to stop it. We are lucky they did not execute him. You must be quick.' He opened the flap and Cassius went inside.

An elderly man was kneeling by a straw mattress at the far end. The stuffy air was heavy with what smelt to Cassius like fried pork. Beside the bed was a small brazier, still smoking though it had recently been put out. Below it were several iron implements and a pile of bloodied rags. The old man stood and walked past Cassius without a word.

Khalima was naked from the waist up, his dark, heavy frame running with sweat. His hair was wet through too, his face almost yellow. The stump of his left arm was laid out on the sheet. The hand had been taken off two inches above the wrist. The cauterised end was scaly and black, the rest red up to the elbow.

The Saracen was propped up on several pillows, head turned away from his mutilated arm. He watched the old man leave.

'One of the best, so they tell me. He says I have three chances in four of living. Not bad.'

Cassius barely felt the ankle as he dropped to his knees. No words came until he had fought off the tears. 'You must wish you had never set eyes upon me.'

'The gods move in strange ways, Roman. Adayyid and the others died fighting for me and for each other. A noble death for every one.'

A great shout went up from beyond the inner gate.

'They tell me Oblachus is dead,' said Khalima. 'They are pursuing Ilaha and his most loyal followers through the caves. A secret compartment was found upon the platform. One of his

438

men must have hidden there, produced the voice of the god. You were right.'

Cassius barely heard him. He fixed his eyes on the Saracen's face, determined not to look again at the arm and have that vision seared into his mind.

'They will tear him to pieces,' added Khalima. 'In time, I believe Adayyid and Uruwat and Enzarri and all the others will be remembered as heroes.'

'I am sure of it.'

Cassius had the satchel over his shoulder. He reached inside and pulled out a bulging bag of coins – one hundred aurei from the barrel. 'For the dead men's families. Please accept it.'

He put the bag down by the bed. 'Is there any news of the German? Of the stone?'

'Some of his men returned – their horses had been lamed. They said others had been killed during an ambush in the night. It sounds like your friends have put up quite a fight.'

Cassius thought of all the hours that had passed. Surely there was a chance they had made it.

'Yemanek is a practical man,' continued Khalima. 'He will see to it that stability is restored.' The Saracen reached out and grabbed Cassius's arm. 'But you *must* talk to Calvinus, you *must* persuade him to meet with them and make peace, or all this could just start up again.'

'I will do everything I can. I give you my word.'

'Kalderon knows he is in the minority for now but he is still dangerous. Do not take the road, take the Goat Trail.'

'I know.'

'There is one of your customs officers at Leuke Kome. He will help you. Go now, while the others are all occupied.'

Cassius got to his feet.

'Tell me,' said Khalima. 'What is your true name?'

'Cassius Quintius Corbulo.'

'Farewell, Cassius.'

'Farewell, Khalima.' He turned away.

'No, no, that is not how a Saracen says goodbye to a friend. Come.'

Khalima put his good arm around Cassius's neck and pulled him in closer. He kissed him on both cheeks, then held him by his shoulder. 'You are young for work such as this, Cassius. Too young.'

—◀●▶—

There were no guards left at the Goat Trail. The nearest of Ilaha's men were down at the road. They had found some wine from somewhere and were sitting, drinking, watching the inner gate – where the warriors of other tribes now stood guard.

Zebib stopped at the foot of the trail. He pointed up the steep slope then silently walked back towards the road.

'I think I shall walk, sir,' said Simo as he dismounted and checked the rope to which Patch was tied. 'Are you going to try it?'

Cassius looked at the trail, which seemed to have been carved out of the canyon wall. No more than seven or eight feet wide, it went straight up for twenty yards then zigzagged sharply to the top. Cassius put his head back, trying to assess the angle of the slope and the difficulty of the path.

He stroked the horse's neck. It was a young black mare, a bit twitchy but strong and agile. Better still, Simo had managed to find a saddle.

Cassius had been riding since he was four. Another pulse of pain from his ankle made up his mind for him.

'Stay back, Simo.'

They started well but as the trail steepened and wove its way around jutting clumps of rock, the sandy ground gave way more easily. Thankfully the mare was a natural climber and kept itself moving. Cassius let it find its own way, reining in only when the animal needed to regain its breath. About halfway up came the most dangerous section – a narrow stretch that ran alarmingly close to the edge. Unnerved by the drop, the horse shuffled its way along, twice almost losing its footing. On one occasion, Cassius was convinced he was about to be thrown straight down the cliff but the animal held its nerve. After a brief rest beneath a shady overhang, they covered the final third without incident.

As the horse's hooves clattered across the ledge at the top, Cassius let out a long breath and gave a brief prayer of thanks to Jupiter. Looking around, he realised he was in some kind of holy place. Several yards back from the edge, a large rectangle had been cut down into the rock. On the far side were steps up to a pedestal and altar. Upon the altar was a hollow for some religious icon but it was empty. On two sides of the rectangle were benches, also made from rock. Cassius carefully dismounted then tied the mare to one of them.

Though he would have liked to rest while he waited for Simo, curiosity drew him back to the edge. Galanaq itself still looked almost deserted, the compound and the encampment too, but from this high vantage point he could now see over the inner wall.

What looked like more than a thousand men had gathered outside the cavern. In amongst all the pale robes, only a handful of the coloured cloths remained. Suddenly more of the warriors poured out of the cavern, then the mass moved backwards.

It took Cassius a while to work out why; they were retreating towards the gate because they wanted to look up.

The two figures were walking across a plateau like the one Cassius was standing on, three or four hundred feet above the canyon floor. Ilaha still wore his purple cloak. Beside him was the old woman, white hair blowing around her face.

Angry cries rang out from the Saracens below.

The pair stopped, raised their hands to the sky, then bowed to the sun. They walked on, slow but strangely purposeful. Cassius couldn't be sure because of the distance but it seemed to him that they were holding hands.

Their last step took them over the precipice.

As they plummeted towards the ground, Cassius saw only a streak of purple and another of white.

The Saracens cheered.

Though in their haste they had forgotten to take torches or lanterns, they rode on through the darkness, eventually arriving at the mushroom around the fourth hour of night. They found Damon and the other wounded auxiliary where they had camped with Khalima. The first thing they did was take down the dead and lay them out.

The second injured man, Ingennus, was in a bad way. He had been stabbed in the thigh and lost a lot of blood. Damon had done his best to clean and bandage the wound but had no wine. Ingennus immediately downed what spare they had.

Both men were immensely relieved that the others had survived and they listened keenly as Nobus described what had happened at the Scorpion Pass. Damon declared that they would all receive decorations for the action but showed little regret that he had missed it. Ulixes also related his tale and proudly showed them his hand – which now looked almost normal. They didn't dare start a fire but used a lantern for Ulixes to stitch Mercator's wound.

Though he wanted nothing more than sleep, Indavara found his figurine and left the others. He knelt in the darkness and prayed for Corbulo and Simo once more, and asked Fortuna to deliver him and the others to Humeima safely. On the way back to the small camp, he passed the cart. Without thinking about it, he reached inside and touched the black stone. He didn't know why.

——8——

'Do you think they're still alive?'

Simo was squatting by their fire, heating a pan of wine. 'I don't know, sir. All we can do is hope.'

'And pray?'

'I have prayed for Indavara. And Master Mercator and the men.'

Cassius stood and warmed his hands above the flames. They had pressed on along the trail throughout the day. The deserted path remained precarious and slow, twisting up and around steep faces, then plunging deep into shadowy crevices. Both men – and both horses – had cut themselves on the unforgiving rock. Just before dusk they'd come across a hollow, protected from three sides.

'And the man in the outhouse?' said Cassius. 'You prayed for him too, I expect?'

Simo hesitated before answering. 'Yes, sir.'

'To you I am a sinner now, I suppose.'

Simo stirred the wine.

Cassius glanced down at the spearhead, which was lying on the satchel next to his pack. 'I had no choice. Say it – I had no choice.'

Simo looked up.

'Say it or by Jupiter I swear I'll hit you again.'

Simo answered softly. 'You had no choice.'

Having got what he wanted, Cassius now found it made precious little difference.

'I've never had a choice. Never. My bloody father, the army, Alauran, this. I didn't want any of it!' His shouts echoed around the hollow. 'The fear, the killing. I *hate* what I have to see, what I have to do. I hate it!'

Cassius snatched up the spearhead and threw it at the rock. It struck with a metallic clang then fell to the ground.

Simo stood up. 'Master Cassius—'

'Do you think he survived? Really?'

Again the Gaul did not answer.

Cassius walked around the fire. 'Come on, Simo, you know as much about these things as anyone. After the fit, might he have survived?'

Simo seemed about to answer but he stopped himself and stared down at the fire. The wine was bubbling.

'Just tell me the truth. Whatever it is.'

'Master Cassius, when we left he was . . . he was not breathing.'

'He may have died, then. But there's a chance—'

'Sir, I think – I think he was dead when we left.'

Cassius nodded slowly and backed away.

'Only to me would this happen. Only to me would the gods do this. Not some heroic bit of swordplay, not even a fight. But some horrible bloody accident in a shit-stinking hole. That is what they have given me.'

Cassius had reached the side of the hollow. He leaned back against the rock and covered his face with his hands. 'And poor Khalima. I can't take it. I can't.'

Simo walked over to him and put a hand on his arm.

Cassius threw it off. 'You should have helped me. You did nothing. *Nothing!*'

Simo retreated.

'Damn you, you coward.' Cassius nodded at the fire. 'Take that wine off there and pour me a mug. But do not speak to me. Do not speak to me at all.'

XXXVII

Every sight of approaching riders worried them. Clear of the mountains and back on the Incense Road, they had nowhere to hide and could only watch and wait. But so far every party had turned out to be merchants heading south, who took little notice of the four men on horseback and the heavily loaded cart.

Ulixes drove the vehicle. Unlike the auxiliaries, he wasn't concerned about being close to the stone or the dead men. Poor Ingennus had no choice. The wound in his thigh was far too big to be stitched and though the bleeding had slowed, he was still in a lot of pain. But what he complained about most was the smell. They had wrapped up Andal and the others as best they could but they were already rotting in the heat. Mercator remained determined that his men be buried at Humeima.

Five days after their flight from Galanaq, they still hadn't reached the fortress. Indavara rode at the front, trying to keep them going, but he could tell the others were exhausted. Mercator barely spoke, and Indavara knew it wasn't just because of his hand. When they stopped, the optio would look at the dead men or gaze up at the sky. The three auxiliaries were simply desperate to be rid of the stone and reach safety. Only Ulixes kept up his spirits – he just seemed happy to be alive.

In the quiet moments, Indavara thanked Fortuna. He had fought many men and come out with little more than a few scratches. The only pain came from his left shin. Somehow he had scraped off the top layer of skin; it would have to heal all over again. He continued to pray for Corbulo and Simo. He couldn't shake the feeling that they would be waiting at the fortress, though he knew it was impossible.

'As afternoon became evening on that fifth day, they still couldn't see Humeima's white walls. Nobus had already fallen from his horse twice and Ingennus was ailing. Mercator sat silently hunched over on his mount and even Ulixes was cursing, knowing they faced another cold night in the desert. Indavara was about to call a halt when the gambler gave a triumphant cry.

'Look. Look there.'

In their weary state, none of the others had noticed the column approaching the Incense Road from the east.

Ulixes stopped the cart and stood up. 'I think it's the camel-riders.'

The column was heading almost directly for them and within a few minutes they could clearly see the well-organised ranks of cavalry.

'Thank the gods,' said Mercator.

They rode on another quarter-mile; to make sure the cavalrymen would come right past them. There were fewer this time, perhaps only forty, but Viridio was there. Mercator slid off his saddle and waved both arms at him.

Just as the column was about to turn onto the road, the decurion halted his riders. He didn't bother to get down himself but sent another man to speak to the strangers. But when Mercator explained that they were on army business and in need of escort to Humeima, the cavalry commander dismounted. He removed the gloves he was wearing, brushed sand off his scarlet cape and strode over to Mercator.

'What is so bloody important that you should halt a detachment of imperial cavalry?'

The optio quietly told him what was in the cart.

The decurion's eyes widened. He looked at Ulixes and Indavara. 'You don't look much like soldiers to me.'

Mercator glanced helplessly back at the others. Not one of them had any papers or anything else to identify them.

'Trust me, sir,' said Ulixes, jumping down from the cart. 'They're soldiers.'

He walked up to the decurion and pushed up his tunic sleeve.

Viridio looked at the four green letters etched on his arm. *SPQR.*

Ulixes grinned. 'Me too.'

▬8▬

Cassius and Simo spent two more days and nights in the mountains. As ordered, the attendant did not speak to his master. Cassius half-expected himself to weaken but he did not.

He hardly noticed the howls of wolves at night, nor worried about the dangers of the undulating trail. Even when they overtook two desperate-looking men armed with spears, he simply hurried his horse past and didn't look back.

When they stopped he drank wine and ignored the water Simo offered him.

When he saw the young guard lying on the outhouse floor he looked up at the sun until it hurt – anything to burn the image away. He pushed the pace as hard as he dared so that he was exhausted at night – so he would sleep.

Once the trail finally took them beyond the last of the high peaks, they descended through wide hillocks covered with thick, pale grass. Nestled between two of them was a hamlet where Simo bought food and Cassius bought more wine. They had to use gestures to communicate; not a single person spoke a word of Greek.

Just after noon on the next day, the trail ran down to a sandy plain dotted with strange, bright orange shrubs. A haze hid the coast but a passing merchant (who did speak Greek) reckoned it was no more than twenty miles. Relieved he would reach Leuke Kome by sundown, Cassius continued on without waiting for Simo, who was having some problem with his horse.

At what he guessed to be around the ninth hour, he stopped in a village to rest. He'd at last regained a little appetite and bought some cooked fish from a stall. Without any plates or cutlery, he sat on a barrel and ate it from the leaf it had been served on. It was a white fish, the flesh soft and sweet and flavoured with green herbs.

He was about ready to set off again when Simo finally arrived towing his horse and Patch.

'Sir, my mount cut its leg two days ago. I think the wound is going bad. I can't ride it any farther.'

'You can walk.'

'And the horse, sir?'

'Just leave it here.'

Though the fish was delicious, Cassius couldn't finish it all. He handed it to Simo.

'Move those bags onto the mule. We're leaving in a quarter-hour.'

— 8 —

As they neared the coast, the smell of the sea grew stronger, as did the cool, fresh breeze. They reached Leuke Kome an hour before twilight. Cassius knew the port had once been a centre for the seaborne incense trade but it had evidently fallen on hard times. Beyond the unadorned arch that marked the town's perimeter, the trail became a solid road but many of the hexagonal flagstones were missing.

The streets were quiet, perhaps only a third of the dwellings occupied. The colonnades leading off the central square were still standing, but the only building of any quality was boarded up. Blocks of marble had been removed from the wall surrounding it and green water had stained the façade. A conversation with a local revealed that this was the old customs house but the last Roman administrator had left two years previously.

Cassius and Simo continued through the town until they reached the port itself. Leuke Kome was protected by a headland, the harbour enclosed by two curved moles. There were a number of craft tied up or at anchor, rocking gently on a slight swell. Cassius observed three high-masted vessels of fifty feet or more. He wearily dismounted and led the way across the main quay, past wooden stalls containing fishing nets strewn with weed and dead crabs.

There were several inns with lanterns alight. Outside the largest

448

of them was a woman putting worn, flaking benches on equally worn, flaking tables. She spoke Greek and told Cassius there was a room free for the night. She called out to a boy who helped Simo take the mounts around to the stables.

Once inside, Cassius removed his cape and ordered a mug of wine. There were a handful of men – fishermen by the looks of them – eating in the parlour. Cassius questioned the woman about the owners of the three large ships and she in turn asked the men. One vessel was known to be awaiting repairs. The other two were coasters that made regular trips up to Aila. Cassius gave another boy a sesterce to find the captains and ask if their boats were available for hire.

Once the mug was finished he ordered a large flask. The woman's husband – also the inn's proprietor – showed him up to the room. Cassius took his boots off and lay on the bed closest to the window. There was no dagger sheath or sword belt to remove; he had discarded them days earlier and Simo had packed them away. Sipping from the flask, he watched the sky darken.

He was still awake when Simo came up but he pretended to be asleep. The attendant moved remarkably quietly as he unpacked the saddlebags. After a while, Cassius couldn't be bothered to pretend any more.

'Sorry, sir. I did try not to wake you.'

Cassius sat up. 'Pass me my satchel.'

From it he took the map, checking the distances up the coast and from there along the Via Traiana. He thought it unlikely he'd be back in Bostra in under two weeks, though he would at least be able to use the imperial post once at Aila.

Cassius knew he would have to reconcile himself to yet more uncertainty; he just had to stop himself thinking about Indavara and the others and the black stone. There were two ways to achieve that; drinking and sleeping.

'Your horse went down almost straight away, sir. It didn't even want any food.'

'Tomorrow you will sell it. The mule too.'

'Patch?'

'Of course.'

Simo thought about this, then reached for another of the saddlebags and took out the spearhead. 'Sir, I don't think I can repair the damage. It may need to go to a metalsmith.'

Cassius lay back again. 'You do understand what this is about, don't you?'

'Sir?'

'I came back for you. And how did you repay me? By doing nothing to protect us, then condemning me.'

'Sir, please. I did not condemn you.'

'Of course you did. Through your silence. I thought better of you, Simo.'

Already on his knees, the Gaul clasped his hands. 'Master Cassius, I cannot wilfully cause suffering to another. Our Lord tells us—'

'I don't care about your Lord. You know that. You belong to me and you should think of me first but I see now that's impossible. Abascantius told me I shouldn't keep you on while working for the Service. He was right.'

'Master Cassius, please. Think of all we have been through these last few years. I have known only two masters in my whole life.'

'How much money do you have – your savings?'

'Not enough, sir. Nothing like enough.'

'Then we both know what must happen. Get up off your knees.'

'Please do not sell me, sir. I beg you.'

'I will do what I can to find you a reasonable new owner. I promise you that much at least.'

Simo sat down on the other bed.

Cassius drank again and turned away from him. 'I'm sorry to say it but I should not have gone back for you. If I had not, you would be in your precious Kingdom and I would have escaped with the others. That poor bastard in the outhouse would still be alive and I would not have to live with what I did to him.'

An hour later came a knock on the door. It was the proprietor's wife, announcing that one of the captains was downstairs. Cassius took his money bag with the twenty aurei he had left. The skipper was sitting at the bar. He was surprisingly young but – judging by his clothing – a man of reasonable means.

'Good evening.'

'Good evening,' said the captain in Latin. 'I am Endymion, captain and owner of the *Tyrus*.'

'My name's Crispian. I need passage to Aila. Immediately.'

'Unfortunately I am heading south tomorrow. I could take you north next week.'

'That's not good enough.' Cassius waved at the proprietor. 'What about the other ship?'

'No reply yet. But the captain's been laid up with fever for the past few weeks. Half his crew too. I wouldn't expect much help from that quarter, sir.'

Cassius turned back to Endymion. 'What if you were to delay your trip south? Add compensation to your price if you must.'

'My hold is already half full. Some of it is perishable and will have to be unloaded if I head north.'

'Just give me the price.'

'How many of you?'

'Two.'

'Two hundred and fifty denarii.'

Cassius didn't have the energy to negotiate. 'Fine.'

He counted out five gold coins and handed them over.

'You'll get the other half when we arrive.'

'Fair enough.'

'How long?'

'The weather is set fair. Depending on the winds, between four and six days.'

'When will you be ready to depart?'

'Let us say the fifth hour.'

Endymion was true to his word and the *Tyrus* left Leuke Kome on time under clear blue skies, the sun sparkling on the water. There were just six crew; apparently all either brothers or cousins of the captain. There was only one piece of cargo for the newly emptied hold – Patch. Cassius hadn't the energy to argue about this either; he half-expected the captain to refuse but Endymion had transported livestock before and was convinced the weather would be kind.

The *Tyrus* had only a single sail but with a twenty-knot south-westerly to help them up the coast, they covered the miles swiftly. Cassius spent most of his time sitting at the mast, sipping from his flask. He had bought an entire barrel of the inn's finest wine and doubted there would be much left by the time they reached Aila. The ankle still hurt but the swelling had lessened and he could negotiate the deck unaided.

The water that streamed past was the clearest he had ever seen. He spied schools of orange and yellow fish and so many dolphins that after a while he didn't even bother to get up and watch them. The *Tyrus* passed sandbanks and small islands, all uninhabited. They encountered only a handful of other ships, some larger and farther out to sea, most much smaller – fishermen not venturing far from the coast.

When the morning mists cleared, Cassius sometimes caught sight of the Hejaz mountains. He looked away and kept drinking, as he did every time his thoughts turned to Galanaq. He grew to appreciate the beautiful blankness of the ocean and he used it to drive away what dwelt within him. It worked for a while, especially when he drank. At night he slept on deck, except when the ship was rolling and he had to wedge himself somewhere safer.

Strangely, he hardly dreamt. But when he awoke, the thoughts were there. The dead auxiliaries lying by the gate. Adayyid in that tomb. Khalima. And that poor bastard lying on the ground, shaking until he died because Cassius had struck him. Someone's brother, someone's son.

Simo spent much of his time checking on Patch and they barely spoke until the third day at sea. When the Gaul came to up collect Cassius's breakfast plate he squatted next to him and asked whether he had reconsidered. Unusually, Cassius hadn't yet started on his wine. He looked at Simo, at the round, kind face that had greeted him every morning for almost three years.

'Sit.'

Simo did so.

'How's the mule?'

'Off his food, sir, but he's drinking well. Sleeping most of the time.'

Cassius looked out at the sea. 'You must understand. This is not something I want to do. But you belong to me and a slave must do as his master bids. You have another master.'

'Sir, I believe I have served you well.'

'Indeed you have. In many ways, most ways, I could not have asked for more.'

'Sir, I know that my beliefs seem strange to you. But I have committed myself to the faith. That means helping others, easing suffering. Not causing it.'

'Unfortunately, those beliefs are based on a false assumption: that others share the same attitude to life. If your time with me has taught you anything, surely it must be that they do not. Sometimes we have to kill or be killed. Without Indavara, I expected you to stand by me. You have done so before, but not this time.'

'It is true I have protected you before, sir. But a man lost his life. I cannot – I must not – kill.'

'And that is why we must go our separate ways. I am not suited to this life but unfortunately I have no choice. I *do* have a choice about who I have around me. By the gods, Simo, I work for Imperial Security. A decade ago an agent like me would have spent his time hunting down people like you. It is better for us both. You must accept it; and ready yourself.'

'But a new master, sir. I wouldn't know—'

'You will not make me feel guilty, Simo. I have had my fill of guilt.'

Simo remained there for a while but there was nothing more to say.

Some time after he left, Endymion came up to the mast. 'Your slave seems very efficient. I aim to have one myself – within five years if the gods are willing.'

'Choose carefully,' said Cassius. 'They can be more trouble than they're worth.' He pointed north. 'Those sails seem to be converging.'

'The mouth of the Gulf of Aila. From there it's only two days if the wind doesn't shift.'

Cassius imagined the captain and his crew must think him a drunk so he waited until Endymion left before drinking once more. He tilted his head back against the mast, the sun warming his face. He closed his eyes and listened to the *Tyrus*'s bow cutting through the water.

What frightened him now was the prospect of returning to Bostra. He would at least know what had happened to the others but what if the news wasn't good? And how could he even function in his present condition? Could he ever get back to something approaching normality after what he had been through? What he had done?

For the first time in his life, Cassius would have been happy to stay at sea.

Bostra, May AD 273

'An odd place to keep such a sacred thing but we didn't want to attract any attention.'

Governor Calvinus opened the door and led Cassius into the room, which was spacious and secure, with only two high grilled windows.

'I believe this is where King Rabbel kept his treasures. My wife colonised it with our old statues.'

The six mounted busts were in a corner. All but one – Caesar, by the looks of it – were covered. Calvinus nodded at the broad, reinforced door at the rear. 'Got the wide access there. Nerva's centurions were able to wheel it up close then move it inside on rollers. Only he – and they – know it's here.'

The governor pulled away the white sheet.

There sat the stone on a wooden pallet, its dark surface glittering under even the weak rays of light coming in.

Cassius almost swore aloud at how pointless the whole affair now seemed. A lifeless piece of rock had been moved from one place to another; and how many had died and suffered because of it?

'Sick of the sight of the thing, I suppose?' said Calvinus.

'Something like that, sir. When did they arrive?'

'Three days ago. You've not seen them?'

'No, sir. I would very much like to.'

'Of course. Once we're finished here.'

Calvinus carefully replaced the sheet over the stone, tugging at the material until it hung straight.

Cassius was still staring at it.

Calvinus ushered him away and out into the corridor. 'Come. Shall I have some food prepared for you, Corbulo? You look terribly thin.'

'No, thank you, sir.'

Calvinus locked the door. They were in a quiet quarter of the residence; there weren't even any servants around. The governor replaced the key in a pocket within his toga then put a hand on Cassius's arm.

'Are you all right, lad?'

'Please, sir, do not show me too much kindness. I fear I might embarrass myself.'

'As you wish. We shall be as swift as we can.'

They spoke in the Table Room, sharing a small jug of expensive-tasting wine. It was late evening and outside attendants were closing doors and shutters.

Calvinus listened carefully, occasionally asking for details and waiting patiently when Cassius hesitated, which was often. It was not only emotion that halted him but the state of his mind; he'd kept up his consumption of wine on the road back from Aila, stopping only when they were in sight of the capital. He told Calvinus everything – except what had happened in the outhouse. When he finished, the governor leaned back in his chair, his florid face even more flushed than usual.

'By Jupiter, Corbulo. You, Mercator and the men worked wonders down there.'

Cassius finished his wine.

Calvinus refilled his glass. 'I look forward to telling Tribune Pontius about you raising the spearhead in the middle of that crowd of bloodthirsty Saracens. I doubt he would have had the courage for that, and I *know* he wouldn't have had the wit.'

The governor filled his own glass almost to the brim. 'There'll be decorations. If not from Abascantius then from me.'

'Sir, has there been any word from him?'

'Not yet. But my letter should have reached him by now. I don't think it'll be too long before we see him in Bostra again.'

Cassius leaned on the table. 'Sir, this business with the import tax. Forgive me, but I noted the expression on your face when I mentioned it. Please tell me we can do something.'

'I would do it in an instant. But such a step would require the permission of Marshal Marcellinus and he has wider concerns than my Arabia.'

'Governor, I must also ask you about the agreement with Khalima. The man lost his son, he was mutilated, they—'

'All right. Calm down. Take a deep breath.'

Cassius followed his advice.

'I agree that we owe the man a debt. And as long as he keeps quiet about it, I will honour the agreement. But a concession to the entire Confederation?'

Calvinus ran a hand through his silvery curls.

'You will meet with them, though, sir?'

'Of course. I will send out messengers at dawn and make preparations to leave for Petra. For months I have wanted to see my old allies face to face and you have made that happen, Corbulo. I shall also enjoy telling Pontius and Nerva that it was you who brought the Tanukh back to the table.'

The governor took Cassius's forearm and shook it hard. 'I thank you. Rome thanks you.'

Cassius heard the words but they washed over him. 'Sir, even though Ilaha is dead, the situation remains dangerous down there. Again, forgive my impertinence, but I would advise the utmost haste.'

'Young man, I have seen and heard enough to know that your advice is worth listening to. For that reason – and the fact that the Tanukh clearly respect you – I would like you to come with me.'

The governor stared searchingly into Cassius's eyes, then gave half a smile.

'But I will not ask you to. I see that you need to rest. We will talk again but not now. If you feel troubled, talk to that bodyguard of yours, or perhaps Mercator. Only they will understand what you have been through these last few weeks. Fellowship is all that helps at such times.'

—❋8❋—

Simo was waiting for him at the East Gate. Their ride up from Aila had taken nine days. Three times more Simo had begged him to reconsider until Cassius had finally snapped at him to be quiet. Now the Gaul seemed to have accepted his fate, which Cassius somehow found even more upsetting. He wished Simo could realise this would affect him too but there could be no doubt it was for the best. Even having him around was a reminder of what he was trying desperately to forget.

They walked back to the house, Simo leading their horses and Patch. The streets of the capital were quiet but Cassius drew a little comfort from the familiar sights. Yet everything seemed slightly different now, as if viewed through new eyes.

He turned to Simo. 'I will take you down to the market tomorrow so I suggest you get your affairs in order tonight. You should take a sample of your writing – that will help you get a decent post. Do not mention the matter to Indavara. Is that clear?'

Simo kept quiet.

'I said is that clear? I remain your master until you are purchased by a dealer.'

'Yes, sir.'

Cassius threw up a hand in frustration. 'Gods, it's not all bad, man. You would prefer a quieter life. If your new master lives here you might even be able to continue attending the church-house.'

'I have seen what other slaves are put through, sir. It is one of the great blessings of my life that I have worked for two kind masters. I could not possibly be so fortunate a third time.'

'Do not try to make me feel sorry for you,' said Cassius as they turned onto the Via Cappadocia, the walls of the fortress looming up ahead.

458

He was glad to reach the house without seeing Lepida or anyone else. The only thing he was looking forward to was meeting Indavara and Mercator and whoever else had made it back alive.

Muranda opened the door. 'Master Cassius!'

He walked straight past her.

'Master Indavara has been worried sick. He was so relieved when that messenger came from the governor.'

'Where is he?'

'He waited here all day but that soldier came round about an hour ago with some other men. They were going to a tavern, I think.'

'Soldier? Mercator?'

'Yes, sir.'

Cassius unclipped the brooch holding his cloak together and handed the garment to Muranda.

She looked past him at the street. 'Ah, and Simo too.'

'They didn't say which tavern?' asked Cassius.

She shook her head. 'You really have caught the sun, sir. My, you've lost some weight too.'

'Make sure my bed's ready.' He walked back outside and spoke to Simo. 'Get unpacked then get the horses stabled.'

'Yes, sir.'

Cassius lowered his voice. 'Indavara will be back here later. You will not tell him. I don't want any fuss.'

Simo gestured at the mule. 'Sir, what about Patch?'

Cassius was already on his way.

■8►

They had raised a toast to every dead man, each of them speaking his full name. Nothing was said after that and when some loud drinking competition began on the other side of the tavern, Nobus, Damon and Apollinaris drifted away to investigate. Most of the drinkers were Viridio's men. Once the decurion had heard they were heading north with their precious cargo, he had volunteered to escort them up the Via Traiana. Entering the city with one

459

hundred camel-riders had been an experience Indavara would not forget.

'Thanks for coming with me today,' said Mercator as he took a pickled walnut from a bowl with his left hand (the right was still heavily bandaged). 'I don't think I could have faced a second day doing that alone.'

'It's a shame Corbulo wasn't here. He's good with words. Women too.'

They had been to visit the wives and parents of all the dead auxiliaries. Indavara hadn't spoken, just stood alongside Mercator. The optio had said they'd been on a scouting mission for the governor. Essential work. The men had died fighting enemies of Rome and Arabia; died bravely, died well. More than one wife had asked about the money but Tribune Pontius wouldn't release the funds yet – not until Corbulo returned.

Indavara could not forget the last visit, to Yorvah's sister Marcella. She had heard from the other relatives that her brother had been lost and that Mercator would be coming. Even though she knew him, she had refused to open the door, as if she could somehow stave off the news. But she had listened as he spoke, and they'd heard her slump to the floor, weeping. Despite Mercator's pleas, she still wouldn't let them in.

Indavara had mixed feelings about what he guessed he could now call his fellow soldiers. Unlike his time as a fighter, he had allowed himself to grow close to them and the loss of men like Yorvah and Andal was hard to take. Then again, he'd made new friends in Mercator and the other surviving auxiliaries. They'd known each other only for a few weeks but – as with Corbulo and Simo – the bonds of those who'd fought together were strong. Though memories of his old life remained lost to him, the feeling was somehow familiar.

'Perhaps I should go back to the house,' he said. 'They might be there by now.'

'Stay and drink with me. I've got to report back to my unit tomorrow.'

Indavara nodded and sipped his wine.

Mercator said, 'I must admit I'm curious to hear how in Hades they got out of Galanaq.'

'No more talk about what's happening down there?'

'Not that I've heard. I hope the governor finds a way to keep the peace. I don't want to ever see those mountains again.'

'Do you think you'll get your promotion?'

Mercator waited for a roar from the revellers to die down. 'I've been thinking about that. Maybe I'm better off as an optio.'

'You're a good leader. Good fighter too.'

'It's not the fighting that worries me. It's days like today.'

— 8 —

Cassius had already checked three taverns. Most of the soldiers' hostelries were in an area not far from the fortress. One street was known to be popular with the auxiliaries, particularly a big place called the Grass Crown.

He was almost there when he heard a soft voice call his name. Standing in the doorway of another tavern was the Persian bar girl. She was wearing a long, pale blue stola, her slender arms weighed down with bangles. Her hair was laced with ribbons and huge gold rings hung from her ears. She really did look like Golpari.

'Cassius, isn't it?'

The doorman rolled his eyes as she sashayed out to the street. 'It is.'

'Surely you haven't forgotten me. I'm Delkash.'

'Of course.'

She took his hand. 'I thought you were going to come and visit me.'

'I was.'

Even though the doorman and several passers-by were looking at him, Cassius was almost tempted to go inside with her right away. Even if he'd been in uniform he wouldn't have cared if anyone saw him. The stola was cut low across her pert, tempting breasts and tight against her long, shapely legs. Perhaps this was the way to drag himself out of this fog of guilt and misery?

461

'Why not tonight?' she said.

'Why not? But don't see anyone else. I'll make it worth your while.'

Delkash smiled. 'I'll be waiting.'

He continued along the street to the Grass Crown. The doorman questioned and searched a rough-looking pair ahead of him but waved Cassius straight through. It took him only a moment to spy Indavara and Mercator.

Cassius hesitated; he wasn't sure why.

But then they saw him.

'Corbulo!' Indavara jumped up.

Cassius walked over to him and they grabbed each other by the shoulders. When he saw a rare beaming smile on the body-guard's face, Cassius had to swallow back the lump in his throat.

'By the gods, it's good to see you, Indavara.'

'You too. Are you limping?'

'Twisted ankle. You?'

'I'm fine. Is Simo with you? Is he hurt?'

'Simo's all right. He's back at the villa. You'll see him soon.'

Indavara seemed disappointed. Cassius moved past him and gripped forearms with Mercator.

'Sir, welcome back to Bostra.'

'Mercator. What happened to your hand?'

'Not much. I'm grateful to have nothing worse. Come, sir, have a seat.'

'I shall. No more of that "sir" nonsense, though, please.'

Cassius spotted Apollinaris and the other two auxiliaries. 'That's it? I heard there were seven of you.'

'Ingennus is at the hospital,' said Mercator.

'I'll fetch you a mug.' Indavara hurried over to the bar.

'We got him a bed next to Druz,' added Mercator.

'Druz, of course.' Cassius sat down. 'How is he?'

'The surgeon says we'll just have to wait and see. Ingennus should be all right. His wounds are clean – should only be a matter of weeks.'

'Only five of the twenty.' Cassius let his eyes close for a moment. 'I am sorry, Mercator.'

'Not your fault. They knew what they were getting themselves into.'

'And Ulixes?'

'The first thing he did was head for the nearest dice den. He said he needed to play while his luck was in. We haven't seen him since.'

Indavara sat down and filled their mugs from a jug.

'Well, how did you do it?' asked Cassius. 'How did you get away from that bloody German?'

'He surrendered, would you believe?' said Mercator.

'What?'

'After we'd taken out about thirty of his men,' added Indavara. 'Your surprises came in very handy.'

They went first; each weighing in as they described the events of the previous two weeks, ending with the return to Bostra with Viridio's cavalry. Then Cassius took his turn, again missing out just the one event. He struggled only once; when he told them about Khalima – meeting him in the tent after he had lost his hand. It wasn't the death of Adayyid or the punishment he had suffered; it was the kindness the Saracen had showed to Cassius when he could so easily have hated him.

Later, the other auxiliaries joined them and happy greetings were exchanged. The six of them drank on through the evening, recounting further details and lightening the mood with japes and banter. By the third hour of night, Cassius's eyes were fogging over.

When Damon fell asleep and Mercator fell off his stool, Indavara decided it was time to see Simo. Cassius knew there was no way of stopping them meeting but he could at least wash, change his clothes, then get out of there. Delkash was waiting, after all.

Once Damon had been roused they left, parting company at the top of the Via Cappadocia, Mercator and the men singing a filthy marching song.

Indavara put his arm over Cassius's shoulder as they wove their way down the darkened street. 'Sorry, Corbulo. Wanted to say sorry.'

'What for?'

'Leaving you two. I should have come back. I wanted to.'

'I gave the order and I'm glad you obeyed it. If you hadn't, the German would have got the stone back to his master and who knows where we'd be now?'

'Even so, I'm supposed to be your bodyguard. Sorry.'

'Think no more of it.'

'At least you had Simo to look after you.'

Cassius was glad they had reached the house.

'Eh, Corbulo?'

Cassius opened the front door. Once in the atrium they could hear voices in the kitchen.

'Go and see him,' he told Indavara. 'I'm heading out again.'

'Where?'

'Prior engagement.'

'A woman,' said Indavara. 'You sly dog. Well, you deserve it.'

He hurried into the kitchen and gave a great shout.

Cassius took an oil lamp into his bedroom and undressed. The water in the bowl by his bed was cold but he cleaned himself then dried off with an old cloak. He dabbed a pit of perfume on then found a fresh loincloth in his chest of drawers. There was a spare tunic there too.

Back in Aila, a sight of the spearhead (damaged though it was) had been enough to persuade the local procurator to loan him a hundred denarii and he still had much of it left. Once he'd secreted his money bag in his tunic, he hurried across the atrium.

His hand was inches from the door when Indavara came rushing out of the kitchen. The bodyguard grabbed him by the shoulder and spun him around.

'Why? Why are you doing this?'

Cassius looked past him at Simo.

'I'm sorry, sir. I had to tell Muranda and she—'

'It's not my fault!' wailed the housekeeper.

Cassius turned away and opened the door.

Indavara's boot connected with the bottom and slammed it shut.

'I want to know why.'

Cassius turned back around. 'You're drunk. Calm down.'

Indavara's words were uttered from behind gritted teeth. 'Tell me why you're getting rid of Simo.'

'I shall not. Nor do I have to. He is my concern, not yours.'

'He is my friend. You will not do this.'

'I will do as I wish.'

Indavara smashed his hand into the door close to Cassius's head. He leaned in close. 'You bastard. You don't care for anyone but yourself.'

'Don't even think about striking me. You have taken an oath. Strike me and you would face a military court.'

'I couldn't care less.'

'Indavara, listen. We've both drunk a lot. I'm not happy about the situation myself but something happened and I've decided to let Simo go. I know he's your friend but I'm afraid it has to be this way.'

To Cassius's surprise, Indavara stepped back. He then surprised him again by using his first name – one of the handful of times he'd ever done so.

'Cassius, come on. Whatever it is, I'm sure it can be fixed. You two have always been together.'

'Not always. Please move back. Let me open the door.'

'Don't do this.'

'Please.'

Indavara let him leave.

------8------

Cassius was almost at the top of the Via Cappadocia when he heard someone running along the street behind him. He turned around and saw Indavara charge out of the darkness. For a moment he thought the bodyguard might hit him but he stopped a few yards away.

'Tell me why or that's it.'

'What do you mean,"that's it"?'

'If Simo goes, I go.'

'Try to get this through your head – you took an oath to the army. You must do your time.'

'Do you really think that will keep me here?'

Cassius guessed it probably wouldn't.

Indavara pointed at him. 'Tell me, or the next time Abascantius comes calling, you'll be on your own.'

'I'm afraid you're not indispensable either. I can find someone else.'

'Fine. I'll leave tomorrow too.'

Indavara set off back down the street.

He hadn't gone far when Cassius spoke. 'All right. All right, damn it, I'll tell you. But not on some street corner.'

———◆8◆———

The Temple of Jupiter was close. It was locked up and quiet and the only people around was a pair of urchins who fled when they saw Cassius and Indavara walking up the steps. Cassius sat down at the top, head buzzing.

Indavara stopped three steps below and looked up at him. 'Well?'

'Galanaq. I told you we hid in this outhouse and escaped through a house next door. What I didn't tell you was that while we were hiding there a guard came in. I intended to stab him but I changed my mind. I hit him with the handle of my dagger. I thought it would stun him, knock him out. But he fell and began to shake. It was some sort of fit. Simo tried to help him but he could do nothing. He stopped breathing.'

Cassius was glad of the darkness. 'I killed him.'

'Doesn't sound like you had much choice.'

'He was young. He sounded scared.'

'You're young,' replied Indavara quickly. 'You were scared. You know as well as I do what they would have done to you. You did the right thing.'

'You say things like that as if it has no meaning. It is easy for you – killing is what you do.'

'You think I enjoy it?'

'I didn't say that.'

'I don't understand what this has to do with Simo.'

'He did nothing. Just stood there and let *me* do it. He wouldn't even say what you said – ease the pain of it for me. How dare he sit in judgement of me? He is my slave. He *belongs* to me.'

'You're angry.'

'I'm tired. Tired of thinking about it. Tired of drinking to stop thinking about it. But I can't. To end another's life . . . by the gods, Indavara. I was supposed to be an orator. To have killed . . .'

Indavara took a while to reply. 'It's not the first time. What about Africa? The legionaries at the bridge?'

'This was different.'

'Up close, you mean.'

'Why did he have to come in there? If only he'd just kept walking along the street.'

'There is no if,' said Indavara. 'There is only what is. You must live with what you have done. So must we all.'

'Not me. I *can't* live with this.'

'Stand up.'

'Why?'

'Just do it. We're going to the hippodrome.'

'What?'

'Do you want me to help you or not?'

Neither of them said a word as they walked out to the edge of the city. The only light at the hippodrome came from the gate-house. An elderly man appeared when they approached the open door.

'We'd like to go inside,' said Indavara.

'No chance, son.'

Indavara took a denarius from his money bag.

The gatekeeper looked tempted. 'Why do you want to go in there? It's empty.'

'That's our business. We won't be long.'

The gatekeeper reached for the coin but Indavara kept hold of it. 'And you make yourself scarce. Come back in half an hour.'

The gatekeeper considered the offer.

Indavara took out a second coin and handed them both to him.

With a grin, the old man went to fetch his keys. Once he'd opened a side gate and left, they entered the stadium. Stopping once they felt sand under their feet, they could just about see the spine and the curve of the great arched walls high above. Cassius waited for Indavara to speak.

'The first man I killed – he was very young, very weak. I wasn't up to much myself then but I was better than most so they made me fight a pair. I knew I couldn't mess around because the other one was dangerous. But this first one, when I went for him he didn't even move, didn't even get his sword up. He begged me not to hurt him, begged me to let him live.'

It was so dark that Cassius could see nothing of Indavara's face. Only his words mattered.

'I stuck him in the stomach and he fell right in front of me. It took him a while to die – until after I'd killed the other man. He just kept calling for his mother. It was five months before I fought again. I couldn't get him out of my head. I couldn't sleep. His face, his voice. I thought of nothing else. After a while, one of the trainers noticed the state I was in. He knew how to help me.'

'Yes?'

'You must talk to him.'

'What do you mean?'

'To him, the man you killed. The gods too if you wish.'

Indavara put a hand on Cassius's shoulder. 'Walk out into the stadium and say whatever's inside you. You can apologise, or explain. Shout or scream if you have to. But leave nothing inside.

Let it all out. And when you leave this place, try to leave it behind.'

Indavara walked back towards the side gate. 'I'll be waiting.'

———⚬———

He had no idea how long Corbulo was in there. He sat down against the wall, wishing he had some water to quench his thirst. Several times he heard a cry echo around the stadium but he couldn't make out a word.

He felt sorry for the poor bastard; and not only because he knew what he was feeling. Corbulo had seen a lot but he wasn't cut out for killing. He thought too much; and lacked the guts of those who'd had to fight their way through their whole lives.

Indavara still didn't really understand why Corbulo thought he had to get rid of Simo, but he knew he had to do something. He wanted to help his friends and keep the three of them together.

———⚬———

Eventually Corbulo returned.

Indavara stood up and walked over to him. 'Do you feel better?'

'I – I don't know.'

'You will, trust me. And if you don't, we will do this again and again until you do.'

They set off back towards the city and soon passed the gate-keeper, who cheerily bid them goodnight.

'Well,' said Indavara after a while, 'what about Simo?'

'I'd like to keep him on. I would. But he is not suited to this life and he will not change. He is a coward.'

'That's not true.'

'I don't claim I'm all that different,' said Cassius. 'But I will fight for my life, and my friends.'

'Back in Antioch, when you were trapped on that ship – I wanted to leave. I did in fact. Simo came after you alone. He risked his life to help you. There is more to courage than killing. And now you will punish him because of what you have done?'

Cassius did not reply.

Indavara stopped and turned towards him. Surrounded by darkness, they could barely see each other.

'Simo doesn't need to fight. Whatever comes at us next time, I'll be there.'

'If he stays, you'll stay?'

'I will. You'll come home and tell him?'

'No,' said Cassius. 'You can. I'm not going home tonight.'

—●8●—

An hour later, Delkash locked the door of her room and sat beside him on the bed. Cassius was naked, holding another mug of wine.

Delkash ran her hand across his back and kissed him softly on the cheek. 'You are handsome but you look like a boy. Not like a soldier at all.'

Cassius put the wine down, bent his head against her chest and wept until he could weep no more.

Historical Note

According to Herodian (a third century historian), The Black Stone of Emesa was indeed taken to Rome by Elagabalus and returned to Syria after the emperor's demise. It's theft and the subsequent events of this novel are however of course inventions of mine. The stone was a 'baetyl': a sacred monolith of the type revered in numerous cults and religions throughout history. Some worshippers clearly believed that the object had been 'sent from above' but the unusual composition of the rock was almost certainly earthly in origin.

Cassius's description of Elagabalus as 'one of the worst emperors of all time' reflects the attitude of commentators like Herodian who revelled in describing the young ruler's excesses, which apparently included harnessing naked women to a wheelbarrow and driving them about and torturing his dinner guests on a water wheel! He is also portrayed as a weak leader frequently manipulated by others, his mother in particular. It is thought that his elevation of the solar cult above the traditional Roman pantheon contributed to his downfall.

Aurelian - ruling half a century later - took care to avoid the same mistake. By the summer of AD 273 he had established a strong relationship with a solar deity, the precise identity of which is unknown. But Aurelian was not intent on supplanting the 'great gods'; he was by nature conservative and must have known that do so might fatally undermine his position. Although there is no direct evidence that he returned the stone to Rome, he did collect numerous other items of religious significance, particularly those related to the solar deity.

Arab historical texts confirm the existence of the Tanukh; the confederation of tribes that fought with Rome against the Palmyrans. We also know that there were ongoing diplomatic relations, even though those the Romans termed 'saracens' were often viewed as mysterious nomads who might easily cause unrest. The incense road and the associated trade existed as described, though by the third century sea transport had claimed much of the Arabians' business. The one quarter import tax (known as the *tetarte*) was a long-standing arrangement in the eastern provinces, though we can surely assume that Khalima and his like never have been particularly happy about it. After the failed invasion of Aelius Gallus in the first century, it seems that the Romans let the trade run its course and settled for the considerable profits of taxation; the primary reason for their continued occupation of Arabia.

Some minor issues of note: the inspiration for the character of Gutha comes from an inscription found in Arabia mentioning one Guththa (a German name) who was apparently a commander in charge of local soldiers. The inscription dates from 208 AD and Septimius Severus's second campaign against the Parthians. The valuable face mask that Gutha finds so appealing comes from Gerrha, the ancient Arabian city renowned for gold-working.

The 'wine cart' used by Cassius in Galanaq might seem like a convenient invention but such vehicles did exist in Roman times; a large leather bag was sometimes used because it was simply a lighter method of transporting liquid than amphoras.

Scooping bitumen out of the Dead Sea sounds similarly outlandish but this is also based in fact. The precious substance had been exploited since the Babylonian era and also by the Nabateans. The Greek historian Diodorus Siculus tells us that the bitumen was easily collected and that its arrival was indeed preceded by a widespread stench.

Haboob is the Arabic name (meaning 'blasting') for the intense dust storms that afflict the desert.

Contemporary readers (and writers) find slavery both alien and repellent but it is perhaps worth highlighting just how ingrained it was in the Roman world, if only to illustrate that Cassius's attitude towards Simo is essentially a product of the time. In this era, there was no serious challenge to the existence of slavery and the Christian Church did not oppose the institution until centuries later. Even those writers who had been slaves rarely wrote of their experiences or suggested that the practice be ended.

Acknowledgements

'The Black Stone' was completed between January and September, 2013. I'm still surprised it got finished in that time – the length and nature of the story made it a more complicated undertaking than the previous novels.

Thanks are due once again to my agent David Grossman, for continuing to guide me through the complicated world of publishing and helping me cut a long initial draft down to something far more dynamic.

Thanks also to my editor Oliver Johnson; firstly for running his expert eye over the manuscript and secondly for buying three more in the series! The work of Anne Perry and everyone else at Hodder & Stoughton is greatly appreciated.

Four books in and a fourth striking cover from the extremely talented Larry Rostant. Thanks also to cartographer Rosie Collins, who faced a tough job in producing the map of Arabia.

Professor Kevin Butcher of the University of Warwick deserves a mention for answering my (often inane) questions with patience and expert knowledge.

Novels like this are impossible without the work of the historians advancing our understanding of the ancient world; I am indebted to all those whose texts I used.

Lastly, I must express my gratitude to three reviewers whose unstinting support for the series has been extremely helpful and is very much appreciated: Pam Norfolk (Lancashire Evening Post), Kate Atherton (forwinternights.com) and Robin Carter (parmenionbooks.com).

For a thrilling exclusive extract from the next
AGENT OF ROME novel,

THE
EMPEROR'S
SILVER

Read on!

The humid summer air and his swift pace had left Simo sweating. He sighed with relief as he approached the rear corner of the property; he was glad to be home. He put his hand inside his tunic to retrieve his keys but his fingers never reached them.

He took one more step then froze.

Three dark figures had just scuttled across the street at the back of the villa. As they disappeared behind the rear wall, Simo walked carefully up to the corner. He could hear the men whispering to each other but he couldn't be sure of the language.

He peered around the corner in time to see one of the men spring upward. Grunting as he gripped the top of the wall, he then pulled himself onto it. The next man was given a leg up and, once he had joined his compatriot, they both reached down to help the third man.

Simo withdrew, throat dry with fear.

The rear door is secure. I locked it myself before I left. The bedroom windows face the back but they're too small to fit through. But the kitchen window is big enough - and the shutters have been left open since the hot weather came.

They can get in. Whoever they are, they can get in.

Simo looked back around the corner. Only one man was still visible atop the wall. Then he too disappeared. They hadn't even tried the door to the yard; they must have known it was always locked.

Open it? No, they'll hear me.

Go round to the front? No time.

There was only one thing he could do.

◄█8█►

Cassius Quintius Corbulo put the oil lamp down on the table and stared at the jug of wine. He was trying to cut down, especially since Abascantius had arrived. Three un-watered mugs a day was supposed to be his limit. This would be his fourth. He didn't want to break the new rule but he just couldn't sleep.

He was surprised Simo hadn't heard him get up. Perhaps the attendant was still at the church-house, doing whatever he did with his fellow believers.

Cassius picked up the jug.

'Indavara! Master Cassius!'

'Simo?' Having spilled the wine, Cassius put down the jug and walked around the table to the window.

'Wake up! There are men here.'

Definitely Simo, but what –

'At the back of the house. Wake up!'

'What - '

Cassius heard hissing voices, then feet scuffing the ground.

A man clad in a dark, hooded tunic vaulted through the kitchen window, shattering the amphora he landed on. Before Cassius could even move, a second man came through. He landed cleanly, hood dropping from his head. Cassius could see enough of his eyes to know he had spotted him.

'Indavara!'

Unarmed and wearing only his sleeping tunic, Cassius turned and ran. His left foot caught a chair leg. He lost his balance and came down on his knees, sliding on the smooth tiles. As he hauled himself up, he half-expected a blade to sink into his neck. He was almost through the kitchen doorway when scrabbling fingers grabbed the back of his tunic. He tried to pull free but the hand swung him to the right.

Cassius bounced off the side of the doorway and spun into the atrium. Tripping over his own feet he landed on his back in the ghostly pale blue rectangle below the skylight.

The intruder was already on him. Because of his black clothing, his head appeared disembodied and the long wooden club seemed

480

to be floating in the air. He lifted it with both hands, ready to swing down.

A fast-moving shape appeared from Cassius's right. Something cracked as the shape hit the intruder, catapulting him across the atrium and into a wall.

'Uff!'

The shape shook itself then straightened up. Cassius found himself looking at Indavara's broad, naked backside; the bodyguard's bulky frame seemed white under the moonlight.

'How many?'

'Two at least.' Cassius scrambled to his feet and backed towards the window that faced onto the Via Cappadocia. Somewhere near there was a candelabra. He was relieved but not surprised to see Indavara had his dagger, which he slept with.

The second intruder leapt into the light, swinging his club at the bodyguard. Indavara retreated; there wasn't a lot he could do with the little knife.

Cassius reached the wall and turned. The window shutters were closed so there was hardly any light coming through but he found the candelabra. He grabbed the iron shaft with both hands.

A third man ran under the skylight and cut off their path to the other rooms.

'Here.' Cassius put the candelabra in front of Indavara so he wouldn't have to turn. The bodyguard clamped the knife between his teeth and grabbed the five foot length of metal. Cassius had struggled to lift it but Indavara wielded it as easily as a sword.

From outside came a shout; Simo calling to the sentries for help.

The first man was back on his feet. He ordered the others forward in Greek.

As the pair prepared to strike, Indavara swung. He narrowly missed the head of the man to his left but struck the second warrior's club, knocking it out of his hands. Before they could counter, Indavara heaved the candelabra at them. It caught both men by surprise and sent them tottering back into the light.

Cassius didn't see the bodyguard take the blade from his mouth but he saw him dart forward and stab the closest man in the chest. The intruder gasped as he went down. The second warrior tripped over him but managed to roll away as the third man took up the attack.

He jabbed his club at Indavara and stepped over his dying compatriot, who was clawing at his wound, mouth fixed in a silent scream.

Indavara threw the knife into the intruder's face. It was not a throwing blade and bounced off his brow, but the moment's distraction was all the bodyguard needed. He leaped forward and launched his right foot straight into his foe's groin, connecting with a heavy slap. As the intruder crumpled, the man who had tripped flew back into the fray.

He drove an elbow at Indavara's face, striking his jaw with a shuddering crack. Cassius thought the prodigious blow might fell even the bodyguard. Though dazed, Indavara somehow stayed upright, grabbing his foe's tunic and holding him so he at least knew where he was. They struggled on for a moment, then stumbled over the candelabra and fell in a heap below the skylight.

Cassius circled them, peering at the ground, looking for a club or Indavara's knife.

Just as the naked bodyguard got one brawny arm around his foe's neck, his second victim found enough strength to give him some of his own treatment: he scrambled across the floor and punched Indavara's unprotected groin.

Cassius had never heard him shriek before.

The sheer shock of it propelled him into action. He grabbed the club he had just located and heaved it down at the intruder, catching him between the shoulder blades. Breath flew out of the man as he pitched forward onto Indavara's legs.

The bodyguard was panting like a dog, spitting indecipherable curses. His arm was tight under his victim's chin. Cassius almost felt pity for the poor bastard as his eyes bulged and his head spasmed.

'Yaaaaaahhhhh!'

The neck bones crunched like twigs underfoot. Indavara head-butted him for good measure then pushed the broken body away. Without a moment's hesitation, he kicked the last man alive off his legs, then crawled after him. He pulled the intruder's hood off and gripped the back of his head, hair springing up between his fingers.

'No, wait,' said Cassius. 'We need -'

Indavara drove the head down into the tiles. The noise of the skull cracking made Cassius gag. He staggered backwards and reached for the wall. Holding himself up, he stupidly looked back and saw dark blood seeping from under the crushed head. Cassius put a hand to his mouth but somehow stopped himself vomiting.

The key turned in the door. Lamp light flickered across the room as half a dozen legionaries piled in. They stood over Indavara, who was lying on his back, top half in the light, sucking in breath.

'It's all right,' said Cassius. 'We're all right.'

'Speak for yourself,' said Indavara.

One of the soldiers cursed as he slipped in a pool of blood.

'Excuse me.' Simo pushed his way through.

Cassius pointed at the bodyguard.

Simo knelt beside him and examined his damaged jaw.

'Forget that,' said Indavara. He nodded at his groin. 'Check there.'

One of the legionaries came forward: Leddicus, a friendly veteran who Cassius knew quite well. The soldier pulled back the assailants' hoods and examined their various wounds. Cassius had recovered himself sufficiently to note that all three were between twenty five and thirty years of age and wearing similarly dark clothing. Judging by their features, they could have been from anywhere from Thrace to Arabia.

'All dead,' said Leddicus.

'See what they have on them, would you?'

Indavara was on his side, eyes screwed tightly shut. 'Sweet Fortuna, please help me. Simo?'

'It's ... well, it's very red. But everything's where it should be.'

Cassius put a hand on the bodyguard's shoulder. 'Thank you. A shame you had to kill them, but thank you.'

'If that whore-son's done any permanent damage I'll kill him again.'

Simo took off his cloak and covered Indavara. 'I'll get you some wine.'

'Strongest we have. By the gods it hurts.'

Leddicus walked over to Cassius. He had searched the assailants and was holding several lengths of rope, a hood and a gag. Cassius realised why the trio had been armed with clubs instead of swords.

'Clear what they were here for, sir. Any idea who might want to capture you?'

'No.' Cassius stared down at the rope. 'Or why.'

H

HISTORY LIVES
at Hodder

From Anya Seton and Mary Stewart to Thomas Keneally and Robyn Young, Hodder & Stoughton has an illustrious tradition of publishing bestselling and prize-winning authors whose novels span the centuries, from ancient Rome to the Tudor Court, revolutionary Paris to the Second World War.

———

Want to learn how an author researches battle scenes?

Discover history from a female perspective?

Find out what it's like to walk Hadrian's Wall in full Roman dress?

Visit us today at HISTORY LIVES for exclusive author features, first chapter previews, book trailers, author videos, event listings and competitions.

@HistoryLives_

tumblr historylivesathodder.tumblr.com

www.historylives.co.uk

Do you wish this wasn't the end?

Join us at www.hodder.co.uk, or follow us on
Twitter @hodderbooks to be a part of our community
of people who love the very best in books and reading.

Whether you want to discover more about a book
or an author, watch trailers and interviews, have the
chance to win early limited editions, or simply browse
our expert readers' selection of the very best books,
we think you'll find what you're looking for.

And if you don't,
that's the place to tell us what's missing.

We love what we do, and we'd love you to be part of it.

www.hodder.co.uk

 @hodderbooks

 HodderBooks

 HodderBooks